By Dean Murray

Broken

Dean Murray

Copyright © 2011 by Dean Murray

Published by Fir'shan Publishing

ISBN 978-1-9393630-6-0

www.FirshanPublishing.com

Second Edition

For all of the fans of the series

None of this would be possible without all of you

Chapter 1

Stepping back out into the relentless desert sun, I once again wished we were still back in Minnesota, or at least that we were done moving. Then again I might as well have been wishing that Mom had decided on somewhere other than Utah, or that we'd had some long-lost relative die and leave us a small fortune, or even better that Dad and Cindi...

The thought was much too dangerous to complete. My breathing had already sped up, and my balance degenerated so quickly it was a small miracle I made it over to the U-Haul before I keeled over. I'd hated the battered vehicle that had spent the last two days carrying us west across I-80. It was hard to keep up the feeling though when it was the only thing protecting me from a concussion.

Half of the horizon was green and beautiful, not land-of-ten-thousand-lakes beautiful, but still not bad. I, of course, ended up on the wrong side of the truck; barren dirt and rocks, only occasionally relieved by scrubby plant life, as far as the eye could see.

I still didn't buy into my mom's oft-repeated claim. I'd told her before that Utah would be a lousy place to try and make her way as a photographer. Only very sick, masochistic people buy calendars with this kind of crap on it. Sane people take pictures of furry little animals romping around green landscapes and sell those.

That helped a little, my breathing was starting to slow back down, but that was too related to the other reasons we'd moved. I wasn't mentally back in safe territory still. I sought refuge in something even more mundane. Namely the fact that tomorrow I would have to go enroll in school and try to blend in with a bunch of small-town juniors who'd all probably known each other since they could walk.

Going to a new school after missing the first month of classes was a prospect likely to generate anxiety in the most outgoing of teenagers, and I was far from that, but it was a different kind of worry. As I mapped out all of the things that could, and probably would, go wrong, I could feel my heart slowly settle back down out of my throat.

If I were pretty or athletic I'd probably manage to fit right in. It always seemed like the kids who moved in partway through the year usually had some kind of instant in with the cool crowd, but that probably wouldn't happen for me. It wasn't that I didn't want to make friends; I just wasn't very good at it.

My equilibrium seemed to have returned, so I took a few unsteady steps around to the back of the truck. If I didn't return with a box soon Mom would rush out expecting the worst. Unless she got caught up visualizing some new project, in which case it would be hours before she thought to come check on me.

We'd moved the beds and most of the other heavy items in earlier, which helped explain my exhaustion, but that didn't make the pile of remaining items in the back of the truck any less foreboding. I decided to take the easy way out, and picked up a couple of blanket-wrapped mirrors.

I didn't unwrap either of them. That was dangerous too. The face that'd look back out of the glass would look almost more like hers than mine. Shoulder-length blond hair and blue eyes still seemed to be all the rage, but mine were ruined by pale skin that burned instead of tanning, and a build that had retained its baby fat long after most of the other girls had started slimming down.

Those extra inches had evaporated recently, but of course it couldn't be a cause for celebration. When Mom surfaced enough to notice how much weight I'd lost, she worried I was developing an eating disorder. She couldn't seem to understand that I hated the new me more than she did. Cindi was the skinny one. I'd tried to make myself eat enough to fill back out, but I'd had a hard time remembering meals lately. It was easier to just cinch my pants up a little and avoid mirrors. Even when I did remember, the calories in didn't seem quite able to keep up with the calories my body routinely burned up. I guess panic attacks are harder on your system than most people realize.

My body had already started spiraling down to an attack again, but before I could get too wobbly, I made it inside the house. Mom met me at the bottom of the creaking stairs with a big smile on her tired face. "The view from the rooms as the sun starts to set is even better than I thought it would be. Coming here was the best idea we've ever had."

Normally Mom's enthusiasm was fairly catching. You expect that kind of energy in a child; when it comes from an adult it's hard not to react in kind. It didn't manage to infect me this time, but it did help focus me on the here and now. I figured I owed her for that, so I tried to suppress my generally ungracious nature. I even let her lead me up the creaky stairs to show me the 'amazing view' for the third time.

Mom pulled the mirrors out of my hands as soon as I reached the larger bedroom, and nudged me towards the window. "Admit it, Adri, we didn't get sunsets like this very often in Minnesota."

"Adriana," I corrected automatically, trying to avoid thinking about where my nickname had come from. The sunset was beautiful, just starting to turn the sky pink as a prelude to the glorious oranges that would no doubt follow. It was the kind of thing that Mom was always trying to capture with her camera, but which never seemed to turn out quite as good as the real thing.

The sunset wasn't what captured my interest though, it was the greenery. Mom's room looked out to the west, the gorgeous side that reminded me of the place and people that would always be home. Mom carting me off to the middle of nowhere wasn't going to change that.

There was a huge tree on the far edge of the yard. It was a species I didn't recognize, but it still called to me. For a second I could almost hear a familiar voice whispering in my ear. "Come on, Adri. Cindi's already climbed up to the second set of branches. You can do it, but you don't have to do it all by yourself, let me help you." My vision was growing blurry. I tried to wrench my thoughts back to safe territory, but it was too late, Dad's face was already filling up my vision.

Cindi and I looked nothing like Mom. She was all dark, wavy hair, olive skin and at five-three hadn't been able to kiss Dad unless he bent down. Dad was the one who gave us the blond hair and a shot at maybe hitting an average height. I could see his handsome face smiling at me now, trying to coax me up into the tree with Cindi. The vision lasted only as long as it took me to hit the floor.

I could always judge how long I'd been out by my mom's expression when I came to. That and whether or not I'd seriously injured myself on the way down. She looked concerned, but not desperate yet. Her cell phone was in her hand, but not yet flipped open. It probably hadn't been more than eight or nine minutes.

"Adri, what just happened?"

She knew already, the psychiatrist had some fancy name for it complete with a whole list of symptoms and psychobabble garbage. It all boiled down to the idea that the more Mom could get me to talk about it, the sooner I'd shake off the fainting spells. Yeah right. Talking didn't make anything better; it just let him rack up a bunch of fees while I was passed out on his couch.

"I'm fine, Mom. I just got a little dizzy." I didn't want to talk to her. What I really wanted to do was enjoy the short immunity fainting usually granted me. For a minute or so I could think about Dad and Cindi with impunity.

I think Mom had figured that out though. Nothing I'd tried recently had been equal to the task of getting her to leave me alone, or at least in silence, right after an episode. She was probably worried I'd go back to how I was immediately after it all happened. I'd lost a couple of weeks there, alternately triggering a panic attack and then thinking about Dad or Cindi until the immunity wore off and another attack ensued.

Mom had flipped out. I'm not sure what brought me out of that black hole. I think maybe it was when I looked out the window one day and realized I'd somehow missed fall. Fall had always been Dad's favorite time. Cindi's had been spring—she hadn't minded the mud.

My immunity was wearing off; the racing heart was a sure sign. I focused back in on what Mom was saying.

"...you were doing so well. Don't worry; this is just a little setback. You'll see. Being in a different environment will do wonders for us both."

I knew the rest of Mom's speech by heart, there was no reason to listen. Next she'd run through all of the famous, marginally well-known, or even really obscure photographers who got their start in the West. It didn't really matter.

I waited the requisite fifteen minutes and then went back out to the U-Haul and got another box. Mom followed me out this time. I guess she was worried again.

Even worries about school wouldn't cushion me now that I'd had an attack today. There was nothing left but to wrap myself in numbness as I traveled back and forth between the truck and the house in a slow-moving haze.

The truck was the smallest one they rented, and we hadn't come even close to filling it up, but it was still dark by the time we finished. Mom looked at the mass of boxes, groaned dramatically, and then went to the fridge and broke out the sandwiches we'd purchased when we stopped in town for directions.

An hour later our beds were made, and I had an outfit laid out for school the next day. The clothes weren't mine. They'd nearly triggered a full-scale blowup. Mom thought I just wanted new clothes. I knew we couldn't afford a new wardrobe just because I was temporarily skinny. I didn't mind wearing my old stuff, I just didn't want to wear Cin...wear her clothes. My near attack ended the conversation, albeit with my old clothes still packed away in some anonymous box.

Mom's enthusiasm couldn't be damped for long though. It had fully returned by the time she turned my light off. "Have a good night, Adri...ana. You'll see, tomorrow will be like the start of a whole new life."

I kept the tears back until the door was shut, and then they came in a hot rush that left me depleted and sore. It was like Mom had already forgotten about the other half of our family.

Chapter 2

The sound of my alarm pulled me from an uneasy sleep, full of dreams where I was running in terror from some unseen horror. I couldn't decide whether I was happy to be free of them, or mad I had to get up.

My radio hadn't been in any of the boxes we'd unpacked last night, so I knew I'd have to get ready in silence. I forced myself out of bed regardless. Mom wouldn't be in to wake me up; she might not even be home.

It still wasn't light by the time I finished showering. The fact that my body was, at least partly, still on Minnesota time should have helped, but the morning was just as unbearable as normal.

Fighting back a yawn, I flipped on my bedroom light and examined the half-dozen boxes that might contain my clothes. I debated searching through them all, but it would just mean another fight if I did find them.

With a sigh of resignation I walked over to the chair where I'd left my selections from the night before, and pulled the faded jeans up my frail-looking legs. I finished up with a tank top, covered by a light blue blouse. All Cindi's stuff. Thoughts of her were just as dangerous as they'd been last night, but maybe I was getting a little better. Feeling like a traitor, I headed my skittering thoughts off before they could start affecting me physically, and focused on the next step in getting ready.

There was a lot more at stake this morning than last night. If I fell apart now I might not make it to school, and then I'd have all kinds of trouble calming Mom back down when she returned from wherever she'd gone.

My hair hung as limp and straight as always. No amount of styling ever made it look any better, just more contrived. Makeup was the same way. A touch here or there made me look marginally better, but I sincerely envied the girls who were skilled enough to transform their faces into something breathtaking after a session in the bathroom. Mom wasn't any help. Most days she didn't even put on mascara.

With the most depressing part of my routine now done, my mind wandered forward. It seemed only a second later that I was on the bus. I ignored the thought that Mom would be mad if she knew I'd skipped breakfast and hadn't brought any lunch. I pulled out my old, unabridged copy of Les Misérables.

Every so often I'd try to make it through Victor Hugo's weighty classic, but so far I'd never made it past Marius' introduction. Having just finished up Pride and Prejudice for the third time, I was once again due to try and make it through the written inspiration to some of my favorite music.

I hardly noticed the slow journey into town, instead caught up in a different time and place as Valjean's story started to unfold.

All too soon, the bus pulled up to a medium-sized, two-story brick building, and five kids my age stood up to leave. I followed them, my heart beating a little faster with each step. Other kids were trickling over to the door, either from one of the other two buses, or from the smattering of cars in the parking lot.

Before we'd even made it inside I'd realized just how much I stuck out. Shorts seemed to be the order of the day, knee-length khakis for the boys, and everything from mid-thigh on up for the girls. The only people in jeans seemed to be the debate-club types.

Silently groaning at my fashion faux pas, I located a sign pointing towards the office, and slipped around a couple of jocks who paused in their manly mock boxing match just long enough to check out the new girl. I silently hoped they slipped and hit each other in the nose.

I wandered down the white-walled corridor until I found another sign and turned left. There was a tall brunette already waiting, so I took a seat in one of the hard-plastic chairs. The other girl had shorts on just like everyone else, but hers were the shortest I'd seen yet. In Minnesota you could always pick out the alpha females by the length of their shorts, and this one seemed to think she was at the top of the food chain. That or a complete slut, but with her tan skin and perfect wavy hair, I figured it was probably the former. She didn't look like she had to put out to get attention.

Two minutes later, a smiling blond secretary came waddling out of what was probably the principal's office. I spent the time wondering if I should try to make small talk; the gorgeous girl spent it staring out the window.

The secretary took in the two of us, frowned almost imperceptibly at the length of the shorts and then signed a form for the other girl.

Determined to at least try and make friends, I started to smile as she turned towards me on her way out, but the expression died as soon as I met her flat green eyes. My heart immediately started to race, but she was already gone, moving with grace and confidence out of the suddenly too-small office.

I'd expected some degree of cliquishness from such a small-town, but this was bad. I'd never seen her before, so there wasn't any way it could be some kind of misunderstanding.

BROKEN

The secretary smoothed her blouse down over an ample stomach and smiled at me. I told myself I was just imagining that the smile never reached her eyes. She seemed to know who I was, and after identifying herself as Mrs. Pendely, proceeded to quiz me about which classes I'd been in at my last school. She stumbled a bit when I told her I hadn't enrolled in classes before moving. I didn't offer any additional information, so she tried to defuse the awkwardness by asking about electives.

I answered numbly, picking out classes nearly at random. I already knew a school this size wouldn't have anything truly interesting. I'd never been willing to dedicate the time required to learn a musical instrument. I've always been passable at drawing scenery, but anything more complicated than a stick figure gives me fits, so art was out too. Unless possibly the teacher liked Neolithic cave drawings.

By the time I surfaced from my musings, Mrs. Pendely had printed my schedule out on an ancient piece of machinery, handed me a map of the school and a locker assignment, and then dashed off a handwritten note to my first teacher.

I somehow found my first class before the bell rang. Mrs. Sorenson, my biology teacher, was a skinny old woman with curly white hair that looked like Greek paintings of Medusa. She made me introduce myself to the class and then let me slink over to my assigned seat.

I left the class even more depressed than I'd been when I woke up. I'd kind of known I'd have an incredible amount of material to catch up on from the first part of the semester. I hadn't anticipated that every other student was going to spend the class carefully ignoring me.

I'd never really fit in, but this was unbelievable. New students could always count on someone to offer to be their friends. I'd seen it a dozen times before as people had moved in. The really attractive people got drawn into the popular circles, less cool people were offered a place with the punks, the nerds, or at least with the drug users, who didn't care as much what you looked or acted like as long as you were hooked on something illegal.

I knew I had serious problems, but I didn't think they were obvious to everyone that looked at me. English was next, and odds were it would be a nearly exact repeat of Biology, possibly minus the awkward introduction.

The thin, distinguished looking teacher absently accepted my proffered form, starting a little when I didn't leave. "Right then, I suppose you need a signature?" The accent was so British I half-wanted to ask him how he ended up in Sanctuary.

I nodded, scanning his desk while I waited. Whethers, Mr. Whethers.

"Right then, I believe there is a vacancy next to Ms. Samuels in the back."

People were still trickling into the room, so at least I was spared the full gantlet, but the few gazes I met were still unfriendly until I reached the last table.

The skinny-ish blond girl already at the table smiled at me as I sat down. "Hi, I'm Britney."

I didn't know what to make of her. She looked like the type who was always on the fringe of the popular crowd. She was the girl who was the first to follow whatever fad happened to be in, and the first to turn on someone if it would make her just a tad more acceptable to her peers.

I mumbled a response, something that wasn't rude, but which couldn't be mistaken as pleading for friendship. Those kinds of girls loved to laugh at the 'poor, desperate, friendless' types behind our backs.

"You must be Adri Paige. I hope people haven't been too terrible to you."

"Adriana." I spent too much time correcting my mom. It came out a little rude. I would have tried to smooth things over but I was too busy trying to brace myself against the panic attack I was sure was coming. My vision swam for a moment, but all the practice compartmentalizing my mind seemed to be paying off.

I looked up. Britney looked a little crestfallen. She was probably deciding to ask for a different seat assignment after class.

"Sorry about that. I don't really like it when people shorten my name. Bad associations with nicknames and all that."

Britney's smile was only a pale imitation of the brilliant thing she'd flashed a few moments previously, but it signaled a willingness to try and make small talk at least.

"How did you know my name?"

"Oh, that's easy. Sanctuary is the smallest town on the face of the world. Anything out of the ordinary is instantly gossip fodder. I'll bet half the town knew you and your mom had purchased the old Anderson house before the ink was dry on the mortgage. The other half learned about it at church the next day."

I tried to smile, but I found it more than a little unnerving. Big city life hadn't been so intrusive. I hadn't even known my neighbors growing up. In Minneapolis the people you lived next to and the people you associated with were always kept properly segregated.

I tuned back into what Britney was saying just in time to answer a question with something safely non-committal. She didn't seem to need much in the way of responses to keep her talking. Probably for hours if she could get away with it.

"I'm glad you feel the same. You'd think they'd be a little more welcoming. Instead it's like they go out of their way to make sure you know you don't really fit in. We've been here a year, and I still can't get invited to any of the really cool parties."

I'd never been invited to any parties, let alone cool ones. I'd never felt the lack too strongly, but I smiled and let Britney keep talking until Mr. Whethers realized it was time to start class.

I quickly gathered we'd be reading Wuthering Heights, a prospect that both elated and disappointed me. After seeing how far behind I was already in Biology, it was nice to know we'd be working on something I'd already been through twice. On the other hand I hadn't liked the novel the first time I'd read it, and when I'd gritted my teeth and sat down for a second attempt I'd found I liked it even less. Maybe I just lacked the maturity to appreciate Bronte's so-called masterpiece, but I couldn't stand that her characters were almost all really nasty people.

I wondered what else we'd be reading. I could always ask Britney, but the odds of her knowing anything useful seemed pretty slim. When the bell finally released us from an analysis of Heathcliff's early depravity, Britney asked what my next class was.

She was elated to find we were both headed to Algebra. As we trailed the other students out of the class, I wasn't so sure I was equally enthused. Nobody had said anything to either of us. It was starting to look like Britney was receiving just as much of a cold shoulder as I was. And she'd been here an entire year.

It was bad enough not fitting in because you preferred your own company over that of your peers. It sucked a lot more when you didn't have a choice.

I tried to amuse myself by people-watching with the half of my mind that wasn't paying attention to Britney's chatter as we went back to our lockers. We passed one of those gorgeous, skinny redheads who always look good without looking like they spent much time in front of the mirror, then Britney exchanged smiles with a couple of artificial blondes. I'd seen the type before in Minnesota, girls who have a perfectly acceptable figure, but who throw money into their wardrobes, makeovers and accessories in an effort to achieve the cutting-edge look, when they'd be much better off just picking outfits that didn't try to compete with the anorexic-looking beauty queens.

A surprisingly adorable-looking nerd in jeans and a tee-shirt ducked out of our way, and I felt a pang of sympathy. He was the kind of boy Mom pointed out when she surfaced from one of her projects. She hadn't ever managed to really pique my interest in any boy, but I could see how a few years from now, he'd probably be fairly popular among college girls.

Britney stopped before one of the top lockers and started spinning the tumbler. She was still relating some story about her old school, but suddenly I couldn't hear a word.

The crowd of students had drifted to the sides of the hall, like worshipers making way for a pair of pagan gods. Even so, there still wasn't quite room for them to walk side by side. The girl was leading. Her dark, wavy hair and flawless skin would've made her pretty in any crowd, but she also had perfectly symmetrical features and one of those bodies that required hours each day in the gym to maintain. I wanted to hate her. It didn't make any sense, she could hardly be blamed for taking care of herself, but it just didn't seem fair. Simply by being in the same town as us, she automatically made every other girl in school feel like bloated, heifers. Surely she was somehow cheating to be doing so well in the subtle, nasty game in which every high-school girl ranked herself against every other female.

I probably would've spent the rest of the day depressed, but once she was out of my line of sight I was able to see the boy following her. He was incredible. Just looking at him drove every other thought out of my mind.

If the girl who'd just walked by me without acknowledging the existence of any of us lesser beings was every boy's ideal physical specimen, the boy was every girl's dream. A gorgeous fantasy breathed into life by some merciful goddess, one who wanted to give us each a glimpse of what awaited good little girls in the afterlife.

Skin that was a gorgeous shade of tan, not at all artificial-looking, disappeared into the collar of a thin, light-blue button-down shirt. The cut of his clothing hinted at designer origins, but the garment was mostly notable for the way it stretched over a pair of broad shoulders that looked like they'd been chiseled from marble, or possibly cast in bronze.

My eyes made it as far as the equally impressive chest before I forced them upwards. Anyone built like that should be ugly to keep things in balance. Not him. His square jaw and even features were nothing less than perfection. If he ever chose to model, the editors of every major fashion magazine would have pulled out all the stops to land the contract for his debut appearance. The whole issue would have to be pictures of him though. No amount of airbrushing would suffice to allow other men to ever share the same magazine with him.

I expected to begin hyperventilating any second, but my lungs seemed frozen. My body should have been screaming for oxygen. Instead every part of me was screaming for more of that divine face. He'd been looking to his left; I pried my gaze away from his profile just long enough to take in a casual tangle of dark, curly hair, and then he was turning towards me.

Vague, traitorous hopes that the other side of his face was marred with a birthmark, or a series of ghastly scars evaporated away as I took in eyes just a few shades darker than the blue of his shirt. Somewhere a cosmic force was trying to fix a pair of large, intangible scales. Scales that'd been twisted into a mangled mess and then torn into two pieces.

I'd expected the shallow, narcissistic eyes of a runway model. Instead, the eyes that connected with mine hinted at depths I'd never even imagined existed.

My lips, acting of their own volition, started to pull back in a tentative smile, but before they could complete the action, the heart-wrenching eyes narrowed. The emotions swooping across the surreal face were too quick to identify, but the way he turned slightly away as he passed all but proved they'd been a close cousin to distaste.

Chapter 3

For a moment I was too busy mentally flogging myself to hear Britney's question.

"Have you been to Vegas yet?"

"No, we just got here last night." And I'd been too busy making doe eyes at gorgeous boys who were completely out of my league to do anything like take a shopping trip.

Britney perked up at my answer. "We *so* have to go down there soon. It's the only place within an hour and a half where you can do any decent shopping."

Normally the prospect of driving for hours to watch someone else spend money I didn't have, sounded roughly as appealing as laying out naked at the pool until I had second-degree burns on my whole body. Then again, maybe burns wouldn't be so bad if they let me disappear into the anonymity of a large crowd in an actual city rather than dealing with hick hostility.

"That sounds great; I can't wait to get out of this stupid town."

A couple of people started a bit, and I heard a locker slam shut with surprising force. The eavesdroppers were predictably pissed I was dissing their home, but I didn't care. It served them right. Don't listen in if you aren't prepared to hear something you won't like. As long as my comments hadn't offended my new pseudo-friend, I was just fine.

Britney laughed. "You said it. There is *so* nothing to do here. You can't even go hiking anymore..."

I'd already realized Britney wasn't the type to think twice before words actually left her mouth. Curious.

"What do you mean we can't go hiking?"

She was looking around at the other students. "Nothing, come on. We're going to be late for class."

I followed without a word, even more intrigued now. 'Cool' people don't sweat tardiness and Britney really wanted to be cool.

A slender, frumpy-looking woman looked up from her desk as Britney and I walked in. I held up my form, which she took without reading it. "No doubt something to ensure I know you're my newest student. Sit over there where you won't distract Britney from just how poorly she's doing in my class. There's an extra book on the shelves in the back."

Britney rolled her eyes as she went to her assigned desk, but I suspected she was actually relieved we'd been split up. Mrs. Campbell didn't seem like the kind of teacher you could get away with ignoring, so I retrieved an algebra book from the back of the room and sat at my desk.

Any thoughts about finding out why hiking was off limits quickly melted away once class started. Math had never been my favorite subject. I'd always managed to pull A's or at least A-'s, but hated all of the little nitpicky rules.

Unfortunately, after missing a whole month of classes, I was at least as bad off in Algebra as I was in Biology. Mrs. Campbell was solving problems with so many variables in them it was like watching alphabet soup spontaneously re-arrange itself on her overhead projector. Not only that, things were being squared and cubed, an operation with which I had only passing familiarity.

I struggled valiantly to understand what was going on. I got the sense the operations being applied to the formulas were being explained very well, I just didn't have the vocabulary to follow what she was saying.

By the time class finally ended I was fighting not to become emotional. The fact that Britney looked for a moment like she was debating whether or not to wait for me before finally stopping next to the door with her arms crossed, didn't help.

I threw my book and binder into my backpack and tromped up to the front of the classroom. Mrs. Campbell looked up when I reached her desk. "Here's your form, among other things."

I verified that the top sheet had her signature on it, and then turned to go. She didn't let me get very far.

"From your bewildered expression during class it appears you aren't transferring in from another school. I expect most of your other teachers are just letting you pick up from where they are now. I'm afraid this class builds on itself, so I'll be testing you on everything we've covered in the past month. I'm sure you've got a full class load, but we haven't gotten into anything truly difficult yet. The sooner we get you caught up, the better off you'll be. Shall we say a month from today?"

The prospect of trying to catch up, all the while needing to master new material and deal with a full schedule of other classes, was too much. I felt tears rising to the surface even as my heartbeat sped up to near-panic attack levels. That was the last thing I needed, but I could only fight off so many worries at once, and I was quickly approaching my limits.

"Now don't come unglued on me. The school has set aside some discretionary funds for a math tutoring lab after school every day. We're not fully staffed yet, but if you swing by we should be able to help clear up any questions you might have. You'll have to do the majority of the work. I expect you to actually read your math book, but if you give it an honest effort I'm sure you'll be just fine."

That helped a little. It was still a daunting prospect, but knowing I had somewhere to turn for help comforted me more than I would have expected. I mustered a half-hearted grin and followed Britney out into the hall.

"She's a complete monster. None of the other teachers are nearly as strict as Campbell. Making you catch up on all that homework is ridiculous."

My silence seemed to leave my new friend at a loss for words. I guess she was used to people agreeing with everything she said. I didn't like to lie though, so when I didn't agree with someone I tended not to say anything. I guess I didn't think my new task was as unreasonable as it'd first appeared?

"On the plus side, at least we'll both be at the math lab together. I've had to spend an hour there every evening since Dad found out I had the class low on the first test. Stupid Internet. I can't believe they give our parents an account where they can see how we do on every test."

Britney had my sympathy there. Nobody liked their parents knowing too much about their school life, academic or otherwise. "Wow, they talked about doing that at my last school, but I wouldn't have expected a town this small to have something like that implemented."

We dropped our books off and started towards the cafeteria. Being back at my locker, back where I'd seen Mr. Gorgeous, made me wonder about him. Britney had to ask me a question twice before I realized she'd been talking.

"Sorry, I was thinking about something."

"Hmm, what distracted you?"

I debated dodging the question, but it was normal to talk about boys. "There was a guy and a girl who walked by earlier when we were at your locker."

A knowing look flashed across Britney's face. "Oh, their royal highnesses Alec and Jasmin. They're pretty distracting all right, but don't waste your time. They'll never waste a thought on you or me, or pretty much anyone."

The way she said their names implied they were a couple. Even if they weren't, she was probably right about not getting my hopes up. Especially considering the way Alec had looked at me there at the end. Despite my best efforts the question still slipped out. "They're together then?"

Britney smirked. "You really are masochistic, aren't you? That's the rumor. Nobody really seems to know, at least nobody who's talking, but they're almost always together. You really shouldn't go there; he's brutal when it comes to breaking girls' hearts."

There was a story there, but I wasn't about to ask now and expose myself to further ridicule.

Britney was oddly quiet as we entered the lunch room. I was a little hungry, but the pangs were a distant kind of discomfort. The real suffering for not eating wouldn't come into play until we hit the tutoring lab. Oh well, when I got home ravenous and ate a decent-sized meal Mom would probably be ecstatic. Or too wrapped up in some project to even notice. It was hard enough anticipating what I was going to do from day to day. Trying to figure Mom out was truly futile.

Being held up by Mrs. Campbell at least had one advantage; the line for Britney to get food was nearly non-existent. Britney was talking again, but it was still the kinds of things I could respond to with half my attention. I took the opportunity to get a good look at the cafeteria. It was incredibly small. It was probably on its second generation of students, but looked pretty good still. The linoleum floor was faded, but still relatively clean, and the white paint on the walls was conspicuously free of tags and gang signs.

The students even seemed to be mingling fairly easily with each other. I actually kind of missed the feel of armed camps. My school hadn't been bad compared to some stories I'd heard from California, but there'd still been some kids beaten pretty severely for crossing the wrong group of wannabe gang members.

Britney had a piece of pizza, and looked like she was eyeing a piece of cake until she noticed I was trailing along behind her without a tray of my own. She actually sighed as she passed the cake. The urge to giggle was so strong I uncapped my water bottle and turned slightly to the side in an attempt to disguise my amusement.

It was one of those moments I'd try to reconstruct in my head again and again. I think I must have heard the cash register till close, or maybe Britney said something. Whatever the reason, I took a step in her direction while still looking away, my bottle half raised, and ran into the biggest junior I'd ever seen.

My clumsiness would've been embarrassing enough all by itself. Unfortunately my mostly-full bottle of water splashed all over both of us.

I felt my cheeks go hot. Britney gasped and giggled. I silently told myself things were as bad as they were going to get. I was wrong. The boy wasn't as cute as Alec, but he was so close I could hear those cosmic scales being melted down into something useless again. Paperweights maybe.

I didn't want to see the mess my water had made of his shirt, so I started at the top and worked my way down. I'd seen better hair in a couple of fashion magazines, but not very many. Casually windswept, straight blond hair had become iconic sometime in the last few years, and this boy either spent an hour on his hair each morning, or the wind in Utah was kinder and gentler than the wind in Minnesota. Kinder, and currently working on its cosmetology license.

His skin was exquisitely tanned, lighter than Jasmin or Alec's, but exactly suited to his lighter hair tone. Friendly gray eyes perfectly spaced above some of the most natural looking white teeth I'd ever seen. My heart would have started slowing down if I'd been sure the display of teeth was a smile, but there was something about the expression that defied classification.

Gritting my teeth slightly I let my gaze continue on down to assess the damage, only I couldn't. I could see the wet spots on the shirt. My mind was classifying it as a dark green polo with some kind of designer insignia but I couldn't *see* anything other than how huge he was. I'd seen linemen on high-school football teams whose shoulders weren't as broad even with their pads on. The shirt was snug enough to see that the rest of him was built along the same lines. No wonder I'd bounced right off of him, a small car would've probably done about the same thing.

My blush deepened slightly as I realized I was wondering what it would feel like to have those arms wrapped around me. I jerked my gaze back up to the handsome face just in time to see the expression settle into a genuine smile.

"I'm so sorry. I should have been watching..."

He gently cut me off with a gesture. "No, please. It was entirely my fault. I shouldn't have tried to squeeze past you like that."

The smile was still there. That had to be a good sign. Usually when people said something nice and didn't mean it their smiles only lasted as long as they were speaking. I tried a tentative smile in return and his widened slightly.

"I'm Brandon."

Feeling more than a little nervous, I allowed him to capture my right hand in his.

"I'm Adr...Adriana."

Our handshake had ended, but my hand was tingling slightly. It was a pleasant, if illusionary, reminder of the contact, one I was hoping would last for about the next three days.

"You must be the poor soul who's got everyone buzzing with curiosity."

Brandon reached into the tall, glass-fronted fridge next to the cashier while he was talking, and pulled out a bottle of water and one of those aggressively-colored energy drinks. He slipped some money to the cashier while I was still trying to come up with a response that didn't sound stupid.

"Um, yeah. We just got into town last night."

He handed me the bottle of water. "Well I hope you'll like it here."

"Wait, what's this for?"

The grin was back, and his teeth were still perfect. "I just made you spill yours, it's only fair."

Brandon nodded at Britney, who stood there with her mouth slightly open, as he walked away.

After a second or two of both of us staring blankly after Brandon, Britney grabbed me by the hand, the one holding the new, unopened water bottle, and pulled me over to a table in the corner.

"Oh my gosh, you just poured water all over Brandon Worthingfield the Third. And then he talked to you. This is *so* incredible."

I more or less fell into my seat, staring at my new bottle of water as Britney's chatter poured over me. It was pointless to try and pay attention to anything she was saying. It was all I could do to remember to nod when she paused and looked at me expectantly.

Lunch passed all too quickly. Before I knew it we were back at Britney's locker and she was promising to give me a ride home from school after Spanish.

History was about as dry as I'd expected, which was really too bad. I'd had a good history teacher in junior high, and it was an incredibly interesting subject when taught right. Unfortunately Mr. Simms was possibly the worst teacher I'd ever had. I mentally shrugged when we were told to open our books and read the chapter to ourselves. At least I wouldn't have any worries when it came to catching up in this class.

Thoughts of Brandon made it hard to really get into the chapter. Also, it was hard not to notice the borderline hostile stares from the other kids. I sighed in relief when the bell rang, and pulled out my schedule and map to see where I'd be going next. Physics? I mentally reviewed my conversation with the secretary, but couldn't remember either of us mentioning the class. As if trying to catch up in Algebra wasn't going to be bad enough, I was going to face the same kind of problem in physics.

Grumbling to myself, I promised to try and switch into something better first thing tomorrow morning. The class was in a section of the building I hadn't been to yet, one apparently older than the rest of the building. The lights were spaced further apart and the cinder blocks in the walls were a slightly different size.

Good thing I still had my water. The old part of the school was just as hot as the rest. You'd think functioning air-conditioning would be a necessity for a school so far south. At least it should cool down a little in the coming months. Assuming of course I lasted that long without losing it from dealing with all of the crazy small-town people in this school.

I entered the classroom and was immediately greeted by a portly, white-haired woman. "Hello, hello. My name is Mrs. Alexander, and you must be Adri. Oh, not Adri? Very good then, Adriana it is."

I watched bemusedly as Mrs. Alexander searched through her pockets for something to write with for at least half a minute before realizing she'd placed her pen behind her ear. The form now signed, the pen went back behind her ear for safekeeping, and she motioned me to a seat, predictably at the back of the classroom.

As I negotiated the crooked path between desks, I found myself looking forward to the class. Right up until Alec slipped into the classroom a few seconds before the bell rang.

If there'd been any justice in the universe, he'd have somehow gotten uglier over the last few hours. That or I'd have developed some kind of partial immunity to him. Neither was the case, he was just as unearthly gorgeous as he'd been in the hall. The sight of him was almost overwhelming.

As he slipped into a desk an aisle away from me, I tried to breathe deeply and slowly in a futile effort to calm my racing heart. It helped a little when he slid the desk back a few feet. As long as I watched Mrs. Alexander I couldn't see Alec anymore. It seemed like I could still feel him though. The right side of my body hummed and tingled, almost imperceptibly, telling me he was there.

I did my best to ignore the sensation, concentrating on the pictures rapidly forming on the ancient blackboard as Mrs. Alexander diagrammed the conceptual model of a wave, and started dissecting the various parts. Crest, trough, period, amplitude. None of it was hard to understand, not particularly interesting, but still a welcome distraction.

After what seemed like an eternity, Mrs. Alexander placed the piece of chalk she was using behind her other ear and smiled at the class. "Okay, that's your introduction to light. Form up into your usual groups and take a project summary; you'll be working on this for the next few days."

I joined the class in filing past the teacher's desk, and then watched as everyone started moving desks around. Mrs. Alexander saw me walking hesitantly back to my desk, and intercepted me before I could get there.

"Miss Paige, you'll have the good luck of working with Mr. Graves."

It wasn't until Alec looked up, annoyance clearly evident on his handsome face, that I realized I was supposed to work with him. It was yet another sign of rejection in a day that'd been largely filled with everything but acceptance. It shouldn't have bothered me, not considering how poorly I'd always fit in; but whether because of his good looks, or for some other unrelated reason, I found myself wanting Alec's approval. My breathing started coming faster, exceeded only by the pace of my heart.

Apparently I wasn't the only one who could tell that working with me wasn't what the school's resident rock star had in mind. There was a scattered chorus of badly stifled giggles off to the front of the class. Not the normal kind people use when they're amused, but the high-pitched ones girls use to embarrass each other.

Alec's face unexpectedly softened for a moment, his expression still unwelcoming, but now mixed with a trace of something else. While I was busy trying to understand the sudden change, Mrs. Alexander looked at the front of the class with a frown on her face for a moment. I suddenly realized that she knew the difference between the two kinds of giggles. That was unusual in someone so old. The younger teachers usually kept the girls from being too awful to each other, but the old guard didn't really catch the subtle differences high-school girls used to emotionally traumatize each other.

Her kindly face taking on a stern cast, Mrs. Alexander turned back to Alec. "I'm sure you'll enjoy working with Miss Paige, Alec. After all, you can't really expect to do everything by yourself. Occasionally a helping hand is exactly what's called for."

The words reached inside me, pulling on something that was already bleeding, tearing it further. The classroom rocked back and forth at the same time my legs lost the ability to support my weight. Alec lunged toward me, moving incredibly quickly as my mind spun away back to our kitchen table.

I was fourteen and trying to understand geometry proofs. Mom had given up trying to help me with homework about the time I turned twelve, so she kept telling me to just read the book and figure out what they were doing in the examples.

By the time Dad got home from work tears were streaming down my face and I couldn't even see the diagrams anymore. "I can't do it, Dad. Missy Jeffrys already did the entire assignment before we even got out of class, and I can't even figure out one problem. I'm not good enough; I'm never good enough."

Rough fingers had appeared from outside my peripheral vision, gently smoothing away tears. "Come on honey, you really can't expect to do everything by yourself. Let's take a break for dinner, and then I'll help you."

He'd forestalled my next excuse as if reading my mind. "There isn't anything wrong with letting someone help you. Sometimes a helping hand is exactly what's called for."

The memory had a vividness that'd been lacking lately. It was the same aching realism that'd devoured nearly a month of my existence before I finally decided I had to try and go on with my life, for Mom's sake if for no other reason.

I panicked when I realized just how badly I wanted to slip back into that twilight world where nothing hurt, where it didn't matter if people liked me or not. The one where I still had all three of the most important people in my world.

The fear that I'd give in, that I'd end up in a hospital during the day or two it took Mom to realize I hadn't made it home from school, pulled me back sooner than normal. For a second my mind inhabited a body that wouldn't obey any of the normal commands. Fear snaked out from my center when my eyes wouldn't open, but before my heart could really start accelerating, my eyelids started functioning again.

The desks on the route between Alec and I were lying haphazardly on their sides, but there wasn't any sign of Alec. Mrs. Alexander was looking down at me, concern etched into her features, and the beginnings of a crowd was starting to form as the rest of the students came over to look at the freak. Only something wasn't right. They weren't towering enough. When you pass out on a regular basis, you get used to finding yourself on the floor surrounded by concerned-looking people, but none of these people were looming properly.

Everyone else having somehow gotten too short suddenly wasn't as important. The room was still swinging around, only now it wasn't moving, I was. A pair of muscular arms encircled my tingling waist and legs, holding me tightly to a near rock-hard chest as Alec deftly weaved through the approaching crowd of students.

I closed my eyes as a wave of heat started at my collarbones and rushed up to the tips of my ears. I wanted to throw up, except that would be even more embarrassing than being carried out of class by the most popular boy in school.

I opened my eyes and found we were already out in the hall. Alec's stride was so smooth it was hard to believe we weren't still back in the classroom.

"Put me down, I mean please put me down."

Those clear, deep eyes met mine for a second, seeming to look past the surface and all the way down to the bleeding mental gash that'd just triggered my most recent collapse. I was trying to marshal my arguments, but his eyes wiped my mind clean. I couldn't form another coherent thought until he shook his head and looked away.

"You need to see the nurse."

My mind hiccupped for a second. There should be some kind of law requiring him to hide those things. Sunglasses, or maybe a blindfold.

"I'm fine. That wasn't anything; it didn't mean anything. Please put me down."

I tried to put the right amounts of sincerity and confidence in my words, but I wasn't a very good liar. Something changed though because Alec slowed his ground-eating stride.

"What do you mean you're fine? People don't just collapse with no warning. You seemed fine and then you were falling. You s...you seemed hurt."

I shook my head gingerly, surprised when I didn't feel the twinge I knew was coming. The attack had been more sudden than usual and nobody had been close enough to catch me. In those circumstances experience had shown that I led with my head.

"It was just the heat here. I'm not used to it. Now *please* put me down."

Alec looked at me doubtfully, then took a deep, no doubt calming breath, and shrugged. The movement seemed too casual, almost as if he was angry, but trying to hide it. I wanted to try and make eye contact to test my hypothesis, but was afraid of what I'd see. The tingling was spreading, no doubt a bad sign. Maybe I'd hit my head even harder than I thought.

"It was all just a game for you, wasn't it?"

There was anger behind the voice now, subtle, like the scent of rain the night before a storm, but definitely there. I started to bristle; I even took a breath to explain what'd really happened. Only the truth wasn't any better than the story he'd fabricated. It was worse even. I'd much rather this cocky, spoiled, rich boy be mad at me than feel pity. I'd had enough pity from my mom to last years.

"You bet. Think they bought it?"

I tried to inject the proper amount of blonde stupidity into my words, but wasn't sure it worked until I felt Alec's arms tighten almost painfully around me. I gasped, and he set me down so quickly I almost fell over.

Before I'd even regained my balance, he was walking away, moving so quickly I would've needed to run to keep up. Even so, he hadn't turned away quick enough to hide the complete disdain in his expression.

I suddenly found myself wishing I'd told him the truth rather than making him think I was stupid and manipulative.

It was too late. He was already out of sight, and by now his opinion of me was fixed.

Chapter 4

School hadn't gotten any worse after I'd convinced the hottest boy on the planet that I was a complete waste of oxygen, but it hadn't gotten any better either. Mrs. Tiggs, my Spanish teacher, had seemed every bit as mean as my Biology teacher from earlier in the day, and it had been a relief when Britney had finally dropped me off at home.

I watched Britney's little white Saturn disappear down the lane with a complex set of feelings that included a bit of loneliness and more than a little relief. After a minute or two spent staring off into space, I finally decided the discomfort in my stomach was sharp enough to justify the effort of eating.

Given the ridiculous heat, studying was the last thing I wanted to do, but there wasn't really anything else to do so I changed into cooler clothes and made the best of it. Three hours later my brain felt like it was going to run out of my nose, so I wandered upstairs.

It was still too hot for comfort in my room, but unpacking in the heat was better than facing the math problems waiting for me downstairs. We'd partially unpacked things to get my bedspread out, so everything else went pretty quickly. My room wasn't particularly large, but someone had put a long shelf around the top of the room, and the closet had more storage space than my room back home. My meager belongings quickly found new homes.

I looked one last time at the box holding my clothes, and then sighed and shoved it under the bed. My unpacking was all done, which meant I had to go back to my homework. At least now I could listen to my music while I studied.

Fifteen minutes later I was safely ensconced in my room listening to the London Cast version of Les Misérables as I tried to work through my backlog of Algebra assignments. When I finally surfaced from orders of operation as the sun started setting, I was pleasantly surprised things had gone so well. As masochistic as it sounded, I actually enjoyed settling down with a set of academic problems, and working my way through them. Sometimes I entered a Zen-like state where everything else in the world just dropped away. It was nice to know the accident hadn't changed that at least.

My heart stuttered a little, but I wrenched my thoughts away from where they'd been headed, distracting myself by wondering where Mom was. She'd been a little flighty before, but now it wasn't uncommon for her to be gone for twenty-four hours at a stretch. In some ways it was hard not having her around, but in other ways it was a relief. Sometimes she reminded me too much of Dad and Cindi.

A surge of guilt splashed around inside me at the thought, but it was a realization I'd made weeks ago. By now some of the sharper edges to the emotion had worn away. I shrugged, dropping my book and binder on the floor next to my bed. Dwelling on the guilt would just make me think about why I felt guilty in the first place. I'd find myself on the floor with no memory of how I'd gotten there.

By the time I'd brushed my teeth and finished the rest of my nightly ritual, my mind was wholly in the present, and I was starting to get a little depressed. I'd never particularly fit in back home, but there'd been enough other people in various fringe groups that I'd always felt like I had somewhere to go if I ever wanted more friends. I would've had to play a role to a certain extent, which was why I'd never made the effort, but the option had always been there.

It didn't look like that'd be a possibility in Sanctuary. In an entire day I'd had exactly one person try and befriend me. As much as I appreciated the effort, I couldn't shake the feeling Britney was befriending me mostly because *she* didn't have any other options. With Mom becoming less dependable by the day, I was in for a miserable, lonely two years until I could graduate and escape to a big city. Hopefully there I could safely find a niche among the other quasi-loners who didn't fit in anywhere else.

As I turned my light out and got into bed I realized there'd been one bright spot to the day. Brandon Worthingfield III might not really be interested in me, but he was obviously at the top of the social food chain, and he'd already shown me way more attention than any of the boys back home ever had. Maybe there was some hope after all.

I was lost, not just in the sense of not knowing where I was, but because I'd never been anywhere even remotely like this. The breeze was louder than any I'd ever heard before, and was laden with an unimaginable host of scents.

It took me several seconds to sort through things enough to realize I was smelling things I didn't even have a name for. After several seconds of trying to catalog the most delightful of my new discoveries, I realized I'd had my eyes closed since I'd gotten here, possibly an unconscious defense mechanism meant to protect me from sensory overload.

The distant sound of water trickling down a rock face, of leaves gently caressing each other in the breeze faded away as I took in an amazing wonderland of light. The trees I'd been listening to were exactly where I expected them to be, but it took me several heartbeats to recognize them. Gone were the sturdy, brown behemoths I'd spent so much time climbing with Cindi.

Instead, pillars of soft light reached up to the sky, swaying slowly back and forth with the wind, creaking in a rhythm I'd known by heart since I was seven. I felt tears collecting in the corners of my eyes as I reached out and touched the nearest tree. It was as if the world I'd known my entire life had been simply a moldy cover designed to hide the true nature of my surroundings. Now the mask was gone and I was immersed in vivid colors, living lights, and a sense of harmony so strong it nearly overwhelmed me.

It was impossible to say for certain how long I sat looking at the gentle motion of the tree branches, marveling at the way things made up of light could still cast shadows when silhouetted by the harsher light of the sun.

Only somehow the sun had disappeared, replaced by the paler, colder light of the moon. The trees were still graceful strands of light, but the breeze had changed to a harsh thing, one carrying new scents that somehow represented danger.

Something inside me forced my limbs into motion. I was running before the first howl tore through the night. I was moving unimaginably fast, jumping fallen trees and bounding over other obstacles which even my improved vision struggled to make out in time for me to avoid them. The speed of my passage wrung tears from my eyes, but I didn't dare slow.

They were back there, four of them moving with speed only slightly less than my own, noses to the ground to follow my scent, save for the moments in which they let loose their unearthly howls.

A flicker of motion up ahead should have made me pull up in fear, but the smell accompanying it was somehow familiar, somehow safe. I knew if I could reach the shadowy person I'd been unconsciously following, I'd be safe, but he was so incredibly fast and my pursuers were gaining.

The sound of my alarm pulled me out of a whole series of nightmares in which I was running from unknown menaces. Each had been terrifying, but none as vivid as the first. Bad dreams had become a frequent companion since the accident. It'd become nearly passé to wake up emotionally exhausted from what should have been a restful night, but these dreams had been different.

I'd played out nearly every possible combination of events since the accident. Dreams where I was the one driving instead of Cindi. Dreams where I got a ride home with someone so Dad and Cindi didn't have any reason to be on the road. Dreams where I was in the truck that killed them, even dreams where I was in the back seat as a passenger at the moment of impact.

I was used to awaking shaking and scared countless times during the course of a night, but I'd never felt that level of pure, bestial fear.

I stumbled into the bathroom and flipped on the light, only to groan at how ghastly I looked. I was even paler than normal, with dark circles under my eyes that only a crack addict could possibly find attractive.

A hot shower did a little to make me more presentable, I tried to hide the shadows with some makeup, and then finally gave up after botching the second application, and just put on some mascara and eyeliner. The mundane process of getting ready for the day wore away some of the edge to my nightmare. It was already starting to seem more like a normal, safe dream.

I put on jeans and a button-up shirt, and then all but stumbled downstairs with my backpack in hand. Sometime during the night Mom had put our message board up on the fridge.

Went shopping, food in the fridge, don't forget breakfast and lunch. See you tonight after school. Love you. —Mom

I shook my head resignedly; you'd think the message would have changed at least a little over the last few weeks, but it was still pretty much the same. 'Don't forget to eat, I'll be back later, but it might be a couple of days.'

I was tempted to just ignore the message, but that'd just make her testy at some point. It made her feel like a poor mom if we went too long without some kind of communication.

Have to stay late for math tutoring. A friend will bring me home. —A.

Signing my notes with an initial still felt a little like a stroke of brilliance. Writing out Adriana was a pain, but for obvious reasons I couldn't use the shortened version of my name.

I glanced down at my watch and saw it was nearly time for Britney to show up. With a sigh I opened up the fridge and pulled out one of the trendy, meal-in-a-bottle drinks Mom had started getting lately. I didn't particularly like them, but it would keep until I was actually hungry, and Mom would count the bottles as a way of determining how many meals I was missing.

I thought about taking a second bottle, but they were too expensive to pour down a sink, and I knew I wouldn't be hungry enough to finish up the first, let alone a second meal.

The tinny blare of a car horn pulled me out the front door. Britney was waiting outside with her heater going full blast. I was surprised at how cold it was with the sun still struggling to get above the mountains. Of course it wasn't cold enough for me to need a heater, but I also wasn't wearing Britney's shorts, which looked like they were even shorter than the ones she'd worn the day before.

It was amazing what the administration was letting everyone get away with. Of course, if I had legs like some of these girls, I'd probably be joining in.

Britney turned down her rap music just long enough to say "Hi", and then we were off to school. The music was fairly hideous, but it did spare me having to try and be friendly before I was fully awake. Of course it also stopped me from digging further into the mystery of why it was so dangerous to hike. That particular question would probably have to wait at least until lunch.

Mrs. Sorenson looked up as I walked into a nearly empty class, but I was on time, even if only barely. I'd heard of teachers taking an instant dislike to one of their students, but I'd never experienced it first hand until now.

I fielded two questions on the role of phosphorus in photosynthesis before being hit with a third one I couldn't answer. I felt my ears go hot as the three other girls in the classroom giggled.

I slunk out of class as soon as the bell rang. English went better. Mr. Whethers got the class involved in a discussion of Heathcliff's motivations, which kept everyone occupied for the full class time, and distracted me from what was likely to happen when Britney and I got to algebra.

As we walked back to our lockers between classes, I noticed that the halls seemed strangely empty. Britney rolled her eyes when I asked why.

"Of course nobody's here. Tonight's the full moon, and there was a monster party last night. There'll be another tonight and then again tomorrow."

I felt my eyes go big. "You mean to tell me that seventy percent of the school parties for three nights running every month?"

Britney nodded. "It's the only redeeming feature to this stupid little town, and I can't even go since the accident..."

I could see her trying to figure out how to sidestep the issue, but I wasn't about to let her off the hook. "Listen, if there's something dangerous around here don't you think I should know about it?"

She shifted uncomfortably from one foot to another, eyes glancing to each side of us in an effort to see who might overhear us. "We can't talk about it here; you'll have to trust me. Wait until lunch."

I wasn't entirely satisfied, but nodded, and followed her to algebra.

Mrs. Campbell shot us both a glance that didn't bode well for any attempt to get out of class without a stern reprimand, but allowed us to go to our respective seats without comment.

I pulled out the two assignments I'd done the night before, and passed them up with everyone else's homework. Realizing the lecture wouldn't do me any good, I pulled out my book, and started reading the next section in my self-appointed study regimen. Mrs. Campbell either understood what I was trying to accomplish, or was saving up all her venom for after class. She didn't call on me even once.

Britney wasn't so lucky, and I caught a nasty look from her each time I surfaced from my textbook. The glares angered me more than I'd expected. I was having to catch up on a month's worth of assignments; she didn't have any right to get pissy just because she wasn't prepared.

The third time it happened, I stopped pretending not to notice and shot Britney a sugar-sweet look of my own. She didn't quite seem to know how to take that and the rest of the class passed quickly. All too soon, it was time to go up and talk to Mrs. Campbell. I put off the ordeal as long as I could, waiting until everyone but Britney and I had exited the room. Britney looked particularly unhappy.

Mrs. Campbell was looking at my homework when I reached her desk. "I was prepared to tear into you for not going to the tutoring lab last night, but that hardly seems fair seeing as how you went ahead and did the work by yourself."

I felt a small glow of satisfaction flare into life, but her next words ensured it didn't get out of hand. "Of course, you've got the right answers, and technically you're attacking the problems correctly, but you're leaving out a couple of steps that I think will give you problems a bit later on. Please take my advice and spend a little bit of time at the math lab. Even if you can't make it every day, you need to come in a few times a week."

"Yes, ma'am." The scolding actually hadn't been that bad, almost like disguised praise. Britney looked like she was hoping for something similar, but Mrs. Campbell's expression quickly dashed that idea.

"You on the other hand definitely need to spend every night at the math lab. Your homework was incomplete, and of the problems you bothered to attempt, you didn't do a single one correctly. Britney, you're headed towards a failing grade, and while you might not care, your father most certainly does. Make my class a priority, or I'll stop in for a checkup and let slip just how poorly you're doing to dear old Dad, and then you'll find yourself riding the bus to school."

It was a vicious threat, but one almost guaranteed to have an effect. Britney most definitely didn't want to be stuck riding the bus with all of the junior high kids and other assorted 'losers'. Her mouth opened and closed several times and then she nodded and fled the classroom.

When I finally caught up with her she'd recovered enough to complain, but there was a breathless nature to her voice that told me she wouldn't be skipping the math lab for a little while. I made non-committal noises as we waited in line, all the while scanning the cafeteria for two faces.

Actually, scanning wasn't the right word for it. I just kind of looked that way and instantly found my eyes drawn to Brandon. He was surrounded by people, mostly female, all attractive. Taking in all of those lithe, tan bodies, I suddenly felt incredibly inferior. All of the impending skin cancer deaths suddenly didn't seem quite so important.

I looked away before anyone could see me staring. Britney was still looking longingly at a pile of fries. When I looked up again Brandon was looking back at me with a smile that communicated all kinds of things I'd always thought you needed words for.

His expression seemed to say he was glad to see me, embarrassed to be the center of attention, and sorry he couldn't get away from his friends to come over and say hi. I felt my face go hot with embarrassment. I tried to step behind a pillar before he saw me go bright red, but knew I hadn't succeeded.

I bit my lip as I realized how spastic I was being. I'd spent the last sixteen-plus years suppressing my natural tendency to form crushes on one cute boy after another. I'd nearly perfected the art of exhibiting zero interest in the opposite sex. The whole point of my existence had been avoiding the kinds of things that'd result in everyone laughing at me. Why was I setting my sights on a boy who was so far out of my league? Even if there'd been a chance he might like me, I had absolutely no idea how to proceed.

Given the option, I would've just hid behind the pillar until everyone left for class, but Britney had made her decision, and was paying for her food. Essentially out of time, I took a deep breath and followed her to a table. I couldn't help glancing towards Brandon's table one last time. I was hoping he was still smiling. Maybe he'd seen how awkward I was, but didn't mind. Maybe he even thought it was endearing. Failing that, I at least hoped he wasn't chuckling with his friends over the new girl's stupid infatuation.

He wasn't doing either, in fact, he seemed to be very much involved in a conversation with the stocky boy on his right. The rest of the kids at the table were listening just as intensely, all except for the brunette on Brandon's left who was looking in our direction.

My face pulled back in a smile, I even brought my hand partway up in a wave before I realized I recognized her. It was the trendy girl from the office, and she apparently still didn't like me.

I felt my face get even hotter, only now I was both angry and embarrassed. It was a relief to sink down into a chair with my back to Brandon and his friends. Strangely enough, Britney also being so obviously uncomfortable helped calm me down.

"Okay, out with it, why is this such a big deal?"

Britney shifted back and forth in her seat for a couple of seconds before leaning in to whisper. "It really shouldn't be a big deal, but everyone around here acts like it's taboo. Two hikers were killed by some kind of wild animal a few months ago."

I felt my heart skip a beat as a chill ran from the base of my spine all the way to my scalp. Britney's innocuous words shouldn't have caused my mind to immediately sink back to the terror I'd felt this morning, but they did.

For a moment I couldn't focus on what Britney was saying, my heartbeat had become completely erratic from the surge of adrenaline flooding my body as it futilely tried to escape the nameless things that'd been snapping at my heels.

"...out in the south end of Zions. It was Mark Childs and Lessi Arnolds. The bodies were a couple of days old by the time search and rescue found them, but it was pretty obvious they'd been mauled by something."

I opened my mouth to interrupt, but my vocal chords weren't working. Now that she'd finally broached the subject, Britney was unstoppable. "It had to have been a mountain lion, there isn't anything else around here that's both aggressive and big enough to kill people, but neither of them had been gnawed on at all, which was strange enough by itself. Everyone refusing to talk about it would've been enough to make it X-Files weird, but when the coroner threw such a fit, it entered a class of its own."

Britney looked around again to make sure nobody was in hearing range, and then leaned in even closer. "He said the wounds weren't made by anything in the cat family. He wrote up a whole paper on how the teeth marks were made by some kind of new, previously undiscovered predator."

The chills were back, and they'd redoubled in intensity. It was like the howl from my dream was echoing through my soul. "Did he say what it was like? The predator, I mean."

Britney nodded slowly. "Yeah, he thought it was somehow related to a wolf, but bigger and stronger, with claws like something out of a slasher movie. He was causing such a stir in St. George they finally fired him. They said he was sensationalizing the attack to get his fifteen minutes of fame. Daddy tried to get access to the bodies, to provide a second opinion even though that isn't his real area of expertise, but they blocked him cold. He thinks they were worried about scaring away the tourists. They had to make the accident go away, to save the local economy."

My hands had gone cold despite the oppressive heat, just now hitting its full stride for the day. You didn't hang around the fringe without running into plenty of people who were conspiracy theorists. Discussing UFOs, Illuminati, and X-Files had been like air and water for some of the people I'd known back in Minneapolis. I'd never given their wild theories a second thought before, but what Britney was describing sounded like a pretty convincing attempt at a cover-up.

I looked up as I realized Britney had fallen silent, only to realize with a start that a pair of tears were trickling down her face.

"Mark and Lessi were the only ones to really open up when I moved in. Their great-grandparents were some of the first people to settle down here. They used to tell me all kinds of crazy stories. After they were killed nobody would really talk to me. Everyone was polite, but it was like I was shut out, like they blamed me for what happened."

Britney paused for a second and then shuddered. "I was supposed to have been with them."

My shoulders suddenly relaxed as everything started to make sense. There'd been an attack of course. There might have even been a bit of a cover-up by local, or regional, authorities, but Britney's father was probably right in assuming the motivation had been protecting the tourist industry.

That was all straightforward, but even that wasn't as obvious as the fact that Britney was suffering from some kind of survivor's guilt. She felt like she was somehow to blame for not dying with her friends, and was reading all kinds of motivations into people's behavior that weren't even there. That would've been spooky enough, but then I'd turned around, linked all of it to a freak nightmare and been convinced the world was about to end. Silly.

I did my best to comfort Britney after that, but was more than a little relieved when lunch finally ended. That of course made me feel heartless and guilty in turn, but I was still too fragile to deal with her issues. When it's all you can do to get through the day yourself, it's impossible to be a pillar of strength for someone else.

History was a complete waste of time. I hadn't even made it through the reading assignment, and I still got a perfect score on the pop quiz.

Physics was surprisingly full. Apparently Alec was the only hard-core party animal in the class. I was still feeling weird from Britney's story, so unlike the rest of my classmates, who seemed genuinely intrigued by the assignment, I just pretended to leaf through a reference book all hour.

Spanish was as bad as history. Mrs. Tiggs turned on one of the Spanish TV channels within thirty seconds of class starting. Towards the end of the hour I finally started to come back out of my funk, so I put the last few minutes to good use reviewing vocabulary for the quiz on Tuesday.

I felt a momentary surge of relief when class ended, but the feeling evaporated when I remembered I had to go to math tutoring.

I grabbed my math book, and met an equally morose Britney at her locker. There are only so many times one person can say something sucks, and expect the other person to agree with them. Britney quickly used up her allotment of complaints, and then subsided into silence as she led the way to an out-of-the-way corner of the old school.

I'd noticed Britney liked to position herself so she was closest to the middle of the hall. Admittedly, dodging all the people trying to get into their lockers wasn't much fun, but I suspected her real motivation was a desire to ensure she could see and be seen, which was much more easily accomplished by relegating me to the outside position.

Normally I'd have just viewed her theatrics with amusement, but it'd been a long day and I wasn't in the mood. If I'd known for sure where we were heading, I'd have considered cutting her off, even with all of the probable fallout, but I didn't. Instead I just sighed, followed her around a corner, and collided with six-plus feet of muscled goodness packaged in a white polo shirt that looked worryingly familiar.

Brandon caught me as I rebounded from him, easily stopping my momentum before I could stumble into a locker. "We'd better be careful; I'm starting to sense a trend."

I wanted to say something equally witty, but his shirt did wonderful, probably illegal things to his gray eyes, and his perfectly straight teeth were parted in a friendly grin that couldn't possibly be meant for me.

I managed a feeble grin before the silence stretched too far towards becoming uncomfortable, but it was a pathetic attempt. Brandon gently released my shoulders and detoured around me with a grace that should have looked unnatural on a boy, but which somehow exuded more masculinity than any four boys I'd known back home.

Britney shot me an envious look and then turned and stalked through an open doorway. I should have been worried I was upsetting my only 'friend'. Failing that, I should at least be mad she was being so unreasonable, but my racing heart brushed those feelings away. Other than a persistent, imaginary tingling along my shoulders I was strangely numb inside as I followed her into the tutoring room.

There were more kids inside than I'd expected, enough that a normal room would've felt crowded, but this wasn't a normal room. Someone had knocked down a wall or two, creating a space that was strangely welcoming, despite obviously being meant for academic pursuits. A large number of rectangular tables were scattered about the room, situated so that the two people sitting at them would feel relatively isolated.

As I continued my survey, I realized that there was only ever one pile of books at any given table, and in the few instances in which two people were sitting at a table, one of the individuals was obviously explaining something to the other one.

Most of the kids looked fairly run-of-the-mill. There was even the expected contingent of jocks, obviously there just because a coach or parent had delivered some kind of ultimatum. Britney predictably headed over and staked out a table as close as she could get to a group of girls who were probably cheerleaders.

Clustered around the other end of the room were the more studious kids, the kind who were generally pretty smart, but for whatever reason were struggling with math. I wasn't surprised to see a kind of a no-man's-land between the two ends of the spectrum. I was startled to see that the middle ground was inhabited by an attractive girl a year or two younger than me.

Left to my own devices, I would've normally picked a table over on the nerd end of the room, but I found myself relating more to the girl stuck in the middle. She looked up and met my gaze for just a second before ducking back down and concentrating on her homework. Shy, obviously, and not popular. There'd been the hint of a smile on her face, possibly constrained by fear of how her overture might be received.

Obviously a complete social reject just like me. It was nice to finally meet a kindred spirit. Britney's clingy neediness was nearly as bad as the icy indifference or borderline hostility all of the rest of the students displayed. Except for Brandon, but I couldn't quite bring myself to trust him. A boy that cute wasn't nice to a girl like me unless he wanted something from her.

Mrs. Campbell walked over while I was casing the room. She still looked stern, but her face had relaxed slightly. She even smiled as she handed me a green, laminated card. "You'll need to pick out an empty table, we don't let students share here. Also I'd recommend choosing one somewhat distant from Ms. Samuels, she doesn't need any more distractions than she already has.

When you have a question, or need help from one of the tutors, flip the card over to the red side and place it on your desk."

I nodded and headed over to a table near the girl, one where I could watch her without her seeing me. I wasn't going to fall all over myself to become her friend or anything, but I figured it was worth observing her for a little bit. If she really was cool then we might strike up a friendship at some point. If she wasn't, then the sooner I could confirm that fact the better off I'd be.

I pulled out my book, study guide, and some paper, and got busy with my next self-assigned homework set. I was up to graphing now, which was about as straightforward as you could get.

I made pretty good progress, pausing from time to time to stretch my neck and look around. The girl had flipped her card over to the red side, and had a tutor with her, a clumsy-looking boy who looked like he might be a senior. Based on the glasses, and the fact he had to have picked them out without any input from a girl younger than forty, I figured he was in debate, or maybe the chess club. He was probably incredibly nice, and boring as watching paint dry. Exactly the kind of guy my mom would turn cartwheels over. I'd have to make sure they never met.

I took the opportunity to look a little more closely at the girl. Seen from profile, she wasn't quite as pretty as I'd thought originally. She wasn't exactly plain-looking, but her features weren't very remarkable. She did have incredibly soft-looking wavy brown hair though.

It looked like debate boy had pretty much finished answering her question. I looked back down at my book so I wouldn't get caught staring. I was just about to dive back into my text book when someone cleared their throat nearby.

The tutor was standing at my elbow looking over my assignment. "Hi, I'm Albert, and you must be Adri."

I winced again. It was going to take a lot of work to get people to use my full name. "Adriana, but I don't need any help."

Albert smiled. "I know your card wasn't on the red side, but Mrs. Campbell asked me to stop by and go over a couple of steps you left out on your homework assignment from today. Since I just finished with Rachel and was over here already, I thought I'd show you the steps you're missing."

I nodded my assent as I mentally filed away both his name and the girl's. Surprisingly enough, Albert was a good teacher, pointing out the steps I'd been skipping over, and even explaining why they were important. It was rare enough to find a school teacher who could really teach math these days, finding a student who could teach was nearly a miracle.

Rachel packed up her things while I was being instructed in the finer points of inequalities. As she slid the last book into her backpack, Albert stepped away from my desk with another smile.

I flipped over to the next chapter and started in on functions as Rachel exited out a corner door I hadn't noticed before. I saw a flash of the stunted, brown vegetation that the locals called grass before the door swung back closed. Suppressing an urge to just surrender and go outside until Britney finished up, I got started. The roar of some kind of high-performance engine a few seconds later almost changed my mind, but my native stubbornness kicked in before I let the thought get out of hand.

The subject matter was harder than graphing, but I persevered, and managed to make it through all fifteen problems without resorting to the red side of the card. Of course Albert did stop by to see if I was having any difficulties, but since I didn't summon him, he couldn't read anything into it.

When Britney stomped over and asked if I was done, I considered telling her I needed ten more minutes. Her being an attention hog didn't justify me being petty though. I just nodded instead and packed up my stuff.

The ride home was completely uneventful, and mercifully brief. Britney was one of those people who drive fast normally, and even faster when they are pissed off. Apparently having to stay after school to study merited twenty-five over the speed limit.

I normally would have complained—I'd become much more sensitive about speeding in the last couple of months, but I was anxious to get home, and very much not feeling like there was anything particularly special to live for. Not that I was suicidal, contrary to Mom's unvoiced, but obvious fears. I just didn't have much of anything to look forward to.

It wasn't until Britney's Saturn was nearly out of sight that I realized our Jeep Cherokee was parked in the driveway. I sometimes felt I should have outgrown the need to talk to Mom when things were tough, but I couldn't deny that it felt like a big weight had been lifted off me as I walked through the door.

"I'm home, Mom. How did your latest shoot..." Whatever I'd been about to say evaporated off of my tongue as I entered the living room and saw Mom curled up on the couch with bloodshot eyes.

Mom had always been the strong one. I still more or less belonged in some kind of padded room. Mom had simply accepted events and done her best to hold our life together so there'd be something for me to come back to.

"What happened?"

I wanted to comfort her like I used to do with Cindi, but I suddenly realized I didn't know how. Parents weren't supposed to need reassuring. If they did, they were supposed to work it out between each other. Only now there was just her.

"The bank's calling the loan on our house. They called the Mayor's office and were told I didn't get the contract to do the tourism brochure. They're claiming I committed loan fraud. Only I don't understand, Mr. Peters told me I had the job."

I'd pretty much forgotten about the tourism brochure for the city. It'd sounded like the perfect job for Mom, albeit a short term one. Now it was sounding like it'd been too good to be true. The move had been something I'd opposed and then ignored when my opposition hadn't made any difference. I didn't know anything about grown-up things like mortgages. I'd been too self-absorbed to learn. For the first time I felt guilty about making things harder for Mom. Surely there was something I could have done to help out, even considering the attacks.

"They can't do that, can they? I mean, if they told you that you had the job they can't take it away, can they?"

Mom rooted around in a half empty box until she found some tissues, it wasn't the first one she'd been through this afternoon.

"I didn't think so, but Mr. Peters claims there was never any contract signed and I can't find our copy in any of the boxes."

"Mom, what are we going to do? Where will we go if they kick us out?"

She smoothed my hair back from my face. "Don't worry about that, sweetie. I'm sure everything will be okay. I was just over-reacting. It'll turn out to be nothing."

It was just like Mom to misplace something important like that. I opened my mouth to agree with her, but stopped before the words could fully form. I didn't know much, but fraud wasn't the kind of thing you associated with a slap on the wrist. If the worst happened and Mom was going to serve jail time then we had bigger problems than even what she was admitting to.

It looked like the sun must have set hours ago, but it wasn't really dark. The full moon seemed oddly brighter than normal, edging the landscape with a silvery tracing. The cool illumination was strangely complemented by the warm tendrils of light trying to escape from the greenery surrounding the area.

I let my gaze drop, and found an unearthly pool of liquid light at my feet. The quiet murmur of falling water to my right kindled a burning thirst I hadn't realized I'd been feeling since I opened my eyes.

Looking towards the waterfall, I found a shimmering ribbon of light working its way down the rock face. The sight was so incredibly beautiful it took me several moments to realize the tendril was the waterfall I'd been looking for.

I reached into the dancing pool of light at my feet and smiled as my cupped hands came away filled with water that lit up my palms. I couldn't imagine anything more surreal. I might have stayed there for hours if the barest whisper of sound hadn't distracted me.

Alec was staring at me, an expression of disapproval marring otherwise perfect features.

"Of all the places for you to intrude, why did it have to be here?"

For a second, surrounded as I was by such beauty, I did feel like an intruder. He was gorgeous, and his tan skin seemed to have the slightest hint of light playing beneath its surface. I was as plain and ugly as always. My response popped out before I could think about it.

"Only you could see such beauty and think only of keeping it to yourself. Trust me, even with surroundings like this I'd much rather be elsewhere if you're part of the bargain."

The thought of being elsewhere brought our newest crisis to mind, and I realized that it was very likely I wouldn't have to worry about Britney, Alec, or Brandon for very much longer.

"At least you won't have to suffer my presence for much longer; we'll be gone all too quickly."

The fact I was saying these things to Alec when I knew this all had to be a dream was ludicrous, but it wasn't as ludicrous as the way he flinched at my words.

"No, you're right, all too soon you'll go the way of so many others. If I can depend on nothing else, I can rely on that."

A little eddy of wind found its way into our grotto, and for the first time my newly-acute sense of smell registered Alec's presence. His scent was divine, full of subtle themes I wasn't experienced enough to pick out, all of which screamed of warm power and rock-like masculinity. For half a second the torrent of sensation was too strong to leave room for conscious thought.

I realized I'd closed my eyes to better savor the experience. When I opened them Alec's expression had moved from annoyance to sadness. I had a pair of heartbeats to wonder at the strange tricks my subconscious was playing on me, and then the dream started fading away.

The heavenly surroundings were predictably the first thing to disappear, leaving afterimages of light burned into the corners of my vision. Alec was the next thing to go, but the memory of his features clung to my mind long after I found myself in a featureless void. Stranger still, his scent stayed with me even longer. I was just self-aware enough to hope I'd remember it all when I awoke in the morning.

Chapter 5

It was a good thing I'd started school in the middle of the week. If I'd gone to school the next day after all the drama of learning about our mortgage problems I probably would have had a nervous breakdown. As it was, I was essentially worthless all weekend.

I tried to warn Mom about the animals that'd mauled the kids from school, but she told me she was already aware of the incident and left before I could draw her into a discussion of what we should do about the bank.

I saw her for maybe a total of three hours during the entire two days. Even I knew it was wasted effort. If Mom somehow beat the odds, it still wasn't going to result in the kind of money we'd need to save our house. Not in the next two or three weeks at least.

It felt like my whole world had just disappeared down a drain. I didn't suffer any real panic attacks, but more or less spent both days in a kind of despondency that wasn't much better than a full-blown attack.

By the time Monday morning arrived I had vague memories of doing homework and not much else. The only positive from the whole weekend was the way my dream from Friday stayed with me. As I got ready for school I idly wondered if it would be possible to recreate the grotto in real life. Obviously not with the impossible, glowing water, but with the incredible, lush vegetation and the secluded pool. Then again, I'd seen Mom pull off some pretty crazy tricks with her camera, maybe there would be some way to simulate glowing water, some kind of photography trick I'd never heard of.

I walked downstairs as the eastern sky was just starting to change colors.

Mom was already gone. The message board was conspicuously empty, so she was either still frustrated with me, angry at our hopeless situation, or wrapped back up in her quest to become a renowned photographer.

Britney picked me up on schedule and I somehow made it through my first two classes. Mrs. Sorenson was still out to prove to everyone I was an idiot, and Heathcliff was still a psychopath despite Mr. Whethers' best efforts to explain the character's motivation.

Math was actually the high point of the morning. Mrs. Campbell was smart enough to put Britney off in a corner surrounded by the kind of kids she'd never even consider talking to under normal circumstances.

Not having Britney distract me all hour would have been a blessing by itself, but things got even better when Mrs. Campbell complimented me on the homework I handed in.

"Most excellently done, Miss Paige. Albert said you seemed to pick up the concepts quite quickly. I've noticed you've been working on the older material during class, which I very much approve of, but you may want to listen today. We're starting a new section, and it should be fairly straightforward for you to pick up."

I shouldn't have been surprised when she turned out to be right. The new chapter was on probability, which had absolutely nothing to do with the stuff they'd been working on the week before. I quickly decided I didn't like the new stuff as much as what I'd been studying on my own, but it was relatively easy, and almost before I knew it class had ended and it was time to go to lunch.

My doubts about whether or not everyone would be back in school today after three nights of partying were quickly resolved as Britney and I tried to fight through the ridiculous foot traffic on our way to our lockers.

By the time we made it to the lunch room, I was heartily sick of dodging jocks with shoulders the size of an ox. Why on earth did every single one of them think it was necessary to mock fight, throw balls back and forth to each other, or otherwise make a spectacle of themselves?

My mood was further soured as we arrived to find an unmistakable circle of bystanders signaling an impending fight. My first instinct was to go find a teacher before the two idiots hurt each other, but while I was still looking around to see if there was an adult in the room, Britney grabbed my arm and pulled me towards the circle.

It wasn't until we got closer that I realized there was something wrong with the circle of kids surrounding the combatants. Normally everyone pressed in tight for the best possible view.

The spectators in this fight were divided into two groups, with a fairly significant space between them. The rest of the students seemed to be reluctant to fill that gap in. It wasn't until Britney pulled me closer that I understood why.

Brandon stood surrounded by his friends on one side of the circle, with Alec and a smaller group standing opposite them. The tension in the room was like the air before a lightning strike, charged and unpredictable, a living organism on the point of materializing out of thin air and attacking anything surrounding it.

Taking in the two groups, I was amazed at the disparity before my eyes. The kids behind Brandon were half again as many as the gathering behind Alec, and they were eager for the confrontation, watching with excited eyes, and large smiles.

Alec's company on the other hand awaited the coming fight with calm exteriors and a sense they were bowing before the inevitable conflict without conceding anything to their opponents. They were fewer in number, but the men were larger than anyone other than Alec or Brandon, and I somehow knew even the girls were dangerous.

With a sudden start I realized the confrontation wasn't between Brandon and Alec as I'd originally thought. Instead the stuck-up blonde I'd first met in the office, was squared off against a brunette less than three-quarters her size. As Britney pulled us even closer, almost into the dead zone between the two factions, I finally realized the smaller girl was Rachel.

"You're going to get what's coming to you, you little slut."

The blonde's voice sounded exactly like I'd imagined, arrogant, vindictive and only barely controlled. Rachel on the other hand sounded calm, speaking in tones I shouldn't have been able to hear, except the spectators were unnaturally quiet.

"I haven't done anything to you, Cassie, and you know it. This is all just an excuse."

I looked around for teachers, but they were still conspicuously absent. There wasn't time.

Even if they arrived right now, someone was probably going to get hurt.

Cassie tossed her hair and smiled, a plastic expression that bordered on a smirk. "Shut your lying mouth. I'm really going to enjoy this."

Britney had positioned herself so she could see Brandon. As a consequence, I could see Alec's entire group, and I was amazed by their reaction to Cassie's belligerence. Jasmin's pretty lips drew back in something that looked almost like a snarl, and she'd tensed up so tightly she was almost shaking.

For a heartbeat I thought Jasmin would launch herself at the other girl, but Alec reached over without looking, and grabbed her arm. A stocky, Middle Eastern-looking boy to Alec's right looked like he wanted to act as well, but he was looking at Alec, and an almost imperceptible headshake stopped him.

I'd been so busy watching the byplay behind Rachel that I'd missed the last two exchanges between her and Cassie. Whatever had been said must have been bad though. Rachel was shaking, and the blonde looked like someone about to pull the wings off a butterfly.

I could feel my heartbeat climbing, slamming away at my ribs with all the energy of a full-blown panic attack, but I wasn't dizzy, just scared.

The cafeteria workers had all turned around so their backs were facing us, a sight which kindled the first spark of anger, an emotion that burned brighter because of the fear still coursing through me.

There was a gasp as Cassie shoved Rachel, a misleadingly casual motion that sent the smaller girl stumbling back into Alec's chest hard enough to leave bruises.

The typical catcalls were still absent, it was as if nobody viewed this as a normal fight, like there was somehow more at stake.

I'd been waiting for someone to intervene on Rachel's behalf. It was obvious she knew nothing about fighting. Cassie wasn't the kind of girl to fight just to prove a point and then forget about the incident afterwards. Just looking at her, I knew she'd remember any slight for as long as she lived, and she had enough influence in the school to make just about anyone's life miserable. She probably got away with things just because nobody was willing to cross her. Rachel was going to get hurt.

I was still thinking about all the ways *I* could get hurt when I stepped through the no-man's-land and into the circle. The parts of me that weren't emotionally dead, that were still behaving rationally despite the accident, were screaming in terror. There probably wasn't anyone in the school who knew less about fighting than me. I knew I should turn around and run away before Cassie realized I was serious, but somehow I didn't care.

Cassie's arsenal of nasty tricks wouldn't be so effective against someone who'd already been kicked out of their house and moved to another state. All I really needed to do was survive the next few minutes. I'd be out of the state before she really got busy making my life miserable.

A dozen different things I could say blew through my mind, but they were all competing, and none of them fit the situation. In typical fashion, I found myself without anything clever to say. Instead I just stood there and stared at Cassie.

I'd thought things were tense already, but where everyone had been quiet before, now they were motionless too.

Cassie spun around and glared at me. "Take off."

I shook my head and clenched my fists a little tighter. "Leave her alone."

For a second I thought Cassie would go through with it. Her knuckles went white, and her breathing sped up. I knew if she sprang at me, I was going to get really hurt.

When Brandon's hand appeared on Cassie's shoulder to restrain her, I thought for a second my knees would buckle. A few seconds later, it was as if nothing had ever happened. The ring of spectators dissolved as kids quickly returned to their tables. Brandon and his friends left through one set of cafeteria doors, while Alec and his friends departed through the other.

Britney looked like she was trying to decide whether to be mad or impressed, but I felt too sick to stick around and try to nudge her in either direction. I mumbled something I hoped sounded intelligible and headed towards the bathroom. I passed Mr. Simms and another teacher on my way out, but apparently I looked as awful as I felt. They just shot me stern looks rather than stopping me to ask what had happened.

It wasn't until I'd finished dry-heaving and was trying to clean myself back up, that I wondered where they'd been. The school building wasn't that big. If they'd really been trying to break up the fight, they should have arrived minutes earlier.

I thought about hiding in the bathroom for a while, but that was exactly the kind of place a girl like Cassie would want to catch me. Instead I took a deep breath and walked outside.

Britney was waiting for me. By her expression she'd decided on being mad. "Do you realize what you just did?"

I was still fresh out of witty comments. I just shrugged instead.

Britney had been mad before, now she looked furious. "You just picked sides, and you picked the wrong one."

Maybe I still wasn't recovered from my ordeal on Friday; I felt like I was missing something obvious. Britney apparently agreed, and she wasted no time in letting me know what it was.

"There are two in-crowds here; Brandon's group, which consists of all of the athletes and cheerleaders, and Alec's group, which is about half the size, and outside of his immediate friends is made up of a few geeks and misfits. You were on the border of getting in with Brandon, but just threw all of that away to save Alec's little sister when he's too much of a coward to do it himself."

I wanted to protest, to explain why everyone should be able to get along, or point out that despite Brandon's obvious appeal, it was his friend who was wrong, but Britney had already turned and stalked off. I probably would've spent the next few minutes refining my arguments for the next time we talked, but the last thing Britney had said finally sank in.

His sister. Rachel was Alec's sister, and he hadn't made a move to save her. He hadn't even been willing to let his friends step in and stop the fight.

I drifted off to History thinking that I would've done almost anything to save my sister. It would take a real heartless individual to abandon their own family. My anger buffered me just enough to think about Cindi without the usual consequences, but I still wasn't really in top form. I was halfway through my class before I realized Mr. Simms had been shooting me dark looks for the last twenty minutes. They weren't the obvious nasty looks that kids shoot each other of course. They were subtle and infrequent but there was something about the set of his mouth that made it clear he wasn't pleased I was in his class.

I shrugged it all off and gutted my way through class, eagerly planning what I'd say to Alec when I saw him in physics, only when I finally stalked into Mrs. Alexander's class Alec wasn't sitting in his corner desk.

I pulled out my notes and started reviewing what I'd managed to learn about our project, stalling until he arrived so I could give him a piece of my mind. Only he never walked through the door.

I still had my anger, but it wasn't cushioning me as well for some reason. It felt like another attack was on the way. My pulse was skyrocketing and the room wavered as my vision dimmed. It didn't make sense to be having a panic attack right now, but images of Cindi swam into view, alternating with pictures of Alec and Rachel.

It was like Alec's cruelty to his sister somehow meant I was failing Cindi. I concentrated all of my energy on thinking about Alec, about how much I hated him, about what I was going to say to him next time I saw him.

Beyond all expectations, it worked. My heart rate slowed down to something approaching normal, and the room stopped moving around. By the time Mrs. Alexander finished taking the roll, and returned her pencil to its customary place behind her ear, I'd stabilized enough that I could read my notes again.

The group project was due tomorrow, and since Alec hadn't bothered to make an appearance in class since my first day in Sanctuary, it was looking like I'd have to do the whole thing by myself if I wanted to pass. Yet another reason to hate him.

So far I'd had zero luck figuring out why rain puddles in the parking lot sometimes had colors on them, sort of like little earthbound rainbows. I turned around and picked a reference book at random. It was a weighty thing that might or might not have the answer, but at the very least promised to keep me occupied for the duration of the class.

I finally found something promising about fifteen seconds before the bell rang. I probably would've stayed there trying to cram information into my head, but Mrs. Alexander walked by with a smile on her face as the last of the other students filed out of the room.

"If you're really that enthralled by a college physics book, you're more than welcome to take it home with you tonight. Just promise to bring it back in the same condition. Remember, I'm less concerned with your answer, and more interested in the process you take to try and solve the problem. Of course the right answer never hurts."

I smiled and hurried out of class with a 'thank you'.

I shouldn't have bothered rushing. I slipped into Spanish exactly three seconds before the late bell sounded, but Mrs. Tiggs wasn't even there. When she finally did show up, we had a surprise quiz on our vocabulary. Once we finished she turned on the television and told us to listen for conjugation.

I almost wished I shared the class with Britney, her dad seemed like the type to get six kinds of riled up over something like that. He'd probably go straight to the school board and demand a new Spanish teacher altogether.

It was a real relief when I was finally able to leave the drab little classroom. I stopped off at my locker before heading to the tutor room, but Britney was nowhere to be seen. Probably still mad. I mentally shrugged as I swapped out books, and set off.

Rachel was already seated in her usual spot in no-man's-land. I debated where to sit for a second. I'd done the right thing in standing up to Cassie, but I didn't want to further alienate Brandon, or put myself anymore firmly in the group of idiots who looked to Alec as their master and liege. Before I could finish weighing the pros and cons, Rachel looked up and caught my eye.

The smile that appeared on her face was tentative but genuine, and completely resolved my doubts. I returned her shy greeting with a smile of my own, and sat down at the table closest to her.

Britney entered the tutor lab a few minutes later, and frowned at me before going over and sitting at the end of the room containing the jocks and cheerleaders. Apparently I was supposed to have waited?

I sighed and flipped open my book. As I finished up my second assignment for the day, I realized I was parched. My trusty water bottle was empty when I reached for it, so I quietly stood and left the room. I thought I remembered where the closest drinking fountain was. Even so, I planned on getting a little lost before I found it. I didn't, however, plan on nearly colliding with Alec as he slowly rounded the corner in front of me.

The tension of the near-fight earlier had distracted me from just how incredible-looking he was. There was no such refuge now. For a moment I couldn't think of anything other than how the dark blue of his shirt brought out his tan complexion.

If his gorgeousness had stopped there, I probably would've been okay, but the little spirits in charge of keeping the universe in equilibrium must've been momentarily busy with something more important.

The blue buttons that kept his shirt snuggly wrapped around his impressive torso were almost the exact shade of his eyes, which happened to be staring at me with a trace of something different than his normal self-assurance. In someone else I would've almost said gratitude, but his manner was too arrogant for that.

More than anything else, that was what finally shook me from my reverie. He was already talking.

"...wanted to talk to you about what happened today."

Part of me wanted to wait and see what he was going to say, to lose myself in what was sure to be a very convincing lie designed to make him look good, and me feel like I was on heroin for however long he favored me with his presence. Luckily that idealistic, stupid part of me had seen too many girls get used by smooth-talking boys. I interrupted right away.

"You mean when your sister nearly got beaten by that whore, and you not only didn't do anything, you stopped your friends from doing anything either."

Alec flinched a little. I was a little surprised by how satisfying it was to have him, a demigod, on the run, but I didn't let it slow me down.

"The fact that I, a little waif from out of town, could defuse the situation and save Rachel no doubt sticks in your craw, which explains why you're lurking around out here waiting to talk to me. Because only then can you fabricate some reason for why everything had to go down the way it did, and thereby save face!"

He wasn't flinching now. Instead his face had gotten tight and remote. For a second it seemed like he was looking right through me. "You don't understand."

Alec's expression should have scared me. It sent shivers down my spine, but I was too mad to back down over a little thing like my knees nearly shaking. "Of course. That's an easy comeback. I don't understand. You're right, I don't. I would've done almost anything to protect my sister, but you didn't even care that Rachel was going to get hurt."

Now I really was scared, Alec was trembling slightly, and he looked like he wanted to slap me. While I was still trying to decide whether I should radiate smugness at having verbally bested him, or run back to the safety of the tutor room, he lunged forward and grabbed me around the shoulders.

"I was going to offer you my protection against Cassie and Brandon, and you throw your supposed superiority in my face. Fine, but don't come crying back to me when the mask comes off."

Alec abruptly released me and stalked off. He was moving so incredibly quickly he'd disappeared around a corner with one balled-up fist pressed against his side before I'd even started shaking in fear. I'd never before been that helpless. Had he wanted to, I had no doubt but that he could have easily snapped my neck. He was that strong.

I really was trembling now. I wanted to mutter something about overzealous body-builders lifting just to intimidate people, but couldn't get the words out. I think maybe I was afraid he'd overhear and return to finish the job.

My shoulders felt like the skin was on fire, but I knew it was just my imagination. His grip had been rock-hard, but he hadn't actually squeezed enough to hurt me. He'd shown pretty good control for someone who'd just been spanked in a debate, and obviously wanted to rip my head off.

Turning around to return to the tutor room, I almost tripped over my own feet when I saw Britney standing just outside the closed door.

"Are you crazy? First you side with Rachel against Brandon, firmly putting yourself in Alec's camp, and then you turn around and piss off Alec?"

I really wasn't in the mood to argue with Britney, so I tried for nonchalance. "So now I'm not on anyone's side. They'll both leave me alone and I'll be fine."

"Oh, yeah, because that's how things work." I'd only thought Britney was mad before. She was all but shaking with fury now. "Don't you get it? You, me, most of the rest of the school, we survive by staying neutral. For better or worse, we aren't attractive, cool, or rich enough to get in with Alec or Brandon. Once you piss one of them off though, you'd better hope you're in with the other one, because that's the only way you've got any kind of protection."

It was starting to sound like organized crime or something. Of course they could make my life miserable socially, but it wasn't like they were going to really hurt me. I opened my mouth to try and calm Britney down, but she cut me off.

"You don't understand how much influence they have. Three years ago someone tried to start a newspaper in Sanctuary. Things were going along just fine until he pissed off Alec's mother. The city condemned the building and refused to change the zoning laws so he could get another place. When he really pushed the issue, his house mysteriously caught on fire."

My mouth was hanging open, but Britney seemed to think it was disbelief rather than amazement. "I'm serious, Adriana, and I'm not letting you take my family down with you. Find your own way home."

Chapter 6

There was no reason for Britney's actions to come as any kind of surprise, it was exactly in keeping with her character. Even if she didn't believe a word of what she'd just told me, I really was on my way to becoming a social pariah, and her whole existence centered around becoming more popular.

Even so, knowing I was officially stranded at school with no way home felt very much like the end of the world. We still didn't have a phone, and probably wouldn't for weeks to come, even assuming we somehow managed to keep our home through the end of the week. Calling Mom and asking her to come and get me was out.

Presumably if I waited long enough Mom would decide something was wrong and come looking for me. Unless she was out hiking somewhere, in which case it might be a day or two before she realized I was missing.

There was nothing to do but walk. I waited a few minutes to give Britney time to get out of the lab, and then walked in and grabbed my things. The other kids were already clearing out. Nobody even looked up as I left.

Luckily I'd worn sneakers rather than the exotic footwear most girls gravitated towards. If I'd been wearing anything else, I'd have been nursing blisters before I made it out of the parking lot. As it was, I quickly realized my little walk home was going to be twice as unpleasant as I'd expected.

The school most definitely wasn't in the pretty, green part of the region. Every step kicked up a miniature cloud of fine, red dust that drifted into my lungs and slowly coated my clothes. The dust would've been plenty bad all by itself, but the heat made things even worse.

It was only an hour or two removed from the hottest part of the day, and the air was so dry it sucked moisture out of me with each breath. I knew it was stupid to walk home. My one little bottle of water wasn't going to last me five miles in this oven, but I was tired of always having to be sensible about everything. I was going to walk, and that was it. Maybe if I passed out on the side of the road and ended up in the hospital Britney would finally realize what a wench she was.

I was barely out of sight of the school, still vividly imagining Alec and Britney's faces when they found out that they'd put me in the hospital, when I heard a car approaching from behind me. Only it wasn't zipping by, it was slowing down.

Every scary story I'd ever heard about rapists, kidnappers and murderers suddenly flowed through my mind like frayed ropes catching at my insides as they went, pulling out all of the other thoughts and feelings until there was nothing left but a hollow, fear-filled shell.

I found myself praying for the first time since the accident, pleading with whatever might be out there listening to protect me and get me safely home. My heart was pounding so hard it almost drowned out the crunch of gravel as the car pulled even with me.

I didn't recognize the vehicle, which was a bad sign. It was a light-eating black, and emitted the throaty roar of a sports car. The windows were tinted; I could see that much out of the corner of my eye without acknowledging that it was there. That really seemed like the best course. Maybe if I pretended he wasn't there, the driver would just go away.

A hint of motion told me that wasn't going to be the case. The passenger side window was sliding down with the smooth, even motion of power windows.

"I've heard that some of you easterners have some really funny ideas. I guess seeing as how we don't have any mass transit out here you must've decided you needed to walk home. Don't you think it's a bit hot for that kind of environmental responsibility?"

The voice was familiar, but my mind initially refused to place it with a face. It was too unbelievable to be real. I took a couple more steps, and then looked to my left and was rewarded as an infectious grin slowly appeared on Brandon's face.

I wanted to say something witty, but the thoughts all just swirled around in my head without making it down to my mouth. Brandon's smile grew just a little bigger.

"I really think you should let me give you a ride home. Based on our past history, it's only a matter of time before one of us runs into the other, and I'm afraid of what my Mustang might do to you when that happens."

Brandon's voice washed over me like silk, carrying away any desires I might have had to walk all the way home just to prove a point. Not trusting my voice, I nodded and took the couple of steps needed to reach his passenger door.

"I wanted to apologize for what happened earlier today. Cassie can be a real jerk sometimes."

It was too good to be true. I almost looked over at him, but I knew I'd lose myself in a pair of soft, gray eyes. Brandon seemed to understand that my silence meant I wasn't convinced.

"You wouldn't believe how relieved I was when you stepped forward and stopped her before things got out of hand."

My natural pessimism reasserted itself, undaunted by the fact that I could just see Brandon's exquisitely-muscled arm out of the corner of my eye.

"If you knew Cassie was in the wrong, why didn't you stop her? She's your friend; you should have been able to defuse the situation before it got that far."

Brandon took a deep breath. His voice was quiet now, the perfect example of someone admitting something they weren't proud of. "Things are complicated with Cassie. Our families go really far back, it's almost like she's my sister sometimes. She doesn't like to listen to me, and when she gets mad, things get very unpleasant."

It was a weak explanation, but there was something in his voice that made me believe him. The few doubts I still had melted away as I finally met his eyes. I've always been pretty good at reading people, and I'd never seen anyone whose eyes conveyed that level of sincerity. My voice caught, and it took a couple of tries to get actual words out.

"She'll come after me."

Brandon shook his head. "I won't let her. That's part of why I wanted to talk to you. I won't let anyone do anything to you. Think of it as repayment."

The words weren't anything special, but there was something about the way he said them that made me absolutely sure he'd deliver on his promise, that he was somehow completely in control of his surroundings.

The intensity in his stare was too much, and I found myself looking away, trying to buy some time to collect myself. Luckily I wasn't so far gone as to not recognize where we were.

"Oh, gosh, that was the turnoff to my house. I'm so sorry."

Brandon flashed me another smile and quickly maneuvered his car through a U-turn, a feat I was fairly certain was harder than it looked in the bulky muscle car.

"No harm done. You guys bought the old Anderson home then?"

I nodded, staring out at the desolate landscape. "You mean every single person in town doesn't already know everything there is to know about us?"

"Oh, the joys of a small town. Yeah, with as little real news as we get out here, people probably know more about you than you're used to. It has its benefits though."

I snorted, and then felt myself turning red with embarrassment. You would think after seventeen years I'd have learned how to laugh without making those wretched sounds. "As if. I can't think of one good thing about everyone having their noses in everyone else's business."

The smile was back, but it was more mischievous than before. "How about me knowing Britney left you high and dry after school today?"

"Please. That just makes the humiliation more painful."

Brandon shook his head as we pulled to a stop in front of my house. "No, that means I can do something about you losing your ride."

I suddenly felt like there was a joke I was missing out on. "How do you propose to fix that?"

"It was my fault so I'll be your ride back and forth from school every day."

"I don't know about all of that, but thanks for the lift just now."

I fumbled for a minute with the unfamiliar latch, and then invited the blistering heat into the cool interior of the car as I swung the door open.

Brandon gently captured my arm before I could slide out of the passenger seat. "You'll wait for me tomorrow?"

"I don't know—maybe. Anyone that thinks Minnesota is the east instead of the Midwest can't really be relied upon to remember important things like appointments."

I could feel myself blushing again as I pulled free and fled into the house with a single wave goodbye. Normally I wasn't flirtatious. Heck, I hardly knew the meaning of the word, but something about Brandon turned it all into a harmless game. A game with rules that were nearly comprehensible for a change. One where there was very little to lose and an undreamed-of potential for achieving amazing things.

As soon as the door was shut I ran to the window and hid behind the blinds, watching as the black Mustang drove up our lane. Overcome by the sudden urge to giggle, I ran upstairs looking for my mom. I made it all the way to her door before remembering the Jeep hadn't been downstairs.

Typical. The one time I had good news, and she wasn't around.

I wandered back downstairs, more because it was cooler down there than because I had any real desire to work on homework. Once I was down there though, I grimly decided to open up my bag and make some progress before Mom got home. I pulled my feet up on the couch, leaned back against the arm and rested my Spanish book on my knees. I momentarily wondered if I should make myself quite so comfortable as my eyes closed.

The doorbell came as an abrupt surprise, waking me from the nap I hadn't intended on taking. I'd been in one of the surreal, vivid dreams. It was already too distant to remember details, but I had the impression of being on a mountaintop during the day with vision so acute that I'd been able to see the individual motes of dust. Oddly enough it almost seemed like Alec had been there too.

The person waiting outside wasn't anyone I recognized, but he had the cultured, high-brow appearance of someone who was either really rich, or who moved in the kind of circles where you didn't get seated unless you were properly attired.

"Why, hello, you must be Adriana. Can I call you Adri?"

I shook my head. "I prefer my full name, Mr..."

"Wilkenson, Mayor Wilkenson. Is your mother home?"

Suddenly struck by the fact that living in the country meant there wasn't anyone around to hear your screams, I almost lied, but for whatever reason I believed him. Maybe because he exuded the false, overabundant sincerity I'd come to associate with both the class presidents I'd known back in Minnesota.

"She's out photographing one of the parks. Is there a message you'd like me to pass on?"

He looked surprisingly uncertain, almost like he was used to working from a script, and didn't know what to do when things didn't go as planned.

"Do you know when she'll be back?"

My headshake seemed to unnerve him a little more. Presumably he was having a hard time believing in a world where people didn't have fixed schedules, where moms didn't let their daughters know when they'd be back from their outings.

"The message really is quite urgent. Are you positive you don't have a way to contact her? Well then, I suppose I've no choice."

Most people say they don't have a choice rather flippantly, but he seemed rather more like he had his back against the wall than I expected.

"You know, I presume, that there was some confusion regarding the tourism project she bid out for the city? Well, I've managed to get to the bottom of the situation and it appears we did indeed award the contract to her."

The news seemed too good to be true. "You mean she's got the job?"

"Technically it isn't an employment offer. It's more in the way of a consulting project, but yes, she'll be in a sense working for the city. I've asked my staff to make sure that the confusion is cleared up with the bank as well so you shouldn't be in any kind of danger of losing your house anymore."

I almost clapped for joy, only there was something off about it all. Since when did the mayor personally come to deliver a piece of relatively insignificant news? Not only that, why would he be so shaken up? He'd actually seemed to be trying to determine whether or not it would be okay to just leave a message. Like he was operating by a set of rules he didn't completely understand. Or maybe at the order of someone else?

Normally I wouldn't have been brave enough to press, but the words were out of my mouth almost before I realized what I was doing.

"That's great, sir. Do you often work so closely with the local bank? I mean when the loan officer talked to my mom he said that there was no way to keep us from losing our house. I think she said his exact words were that it would take an act of God to change things now."

A tiny fragment of memory rose to the surface of my mind. A time when Dad had been talking about negotiating with someone for work. "Don't be afraid of silence, Adri. Especially not when you know you're right. Let the silence work on people for a little while and they'll usually start to crack."

That was the last thing I wanted to do right now, but I kept my mouth shut anyways. It was almost like I could see the gray matter starting to heat up as the mayor tried to figure out exactly what I knew and how much I just suspected.

"Act of God indeed. Fancy that. Well, surprising as it may be, Fredrick doesn't know everything there is to know about the world."

He was turning to leave, and most of me was screaming to just thank him and wave goodbye, but there had been something in his eyes that had me convinced he'd been lying.

"Thank you, sir. I guess I need to learn more about civic government. I can't wait to go into whatever records are public and learn about all of the ways the mayor works with the banks. I'll bet there are plenty of other people who'd be interested too. Maybe I can start a club at school."

It was like someone else was doing the talking for me. I'd never been this bold, and to do so now with someone who could arrange for my mom's job to disappear again seemed like the worst kind of stupidity, but I couldn't fall apart now.

I almost couldn't believe my eyes when his face turned red. "Listen here, Missy. I've been in politics longer than you've been alive, and it takes a whole hell of a lot more than a precocious teenager to blackmail me. So, you can just drop your veiled threats and pretend like we never had this conversation, or I *will* see that your mom is once again unemployed, and we'll just see whether or not your protector is bluffing."

Stepping out of my front door and being hit by a cement truck would have been less of a surprise. I'd thought something odd was happening, but the idea of someone protecting us was almost unbelievable.

The mayor took my shock as a sign he once again had the upper hand. Smiling smugly, he turned to leave, but not before I could grab at the sleeve of his sport coat. "Wait. Who is it? Who's helping us?"

The smirk hadn't left. "No, he was very clear on that point. You're not to know. That's the one thing guaranteed to make him go through with his threats. You'll just have to be satisfied with the fact that you'll both continue to be able to live in our fine city."

Normally I would have just acquiesced, but I couldn't bear the thought of letting him leave, taking with him the identity of the only person besides my mom who really cared what happened to me. I tightened my grip in an attempt to stop him.

"Please, if you won't tell me who it is, let me write a thank you note. I have to do something. He's done so much for us."

He stopped partway through shaking his head. "I can't promise he'll even bother to read it, but I'll take it to him if you promise never to talk about this again. I don't want to hear even the slightest rumor anything unusual happened in association with this project."

I nodded, relieved I'd have a chance to jot down a couple of lines, that I'd at least have that much of a link with our protector.

Mayor Wilkenson waited at the door, almost the perfect picture of a gentleman at his leisure, but his desire to be done with this whole affair was almost palpable. I hurried back to the kitchen counter and tore a piece of paper off of the tablet I'd been drawing on.

Whoever you are thank you so much for what you've done. Not just for the job, but for smoothing things over with the bank as well. I wish there was some way I could repay you for everything.

—Adriana

Chapter 7

My alarm clock jerked me out of a thankfully dream-free slumber. Actually, as I pulled myself out of bed I realized I'd had a virtual torrent of dreams, but none of them had been possessed of the strange vividness that'd begun haunting my waking moments. I hadn't had one of the special dreams, ergo I hadn't had any dreams last night.

I really needed to get out of this town before whatever was in the water drove me completely crazy. Actually, I probably didn't have much time in which to affect my escape. When it came to craziness I was already halfway there. After all, I'd already been diagnosed with the kind of clinical condition nobody with less than eight years of school could even pronounce.

As amusing as my internal monologue was, I didn't let it slow my normal morning preparations. Almost before I knew it, I was downstairs and once again facing the dreaded decision of whether or not to eat breakfast. I already knew I wasn't hungry; the only real decision was how much of Mom's wrath I was willing to face later on.

It wasn't until I had my hand on the doorknob that I remembered Brandon's promise to pick me up. I was so tired I actually considered for a second that he might have been serious. Sitting in his car, fighting not to look at his smiling gray eyes, it'd all seemed so reasonable. I'd lost my ride and he was grateful I'd saved him from having to interfere with Cassie, so he was going to become my personal chauffeur for the rest of the year.

Looking at my empty lane, the school bus only minutes away, it seemed more likely Brandon wouldn't even remember talking to me. Just like every hot boy with every loser since the dawn of time.

The thought hurt a little, but I'd had plenty of years to come to understand boys like that didn't go after girls like me. Instead of dwelling on it, greenhouse gases or anything else I couldn't change, I simply shrugged my backpack a little higher and started down the lane.

Some kind of bird was merrily announcing to the world that he was ridiculously happy the sun was just rising, and that it was already pushing eighty degrees with the promise of something much, much worse before lunch.

I hadn't been waiting for more than a minute when a pair of headlights rounded the bend in the road coming from town. I was so busy worrying how I'd deal with Cassie when I saw her that it took me a minute to realize the car had slowed as it approached.

"Wow, I drive all this way, and then you deprive me of the pleasure of the last hundred feet."

The deep, smooth voice was unmistakable even if the light was still too poor to make out anything else. I slipped inside the Mustang with a grin playing at the edge of my lips despite my best efforts to remain cool and collected.

"Well, I didn't want to start your day off too well, or everything else would be anticlimactic."

"Really? You weren't just worried I wasn't going to show up? Because you understand how someone could've been thinking you'd walked down your lane so you could catch the bus if I'd forgotten about you?"

I'd been giving Brandon my crinkled-nose glare for a solid three seconds before his easy laugh made me realize what I was doing. I hadn't done that to anyone in months, it'd been my trademark expression for when a family member had made me mad.

"Okay, you're right. I didn't think you'd show."

"I should be very hurt by your lack of faith, but seeing as how you've been through so much lately, I'll forgive you."

My heart was suddenly trying to hammer its way out of my throat, which had constricted so tightly I couldn't seem to get any air down to my starving lungs.

"How did you...nobody knows..."

Brandon's hand was on my shoulder despite my inability to remember how it had gotten there. "Are you okay? I was just kidding, you know, about the near fight and then telling Alec off and having Britney decide she was moving on to greener pastures. I didn't mean anything by it."

The attack was still trying to overwhelm me, but Brandon not knowing the full extent of my weakness robbed it of some of the momentum necessary to roll me all the way under.

I managed some kind of reply, one that might've even been witty, but which apparently didn't manage to cover up the fact I wasn't really okay. We drove in silence the rest of the way into town, and by the time we turned into the school parking lot I'd come back to myself enough to be desperately looking for something else to say. I needed something cool enough Brandon wouldn't write me off as a lost cause.

Wish-granting fairies somewhere were working overtime, because as Brandon turned off the engine, I saw a mob of people over by one of the smaller entrances to the school.

"Wow, I wonder what's going on over there."

We were both out of the car now, and it seemed the most natural thing in the world to grab Brandon's arm and tug him over to the crowd. It wasn't until I felt the iron-hard muscles under my now-tingling hand that I realized what I'd done.

I felt a surge of heat wash over my face and neck. Brandon for once didn't have an easy comeback to defuse the awkwardness. If anything he looked slightly uncomfortable himself.

"I'm sure it's nothing important..."

He trailed off as my traitorous hand found his arm of its own accord and started pulling again. I wasn't sure why I was so anxious; usually I avoided crowds like the plague. Maybe I was just trying to prolong our time together.

I let go as soon as we reached the fringe of the crowd, and prayed it was only my imagination that made me think Brandon was just the slightest bit relieved. Luckily there was plenty to distract me.

It looked like there'd been some kind of war behind the school. The flagpole had a massive dent in its base, and actually looked like it was leaning slightly to one side. The straggly grass, kept just barely alive by the nearly non-existent rain and infrequent watering by some anonymous grounds keeper, had been torn up. Large patches of reddish dirt had been exposed and the ground was scarred by gouges that looked like they'd been made by some kind of farm machinery except for being so irregular.

My eyes were momentarily pulled back to the ground. Something about the gouges was tickling the back of my mind. Had I seen something like that before? Hiking maybe? Only I could count the number of hikes I'd actually participated in on one hand. Surely something like that would've stayed with me.

Someone gasped as the crowd shifted around, distracting me from my half-formed suspicions. I looked over at the exterior wall of the school and felt my jaw drop. Maybe Mom had read the story about the three little pigs a few too many times to me when I was growing up, but I'd always thought of brick as the strongest possible building material. I didn't have any idea if it really was, but it seemed incredible that anything could've wreaked such damage.

The bricks on the wall next to the door were cracked and set back in the wall, almost like they'd been hit with some kind of wrecking ball, and the concrete of the sidewalk had gouges crisscrossing its surface like some kind of abstract painting.

"There's nothing to see here, kids. I want you to all disperse and go to your home rooms."

The short, mostly bald man who'd ordered us all to leave was just visible through a gap in the crowd. He walked like an administrator, but I hadn't ever seen him before.

"Who's that?"

Brandon started just a little, like he'd been thinking of something else. "Mr. Rindell, the assistant principal."

Now that my complete attention wasn't on the various destroyed bits of school property, I noticed how much whispering was going on. Most of it was too quiet to catch more than bits and pieces, but I heard more than one 'completely jacked up', and a few people wondering what could have caused that kind of destruction. Mr. Rindell apparently heard much of the same snippets of conversation.

"You would think by now you'd all be old enough to figure some of this out on your own. The flag pole was obviously hit by some kind of vehicle, probably one of those big 4x4's that you kids seem to love so much down here. The damage to the brickwork was no doubt the work of those stupid potato guns. Now get out of here before I start handing out detention assignments."

Brandon was tugging on my arm now, not hard enough for anyone to think he'd been driven off by a mere school administrator, but urgently enough I allowed myself to be guided away. We hadn't gone more than a step or two before his grip on my arm grew painful.

I hissed in discomfort and he released me, but not before I noticed that his other hand was white-knuckled and his jaw was clenched.

"Sorry, I just don't like to see that kind of needless destruction. It makes everyone look bad and costs the town a lot of money."

Brandon's smile was back, but it didn't have his trademark easy carelessness.

"Now you sound like my mom."

We rounded a corner before Brandon could say anything else and nearly ran into Britney.

"Guys! Did you see the back door?"

I could almost see the wheels turning in Britney's head. First she went red as she remembered she'd stranded me at school, then her eyes got a little wider as she realized it was still about five minutes too early for me to have arrived on the bus.

Brandon's normal smile was back. "Yeah, Adriana noticed it almost as soon as we pulled up to the school."

Her suspicions that Brandon had given me a ride into school satisfied, Britney managed a sickly smile and mumbled something about seeing us later as she disappeared around the corner.

I managed to make it another twenty feet before I couldn't restrain my laughter anymore. Brandon joined in with a chuckle that was more restrained, but no less heartfelt. We both wound down about the same time, and I wiped a tear off of the corner of each eye.

"I should feel bad for laughing at her, but she's so transparent. It's nice to see her served with a little justice."

Brandon nodded with a smile. "It's a little ironic. She threw you overboard because she was worried you'd limit her upward mobility, and then the next day you arrive with the guy she's had a crush on since the day she moved into Sanctuary."

I punched him on the shoulder. "You knew all this time?"

Another laugh, and a smile at the way I was trying to conceal how much the punch had hurt my hand. "Of course I knew. It isn't like I could do anything about that. I've never led her on, but I've always been aware she liked me."

There didn't seem to be much else to be said, so I thanked Brandon again for the ride into school, and headed off to my home room.

Everyone had pretty much just pretended like I didn't exist before. Now, with Brandon having taken an interest in me, I got everything from simple acknowledgment of my presence to obvious dislike, and even a couple of people who looked like they wanted to take Britney's place.

I suppose some people would have been thrilled by the chance to join the top of the social food chain, but it mostly just disgusted me. I politely rebuffed the scavengers, ignored the haters, and carefully acknowledged the rest without giving them anything else to go on.

It was a rather depressing exercise. By the time Mrs. Sorenson had fired a couple of ridiculously obscure questions at me, I found the good feelings I'd managed to carry away from the mayor's visit the night before had pretty much evaporated.

English should have been better. Wuthering Heights wasn't ever going to be my favorite book, but Mr. Whethers had made the characters more real in the last few days and I was actually excited to see what he had in store next.

Unfortunately, Mr. Whethers wasn't there. The substitute teacher sitting at his desk didn't even take roll; he just shut the door, told us to keep it down, and flipped open a magazine. While I was sitting at my desk wondering what to do with the next hour of my life, something I'd read in the physics book suddenly clicked.

In a perfect world I would've been left in peace to finish reasoning out the answer. Instead, Britney leaned over and smiled.

"So I was really surprised to see you with Brandon. I thought for sure he'd be pissed after you made Cassie back down like that."

"Surprise, surprise, maybe he isn't as shallow and vindictive as you thought." The words were mean, but they felt good. There were a lot of other, even worse things on the tip of my tongue, things I really wanted to say. For a moment, my anger warred with the fear of being completely friendless.

I'd always thought I didn't need any friends, that I was fine making my own way. I was starting to realize I'd never really been alone before now. I'd always had the best friend a girl could've wanted. I'd just never recognized how much I'd depended on her.

Even that oblique thought was almost too much. I felt my pulse quicken a little as the air seemed to vibrate.

"Look, I'm sorry about how I reacted yesterday. I shouldn't have left you here like that."

Britney's voice was coated with sincerity, but it was the thinnest of layers, one which poorly disguised all kinds of nasty little feelings. On the other hand, it distracted my mind from the string of thoughts I'd otherwise have followed all the way down to a full-blown panic attack. It was a small thing in the grand scheme of the universe, but it was just enough to tilt the balance in her favor.

I still didn't like her any more than she really liked me, but I was willing to tolerate her. To pretend we were friends so that neither of us had to face the scary world entirely on our own.

"Okay, apology accepted. It wasn't very nice, but I suppose everyone makes mistakes."

Britney's eyes grew bright, even after such a short acquaintance, I knew she was about to launch into a blow-by-blow account of the last twelve or so hours.

"Listen, I don't mean to be rude, but I've got to finish up my physics homework. Can we catch up during lunch?"

Britney looked a little crestfallen, but her eyes quickly lit back up, and before I could get my notebook out and start writing, she'd already switched seats to one closer to a gaggle of cheerleaders.

It was amazing that I hadn't made the connection between light, the fact that light acted like a wave, and the rainbows on the parking lot puddles, but it was all making sense now. By the time the bell finally rang to release the circus back into the halls, I'd finished up a reasonable outline, and was feeling pretty smart.

Alec probably expected me to have been totally stumped, but I'd figured out the exact answer to the assignment, and I was so going to show him. The glow of satisfaction more than made up for the fact that Britney chattered non-stop on our way to Algebra. I felt like I should feel guilty for not liking her, but I was starting to notice how much of her conversation revolved around nasty gossip that made everyone else in the school sound like rejects or sluts.

When we finally made it to Mrs. Campbell's class, I slid into my seat with a sigh of relief. This was the one class all day where I could virtually guarantee I wouldn't be talking to anyone. Mrs. Campbell wasn't ever really mean, but she gave off an air that made you absolutely sure she wouldn't put up with any crap.

We were still working on statistics, which was nice in that I could follow what was being said and wasn't falling any further behind, but kind of a bummer because it meant I couldn't do a bunch of makeup work during class. It was a relief when Mrs. Campbell finally capped her marker and turned us loose to work on the homework assignment.

I was midway through the first assignment when one of the aides slipped into the room and whispered into Mrs. Campbell's ear. There was a kind of muted, collective gasp that made me look up just in time to see the color drain out of her face. Before the aide had even finished whispering, Mrs. Campbell was out of her chair and headed towards the door. Thirty seconds later we were all still looking around and wondering what had happened.

It was a testament to our respect for, or in some cases fear of, Mrs. Campbell that nobody spoke in anything above a whisper for an entire five minutes. Every terrible thing that could possibly happen to a person flowed through my mind, and all I could do was hope I was overreacting. Mrs. Campbell had scared me a little that first day, but she'd been pretty nice since, and she'd always been fair.

"So what do you think happened?"

"Britney, what are you doing?"

"What? You finished up your homework already and she left. We can totally talk right now. What do you think happened? I'll bet she just got some really, really bad news."

BROKEN

I felt a dull ache starting behind my eyes. "Just because I finished my Physics doesn't mean I don't have other stuff I need to do, and I don't even want to guess at what would make her go that white. I just hope whatever it was turns out not to be as bad as she thought it was."

Britney rolled her eyes. "Please, like you don't have just as much reason to hate her as me. Besides, what other homework could you possibly have? You're like the most anal person I know when it comes to doing your homework. Therefore you finished it all last night, and have nothing that could possibly be more important than talking to me."

Her logic sucked, but that didn't bother me even half as bad as how sure of herself she was. I held up my math book with a look that I hoped conveyed how ridiculous she was being.

"Oh, that's perfect. I don't understand any of this junk, so you can explain it to me now and then we won't have to spend as much time in that stupid tutoring lab."

The old me would have told Britney she was a self-centered wench, but the new me, the one that was all too aware of how much it would suck to go through the next two years of school without a single friend, just forced my face into something approximating a smile and tried to explain why drawing something at random from a bag with replacement was different than drawing something from a bag without replacement.

It was a fairly straightforward concept that we'd seen twice now. I was pretty sure Britney was capable of understanding, she just didn't care, which was the one thing virtually guaranteed to make me mad. Stupidity was bad enough; laziness would be a hundred times worse.

Still, by the second time through I'd clarified a couple of points I'd been a little fuzzy on, and was almost ready to believe Britney might actually apply herself to listening. I was so caught up in what I was doing, and the ever-so-slowly growing light of interest in Britney's eyes, that the rest of the class had fallen silent for a full twenty seconds before the drop in noise registered for me.

"I want everyone back to their regular desks and hard at work on their assignments."

Mrs. Campbell wasn't as pale as she'd been when she'd left, but she still looked unsettled and more than a little unhappy, presumably with both whatever had caused her to leave so quickly, and the fact that she'd come back to a class where almost nobody had been doing anything productive.

I had a couple of heartbeats to hope she'd realized I'd been trying to help Britney with her homework, and therefore not deserving of any punishment. "Britney, Adriana, I'll need to speak with you both after the bell."

Apparently the whole justice thing was on the fritz right now. It would probably start working again just in time to punish me for whatever bad thing I did next. I tried to work on my homework some more, but my heart wasn't in it, so I just sat at my desk and tried not to look like I was pouting.

All too soon class was over, and I found myself trailing Britney up to Mrs. Campbell's desk. She still didn't look very happy, but there was a trace more self-control to her face than a few minutes before.

"Britney, despite spending at least an hour at the tutor lab each afternoon, the quality of your homework hasn't come up in the slightest, so I took the liberty of talking to your father yesterday."

Britney's gasp had all the dramatic effect you'd expect out of someone who'd spent the last decade of her life getting away with pretty much whatever she wanted. She was obviously pretending to be sorry, all the while figuring her current trouble would blow over quickly enough if she just played her cards right.

"Your father agrees with me that your studies should be your highest priority, so you'll be staying an extra hour starting today, and ending once your performance improves. Of course you can always continue to just waste your study time, but if you choose to do that I've been assured that additional penalties will follow quite rapidly starting with the loss of your car."

The next gasp was less impressive, but tangibly more genuine. Even my being next couldn't stop a flash of satisfaction at the way Britney was finally having to face some of the consequences of her actions. Mrs. Campbell dismissed her with a wave, waiting until she'd left, shutting the door with a tad more force than strictly necessary.

"While I can't for a moment understand why you've chosen to befriend Britney, I can't fault you on your willingness to help her despite her flaws."

I should have been overjoyed I wasn't in trouble. Instead I felt guilty for being given far more credit than I deserved. I opened my mouth to object, but was waved back into silence.

"Obviously I don't want you to make disrupting my class a habit, but that isn't why I wanted to talk to you. Your studies are coming along nicely, and I've heard quite a few good things about you from other sources, so I'd like to offer you a job."

Now that I had a chance to talk, I wasn't sure what to say. Nobody had ever wanted to hire me. Mrs. Campbell gave me a tired smile. "The tutor lab is still understaffed. Obviously you couldn't spend your whole afternoon tutoring, as that would negatively affect your efforts to catch up. I'm thinking just an hour or so per night. It would just be minimum wage, but I think you'll find you quite enjoy teaching."

Still at a loss for words, I just nodded. I started towards the door as soon as I was dismissed, but stopped at the threshold. "Is everything okay Mrs. Campbell? I mean it seemed like you were really worried when you left."

I trailed off, worried by the measuring look that she gave me. "I don't suppose you're one of the gossipers, and I guess it wouldn't really matter if you were. I got a call that my daughter had been in a car accident. By the time I made it out to my car she'd called to tell me she wasn't hurt, just shaken up. So, in answer to your question, yes, everything's all right. I'm just a little unsettled."

Lunch was an awkward affair. Britney was still upset. I, on the other hand, was extremely happy I'd made a good enough impression to get a job. I didn't like sitting there while Britney badmouthed Mrs. Campbell.

I looked up during one of Britney's infrequent pauses for air, and caught Alec staring at me. Staring wasn't quite the right word though. Strangely enough, it didn't seem like he was necessarily mad, but he didn't seem happy either. I only caught his eyes for a few seconds before he looked away, but even his normally riveting blue eyes couldn't distract me from my inability to identify the look.

I was used to people disliking me, ignoring me, or even occasionally liking me, but this was the first time I'd met someone who seemed to be still trying to decide what camp to join long past the time when most kids our age would have either made a decision or just decided I was weird and started ignoring me.

Britney seemed to be getting suspicious that I wasn't really listening, so I had to make a lot of eye contact over the next few minutes. When I finally got a chance to look back up, Alec and his friends weren't at their table.

Cassie caught my eye before I looked down, but she was definitely glaring. Not the typical I-hate-you-and-I'm-going-to-do-everything-I-can-to-smear-your-reputation-and-get-you-in-trouble-because-we're-in-high-school-and-that's-all-I can-really-do type glaring. Instead her eyes seemed to warn me never to go out alone at night because if she ever found me somewhere without any witnesses, they were going to have to hospitalize me.

I felt a chill run through me, and dropped my eyes out of involuntary reflex. I probably would've started shaking if someone hadn't grabbed my shoulder and startled some kind of twisted cross between a shriek and a gasp out of me.

I turned to give whoever it was a piece of my mind, but Brandon's laughing gray eyes made the words tangle up before they made it down to my tongue.

"Hey there. You still going to that tutoring lab after school?"

I managed a nod that I thought nearly looked casual.

"Good, I need to start tracking your movements so you don't keep running me over."

The rest of lunch and all of history passed in a blur. My mind kept returning to Brandon, and the question of why he was taking such an interest in me.

It wasn't until I'd returned Mrs. Alexander's reference book to its shelf and sat down at my desk that I remembered I'd had to do the entire 'group' project by myself. Alec hadn't even bothered to come to Physics since the assignment had been given. My entire life I'd had people try and sponge off of my work, and I was way beyond sick and tired of it.

By the time Alec strode into class looking like the inspiration for every romance novel ever written, I was really mad. I hardly waited for him to sit down before I pulled my desk a little closer and hissed at him.

"So very nice of you to come to class on the day our stupid assignment is due."

Alec's expression was remarkable in that I'd never seen anyone look so full of life while simultaneously failing to betray even the slightest hint of emotion. He didn't even open his mouth as he reached into his bag and pulled out a bundle of densely-packed typewritten pages.

The arrogance of it all. He hadn't even bothered to consult with me before typing up an answer that was probably completely off base. I pulled out my shabbier, but correct, answer and mirrored his action, tossing my bundle on his desk before looking down at his report.

I skimmed through Alec's answer and felt my anger joined by surprise and just the slightest touch of admiration. He struck on exactly the same theory as I had, and done at least as good of job explaining it. Maybe even better considering that he took the time to review some of the underlying theory we'd been taught in class. I'd just jumped right into the answer.

"You're right. You never even came to class, and you got the right answer. Did you cheat? Is the answer to this problem out there somewhere on the Internet?"

Alec's face tightened with something I was willing to bet was anger. "No, I didn't cheat. I did the research to find the answer, presumably just like you did. Next time you feel like insulting me, please suppress the urge."

I had at least one nasty comeback on the tip of my tongue, but I swallowed it. I didn't like his tone, but he did have a right to be mad.

Luckily, I was saved by Mrs. Alexander's appearance at the door, a dry-erase marker behind one ear, a pencil behind the other.

The rest of the class period should have been enjoyable. My group had the right answer, which I'd come up with on my own, and we were now learning about leverage, mechanical advantage, and friction, all of which were actually pretty interesting.

I studiously ignored Alec, even though I could all but feel him glaring at me the entire time. When the bell finally rang, Mrs. Alexander looked up from her white board with a startled expression. "I suppose that's it then. Don't forget to turn in your assignments on your way out."

Anxious to make sure I got credit for all the work I'd done, I hurried up to the front of the class before Alec could get to his feet.

"Oh, Adriana. It looks like you've been busy."

She took my handwritten report, and then held out a hand as Alec approached. "Somehow I rather suspect you both have the same answer, Alec just used twice as many words to get there."

I shot Alec another dirty look, but it slid right off the armor of his arrogance. He nodded to Mrs. Alexander, and then slipped out of the classroom.

"Run along, young lady, we wouldn't want you to be late for your next class."

Spanish went about like I'd expected. There was a brief discussion on a new grammar concept, some vocabulary, and a whole lot of television. Britney caught up with me at my locker, still complaining that she was going to have to start doing her homework instead of trying to flirt with football players.

"It's completely unfair. Nobody else's parents get called. It's like I'm back in grade school and have to deal with parent-teacher conference every month. I thought the whole point of high school was to give us the chance to start making some of our own decisions."

I grunted something noncommittal as we turned the corner. It probably wouldn't have been good enough to save me from having to actually say something, but Brandon was leaning against a wall.

"I thought it much safer to stay in one place and wait for you rather than wander around and risk getting knocked down."

I felt my skin flush with embarrassment. It was fairly gentle as teasing went, but I hated how my skin looked when I was blushing which meant I blushed more than any two other people. Not only that, I couldn't ever come up with anything good to say when someone teased me.

Brandon seemed to sense my unease, and flashed another gentle smile. "I just wanted to find out if you had a way home tonight after you finished up with your math stuff."

Britney was almost jumping up and down. "Oh, don't worry, Brandon, I'll give Adri a ride home. The poor thing lives all the way out in the Anderson home. I've been giving her a ride into school and home almost every day since she moved."

Brandon was still smiling, but I got the feeling that it was a little more forced.

"Perfect. I'm going to go take care of some stuff then, but I'll see you both tomorrow."

Mrs. Campbell looked up from the plant she was watering as we walked into the tutoring room. "Ah, there you two are. Britney, you'll be sitting over there from now on. Adriana, go ahead and get started on your homework. When you finish come find me and we'll get you situated."

As always, Rachel was sitting at her table in the middle of no-man's-land. She looked up at me and smiled as I took my usual spot and started on my homework.

For the first time all day I felt like I could relax. The few times I looked up, I saw Britney, who seemed determined not to give in and actually do her homework.

I finished my two assignments about the time I normally did, and walked over to where Mrs. Campbell was trying to explain a story problem. The sophomore she was helping looked like he wanted to be anywhere other than trying to figure out how long it would take Sally to mow the lawn given a certain width of lawn mower moving at a given rate of speed.

"Oh, Adriana. Go ahead and walk around looking for students who need help. Most everyone will leave in the next ten minutes or so, but we're actually open for another hour."

She was right. Nearly everyone left over the next little while as they either finished up their assignments, gave up, or finally filled whatever quota of study time they'd been given by their parents. I did get to answer a couple of questions, which was surprisingly fun.

When there was only half an hour left Mrs. Campbell walked over. "Good job so far. Albert, the other tutors, and I are all going to head out. Stay here until closing time, and then you're free to go. We'll see you tomorrow."

I watched as my new co-workers trickled out, and then looked around at the nearly empty room. Rachel was still sitting at her desk in the middle of the room, and Britney was still pouting from her new, assigned seat.

"Let's go."

I shook my head. "I told Mrs. Campbell I'd stay the whole time. I'm not lying for you or anyone else."

Rachel piped up unexpectedly. "It's okay, Britney. If you want to leave we'll give her a ride home."

I could see the wheels turning in her head. If I really did have a ride, she could leave without ruining things with Brandon; but if I wasn't going to lie, then there was a good chance that Mrs. Campbell would find out she'd left early.

Parents were relatively easy to fool. Leave the tutor lab early, go somewhere else and kill some time until you were supposed to come home, and they'd never know the difference. Teachers were a little harder, but if you didn't have the help of your 'friends', then they became an insurmountable obstacle.

The gears finally ground to a stop and Britney sighed as she put her head down on the table. I tried to stop from smiling at her theatrics, but happened to look over at Rachel just in time to see a matching smile on the younger girl's face.

Before I could look away, Rachel held up the red side of her card. "Do you have a minute?"

Happy to be able to do something, I hurried over and took a look at her open book. "Fractions, huh?"

"Yeah, I'm supposed to reduce them after I finish adding, but I can't seem to get to the same answer as the book on this one."

She'd transposed a couple of the numbers when working on one of the intermediate steps.

"Here it is, you've changed the numbers here, it should be fourteen sixty-fifths, not fourteen fifty-sixths."

Rachel's skin was several shades darker than mine, tan enough that it didn't show embarrassment as easily, but it still looked like she'd gone the slightest bit red. "Oh, I'm sorry to bug you with such a stupid mistake."

"Don't worry about it. I'm just glad it was that easy. I've been worried all day someone would stump me on something right out of the gate on my first day."

Rachel looked up at me through dark lashes as I stood. "I've wanted to say thanks for a while. I really appreciate you making Cassie back down yesterday. Nobody else has ever stood up for me like that. At least not people that I didn't already know."

Based on what I'd seen less than thirty hours ago, it didn't look like her friends stood up for her either.

"No worries, it just seemed like the thing to do at the time. Why did she want to hurt you anyways?"

Rachel looked down, but somehow it wasn't a gesture that conveyed guilt. "It's complicated."

I'd spent too much time with emotions and thoughts floating around in my own head that I didn't want examined too closely. I wasn't about to pry if there was something she didn't want to tell me.

"I guess that's fair. Let me know if you have any more questions."

Rachel nodded, and then turned back to her book, apparently having used up her store of courage for the afternoon.

I stopped by Britney's desk to ask if she needed any help, and had to avoid an attempt to suck me into another gripe session about Mrs. Campbell. Satisfied that there wasn't anything I needed to be doing to help either of the other girls, and that they'd let me know if that changed, I broke out my Spanish book and reviewed some more vocabulary.

Despite my growing hatred for Mrs. Tiggs, I managed to get deep enough into my Spanish homework to lose track of time. When I finally surfaced from *abeja*, *camisa*, and *reloj* it was just five minutes before I was supposed to close up for the afternoon.

Rachel pulled her things together and left while I was straightening up the chairs. It was petty, but I waited inside the room until the clock showed exactly the time the lab was supposed to finish, and then joined Britney outside in the oppressive heat.

The air was so dry I could nearly feel it pulling the moisture out of my body as we started around the school towards where Britney had parked her car. As we reached the west side of the building, the high-pitched growl of a performance engine tore a hole in the relative silence.

The edge of the student parking lot was just barely in view now, but it was enough to see the source of the noise. A tiny figure barely recognizable as Rachel, was walking towards a dark-blue bullet bike, which had just roared to life. We had to walk several more steps before I recognized the leather-clad, dark-haired figure on the bike as Alec.

My feet must have unconsciously slowed because Britney was now several steps ahead of me and looking back impatiently. I tried to catch up, but Alec chose that moment to look up and stare in our direction. He was quite a ways away, and his lovely eyes were covered by a pair of sunglasses, but I somehow knew he was looking at me. He handed Rachel a helmet but continued to look at us, at me, while she put it on.

I was moving again, but my pulse sped up as Rachel grabbed a hold of her brother and swung her leg over the pillion seat on the bike. She seemed to see us for the first time as a cold chill arced down my back and the horizon started to vibrate.

I managed to raise my hand in response to her wave, but it was an absent motion. My attention was still on Alec and his unwavering stare. Rachel leaned forward as if to say something to him, and he finally nodded and dropped the bike into gear. A few seconds later the pair was screaming out of the parking lot, and my breathing was too labored for it to be anything other than a full-blown panic attack.

I made it another couple steps, just far enough to grab Britney as I started to fall. I had a split second to be grateful I'd lost all of that weight so Britney wouldn't collapse under me, and then the darkness claimed me.

Even though I knew I wouldn't remember the void when I finally came to, I wanted nothing more than to just float in the darkness. It had been a hard day. I'd....actually I wasn't sure why it'd been a hard day, but something told me I'd unconsciously been at the end of my rope just before I'd collapsed. Unfortunately that same thing told me I couldn't dwell here in the comforting absence, there was a very important reason for me to regain my feet.

The void was reluctant to let me go, stripping me of memories and experiences as I fought my way free. By the time I was near surfacing I no longer remembered just how much I'd wanted to stay.

Britney was pacing back and forth when I opened my eyes. She had her cell phone out and was looking like she wanted to dial 911, but was worried about the possible fallout. I was on the ground, which for some reason made me more irritable than it should have. Didn't she realize how hard it was to make it over to someone before collapsing like that? It kind of defeated the whole point if they then put you on the ground where your clothes would take their normal, instantaneous-collapse beating.

"Oh my gosh, are you okay? I wasn't sure what to do."

"I'm okay, I just need a minute."

Since I was already on the ground, I really did just want to lie there for a moment, scorpions, dirt and all, but Britney didn't seem to understand that concept. Now that my eyes were open and the whole 911 question had been answered, she was determined to get me back on my feet.

Chapter 8

I was midway through brushing my teeth before I realized I'd had another night filled with nothing but regular dreams. I'd walked into two different classes and found out that there were tests I'd forgotten about, been stranded at the side of the road, and been chased through some kind of rain forest, but while some of those dreams had been plenty terrifying, none of them had even a touch of the surreal vividness of the ones I'd had my first few nights in Sanctuary.

Maybe they were just some kind of psychological defense mechanism popping up in response to all the changes. If so, I kind of wished I could be sick still. It's a heck of a thing to not want to be healthy, but I'd gone to bed most every night hoping I'd get to experience another one. It was depressing to think that I probably had one less thing to look forward to.

Looking at the clock, I saw that I was a bit behind schedule. The bus would be here in about ten minutes, and Britney was supposed to arrive just a tad before that. It was sad, but I didn't trust her anymore, so I'd probably take the bus if she didn't show up before it did. I just couldn't risk her leaving me here without a ride. She'd been way weirded out after my collapse. I wasn't sure even the promise of Brandon's continued presence would be enough to convince her to come through on her word.

I hurried downstairs and grabbed my liquid lunch replacement out of the fridge. I was in such a hurry I almost didn't see the new note on the white board.

Sorry I missed you last night. Found a really promising spot. Left early—looked like it might work if I was there at sunrise. —Mom

I wasn't sure what to think. In theory she might be working on stuff for the brochure, but somehow I knew she was busy chasing her dreams once again.

Good luck, I'll see you later. —A.

My backpack creaked and groaned as I picked it up. Luckily most of my classes weren't moving as fast as I'd expected. I was far enough ahead I could start picking a few subjects and working on them every night instead of bringing home my entire locker every day.

As always, it was already heating up despite the sun having only barely cleared the mountains.

It did seem like it wasn't quite as hot though. Maybe it was getting late enough in the year to bring the temperatures down slightly. It was too much to hope it would actually drop to the low seventies, even when December came around.

I made it down the lane and then started worrying. It was like I couldn't win. If Britney drove all the way out here and I was already gone because I'd taken the bus, she was going to be really mad. On the other hand, if she didn't show, I had no other way to get to school, and Mom would freak out. Part of the reason she felt like she could be gone so much ever since the accident was the fact that I always did the responsible thing. If she started thinking I was cutting class, she was going be furious. It would be like I was behaving irresponsibly and taking away her ability to pursue her art, all at the same time.

It was past time for the bus to arrive, and she still wasn't here. A car zipped around the corner driving way too fast, just like Britney always did, but it wasn't white. I looked past it, hoping to see another one following it.

My mouth nearly hit the ground when I recognized the throaty roar and dark paint job of Brandon's Mustang.

"I knew you'd be sitting here worrying she wouldn't come."

It took a minute for the words to make sense. "Fine, but that doesn't shed any light on why you're all the way out here."

The gray eyes just visible in the slowly growing light crinkled up in a smile. "I called her and told her I'd pick you up. She can take you home, I'll come pick you up every morning."

My head was spinning. Why would the most popular boy in school want to pick me up for school every morning?

"You don't need to do that; I can always just ride the bus."

Brandon flipped open the passenger door and motioned for me to get in. I started around the vehicle, stumbling and nearly falling before I finally made it to my destination. Brandon waited for me to get my seatbelt on and then gunned the engine, flipping around a hundred and eighty degrees in a maneuver I'd never seen anyone perform outside of the movies.

"Of course I don't have to pick you up. It's more a matter of wanting to, if I can say that without making things all weird. I have obligations at school, people who depend on me. I can't spend the time I'd like getting to know you there, so it just made sense to free up some time in the mornings to make that happen."

Everything was just too unreal. I couldn't believe it was all happening, so I chose to ignore the implications of what he was saying. Boys like him didn't go for girls like me. They didn't even acknowledge the possibility unless they were after something.

We'd been driving in more or less comfortable silence for several minutes before I decided to act before things got uncomfortable. "So, tell me about yourself."

"There isn't much to tell. I was born here, and I'll probably die here."

"More of the obligations you were talking about?"

Brandon nodded, staring off in the distance for a second. "Yeah. It sounds pretentious, but a lot of people depend on my family. Half the businesses in the town are owned by my family, the other half are owned by Alec's mother."

The revelation was a bit of a shock. I'd known all along they were both ridiculously rich, but them owning the livelihood of nearly every person in the town was mind-boggling.

Brandon seemed to know where my thoughts were headed. "Pretty amazing, huh? Anyways, I've been raised to believe I have an obligation to the town, to the people who work for us. Part of that includes making sure other people with substantial resources don't abuse their power."

It was probably about as good of a chance to find out what was going on under the surface as I was going to get, but something inside me shied away. It was like I'd be entering a new world, one in which some of my illusions would be shattered. I'd have to face a colder interpretation of certain people's actions.

Brandon successfully defused any awkwardness, chuckling as he pulled into the school parking lot. "You really didn't know any of that?"

I shook my head, more or less speechless, and he reached out and playfully tapped the side of my face with one finger. The touch left my skin warm and tingling.

"That's what's so amazing about you. Almost everyone else at school was born here. They essentially look at every action as choosing between Alec and I. Britney, who could have legitimately stayed neutral, has been trying to get in my good graces almost since she arrived. You, on the other hand, couldn't care less who has the most money."

It was an explanation. Not an iron-clad one, but good enough for now. I thanked Brandon for the ride, and was rewarded with one more wide, open smile before we split up and headed our separate ways.

I kept telling myself not to get caught up in the idea of being with someone for the first time in my life, but still went through the first two classes more or less in a daze. Mrs. Sorenson was just as nasty as she'd been every day this week, but I didn't care when she managed to stump me on her second question.

I found myself subconsciously comparing Heathcliff with Brandon during English, and Mr. Whethers had to ask me a question at least twice before I realized he was talking to me. I hardly even blushed at the inevitable giggles. I made a mental note to find out from Britney if I'd caught his question on the second or third repetition, but I rather suspected I'd forget.

In fact, when class finally got out I remembered my question, but just didn't feel like asking. Instead, I just wanted to get away from her and the never-ending gossip. I waited until she stopped to talk to one of the cheerleaders about who was dating who, and then mumbled something about the bathroom, and made a break for it.

Not wanting to out-and-out lie, I ducked into the nearest restroom. It was empty except for a mousy brunette I'd only seen a couple of times before. I smiled and started to open my mouth to say hi, but thought better of it. This was Sanctuary. She wasn't going to acknowledge the new girl was even breathing, let alone sentient.

It should have bothered me, but I just shrugged it off and went to the far stall. A split second after I'd closed the door I heard the heavy wooden outer door open. Normally that wouldn't have caused me to even pause in my normal routine, but it suddenly felt as if the stall was too small.

"I told you to stay away from him, you stupid whore."

I didn't recognize the voice for all that I felt like I should. It was a snarling alto that even distorted by anger had traces of smooth velvet, the kind of voice guys occasionally fantasized about, when they weren't thinking about other, less subtle, feminine features. Something hit the stall next to me, hard enough to leave dents.

I was scared, I should have been terrified, but I was too busy trying to breathe. It was like the air had become thick, and although the fine strands of hair on the back of my neck hadn't moved, it felt like they should be standing on end.

I heard indistinct sobbing, and then the voice returned and made me shiver. The sensation started somewhere on my back, and traveled forward like it was clawing to get out of my face.

"I know you're sorry, just like you were sorry before. Only I don't really believe you, so we're instituting a new policy. If I catch you sniffing around him again, I'll kill you. No questions asked."

My pulse skyrocketed as the raw terror hit. I'd heard death threats a couple of times before. You don't go to a school of any size without seeing fights, and usually by the time girls resort to physical confrontations they really are serious about hurting the other person. When girls say they're going to kill each other, they mean it. This was something else entirely though.

Whoever was on the other side of the flimsy metal door I was hiding behind didn't just believe she would kill the other girl, she knew it, like someone who'd killed before. As scared as I was, I should have been a gibbering wreck, but strangely enough part of my mind was coldly rational. If I walked out right now I might be okay. If however they did kill the brunette, they'd come after me too.

It was possible, it turned out, to be rational but still completely paralyzed by indecision. The girl was sobbing now, and my heart felt like it was about to tear itself into pieces.

The creak of the bathroom door opening should have been a relief. I was expecting the tension to evaporate once there were more witnesses. I couldn't have been more wrong. The air had felt heavy before, now it felt alive, like ground zero of a lightning strike a split second before the soil was blackened by three hundred thousand volts.

"Get out."

"Go to hell."

I expected whoever it was to leave, I would've. I didn't expect for them to tell monster girl off, or that I'd recognize the new voice as belonging to Cassie.

The first girl was still whimpering. It nearly covered up the distant sound of some kind of machinery kicking on and creating a barely-audible two-part growl that made the air shiver.

"You can't get away with this." Cassie's voice was barely recognizable, a tattered shadow of her usual arrogance.

"I already have. I've already told Lucy where she stands with Ben. If you get in my way, if you approach him on her behalf, if you even think of acting on any of the hundred things going through your mind right now, I'll kill you too."

My knees were weak, but I had to get out now. For all that I hated Cassie, there was no way this crazy chick would act on her threats when there were three of us to corroborate each other's stories. I quietly swung the stall door open and felt my eyes go wide as I saw Lucy curled up, sobbing, at Jasmin's feet.

Neither of the other girls even bothered to look at me as I carefully moved to the door. Jasmin took half a step to the side, giving me room to get around her, but there wasn't even a slight drop in the level of menace she was radiating. It was like I didn't even exist.

I was still shaking on my way down the hall. By the time I made it into Algebra, I thought I was going to throw up. I felt like a complete coward, but I wasn't willing to go back there. I rationalized it by saying there wasn't enough time before the bell rang, but I was really just scared.

Britney gave me a questioning glance from across the room, but I just shook my head. I couldn't tell anyone about what'd happened. Not yet at least.

Mrs. Campbell obviously knew something was wrong, but as soon as class ended I dodged out of the room and headed towards the relative safety of the lunchroom. Britney's proclivity towards gossip was a complete godsend when you wanted to find out information about someone.

"Jasmin? I don't know, people don't say very much about her. She's got an incredible temper though."

"She's dating Alec right?"

Britney nodded emphatically. "I've never seen them kiss or hold hands, but they've got to be. She's totally rebuffed everyone, and he's never evidenced even the slightest interest in any other girl. Plus, they're like the two hottest people in the entire school. How could they possibly date anyone else?"

It was hard to argue with that. Jasmin was the kind of brunette who disproved the old saying that gentlemen prefer blondes. Any guy with a pulse would want her. And Alec was like a composite of every gorgeous model ever born. I could get past that and see he was a jerk, but that was just because girls seemed to be wired a little different.

None of it made sense. If Jasmin was dating Alec, why was she so mad at Lucy for talking to this Ben boy? I hadn't seen any other boys who were even close to as attractive as Alec and Brandon, and Jasmin didn't seem like the type to pick substance over form.

Britney had wandered off to other, safer subjects. I nodded a lot and tried to avoid thinking about what life was going to be like if Jasmin was determined to kill me. There was just no way to know if I'd made the right choice in leaving when I did. Would Cassie hate me a little less because we were both potentially in Jasmin's crosshairs, or would she hate me all the more because I'd seen her humiliated and forced to back down?

I finally finished the little can that represented my lunch. I wasn't particularly hungry, but I couldn't lose much more weight without Mom dragging me into a doctor. Besides, it gave me an excuse to try and ignore the fact that half of the people in the room seemed to be staring at me when they thought I wasn't looking.

I finally worked up enough courage to look across the cafeteria as I peeled the label off of the can. Alec wasn't at his usual place, but Brandon was at his normal table, surrounded by a smaller than normal group. The discussion looked way more intense than normal, and seemed to center around him and Cassie.

It was all so crazy. Two weeks ago my life had revolved around my inability to think of certain things without collapsing. That hadn't changed, but now there was a distinct possibility Jasmin was going to hurt me just to ensure I stayed silent. Oh, and I was actually considering opening myself up for some very nasty ridicule, just on the infinitesimally slim chance a boy who was so popular, rich, and gorgeous that he shouldn't even know my name might be interested in me.

Life was supposed to get better as you got older, but it was starting to look like it just got more complicated.

Just before I looked back down at the shiny aluminum of my now-naked can, Brandon looked up and caught my eye. The smile on his face seemed to say all kinds of things. *I'm sorry I can't come over and talk. They all really depend on me. This whole thing with Jasmin is really crazy; we've got to figure out how best to handle it.*

Maybe it really said all of those things, or maybe I was completely deluded, but it was definitely a smile. That alone was enough to make my heart skip a beat, and send a warm tingly feeling lapping through me like a wave of distilled happiness.

I was halfway through History before I realized there'd been something odd about the discussion at Brandon's table. Luckily, Mr. Simms started out the class in usual form. It was virtually guaranteed we wouldn't learn anything which was fortunate or I might have missed something. Once my mind latched on the question of what had been different than normal, I didn't hear a word anyone else said.

It wasn't until I was back at my locker and midway between switching out my History book for my Physics notes that I finally realized what it was. Normal juniors didn't sit at a lunch table and figure out what to do about anything. They complained, they gossiped, they boasted about what they were going to do, but it was all just an exercise designed to reinforce the social order. I'd seen it played out in multiple grades, among groups ranging from the jocks down to the lunatic fringe, and while the details changed, the overall form didn't. It was a universal constant, like the speed of light or maybe gravity.

Only Brandon's group hadn't been gossiping. They'd been discussing, brainstorming even. I didn't know what it meant. I didn't even know if it was a good thing. It made Brandon more intriguing, but he hardly needed any more help there.

With a sigh of frustration, I walked into Physics, smiled at Mrs. Alexander, and took my normal seat. I could pretty much set my watch by Alec's arrival. Apparently it wasn't cool to be caught inside a classroom more than fifteen seconds before the bell rang.

It was a sign of just how far removed from reality I was that he was able to sit down in the other corner before I even realized he'd stepped through the door. I realized I must have been woolgathering for longer than I'd thought, and reached for my notebook.

Only the bell should have rung by now, and it hadn't. I looked up at the clock and it confirmed that there was still at least a minute before class started. A slight rustle to my right brought my head around, and I looked up to find Alec smiling at me. I couldn't remember for sure if he'd ever smiled at me before, but I found myself suddenly positive he hadn't. I would have remembered such a strangely innocent expression.

Brandon's smile was one of the most genuine I'd ever seen, the kind of thing that only the most deceptive person could possibly pull off and not mean. Alec's smile was like the first bloom on a flower, something so new, so unpracticed that there wasn't any possible way it was anything other than sincere. It made me tingle all over, and want to giggle like I was still six.

Several seconds passed before I realized I'd been unconsciously returning his smile. I felt a blush slowly rising past my throat, but I couldn't look away. Luckily the bell broke my strange fit of paralysis, and I was able to regain some of my composure while Mrs. Alexander struggled her way through the role.

"I've been thinking about the fact that I didn't really give you young people a chance to ask any questions that might have come up during the course of your work on our section regarding light. Now's your chance, please ask away. If I don't know the answer, I'm sure that together we can find an adequate explanation for whatever you might have come across."

The class was quiet for several seconds, before a hand finally shot up. I could have predicted who it would be. Every class has at least one teacher's pet. Some of the kids end up that way because they have this bizarre thirst for knowledge, some go that route because they like to make everyone else look stupid. Sammy was in the latter group. She'd probably been saving a question about light since we'd started the unit. Just in case an opportunity presented itself to earn some brownie points.

"Mrs. Alexander, I read something about water around reactor cores giving off a blue light. Can you explain how that works?"

I'd expected something stupid, but glowing water made me think of the vivid dreams. I listened as intently as I'd ever listened to anything, and did my best to follow all of the diagrams as Mrs. Alexander attempted to break a college-level concept down into something fairly average high-school students could follow.

"So, in short, really it's a matter of the hydrogen and oxygen atoms attempting to shed the excess energy they've gained from the radioactive particles emitted from the core. The energized electrons give off radiation in the visible light spectrum during the process of dropping down to a lower energy state."

Hmm, an interesting concept, but still not an explanation for how the water in my dream had given off a soft golden glow, one that had rippled with the movement of the water. Almost before I'd realized it, my hand shot up.

"Is the light always blue? Is it ever a whitish-gold color?"

Mrs. Alexander looked slightly startled, like she'd never thought of such an idea, or maybe just that she hadn't been expecting a question from anyone other than Sammy.

"Not that I'm aware of. The water will actually emit quite a bit of ultraviolet light, but for whatever reasons, the electrons don't ever seem to release any electromagnetic radiation down in the lower energy levels like infrared, or even the visible red. You'd need red and all of the other colors to generate a true white light."

It was obvious we were on the wrong track here. "What about some other mechanism? One that wouldn't just make water glow with a dancing gold light, but plants too. Do you know of anything like that?"

I heard something snap off to my right, but I was too busy blushing from the chorus of giggles coming from the front of the classroom. Even Mrs. Alexander had an amused smile on her kind face. "While there are certain types of vegetation that do indeed glow, I'm afraid I don't know of any natural phenomenon that would create the kind of effect you're referring to. Such a thing is still the provenance of science fiction writers."

I knew I'd gotten a little carried away. The prime rule of high school survival involved avoiding situations people could use to ridicule you later, but I'd really wanted a rational explanation for my dreams. They seemed so real. I needed a friendly face to get me through the rest of class.

Remembering Alec's smile from earlier, I looked over at him, hoping he'd return my sheepish grin. It was almost like he was a different person. The smile was gone. It'd been replaced with a steely mask that almost completely hid his emotions. Only the look in his eyes, and the mechanical pencil in his hand, neatly snapped into two pieces, told me he was mad, that something very much like hatred was washing through him.

I felt like I'd been punched in the stomach. It shouldn't have mattered. I'd known he hated me pretty much ever since I'd met him. Somehow it *did* matter though. To have his friendship dangled out in front of me only to be yanked away a heartbeat later was somehow crueler than I'd ever guessed it would be.

It all fit together though. Jasmin had told him I'd overheard her death threats, and he'd decided to use his good looks to convince me to keep quiet. Only he hadn't been able to keep the act up for more than just a few seconds. I must really repulse him.

Physics was my own little personal hell for the next forty minutes. I absorbed absolutely nothing from the rest of the discussion about calculating mechanical advantage, and when we were finally released into our groups Alec and I didn't even look each other in the eyes. I gutted out the last five minutes by pretending I was completely absorbed in a reference book while Alec started running preliminary calculations.

He was out of his seat and halfway to the door by the time I'd even realized the bell had rung to dismiss us.

Spanish was both better and worse. Better because without Alec sitting six feet away from me I was able to think about something other than him, worse because we had a pop quiz and I barely placed in the A- range despite having spent a fair amount of time on my vocabulary. Math was plain and simply burning up too much time. Something needed to change because my only hope of going to college was to get a scholarship, or load up on student loans, and I had no desire to graduate sixty thousand dollars in debt and spend the next fifteen years trying to pay it all off.

By the time I met up with Britney in the hall I was emotionally exhausted and could feel an attack hovering in the wings. Much as I'd have liked to, I couldn't continue to blow her off. She was my only friend, and I definitely didn't want her spreading the kind of rumors about me that she routinely spread about everyone else.

"Wow, you look like crap. Are you going to collapse like you did last night?"

"Thanks, Brit. You look ravishing too, and no, I'm not going to collapse. I just haven't been sleeping very well lately. I'm probably coming down with something."

Britney shrugged with the supreme indifference of someone whose world extended only a few feet beyond their immediate person. "Just don't get me sick if you do. Ashure Day isn't that far away."

We were halfway to the tutoring lab, and the halls were nearly empty. Everyone was always in such a hurry to get out, to go home, or to a party. Anywhere but here. "Oh, speaking of boys, I saw Brandon between fifth and sixth period. I made sure he knew I'd get you home after tutoring. He's *so* gorgeous. I don't know how you're doing it, but whatever it is, don't stop. He's the surest ticket ever to the A-list."

I wanted to throw up a little, but I managed to smile and hold the door open for her. If I made it through the next two hours without having an attack it would be a miniature miracle.

Halfway through the walk to my normal table I looked up and saw Rachel smiling at me with almost the exact same innocent, convincing smile her brother had used on me just a couple of hours before. My insides simultaneously tensed up with hurt and relaxed in happiness. The best I could really have expected out of the experience would have been to stay on an even keel, but instead it was almost as if part of my frustration evaporated. I still wasn't ready to get up and sing any songs, but it was starting to at least look like I might manage to finish out the day.

Especially surprising considering my current mental state, it only took me half an hour to finish up the two Algebra sections I'd assigned myself. Mrs. Campbell stopped by my desk a few seconds after I finished up. "We don't really need the extra help until later. Is it okay if you just start at the same time you did last night?"

She accepted my nod at face value, but then paused in the act of turning away. "Is there anything wrong? You seemed awfully distracted in class today."

My headshake wasn't very convincing. I'd known it wouldn't be, but couldn't manage anything more. It was a relief when she chose not to press for more information.

By the time people started trickling out and my shift started, I'd spent plenty of time watching Britney pout, and very little time actually working on my homework. I think it was really starting to sink in that she wasn't going to be able to get out of continuing to spend most of her afternoons here.

Albert, Mrs. Campbell, and the other tutor all waved goodbye as they left. One of the cheerleaders, a particularly whiny specimen named Jackie, wanted help, which I was happy to offer, even in my current state. Unfortunately she thought that meant I'd just hand over all the answers. We spent a good ten minutes with her trying to offer a variety of covert bribes ranging from the insignificant to things she couldn't possibly deliver. I kept telling her I wasn't interested and that she'd just have to do the work.

Surprisingly enough, once she accepted that, she actually buckled down. It only took another ten minutes to explain the Pythagorean theory to her.

By the time I stood up from Jackie's desk, there were only four of us left. Britney was staring sullenly at her book. I thought about going over and seeing if she needed any help, but after helping Jackie I was feeling pretty good.

I turned and headed back to my desk, smiling at Rachel as I passed.

"Adri, do you have a sec?"

The deadly nickname. Apparently I'd only thought I was doing better. The good feeling I'd gotten from helping Jackie had just been the deceptive crust of ice hiding the sub-zero deathtrap below. My desk was too far away. I wanted to try and gut it out, but the emotional extremes from the day had been too draining.

I slumped into the empty chair next to Rachel and tried to concentrate on my breathing. Maybe I could lessen its impact, somehow have a mini-attack that made my mind blank out, but left me enough control over my body to remain seated in the chair. Rachel grabbed my arm, disrupting my concentration. "Are you okay? What's going on?"

She had a cell phone out, partially hidden by her desk. Part of me wondered why I'd never seen her with a phone before. Most girls walked around looking like they'd had some experimental surgery that created a two-way graft between their phone, their hand, and their ear. It didn't really matter though. Cell phone or not, the biggest part of me was already floating away to somewhere safe.

"I'll call Alec; he'll know what to do." She was still whispering, but the words sheared through the darkness, arresting my fall. I didn't want him here, didn't want to give him another reason to despise me. What if Jasmin came with him? The thought of lying helpless with her in the same room sent shivers of cold sliding down me.

I couldn't see, so I reached out, blindly trying to find the phone before Rachel could dial Alec. My questing hand finally found the tiny, hard-plastic package, and I grabbed on with all of my fading strength.

The darkness was still beckoning, but alternating images of Jasmin and Alec flashed before my eyes. I was so confused that I couldn't make sense of the flood of emotions that accompanied the pictures, other than the fact that terror came to the forefront as they sped up.

Faster and faster the two figures changed places, and then they disappeared. It was like my mind was a computer that'd overheated and had to reboot. I opened my eyes and met Rachel's worried gaze. My pulse was still elevated, and I was breathing too hard. It seemed impossible for Britney and Jackie not to hear and realize something was up, but a quick look verified that they were still lost in their respective inner worlds.

"You just had another fainting spell, didn't you?"

I felt my eyes go wide. Nobody here was supposed to know about that. The more people who knew, the more pity I'd see in everyone's eyes. All that pity would then make it hard to want to continue fighting, hard to want to do anything other than just curl up in my room so I could avoid them all.

Rachel shook me gently, apparently not convinced I was mentally where I was supposed to be. "Britney's been telling people you collapsed yesterday after school. This makes twice in two days, and I know that yesterday wasn't the first time."

The tired, dreamy remnants of my attack were suddenly burned away as I registered the meaning of what Rachel had just said. Vague suspicions that people had known about

Jasmin's threats vanished, driven away by the truth that Britney had been gossiping about me just the way she gossiped about everyone else.

Rachel grabbed my arm as I tensed up. "I don't know what you're going to do, but maybe you shouldn't get up yet."

I looked over at Rachel's concerned face and opened my mouth to thank her for whispering, for keeping my secret, only the words didn't come out. Instead the image of Alec, the one that had burned itself onto my retinas a few seconds previously just as it had done in physics when I'd looked over to see his broken pencil, flared back into life before my eyes.

"You knew there was another time. Alec told you about Physics."

Rachel opened her mouth, probably to deny it, but the look in her eyes told me it was true. She couldn't possibly be that scared about me putting two and two together if he'd been saying nice things about me. He hated me, and she was scared of him, scared of what he'd do if he found out she'd let his secret slip.

"It's not like that, Adri. It's..."

I didn't even have to cut her off. She couldn't finish her own thought, couldn't come up with a lie that was believable. I shook my head and went back to my desk before my invulnerability wore off and she brought on another attack.

I missed them both so badly. Dad had always been there to listen when I got into problems like this. He'd known how to deal with the world, how to work with circumstances so that what resulted was beneficial, or at least something I could live with. And Cindi. If she were still here this would all be a moot point. I hadn't ever needed any other friends while she was alive, hadn't ever had to really put myself out there where I could get dragged into the kind of stupid infighting I'd read about for so many years growing up.

Author's Note

In some ways it feels like I've been at this for decades, in other ways it feels like I only just sat down to try and put Adri's story down in words. Now that it's live, I can only say that I hope you enjoyed it as much as I enjoyed writing it. If you haven't read Torn yet, please go check it out. When I set out to write Broken, I never expected that I was going to end up writing the same story from Alec's point of view, but I'm pleased with how both Broken and Torn have turned out, both individually and as a combined work.

They are done in very different styles, but ultimately that was exactly what I was after. I think there is plenty of cross-over of guys reading paranormal romance, and girls picking up more action-packed stories. Ultimately I think most of us just want a compelling story, but sometimes the labels that get applied to books get in the way of us discovering them, rather than helping as they are meant to do.

Acknowledgements

A big thanks to all of the fans who are doing so much to help get the word out. I want to make special mention of a few dependable souls that I'm very grateful to know. Cassy & Mark, I'm glad you both turned out to be story addicts just like me. Thanks for everything. Dad, not everyone gets to be best friends with their parents. Thanks for all of the feedback and the ongoing support. Mimi, thanks for sticking with me long enough to get addicted and to fix some of my biology facts along the way. As always, Katie deserves special thanks. Without her, Alec and Adri's story never would have seen the light of day.

Thanks also need to be expressed to Obsidian Dawn, www.obsidiandawn.com, for brushes used in the creation of Broken's cover.

About the Author

Dean Murray is a prolific author with more than thirty titles across multiple pen names and more than half a million copies of his work currently in circulation.

Dean started reading seriously in the second grade due to a competition and has spent most of the subsequent three decades lost in other people's worlds.

Things worsened, or improved depending on your point of view, when he first started experimenting with writing while finishing up his accounting degree.

These days Dean has a wonderful wife and two lovely daughters to keep him rather more grounded, but the idea of bringing others along with him as he meets interesting new people in universes nobody else has ever seen tends to drag him back to his computer on a fairly regular basis.

Keep up to speed on Dean's latest projects at www.DeanWrites.com.

Torn

Shape shifter Alec Graves has spent nearly a decade trying to keep his family from being drawn into open warfare with a larger pack. The new girl at school shouldn't matter, but the more he gets to know her, the more mysterious she becomes. Worse, she seems to know things she shouldn't about his shadowy world.

Is she an unfortunate victim or bait designed to draw him into a fatal misstep? If she's a victim, then he's running out of time to save her. If she's bait, then his attraction to her will pull him into a fight that'll cost him everything.

Splintered

Most girls would have killed to be in Adri's shoes, in fact several people think that's exactly what she did. Of course life with a pack of shape shifters isn't quite what she expected. The time with Alec is great, but now that the rival pack is out of the picture, Alec's wolves are all starting to turn on each other, and Adri is finding there is less and less she can do to help hold the pack together.

Alec's determination to keep her at arm's length physically is just as frustrating as always, but his ongoing refusal to explain the larger world the pack is operating in is starting to become more than just something that keeps Adri up at night. It's starting to look like something that could get them all killed.

Frozen Prospects

The invitation to join the secretive Guadel should have been the fulfillment of dreams Va'del didn't even realize he had. When his sponsors are killed in an ambush a short time later, he instead finds his probationary status revoked, and becomes a pawn between various factions inside the Guadel ruling body.

Jain's never known any life but that of a Guadel in training. She'd thought herself reconciled to the idea of a loveless marriage for the good of her people, but meeting Va'del changes everything. Their growing attraction flies against hundreds of years of precedent, but as wide-spread attacks threaten their world, the Guadel have no choice but to use even Jain and Va'del in their fight for survival.

Chapter 9

I couldn't bring myself to speak to Britney the entire way home. It didn't really matter; she spent the whole time complaining about a dozen different ways in which everyone around her was making her life miserable. She didn't need any kind of response from me.

I had the house to myself again, so I worked on homework until I was too exhausted to continue.

It wasn't until I was almost asleep that I realized I was hoping I *wouldn't* have one of the incredible, vivid dreams tonight. Alec's cameo role in my last two had apparently been sufficient to tie him inseparably to all of the special dreams, and as silly as it was, I didn't want to see Alec right now. Not even just in my dreams.

Maybe there really wasn't any kind of link between him and the dreams. Maybe I'd have one of them tonight without him making any kind of appearance. I sincerely hoped not, but I'd rather not have them right now than see the disdain he'd displayed earlier in the day.

The next morning played out essentially the same as the day before. I awoke to an empty house, and then hurried to get ready and down to the bus stop so I wouldn't be stranded if nobody else showed up to give me a ride into school.

Brandon smiled as he pulled up and found me patiently waiting for the school bus. "One of these days you're going to go ahead and wait for me at your house, and then I'll know you finally trust me."

I didn't feel much like playful banter, but I marshaled a semi-convincing smile and gave it my best go. "Oh, I trust you, I just know that you've got more important things to worry about. One of these times you'll either forget to come get me, or you'll forget to tell me you're not coming by anymore."

Brandon let the silence build several seconds. "I'd try and convince you I'm not going to do any of that to you, but I suspect that's just going to take time."

I was busy kicking myself for having cast such a pall over the morning, when Brandon sighed. "We should talk about what happened to you yesterday."

"I don't know what you're talking about. Nothing happened." Deny everything. It's essentially the motto of two entire generations now. Make them tell you exactly how much they know before you admit to anything, and then only admit to the parts they already know about. It's a crappy way to run a society, but I'm just one kid. I can't be blamed for just trying to keep my head down and survive.

We were already pulling into the parking lot. He must have been driving even faster than normal. That should have triggered another panic attack, but the tension in the black Mustang was high enough to distract my subconscious for now.

Brandon smoothly pulled the bulky car in between a pair of SUVs and cut the engine before turning and hitting me with the full force of his gray eyes. "Adriana, I promised to protect you. I know it's kind of anachronistic, but I take those kinds of promises seriously. Most of us here in Sanctuary do. I need to know what you saw and heard while you were in the bathroom with Lucy and Jasmin, before Cassie arrived."

"You're going to protect me from Cassie *and* Jasmin?"

His face was completely serious as he nodded. "If necessary, but I need to know what else was said so I know how serious things are. Jasmin had a really tough childhood. Her mom was killed while she was really young, and her father was pretty abusive. Alec's mother did a good thing by bringing her into their home and trying to give her a decent life, but she's not completely stable."

My laugh had a touch more hysteria in it than I'd meant to let slip through. Brandon didn't look at me like I was losing it though. "You're not the only one to realize she's dangerous, it's just that Alec's family has a lot of influence, and so far she's avoided doing anything they couldn't cover up."

I drew a deep breath and nodded. "Okay, I don't remember exactly what she said, but she was mad at the other girl, Lucy. Something about staying away from a boy, I don't remember if she said his name. Then Jasmin said she didn't believe Lucy was sorry, and that she'd kill her if Lucy didn't stay away from him."

Brandon nodded slowly. "The boy's name's Ben. I'm not sure why she's fixated on him the way she has, or why she views Lucy as such a deadly threat to her chances with him, but it's essentially that simple."

I felt like my head should be reeling from the sheer stupidity. Even in a town this small, it didn't seem like the competition for the available males should be a matter for death threats. Brandon took my head shaking as denial of what he'd said, rather than disbelief regarding the situation.

BROKEN

"I promise that every word I just told you is true. More importantly, I promise I'll make sure nothing terrible happens to you."

Looking into Brandon's caring eyes, I almost couldn't believe any of it. Being threatened and then having the perfect man come to your rescue didn't happen in real life. Then again, maybe I was due for some happy endings. With a sigh, I thanked him for the ride, and we parted ways.

The only thing of note that happened in Biology was that for a few moments at the beginning of the hour it almost seemed that the near-constant stares had somehow changed and taken on a more sympathetic tone than they'd had previously.

It seemed silly to even entertain the idea. People my age don't really do sympathy very well. We're much more inclined towards ridicule and hasty, usually unfair, judgments. Still, something had changed. I held onto that hope right up until I saw Mrs. Sorenson joining everyone else in staring at me whenever I looked down at my book. There was no mistaking the look on her face; it was utter distaste, possibly with a dash of disdain.

I was so tired of it all. By the time English rolled around my natural embarrassment had given way to actual anger at Britney for starting it all. She tried to catch me at our lockers in between classes, but I pretended not to hear her, and made it safely into Mr. Whethers' class before she could catch up.

Part of me acknowledged how petty it was, but I avoided her attempts at a whispered conversation during class. Mr. Whethers unknowingly helped my cause, when he crossly silenced a couple of girls on the far side of the classroom. He was normally so even-tempered that even his moderate rebuke instantly shut them up. I probably shouldn't have felt quite so happy about it, but I was pretty sure from the way they'd been looking at me that I'd been the source of their gossip.

When the bell finally released us, I couldn't avoid Britney any longer.

"Adri...ana, why didn't you tell me?"

I didn't answer for several seconds, not sure I'd actually heard her right. "Tell you what?"

"Fine, play coy. I just think you should know it's pretty lame for me to find all that stuff out second hand. We're best friends; you should totally have trusted me enough to tell me."

Apparently I'd only thought the anger was under control. It frothed beneath the surface right now, anxious for a reason to bite someone's head off, and Britney was the preferred target. Only I needed her. Not enough to completely dismiss what had happened though.

"I don't know what you're talking about, but I honestly wouldn't have told you anything I wanted kept a secret. Not after the way you told everyone about my panic attacks."

Britney looked like she was having a hard time getting enough air. She gasped a couple more times, and then managed to get some words out. "I'm so sorry. I didn't realize you'd care. I thought it would be okay."

I pinned her in place with my eyes for several seconds to prove I didn't believe her, and then shrugged. "I don't suppose it matters all that much. I just know now that I can't trust you with those kinds of things."

Mrs. Campbell's class served as another safe haven. There were still plenty of looks, but nobody dared gossip, and Britney was safely seated on the other side of the room. I took a little bit of sick satisfaction over the fact that everyone else was frantic about our test tomorrow. I actually couldn't have been happier. This was the first section where I'd been in a position to sit for the exam with everyone else.

Our lecture essentially consisted of an extended review, which I quickly realized I didn't need. I broke out my book and started in on one of my catch-up assignments instead. At the rate I was going I'd be able to take my makeup exam way ahead of schedule. It was a pretty lame thing to be excited about, but just having something going well for a change helped compensate for the rest of my life.

Amazingly enough, the satisfaction from having accomplished so much shielded me for most of the rest of the day. I withstood Britney's varied, mostly unsubtle, attempts to make me feel guilty for not spilling my guts about whatever big secret she thought I had, and even held up through the complete boredom that was Mr. Simms' class. It wasn't until I walked into Physics that I felt the cold hand of reality reach out and caress the back of my neck.

Alec was uncharacteristically early, already sitting at his normal desk. He looked up and briefly met my eyes when I reached my desk, but there wasn't even a trace of acknowledgment in his gaze. Mrs. Alexander started class, reviewed a couple of points that other groups needed clarified, and then released us to work on our assignments.

I waited several seconds for Alec to make some kind of move, and then with a flash of anger stood and carried my things over to the desk next to his. I nearly jumped when he opened his mouth.

"You'll want to review page 89. It contains most of the relevant formulas. We'll need to know exactly how they work. We'll be given an unknown weight, an unknown number of pulleys, and expected to move it all with the most efficient arrangement possible."

It almost didn't seem like he was talking to me. There was no emotion in his voice, no gentle teasing; he didn't even meet my eyes. I sat down with a slight hope that he'd thaw out a little by the time class ended, only to shake my head in disbelief when the bell finally rang and proved me irrevocably wrong.

Maybe he'd go back to normal after a few days. There really wasn't any way to know though. I didn't even know what'd brought on the sudden change. Was he really just angry I'd overheard Jasmin threaten Lucy? Why did I even care?

Spanish dragged by at a snail's pace, but somehow before I knew it, I was walking with Britney towards the tutor lab. I should have been surprised when we rounded a corner to find Brandon casually leaning against the wall, obviously waiting for us, for me.

"You still okay to go home with Brit today?"

He acted like it was all my choice. It gave me goose bumps. Britney almost tripped over herself assuring Brandon that we were still the best of friends, and she wouldn't even think of leaving me without a ride. Obviously if it wasn't convenient for him to take me, she would love to make sure I got home okay.

Brandon's face remained serious through Britney's torrent of words, but he winked at me when she looked down to catch her breath.

"Perfect. I'll go take care of some stuff then. You two enjoy all of that math, and I'll see you tomorrow morning. Maybe you'll even wait for me at your house this time."

It unsettled me a little that such a simple statement could cause industrial-sized butterflies to spontaneously appear in my stomach, so I tried to push the thought out of my mind. I hesitantly returned Rachel's tentative smile, and then dug into my homework.

Mrs. Campbell stopped by for a few minutes, obviously checking to make sure that I was over my aberrant behavior from yesterday. I got the feeling she would've liked to chat for a bit longer, but we had the predictable surge in attendance given the coming test.

I gave her my best reassuring smile as she left, and then watched as she and the other tutors all bounced from one student to the next answering questions. As much as I would have liked to just call it a day, another good effort added to what I'd done earlier would put me two or maybe even three days ahead of my personal schedule.

With a sigh of resignation I found my place on the page again, and started sorting out another set of variables. Forty-five minutes later I'd nearly completed another two sections, and was more than ready for a breather.

Sometime while I'd been studying, most of the kids had left. I hadn't expected all of them to stay until my shift started, but I'd expected more than the two or three I usually had. Only it didn't look like that was going to be the case. Apparently most of them hadn't been serious about learning the material—they'd just wanted to come to the lab, make a half-hearted attempt, and then leave secure in the knowledge that if they failed the test they could whine to their parents about how hard they'd worked. *But Mom, I even went to the lab.*

It sort of made sense though. If they'd been serious about acing the test, they'd have been here every night for the last two weeks instead of trying to cram a few more morsels of knowledge into their heads at the last minute.

Mentally shrugging at the stupidity of it all, I pulled out my Spanish and studied my vocab for a few more minutes until Mrs. Campbell came by to wish me goodbye.

"It looks like most everyone's gone again. The last few will probably leave in the next ten minutes." She dropped her voice to a conspiratorial whisper. "I actually prefer they do. That way when their parents phone in to complain about how poorly they did on the exam, I can point out that the lab was open for another hour, but they didn't bother to stick around for the extra help."

It was a speech that made her sound like a grouchy old lady, but I was starting to know her well enough to take it in the proper context. She would gladly have done just about anything to help a student who really wanted to learn, but was tired of having students try and use her as an excuse for their own laziness.

I waved goodbye to everyone as they left, and then made a quick round of the remaining students. Rachel and Britney were both in their accustomed places, Rachel studying away as always, and Britney making some weak efforts to do likewise. Two of the other three, a boy and a girl I recognized from second hour, but whose names I couldn't even begin to remember, were already packing their books into a pair of book bags, one of which was a fairly utilitarian item, the other of which probably cost as much as my whole wardrobe.

I couldn't place the last boy for all that he looked really familiar. He had incredibly dark skin and features with a slight Middle Eastern cast. When he shifted in his seat, I realized he was built like a football player. Not like a lineman, but like a running back, or maybe a quarterback. He wasn't as big as Brandon, or even as Alec, but he was obviously well muscled, and he moved with an echo of their grace.

None of which helped me figure out where I'd seen him before. He wasn't a regular at the tutor lab, and didn't have the hectic, desperate look of someone cramming for a test. Instead he looked completely at ease sitting in one of the no-man's-land tables with a pair of books open in front of him. By the looks of things he wasn't going to need any help.

Once it was just the four of us, Britney waved me over and held up her homework. "I don't get it. What is the answer to this one?"

I shook my head in exasperation. "Me telling you the answers won't help you on the test. If you have a specific question about how to work a problem I'd be more than happy to help you, but I'm not going to do your homework for you."

Britney looked like she had all kinds of things that she'd like to say, but she showed more restraint that I'd realized she was capable of, and kept them all inside.

"Please explain this one then."

I ran through three different examples of the same problem before she got it, but thirty minutes later she was finally working on her homework for the first time I'd ever seen. I was surprised just how satisfying it was. Maybe I should become a teacher.

Rachel caught my eye before I made it back to my table. She gave me another tentative smile as I slid into the seat next to her. "I'm really sorry about yesterday. I said all of the wrong things. It's just I'm not supposed to talk about what Alec says."

Wow, he sounded like even more of a jerk than I'd expected. Talk about controlling. "It's okay Rachel. I'm sorry I overreacted at finding out my attacks were public knowledge. It was mostly meant for Britney."

She cocked her head slightly to the side and looked at me with incredibly large blue eyes that seemed older than they had a few seconds before. "It really bothers you that everyone knows?"

I shrugged uncomfortably. "I guess maybe it shouldn't, but it does. Nobody likes to be ridiculed, but it's even more than that. The attacks started up a couple of months ago. They...remind me of a really terrible thing that happened, so when people make a big deal out of them it's like it's all happening again."

Rachel nodded slowly, her wonderfully expressive face full of sympathy. "I'm sorry to have pried like that. If I'd known it would make you feel bad, I wouldn't have asked."

I tried to shrug indifferently, but she seemed to see through my pretenses. "I normally wouldn't have said anything, but knowing what I know now, I wouldn't want you to go through the next several days hurting inside because you think everyone looking at you out of the corner of their eye is ridiculing you."

Confident she didn't really need help, and eager to avoid further reminders of just how broken I was, I'd been standing to return to my desk. The words were plenty foreboding, but they had an impact all out of proportion from what they should have. I sank back into the chair and turned towards Rachel. Not enough to actually make eye contact with her, just enough I hopefully didn't come off rude. Maybe the illusion of space would be enough to cushion me from whatever she was going to say next.

Rachel waited a second, giving me a chance to say something before she proceeded. "You should know that someone released another rumor about you, about your attacks."

My heart sank. I'd only thought things couldn't get any worse. Once everyone knew exactly why I was emotionally crippled they'd have even less sympathy. They'd pretend to feel sorry for me. They'd talk about how hard it must have been to suffer such a loss, but they wouldn't understand, wouldn't have the frame of reference to feel what I was feeling. They'd secretly talk about all of the people they knew who'd lost family members and been okay after a few weeks, or a couple of months. How even at their worst, those friends hadn't collapsed at the mention of their departed loved ones.

My pulse was already almost twice as fast as normal, and the room was just starting to wobble from side to side. Rachel was saying something, but I couldn't really hear her. The void was gaping below me, when something grabbed my shoulder and shook me surprisingly hard.

I opened my eyes to see Rachel looking at me. "I'm sorry I had to do that, Adriana, but you need to hear what I have to say."

Half of me wanted to be angry, but the other half just wanted to collapse into the void. Force of habit won over anger and I passively let my defenses crumble, but apparently being shocked out of a collapse functioned much the same as having just come out of an attack. For the next few seconds at least I was safe, could think about anything I wanted without fear of the repercussions. Only Rachel was talking, ruining my concentration, so the only thing I could focus on was her words.

"The rumor revolves around the fact that you tragically lost your boyfriend in a vicious car wreck."

The immunity meant I hadn't expected the words to hurt, hadn't expected the flash of surprise that spiraled up from my center. The words were close to the truth, but not right somehow.

"He was someone special, some of the rumors put him as some kind of model or actor, or maybe a semi-pro athlete. You'd been dating for two years, and were in the car with him when it happened. It was so devastating that you've had a hard time dealing with certain things since the accident. Being in cars that are driven too fast, mention of the wreck, other assorted things, and sometimes things nobody would expect trigger an attack."

The words were striking into my mind with such force I almost forgot Rachel was whispering. None of it made sense, it had some things in common with the truth, but most of it was pure fabrication.

"Why...I don't understand. Who would say that?"

Rachel's face went from a mobile, beautiful thing to a near-perfect mask. Even in my befuddled state it was obvious she was lying.

"I don't know, but you can use this. You're not being mocked or scorned anymore. True or not, that rumor is the most romantic thing anyone here has ever heard. It will transform you into a mini-celebrity overnight."

The haze was starting to evaporate from my thoughts, the story still didn't make sense, but Rachel's explanation did.

"The story's vague enough that nobody can really prove or disprove it. Don't get specific on any details, and you can ride this all the way until you graduate."

The mask was gone, she wasn't lying anymore. She really believed this rumor would change everything for the better. It all made sense, but didn't explain who'd started it, or why they'd done it. Rachel's face told me she wouldn't answer either of those questions.

I finally settled on one I thought she might answer. "Why are you telling me all this?"

Rachel's face tried to take on her liar's mask, but didn't quite succeed. "You risked a lot to stop Cassie from hurting me. The least I can do is tell you anything I know that could save you from getting hurt in return."

She was telling the truth. Not all of it, but at least some of it. I wanted to tell her she didn't owe me anything, but there were so many questions I needed answered still. There was some kind of weird power struggle going on, and her brother was right in the middle of it all, but I couldn't ask her about any of it. She'd already said as much as she was going to.

I nodded my thanks, and went to stand again, but she captured my arm before I could complete the motion. "There are a lot of things I can't tell you, but anything you want to know about me is fair game. I'm sorry about all the rest."

Something about the vulnerability in her eyes convinced me she really meant that. I added one more item to the list of reasons to hate her brother. Anyone who would be so controlling to someone like Rachel had already piled up all kinds of bad karma.

"Fair enough. What's your favorite book that you've never read?"

The question seemed to take her by surprise. "Um, Gone With the Wind. Probably because she doesn't necessarily start out as a bad person, but allows self-interest and events to carry her into terrible actions."

I felt my eyes go wide. "That's a pretty detailed analysis of a book you've never read."

Rachel blushed a little. "I really haven't read it. Maybe because I'm worried that it won't turn out to be what I think it will be. What about you?"

I shouldn't have been surprised by the question, but I was. Possibly because I'd spent too much time around people like Britney who were so caught up in their own lives that they didn't really care about what was happening in mine.

BROKEN

"Les Misérables. The music from the musical is so inspiring that I know the book must be truly wonderful."

I let the statement hang in the air for a couple of seconds, and then finished up with the truth. "Of course I don't really know, because it's so big, and parts of it are so boring, that I may never manage to get through the whole thing."

Chapter 10

The rest of the afternoon finished up on a quiet note. After I went back to my table, Rachel worked on some homework for a few more minutes, and then gathered up her things and slipped out.

I decided the new guy wasn't a football player when he started gathering up his books. No athlete in my experience ever took that many books anywhere. Not only that, he gently placed them in his backpack like someone who viewed the written word as his friend rather than as a necessary evil that interfered with the hero worship due him from the masses.

I was so busy watching him that I forgot to look away when he stood up, and he caught me staring. I expected annoyance, or possibly some of the disdain I'd endured off and on for the last forty-eight hours.

I didn't get either. I couldn't really interpret the look, but he held my eyes for several seconds, until I finally looked away, my face heating up. I tried to run through the entire range of possible emotions, to pin that look down to something that made sense. It wasn't attraction, it'd been too neutral for that. Envy, fear, friendship, none of them fit.

Whoever he was, he quietly left the room while my head was still whirling. I looked up to find Britney frowning at me. "What is your deal? I don't think I've ever seen Isaac notice anyone other than his girlfriend. He isn't like Alec, who notices everyone but is too good to actually speak to any of us. Isaac's just so caught up in whatever is going on inside his head that he doesn't realize any of us exist."

Britney slammed her book. "First Brandon decides he has the hots for you, and then you crack the ivory tower. There's absolutely no justice in the world."

I so wasn't looking forward to the ride home. Past experience had pretty much established that when Britney got like this there was no reasoning with her. Trying to explain that she hadn't seen the look from my end, that Isaac most definitely hadn't been attracted to me, would be useless.

I was pleasantly surprised when Britney's annoyance seemed to have blown over by the time we left the building. Before we'd even made it out of the parking lot, Britney was once again chattering about everyone else in the school and what they were or weren't doing lately. Considering that I still couldn't put a face with most of the names she was tossing around, the gossip wasn't just uninteresting, it was a near ordeal.

It wasn't until I looked over at the speedometer that I realized we really had been driving longer than normal rather than the gossip just making it seem to take forever. Britney caught me registering the fact she was driving under the speed limit for the first time I could remember, and broke off recounting Amy Stevens' supposed fling with one of the football players just long enough to blush.

"I figured I should be more careful of how fast I drive. You know, my dad keeps threatening to take away my car if I get any more tickets. With everything else going on right now he just might do it."

It was actually pretty plausible. I probably would've believed it if not for Rachel's description of the new rumor floating around school. Britney was trying to cater to my supposed fear of being in a speeding car. Only, my supposed fear was actually a very real fear, just not for the reasons Britney thought.

Chapter 11

Brandon arrived just in time to pick me up before I got on the bus. As expected, he teased me about not waiting for him at my house, but it was a small price to pay for not having to worry about how I was going to get to school if he didn't show up. We made small talk and all too soon arrived at school. As we pulled into the parking lot I was desperately looking for something witty or insightful to say. I needed to give him a reason to stay interested in me, but nothing came to mind.

As we pulled to a stop, the quiet hum of a cellphone on vibrate broke the strange paralysis that'd gripped me for the last twenty seconds. Brandon's grin was more than a little sheepish as he fished his phone out of a front pocket and checked to see who was calling. I didn't need his groan to know it was one of his friends. A selfish urge to try and make him ignore the call and continue to focus on me momentarily flared up, but I suppressed it.

It was such a petty thing to do, and even worse was probably the quickest way to demolish whatever interest he might have towards me. I might be almost completely naive when it came to dating, but anyone who'd read more than a couple books, or sat through eight or nine chick flicks, totally knew that the quickest way to drive a guy off was to become controlling and manipulative. Unless maybe you were a cheerleader and you were talking about a guy who was used to dating cheerleaders. Which while I wasn't even close to the former, the latter actually described Brandon almost perfectly.

I almost stopped midway through the action of opening my car door, but it was too late. Even if I'd picked the wrong course, the moment was gone. I had to just play it cool and leave or risk looking like a total loser. He returned my wave with a nod and shifted his focus back to whoever was on the phone with him.

Brandon had parked on the opposite end of the parking lot from where he normally did. Presumably it was because all of the good spots in his normal area had been snatched up by people who weren't running quite as late as us. I was halfway to the closest door before I remembered that it was still closed as a result of the mysterious 'potato gun rampage' as everyone had started calling it.

BROKEN

A normal person, one who was really as self-confident as I pretended to be, would have just turned and headed towards the eastern set of doors. Not wanting to look like a ditzy blonde who couldn't even remember that someone had run a SUV into the flagpole and temporarily rendered one of the four main exits inoperable, I kept walking.

The school was narrower than it was long. I could walk around the west end, and use the closest doors on the north side, and still have plenty of time to get to my locker before Biology started.

I was busy replaying my conversation with Brandon as I walked around the corner of the building. The air was already hot enough to suck the moisture out of rocks, but that wasn't the cause of the sudden rush of heat to my face. I didn't think I'd ever seen the boy before, but Jasmin was easily recognizable, even half-hidden amid all the intermittently-functioning cooling units that lived on this end of the building.

I couldn't see much beyond the boy's wild red hair, but even that was enough to tell he wasn't completely comfortable. I wanted to turn around and go back the other way, but there was a chance that Jasmin had already seen me, and if so I couldn't afford to look like I was scared of her.

The fact I actually *was* terrified she was going to snap and start trying to kill people was irrelevant. If I could convince her I wasn't scared, I was less likely to get hurt.

I kept walking, not necessarily steering closer to the three-quarter wall the boy was leaning against, but also being very careful not to go out of my way to stay further away from them either. As I got close to the pair, a little more of the boy became visible, reaffirming my impression that he wasn't happy to be talking to her. His shoulders looked unnaturally tight and he was shaking his head slowly from side to side.

Locked as I was into my course, I couldn't help but hear them both as I got closer. "I can't do this, Jasmin. I've been meaning to tell you for a while, but I was afraid of how you'd react."

I half stumbled at the raw pain in his voice. While I was still trying to recover my balance, Jasmin looked up at me, and the force of her glare almost made me fall over my feet again. I'd seen plenty of girls try and warn off potential competition, but I'd never seen an expression that intense.

Despite my earlier resolve, I couldn't help myself. I veered further away from the pair as some primitive, survival-minded part of my subconscious sought to create a buffer between me and the girl who looked ready to rip out my throat.

I'd gone far enough I couldn't see either of them, but it honestly felt like Jasmin watched me all the way until I managed to make it safely out of sight. I'd read stories where people claimed to have felt someone's gaze trying to bore a hole in their back, but this was the first time I'd ever experienced it for myself. I hadn't even believed it was possible, but the pins and needles I'd felt starting the second she'd looked up hadn't disappeared until I put a brick wall between us.

Biology would've been unpleasant even without everything else that was going on. The air conditioning was out to part of the building, and Mrs. Sorenson's classroom was one of the ones that apparently were going to go without until they got the regulator or switcher, or whatever it was, fixed.

I bowed out of our little competition even earlier than usual. I probably should have stayed in the game longer, should have kept answering questions until she came up with a real stumper, but I wasn't in the mood. Once I was safely free to let my mind wander, I couldn't think of anything other than the look on Jasmin's face. Even the steadily rising temperatures achieved by packing more than thirty bodies into a tiny classroom with only one door wasn't sufficient to really distract me. I was going to suffer once again for having stumbled into somewhere I didn't want to be.

By the time I made it into English and sat down next to Britney, my heart felt like it was going to seize up. Mr. Whethers walked into class a few seconds after the bell rang, took one look at his already perspiring students, and told us all to go ahead and spend the time reading rather than worrying about trying to focus on a lecture. It was a nice gesture, and normally I would have appreciated it, but I'd just finished Wuthering Heights, and knew that flipping the book back open wasn't going to help distract me. Unwilling to spend another hour in worry, I let my thoughts drift over to another, dangerous area.

Thinking about Brandon wasn't safe anymore. He'd started out making my stomach knot up simply because he was so gorgeous, but lately my insides had started jumping around for other reasons.

I wiped away the light sheen of perspiration on the back of my neck, and wished the world was simpler. If only I was still in Minnesota, or anywhere other than this crazy, secretive town with its ridiculous share of gorgeous boys. Boys who didn't behave much at all like any other popular kids I'd ever known. Alec hated me, Brandon stopped by to give me a ride to school every day, and neither of them should have even realized I was alive.

If I couldn't be at home, couldn't the universe have at least arranged for me to get involved with a nice, normal, uncomplicated, plain-looking boy, or barring that to remain safely uninterested in boys altogether? At the very least, someone out there should have managed to keep the air conditioning working.

By the time English ended, I felt worse, albeit for different reasons than earlier in Biology. Luckily, Algebra was starting to become a real sanctuary. The fact that we had a test made everyone even more focused than normal. Considering how on-task and busy Mrs. Campbell normally kept the class that was a feat in and of itself. I scanned through the first problem, and then picked up my pencil and got started.

Having successfully finished my test with ten minutes to spare, I expected lunch to bring more of the same kind of anxiety that I'd just managed to push out of my mind. It was headed that way. Despite Britney's best efforts to distract me with a point-by-point analysis of what was going on with someone named Sandra, and the two boys she'd been leading on for the last month.

I followed Britney through the lunch line, gripping my meal replacement drink with both hands. We sat down at our usual table, only to be surrounded a few seconds later by an energetic mob of familiar-looking people. It wasn't until Brandon slid into the seat next to me that I realized who everyone was.

"We thought maybe we'd come join the two of you today. That shabby little corner where we always sit was getting a little old."

Brandon's voice was smooth and flawless as always, but even that couldn't distract me enough to miss the flash of dislike in Cassie's eyes as she sat down next to Britney.

Nobody talked about anything important, which was good since I couldn't focus on anything other than the fact I'd just been given one more sign, a really big one, that Brandon was interested in me.

A couple of minutes before the warning bell rang, I looked up from the group and saw another familiar face leaving the lunchroom. Everything suddenly dropped into place, and I grabbed Brandon's arm.

"Who's that?"

Brandon tensed up for a second, and then his massive arm relaxed under my hand as he followed my gaze.

"That's Ben." His voice dropped to a rumbling whisper. "The one I told you about the other day."

It was incredibly obvious, all the while making absolutely no sense. He was obviously uncomfortable this morning, just like you'd expect from someone who was in the unenviable position of telling off a borderline psychopath. Everything I'd seen substantiated Brandon's explanation, but why would Jasmin become so enamored of someone so average-looking? Not only that, what were the odds Ben was one of the eight males in America who would decide they weren't interested in dating the most gorgeous girl on the planet, even if she was a nut case?

I was still trying to sort out all the pieces when Brandon fished his cell phone out of a pocket and checked the time. In an amazing display of herd behavior, thirty seconds later his friends had all disappeared, and he was standing to leave.

"We should do this more often. I'll see you tomorrow."

The words were innocent enough, but there was something in his eyes that made a rush of warmth shoot through me. Britney was so excited she could hardly speak, but I was too excited myself to feel very superior.

I floated through my next class, and would've gone through the rest of the day the same way, if I hadn't had to share a class with Alec. Still, I was so happy that even Alec's giving me the cold shoulder didn't completely sour my day. Rachel had turned my illness into something really cool, and Brandon really did like me. Life couldn't get much better than this.

Chapter 12

I'd all but run through the house, looking for my mom, excited to tell her about my day. Instead I'd been greeted by nothing but half-filled boxes and silence.

I didn't really want to unpack, but it was long past needing to be done and I knew if I left it to Mom that we'd never really get moved in. If I'd had anything even remotely better to do with my Friday night, I would have done it. I didn't, so I started with the stuff that we'd piled in the living room because it was marginally cooler downstairs.

I got into a decent rhythm, opening boxes, pulling out the stuff that I could easily put away, and then consolidating what was left into fewer boxes. I was on my fourth box when it happened. Mom's jewelry box had somehow got packed into a box labeled 'old photography gear'. As I pulled it out to set it to one side, it slipped from my hands.

The glittering deluge of chains and bracelets that went sliding across the floor would have made me feel bad enough all by themselves, but there was a proverbial scorpion nestled in the midst of all that shininess.

I'd thrown mine out shortly after the accident. Part of me hadn't wanted to. It had felt like I was abandoning Cindi by doing so, but just seeing Cindi's half of the twin pendants we'd received two years before had been enough to send me into a tailspin.

A detached part of me noted that it was just like Mom to have lied about having lost Cindi's. She'd known I couldn't handle the reminder of what we'd lost, but she'd been unwilling to give up that link to the past.

The thought slipped away like sunlight skipping across water a split second before the storm arrived.

The attack was a bad one. I lost more time. I must have slept at some point, but the next time I surfaced it was Saturday morning and I was sitting in front of an empty bowl with an unopened box of cereal and a gallon of milk waiting in the wings. At some point I realized I wasn't hungry. I put everything back away and went upstairs for a shower.

It didn't help. By the time I was done, I was clean but just as emotionally numb as before. At least I'd turned the water all the way to cold there at the end. I came out shivering, but it was a welcome change from the oppressive heat. Even that didn't last; it felt like I was sweating again before I even finished dressing.

I finally pulled out my Biology book. A coldly rational part of me knew that however this ended up playing out, I'd still have a test on Monday, and I'd still want to pass.

It'd be nice sometimes to make the kind of dramatic gesture that you see on movies, or read about in books. Instead, I was sitting here with a stupid textbook while everything else inside of me hurt in a funny, cold kind of way. Like it hurt so much I could only feel the edges of the pain.

Spanish followed Biology; then other subjects came and went until I felt like I'd made enough progress, or possibly wasted enough time. I collapsed into bed hours early and slept poorly.

Sunday was about the same, only my insides felt even rawer under the calm surface. Like maybe they'd had something caustic poured on them. I woodenly went through the motions of studying, and then finally pushed all of my books to the side and opened up Les Misérables. I tried to lose myself in the book, but the same worries that'd pestered me while I was trying to study continued to grate against the back of my mind.

I hadn't wanted to come here, but I'd tried to make it work. Mom keeping the pendant felt like a complete betrayal. She'd known how it would impact me, but hadn't cared. I finally gave up on trying to immerse myself in nineteenth-century France, and cried myself to sleep.

It was all I could do to drag myself out of bed Monday morning. A part of me knew this was all stupid, but I couldn't shake the depression. I was just aware enough to register Brandon's concerned glances as he drove me into school.

Mrs. Sorenson shot me a nasty look as I stumbled into class. "Well isn't it nice of you to come to class today. And here we all thought you were doing so well you didn't need to bother with the test."

I took the proffered test and made my unsteady way back to my desk. The class passed in a blur as I made a half-hearted attempt to focus on the questions and remember all kinds of facts about photosynthesis that I'd known just a few days before. It was useless. The separate pieces of information skittered about on the edge of my memory without ever becoming tangible enough to relate to the answer I needed.

By the time class ended, I'd almost completely shut down. I registered the whispers as I made my way to English. I normally would've been mad, or possibly embarrassed, but it was like my feelings were wrapped in layers of cotton candy. If I really pushed, I could faintly feel the hard edges, but there were so many layers shrouding them. I just couldn't seem to muster up enough concentration to care. I was on autopilot now.

I answered Britney's whispered questions without ever registering them and never once worried about whether or not I'd made sense. I parried Mrs. Campbell's concerned inquiries in much the same manner, probably not convincing her that I was okay, but at least persuading her to leave me alone, and then sleep-walked into the cafeteria. I hated the fact that I wanted Brandon to come sit down with me. If he did a convincing enough job pretending to like me and I tried really hard, maybe I'd believe it'd all just been my imagination. It'd be one less piece of my world crumbling out from under me.

Britney slammed her tray down, but my listless gaze didn't move from the vacant corner where Brandon usually sat. A few minutes later a group of girls came to join us. I recognized them, but didn't bother putting names to the faces.

It was like I got hit with another panic attack. Somehow I lost an hour, but nobody was running around calling for an ambulance so I must have at least responded to direct questions.

Alec was sitting in his normal seat as I wandered into physics. I tried to remember whether or not I'd already heard the second bell ring. It wasn't important though. Not compared to the first thing I'd faced in hours that had the potential to hurt me.

BROKEN

I could feel the edge, razor sharp, cleanly parting some of the layers of gauze that'd been wrapped around my emotions. It didn't make sense. Alec was barely even civil. He most definitely wasn't part of the support structure that'd been holding my world in its normal orbit, but suddenly my defenses were in danger of being breached.

He looked up disinterestedly as I sat in my desk, and even that was enough to send little shivers of near pain coursing through my system. It wasn't real pain; I was still too cushioned from the world for that, but my body shied away from it just the same.

I wanted to run screaming from the room, to jump through a window, to do anything to avoid coming into further contact with someone who so obviously hated me. The urges were all very real, but it was like I'd been drugged to the gills. I couldn't gather the energy to do anything about them. Instead my mind reached down and pulled extra layers of gauze over itself.

I looked down at my Spanish test and wondered how I'd gotten here. There were answers on the page. They were unmistakably done in my awkward scrawl, but didn't make sense. I flipped the page over and found more of the same. My eyes idly traced down the page, finding blanks and almost of its own accord my pencil reached out and filled them in with words that seemed familiar, but whose meaning I couldn't seem to pin down.

I resurfaced as I walked into the tutor lab, unsure if I'd passed anyone I should have greeted.

I sat down at my usual spot and pulled out a book at random as Britney stomped into the room and threw her books down. She was obviously mad, but once again I couldn't muster enough concern to figure out what'd ticked her off.

I blinked several times as I realized Mrs. Campbell had been speaking to me for several seconds. She was important, one of the few teachers that actually liked me. It was incredibly hard, but I focused on what she was saying, voluntarily pulling myself partway out of the wonderful cushion and exposing myself to some of the pain.

"Are you sure you're okay?"

My nod and smile must not have been very convincing.

"Listen, there isn't any real reason to keep the lab open so late today, and you've made amazing progress catching up. Why don't you take the night off, and go straight home?"

The idea didn't make sense. I knew all the words, but they wouldn't string themselves together in a way that had any meaning. I nodded anyway, and then put my book in my bag, which had somehow made it into her hands. She was holding it open as if expecting me to fill it.

I found myself outside the school, sitting on the edge of the parking lot without a clear idea how I'd ended up there. There was a vaguely irritating noise behind me that didn't seem to fit with what I expected from school.

I thought about turning to see what it was, but was thankfully too far back into the gauze to act on the thought. I went back to contemplating the pair of ants that were currently trekking across my right foot.

"Adriana. Are you okay?"

My insides were too raw. Just coming out long enough to listen to Mrs. Campbell had opened everything back up. My mind tried to shy away, to sink away from the certainty of more jagged shards being shoved into me, but this voice was an important one.

Rachel looked down at me, her arms wrapped around her waist as if trying to hold herself together. "What are you doing?"

The words stubbornly tried to avoid making sense, but I reached out with my trembling mind and forced them each into their proper place.

"Waiting." The answer fell out of my mouth of its own accord. It took me several seconds to realize it was the truth. I didn't have a ride home until Britney finished up her regular studying stint.

"For Britney? Do you want us to give you a ride home?"

A slight movement, barely seen out of the corner of my eye, gave meaning to the last part of the sentence. A familiar-looking guy was standing a few feet from Rachel. I couldn't place him. I slowly shook my head, trying to jar something loose enough to figure out who he was.

"Please, Adriana. It really isn't any trouble. James, can you get your car, please?"

He looked angry. Like maybe he was going to argue, but as he opened his mouth Rachel turned and glared at him. It seemed odd to see someone only a little smaller than Alec back away from someone even smaller than me.

The image stuck with me so strongly that I considered it until Rachel came over and took my hand. "What's wrong? It's just the two of us now, you don't have to worry about James, and I won't tell anyone else. I swear."

Rachel's promise somehow seemed like it belonged from another time. The sincerity pulled me further out of my safe, numb shelter. Something in me wanted to confide in her, was willing to risk the pain of facing reality, but I was too far gone to be able to put what I was feeling into words.

I shook my head again, not sure if it was a refusal or something else entirely. Rachel took it as the former and sat down next to me, pulling her knees up tight against her chest. A few seconds later I heard the howl of an after-market exhaust fed by a turbo-charged engine.

BROKEN

The green Honda that came screaming through the parking lot was hardly recognizable as an Accord. It was approaching too quickly, but I couldn't bring myself to care. Besides, Rachel seemed unconcerned.

Rachel helped me up as the car came to a screeching halt, all four tires locking up to slide it around so that the passenger side was facing us. The over-tinted windows smoothly slid down to reveal that James was indeed the driver, and he wasn't any happier than he'd been a few seconds earlier.

I started towards the back seat, only to feel Rachel's surprisingly-firm grasp guide me towards the front seat. She got me settled and then slipped in behind me.

James pulled out of the parking lot with a rush of acceleration that pinned me to my seat. Normally I'd have gripped the door hard enough to make my fingers creak, but I was still strangely unconcerned with the possibility of dying. For the first time in months I simply slouched down in my seat and enjoyed the ride.

The little Accord zipped around corners faster than I would've believed possible, its tiny engine howling as the turbos wound up in between shifts. My bemused state was interrupted by Rachel leaning forward and tapping me on the shoulder as she gestured for James to turn his music down.

"I almost forgot. Guess what, Les Misérables is coming to Las Vegas. Not just a local cast, an actual touring cast out of London. It's gotten excellent reviews all over the U.S."

I stared at her blankly, unsure where she was going. Some of her enthusiasm wilted in the face of my incomprehension.

"I just thought maybe you'd want to go. You know. You said you loved the music, that it was what made you want to read the book. It's playing for more than a month, so there's plenty of time to make arrangements. I can set everything up if you want."

It seemed impossible that she'd be so insensitive to my situation. I opened my mouth to tell her off, and then realized she wasn't privy to everything happening in my head. My world felt like it was disintegrating around me, and hers continued on as normal. It should have been depressing, but somehow I found it so ludicrous I giggled. The laugh had a definite edge of hysteria to it, but it still felt good.

"Rachel, my life doesn't work like that. Even if I could afford a trip like that, my mom would never let me go. She's only an absentee parent when I need her."

Rachel's soft blue eyes got really wide as she recoiled slightly. Whatever she was about to say was preempted as we were both thrown forward in our seats. James slid the car through a one-eighty turn that left us facing the direction we'd just come from, only a couple of feet from the start of our lane.

"You're not making her walk!"

It was obvious that whatever magical ability had allowed Rachel to face down the larger boy wasn't working anymore. He looked like he was set for a monster fight.

"I'm not washing my car again."

I expected Rachel to back down as soon as she realized he was spoiling for a fight, but if anything she looked more determined. It was hard to believe this was the same person I'd had to rescue from Cassie so recently.

I stopped Rachel just before she could put the impressive lungful of air she'd just taken in to whatever use she'd planned. "It's okay. I'm better. The lane's dusty and exercise would do me good."

She hesitated, obviously torn, but my fumbling fingers finally found the unfamiliar door release and I made the decision for her. I swung the door open and slipped out of the car before she could respond.

I waved goodbye with a cheery casualness I thought did a pretty good job of hiding my desire to break into tears. It was amazing how I'd let the numbness slip away for nothing. Rachel wasn't any more my friend than she'd been a few minutes before. Instead she was probably freaked out. I'd have been so much better off if I'd just stayed oblivious to everything, and ignored her like I'd done everyone else today.

The hot Utah sun was trying to knock me to my knees as I slowly made my way down our lane. For a moment I thought about what would happen if I fell and hurt myself.

By the time Mom realized I was missing, I'd be a perfectly preserved mummy, sucked completely dry by the harsh climate, exactly as ordered for a pyramid burial.

I hadn't realized some part of me was hoping Mom would be there waiting when I got home. I felt it shrink as I came around the corner and saw the empty cement pad.

I walked through the door and dropped my things on the couch. I could feel myself sinking back into oblivion, but instead of welcoming it, I was suddenly terrified. I'd spent weeks numb to the entire world. I'd even missed Dad's favorite season, the one that'd become mine as well. It'd be all too easy to slip into the same kind of numbness now as a refuge against everything.

What would happen if I failed to surface? It'd been easier to lapse into catatonia this time than last. Would I reach a point where I couldn't come back? There'd been a time right after the accident where Mom had thought I was already there.

I was just numb enough still to think about such things without immediately collapsing. Even so, I felt a pang of dizziness as my mind warned me I'd pushed it too far today.

BROKEN

I found myself in the kitchen, nearly finished making enchiladas with only vague ideas of why I'd started pulling ingredients out of the fridge. I wasn't hungry. I knew I should eat something, but that hardly merited putting together anything more complicated than a sandwich. What was I trying to accomplish?

I slowly put the pan in the oven as I admitted to myself that even after more than two days, the odds were better than even that I'd be eating alone, that most of the food would go into the fridge untouched.

My class work, neglected as it had been all day, really deserved my attention, but I didn't have the heart to pull it out. I knew I wouldn't find any kind of refuge there. Instead, I pulled out a pencil and a sheet of paper from my notebook, and started sketching. The process slowly started pulling me back out of the numbness.

I wasn't actually any good as an artist. Mom had exposed me to enough art for me to realize that early on. I lacked some kind of creative spark necessary to achieve any kind of real beauty. Still, I occasionally enjoyed trying to recreate something I'd seen.

This time I didn't try to guide my hand, I just let it create lines and curves at random, until something tugged at my subconscious, and a half-formed memory began to materialize on the page before me.

I knew that the wavy vertical line off the side was destined to become a waterfall. The scene was starting to take shape, but for the first time in ages I still couldn't place it. A mossy boulder filled itself in with feathery detail, and then I realized the center of the piece was still blank. It was like my subconscious hadn't ever seen that part of the landscape.

Only that didn't make sense. How could I not have seen part of whatever it was I was looking at? Unless it'd been blocked by something. But if so I would have drawn whatever it was that'd been in the foreground. I was even worse than normal when it came to drawing people or animals, but I had a good memory for everything else.

I pushed the notepad away in frustration, and then started shaking as I finally recognized my drawing. It was the grotto from my dream, and the reason I hadn't filled in the center was that I'd never seen it. That was the spot where Alec had been standing.

Chapter 13

Morning came not a moment too soon after a night filled with tossing and turning. Every time I nodded off, I awoke a few minutes later, my mind reaching for something that wasn't there, only to snap back as it didn't find what it was looking for. Each time the backlash woke me up, I tried to figure out what was going on, but I didn't succeed until nearly morning.

I'd been trying to find the vivid dreams again. I'd finally stopped thinking about them, finally stopped yearning for them every night, only to have my stupid subconscious somehow mix them up with real life. That was really the thing that was the most unnerving. I'd only ever unconsciously drawn real places. To draw a pretend place was surprisingly unsettling, but I almost couldn't blame whatever part of me had gotten confused. The dreams were so clear and sharp they sometimes seemed more real than the rest of my life.

By the time I finally realized what was keeping me from getting real sleep it was too late to worry about trying to get anymore rest. I just stared out my window at the light the previous owners had mounted on a pole. It was just close enough to see an amazingly thick cloud of insects swirl around it, captivated by the artificial glow.

When I walked downstairs I found Mom's camping equipment piled in the living room. For all I'd tossed and turned, I must have gotten some sleep to have not heard her come in. I contemplated jotting down a note before just shrugging and skipping outside, happy for once to be shivering. It wouldn't last. Eventually the sun would clear the hills, and we'd be headed for eighty-plus degrees, but I could at least enjoy the next hour or so without worrying I was going to melt right out of my clothes.

Walking down the lane, I tried to decide whether or not I wanted Brandon to show up today. After my mixed signals yesterday I figured there was a better than even chance he'd 'forget' to come get me. Strangely enough that didn't bother me as much as I thought it would. It was like walking down the lane managed to put things back in perspective for me.

How could I be put out about something I hadn't ever actually believed was possible?

I almost refused to believe my eyes when I came around the bend in our lane and saw a black Mustang parked on the side of the road. Brandon stood up from where he'd been leaning against the sports car and flashed me a blinding smile. He moved towards me with a casual grace that made little shivers run through me despite my earlier decision not to let his interest, or lack thereof, affect me.

"I had a bet with myself that you weren't going to wait. Somehow the fact I just lost doesn't matter now."

It didn't seem possible he was talking to me, that anyone so gorgeous could mean something like that about me. I opened my mouth, maybe to laugh the comment off, or otherwise hedge my bets against the humiliation and inevitable mocking laughter. Whatever it was I'd intended on saying evaporated away the instant he reached out and slowly slid his finger down the side of my face.

The tiny part of me that was still screaming none of this could be real was pulled along by the rest of me. I completely abandoned myself to the sensations created by his touch. My nerve endings didn't know whether to classify his finger as icy cold or scorching hot, but before I could recoil in pain the sensation gave way to a tingly warmth that sank down into my center, simultaneously tightening and relaxing parts I didn't even know I had.

My pounding heart seemed loud enough to hear from across the street. I opened my eyes, afraid he could somehow hear the overworked muscle, already flushing red with embarrassment, only to find a gentle smile waiting for me. If there was any insincerity to the expression, I was utterly unable to detect it. I cleared my throat, seeking to avoid the awkwardness that always followed these kinds of moments, but Brandon effortlessly defused all of that by opening my door and helping me into the car.

"I'm sorry I wasn't around yesterday. Some things came up that demanded my attention."

The music was lower than usual, a possible sign he wanted to talk? "Did you manage to resolve them successfully?"

Again that incredible smile flashed across his face. "They were touch and go for a little bit, but I'm most pleased with how everything worked out."

I'd spent all of Monday in a daze, and felt much the same now, only this time it was a daze of good fortune. It hardly bothered me when Britney snubbed me during English. I flew through my Algebra assignment, finishing up the one from yesterday as well as the one Mrs. Campbell assigned, before the bell rang to release us.

The only thing that even threatened my bubble of happiness was when I walked into the lunchroom and saw that Britney was sitting with the cheerleaders who'd come and sat at our table yesterday.

It was blatantly obvious I wasn't welcome. Unsure where to sit, I almost spun around and walked back into the hall until Brandon caught my eye and waved me over.

I had to detour around the tangle of tables that belonged to the closest thing Sanctuary had to real Goths. My wandering path brought me around to where I could see what I'd mentally dubbed 'Alec's corner'.

It was a good thing there was an empty chair nearby. The force of Jasmin's stare was almost a palpable thing; my knees got weak so quickly it was like she'd reached out and pushed me. I steadied myself and then tried to ignore the way my skin crawled as I crossed the rest of the distance to Brandon's table.

"The mongrels unnerve you a bit?"

The scorn on the face that the comment belonged to was unnerving. I'd seen him several times before, but didn't have a name to go with his aristocratic features.

"That's enough, Vincent."

A trace of rebelliousness flared up at Brandon's chastisement, but Vincent buried it so quickly I almost didn't have enough time to classify it before it disappeared. Interestingly enough, I could see Cassie out of the corner of my eye, and she didn't look any happier than Vincent.

The rest of lunch flew by. I'd never realized how much fun it could be to belong to a group. Things weren't ideal; I'd never met a group with so many inside jokes. Half the time I felt like there was an entire conversation being carried on over my head, but sitting next to Brandon left me with such a tingly feeling all along my right side that I didn't really mind.

Not even the presence of a pop quiz in History managed to faze me. Almost before I knew it I was sitting down in Physics.

As usual, Alec slipped into class a half second before the bell. I was so happy I forgot how arrogant he was, and I smiled at him as he sat down. It was like he was looking at something that wasn't even human. My insides seemed to freeze and shrink. I couldn't even muster up my normal blush of embarrassment. I'd had plenty of people hate me since I'd arrived in Sanctuary, but he was the first person I'd met who I was convinced wouldn't have thrown me a life preserver if I was drowning. It wasn't even because saving me would be too much work. He was completely convinced the world would be a better place without me.

I'd never been so unnerved in my life. As Mrs. Alexander took roll and then released us into our groups, I was still trying to pull myself back together. It didn't help when I realized we were being evaluated today.

I fished out my notes and desperately tried to remember how to calculate some of the stuff we'd need to know in order to successfully get our weight up the ramp, over the obstacles, and otherwise to the appropriate destination using the minimum number of pulleys, the shortest ramp, and the thinnest string possible.

Alec hardly even looked up as Mrs. Alexander came by with our particular spool of thread, an array of metric weights, and a note card bearing the amount of weight we'd been assigned to move around.

I was still leafing through my binder when Alec started testing the strength of our 'tow line.' I scooted my desk over and picked up a weight to hand to him, only to see the thread break as he successfully figured out the breaking point.

Again and again it happened. I ran a calculation for how many pulleys we'd need to lift our weight up the thirty-degree incline on a string able to hold only a fourth as much, only to look over at his paper and see not only had he already arrived at the correct figure, he'd already thought to adjust for starting friction.

Not used to being outclassed academically, I got flustered, which led to a misplaced decimal, and then an incorrect conversion from English to metric. Alec just continued on, never seeming to really hurry, never actually making a mistake, but still grinding through calculations with a speed I might have been able to match on a good day, but couldn't even approach today.

It would've been much easier to just stop my efforts and watch him work, but I was too stubborn to give up.

Alec finished up with the theoretical portion of the assignment, and started stringing the pulleys while most of the other groups were still arguing over whether or not they could afford to add a few extra grams for extra credit.

If there was a single person in the class who *didn't* need any extra credit, it was Alec; but he calmly loaded the system with an extra sixteen grams, caught Mrs. Alexander's eye, and then smoothly started the train of weights moving up the ramp, over the wall, through the woods, and right up to Grandma's house.

It wasn't fair that someone who missed so many days of school could be so consistently right. He must have an IQ of 160. That and an ego big enough for someone twice as smart.

Mrs. Alexander shuffled over and smiled at the pair of us. "Sixteen grams. Most impressive, you two. An entire gram more than I would have ventured to risk myself, and done before anyone else. I thought the pair of you would make a great team."

The easiest thing would have been to stay quiet and just let her believe I'd played an integral part of the project, but I didn't like getting credit for something I hadn't done. It was the worst kind of lying.

"Mrs. Alexander, I didn't actually do any of it. I kept making mistakes."

She chuckled so hard, for a second I thought the pencil behind her ear was going to fall out. "I rather suspect you're understating your accomplishments, my dear. Didn't contribute indeed. As if Nora's favorite student would just sit around while there were equations to solve."

I felt like I'd been hit in the stomach. I hadn't realized just how fond of me Mrs. Campbell was. My mind whirling with too many thoughts to sort out, I turned to go back to my desk, only to find Alec staring at me. He still didn't seem happy to be sharing the same room with me, but the complete disgust from half an hour before had been replaced with something more measuring.

In Spanish, Mrs. Tiggs took special delight in telling us that she'd started grading our tests and a couple of them weren't looking very good. I suffered through the last hour of school and then hurried to my locker. I didn't really want to meet up with Britney, but I also didn't want to alienate her any more than I already had.

I shouldn't have even bothered. I waited around for a full fifteen minutes before finally heading over to the tutoring lab. Britney was watching the door when I arrived. She didn't even bother trying to mask the flash of satisfaction that crossed her face when I walked in late, obviously having spent the last little while waiting for her.

I wanted to scream, or maybe cry. It was amazing how quickly a perfect day could go down the tubes. I turned towards my normal table, and Rachel caught my eye. Sitting in a pool of light from one of the overhead skylights, she looked like Britney's antithesis. Smiling, happy to see me, and obviously already having forgiven me for my weirdness from the day before. I smiled back and sat down, relieved the most important parts of my social life had survived.

Britney might hate me, I might have lost the cool factor resulting from all of the rumors about my imaginary boyfriend having died in a car wreck, but Brandon still miraculously wanted to spend time with me, and Rachel was still shaping up to be the best friend any girl ever had.

It was too bad the two nicest people I'd ever met hadn't been born in the same family. Of course, Rachel was so inherently good, and Brandon was so reasonable about everything. If I could get the pair of them to spend some time together it would probably go a long ways towards patching up the stupid feud Alec seemed so determined to keep alive.

I thought about broaching the idea with Rachel, but discarded the notion immediately. She would just clam up, just like she always did whenever anything relating to her brother was mentioned. I'd have to be sneaky to get the two of them together.

Mrs. Campbell needed a little bit of reassuring when she stopped by my desk, which I did happily now that my personal universe was looking up once again, and then I dug into my homework with near-normal gusto.

Time flew by all too quickly. Soon it was just me holding down the fort and trying to take care of a trio of freshmen girls who seemed to be at least slightly ahead of the normal cramming curve. I was glad they weren't waiting until the day before the test to come in for help, but it was looking like tomorrow wasn't going to be any fun. Maybe I'd get lucky again, and most of the lazy ones would give up before my shift started.

I turned around from explaining for the fourth time to the third person why you couldn't prove congruence of two triangles with the nonexistent angle-angle-angle postulate, only to find that Britney had slipped out of the room.

It was possible she'd just gone to the restroom. I tried to remind myself of all of the places she could be, and all of the reasons she might have left that didn't involve abandoning me here. Rachel met me on my way back to my table to gather up my books.

"She left with Rick Anders."

I mustered a grin. "Was my panic that obvious?"

"No, I was just watching her to see who she had in her sights for the Ashure Day Dance.

Then when I saw her leave I realized that would mean you wouldn't have a ride home."

I put the last couple of books in my backpack and shrugged. "I think she's mad. I guess she has pretty good reason to be, but she hasn't even given me a chance to apologize."

The first half of Rachel's comment finally sank in, and I nearly tripped. "Wait, what dance?"

"Ashure Day. It's an...a local tradition. Think of it kind of like earth day, but with a dance. Kind of like a pagan Prom. Or maybe a pagan homecoming since it's still fall."

Prom was my arch-nemesis. There were really only two times a year that the universe managed to penetrate my historical indifference to the opposite sex. Prom, and Valentine's Day. Of the two, Prom was the more deadly. Valentine's Day was usually filled with enough examples of guys screwing up to make me feel okay. They were always picking the wrong present, forgetting to buy one, or otherwise making the day less than perfect. That in turn helped me remember that most relationships seemed to be more fuss and mess than they were worth. Why get something built up so much in your mind that you can't possibly ever realize it?

All of the little things about Valentine's Day that grounded me in reality were overcome by the mystique of Prom. Instead of people fighting, there were dozens, sometimes even hundreds, of couples who all seemed to be very much in love. Everyone got to dress up and go dancing in a place that'd been transformed into another world. Even before I'd gotten old enough to attend Prom, I'd still invariably spent the day grouchy and depressed. Things only got worse as I'd aged, presumably because I wasn't really as indifferent as I liked to pretend, and I couldn't hide behind the excuse of being too young to be asked anymore.

My pulse had already skyrocketed; I almost didn't hear what Rachel was saying over the pounding in my ears.

"...of course it's still a little ways away, but a girl like Britney starts early so she gets as high up the social food chain as possible."

Rachel's words calmed me a little at the same time they sparked confusion. I'd never heard her be quite so cynical. It was completely at odds with the innocent, accepting exterior she usually displayed.

My surprise must have leaked through. Almost as soon the thought crossed my mind Rachel's demeanor crossed back from the older, jaded visage, to one that was more youthful, even embarrassed. "Sorry, I know she's your friend. I shouldn't say things like that, but that's really what she's doing. By the time the actual dance arrives, everyone who is anyone will have a date, most of them picked out by the girl weeks before the boy even started thinking about the dance."

There wasn't really any bitterness in her voice, but there was something, maybe the same kind of longing I felt when I talked about Prom. "You're probably right. That would fit with what I know of Britney so far."

"Do you need us to give you a ride?"

I looked over and saw that James was once again glaring at me, somehow having approached to within a few feet without making any noise. "I should probably make sure she isn't waiting somewhere for me. That's probably half of why she's so mad. I was so out of things yesterday I didn't think to let her know I was headed home with you."

Rachel looked for a moment like she wanted to disagree, but she nodded, in the kind of noncommittal way people use when they don't really agree, but are ready to let you make your own mistakes.

Rachel pulled her books together, and then followed me through the door, James two steps behind, and looking, amazingly enough, even more surly than he had a few seconds before. Rachel didn't seem to be one of those people who always had to be talking about something, but even so, two minutes of silence were enough to leave me scrambling for something to talk about.

"Thanks for telling me about Les Misérables. I mean, I should have said thanks yesterday, but I really do appreciate you thinking of me. It was really nice."

Rachel's eyes lit up brighter than I'd seen them in a while. "You're welcome. Does that mean we can go to Vegas?"

It seemed like a crime to deny her, but I knew Mom didn't have the spare money to send me on a two-hour trip to an opera. I was working now, but by the time I could save up enough to pay for gas, food, and a ticket, the production would've moved on.

"I'm sorry, I'd like to go, but I just don't think I can. If it was running for an extra month or two I could probably save up enough money from tutoring, but it isn't, so it just isn't going to happen."

Rachel nodded, and for a second it was easy to forget that she probably got more spending money each month than I'd see all year.

"That's okay. Things like that are always coming through Vegas. We can just go the next time they come to town."

I nodded and smiled, surprised that the thought of so much time trapped in a car with someone didn't make me want to run away screaming. Cars were scary. All that time with nothing to do but talk, and once you started talking to people they wanted to know things. Things that weren't any of their business, things you weren't ready to discuss. Somehow I knew Rachel wouldn't pry. It was like keeping so many secrets for her brother had made her especially sensitive to other people's secrets.

Another few steps brought us to the door, and I held it open for Rachel to follow me outside. The intense heat felt like a physical blow. I could almost feel my pores open up in an effort to keep me from overheating.

The sensory overload as my eyes tried to adjust to the unfiltered afternoon sun momentarily distracted me. It wasn't until I heard the other door swing shut that I realized James had followed us through, but he'd taken the door on the right instead of the one of the left that I'd been holding open for him. Wow, talk about a chauvinistic pig.

It wasn't worth getting bent out of shape. I let my door swing shut, and walked over to Rachel's side so that I could see the entire parking lot. Empty as it was, it didn't take very long to realize Britney's little white Saturn was gone.

"I thought you might still be here."

The voice caught me by surprise. I probably would've jumped and screamed a little if I hadn't recognized it.

Brandon was walking towards us with his characteristic casual stride, and I felt my heart speed up a little as I remembered our conversation from earlier in the day.

"Brandon! What are you still doing here?"

I heard some movement off to my right, but was so focused on Brandon's response that none of it really registered. The smile gracing his breathtaking face was like the ultimate treat.

"Oh, I was helping out with the new set for the theater class' production of Arsenic and Old Lace."

I was suddenly glad Britney had abandoned me. If it resulted in me seeing Brandon again today it couldn't be all bad. In fact, my life felt pretty much perfect right now. Wait, not quite. If he'd greeted me with a hug in addition to the smile, *then* things would have been perfect.

I felt myself blushing almost as soon as the thought crossed my mind. My family wasn't...hadn't been demonstrative. I wouldn't know what to do if he hugged me. In an effort to cover my embarrassment, I turned back to Rachel and James, only to feel my jaw figuratively hit the ground.

James was standing between Rachel and Brandon, slightly crouched in a posture that looked strangely familiar. I heard footsteps to my left as Brandon finished crossing the last few feet between us. James backed up a half step, one arm stretched out behind him, pushing Rachel back. I suddenly realized why his movements seemed so familiar. I'd seen dozens of celebrities being shepherded out of one award show or another by professional bodyguards who acted exactly like James was acting right now.

Only they usually weren't so obvious about it. The only time I'd ever seen a bodyguard physically push their client around was when some up-and-coming soap star had a bottle thrown at her by the wife of someone she was sleeping with. I looked past Brandon, expecting to see something threatening headed towards us. I even opened my mouth to warn Brandon, but there wasn't anything there, just Brandon, still with the same casual smile as he reached out and squeezed my arm.

"Hi, guys. I just thought I'd see if Adri needed a ride home."

It was like I'd been hit by a bus. My arm tingled at the same time my heart started skipping beats. My body was trying to shut down as a panic attack loomed on the horizon, but not succeeding because it was also revving up from standing so close to Brandon.

I think I said goodbye to Rachel and James. I kind of fuzzed out. The next thing I knew Brandon was pulling onto our cement pad.

"So it looks like Britney's out. Do you mind if I give you a ride home on Tuesdays and Thursdays?"

Did I mind? Of course not. "That would be really great. Thanks for offering."

Brandon ran one finger down the side of my face, and then leaned back with a smile as I reached for the door.

It wasn't until I was out of the car that I realized our Jeep was parked in its normal spot off to the side of the house. Excited to talk to Mom about her last outing, I waved goodbye to Brandon and hurried to the door.

Mom hardly even looked up from her laptop as I walked in. Whew, no need to go through the third degree about Brandon.

"Anything promising, Mom?"

"Hmm? I don't know. Maybe one or two will be okay once I've touched them up, but this brochure is proving tougher than expected. Can we talk after dinner?"

By now I really should have been used to Mom ignoring me when she got buried in a project. I shrugged and went upstairs to change.

Hours later, having finished up all my homework and endured the agony of dinner, I was finally free to do whatever I wanted with the last few minutes of my night.

My room was still miserable, but with Mom sitting down in the living room with her laptop going through the gigs of data that she'd shot over the last few days, it offered the only real chance at some time alone.

I trudged up the stairs, shut my door, and then realized I wasn't sure what to do with myself. I'd spent most of the time since we'd arrived either buried in homework, or borderline catatonic.

The obvious choice was sitting on the rickety table next to my bed, but I wasn't sure if I was up to Les Misérables right now. Maybe in a few weeks, once the production had left Vegas, I'd be ready to delve back into it. Right now it was just another reminder of how many things in my life I didn't have control over.

No, that was right out. I thumbed through Pride and Prejudice for a few minutes, and then just gave up and headed to the bathroom.

A short time later, teeth brushed and face washed, I swung my window wide open and climbed into bed. It would take hours for the air to cool down enough to start leeching some of the heat out of my room, but it was better than nothing. I'd at least sleep better for the second half of the night.

As tired as I was, my mind didn't want to shut down yet. Mom didn't seem to think it was at all odd that the city had flip-flopped so completely on the job. First she had it, then she didn't, now she did again. None of it made sense, but she seemed perfectly ready to accept everything at face value. Maybe her way was the best. I certainly envied her. Not the not knowing, but the fact that she didn't have to worry about what it all meant. How did I get stuck being the parent, while she got to be the kid?

Who'd be interested in helping us? No, that wasn't the right question. The key to figuring this all out was to decide who could've helped us out. Nobody we'd known back in Minnesota could've strong-armed both the president of a bank and the mayor. Especially not from all the way back there.

It had to be someone local, and they had to be either rich, powerful, or both. The answer was so obvious I felt like an idiot for not realizing who it was from the start. Who had I been told, almost from my first day here, were the two most influential families in Sanctuary? The Worthingfields and the Graveses. Both of which had at least one member of the family my age, one of whom seemed to hate me profoundly.

What was it the mayor had said? "I can't promise he'll even read it." It was a he who'd intervened on our behalf, and Rachel and Alec's father had died years ago, while Brandon's father...actually I knew next to nothing about Brandon's parents. I wasn't even sure whether or not they were around. They must be though—if it had been a male who'd saved us, then it couldn't be the Graveses, and that left only Brandon's family.

It was hard to believe that Brandon had stepped in and done so much for us, but the pieces fit together so tightly. Brandon was even more wonderful and amazing than I'd thought before.

Part of me expected this new revelation to keep my mind whirling so fast that it would take me hours to go to sleep. I was only partly right. It took quite a while for me to go to sleep, but this time the culprit was the light outside my window.

Chapter 14

For the first time in longer than I could remember, I woke up two minutes before my alarm went off. I was showered, dressed, and ready to go ten minutes before normal, but after pulling my books together, I just sat down on the sofa.

Today was the day. I hadn't consciously planned it when I went to bed, but circumstances were perfect. If I was wrong, Mom was not only home, judging by the noises filtering down the stairs, she was awake and only a few minutes away from coming downstairs.

Even filled with the near certainty that Brandon's parents, and by extension him, were our secret benefactors, the next fifteen minutes were some of the longest in my life.

When Brandon's Mustang finally appeared around the bend in the lane, I found myself smiling so hard my face was starting to hurt.

Breathing silent but heartfelt thanks that Mom was in the shower and therefore couldn't hear the low rumble of the Mustang's engine, I slipped out the front door and skipped down the concrete steps.

"I figured you were either too sick to get out of bed, or you finally decided to trust me." Brandon's gray eyes twinkled as he made a show of checking me over. "Looks like you're not sick."

I didn't know it was possible to blush and smile at the same time. "Nope, not sick."

After such a beginning, my day could hardly be anything but great. One class after another rolled by, and all of the things that normally would've bothered me just went whipping past without managing to stick.

I couldn't remember the second phase of cell division in Biology. I'd forgotten to reread the last chapter of Wuthering Heights, and Britney went out of her way to snub me. The only thing I cared about was making it to lunch so I could see Brandon again.

I dawdled on my way to Algebra, so much so I was nearly late for class. It wasn't until I sat down at my desk and felt a wave of disappointment slither through me that I realized I'd been hoping to see Brandon in between classes.

Mrs. Campbell caught me before I could leave for lunch. "Adriana, your homework is progressing along very well. At the risk of having you slow down, I'm going to admit that you're well ahead of where I'd hoped you'd be. Another couple of weeks and you'll be caught up and ready for your makeup test."

I shrugged uncomfortably. When teachers praised me, it always made me feel like I was socially deficient. I didn't necessarily mind the fact that I spent hours more on homework than any of my peers, but being praised for it always felt like a backhanded insult.

"It's okay, I'm not going to slack off. I want to be done with extra assignments as badly as you want to be finished with having to grade them."

My feeble joke evoked a smile, but I wasn't quite free to go. "Well, your homework is easier to grade than most. I also wanted to let you know that I'm happy with what you've been doing at the lab, and to give you this."

As unbelievable as it was considering that most of my classmates seemed more concerned with working their fast-food jobs than with doing homework, the plain envelope she handed me contained my very first paycheck. Ever.

I all but skipped out of the classroom. Later I'd probably complain about how small it was and wish I had enough to go shoe shopping, but for now it was just nice to know I had some discretionary money.

Brandon looked up as I walked into the cafeteria, and waved me over. As I threaded between a pair of closely-set tables I noticed that

Alec's table seemed unusually unsettled. If a shouting match could be conducted in whispers, it was being done by Jasmin and James, neither of who looked like they were happy about whatever was being discussed. Alec wasn't talking, but from the way he was scanning the room, he didn't want to be there anymore than the rest of them.

I made it to Brandon's table, and was still pulling my meal replacement drink out of my bag when the loudspeaker clicked on with the obligatory burst of static.

"This is Principal Gossil and I've got an exciting announcement. The school is sponsoring a trip to Las Vegas to see the production of Les Misérables that just started. Tickets are available at a discounted rate in the office for the next two days."

It was like someone had rifled through my mind to pick out my biggest disappointment in recent days, pulled it out and rubbed salt on the wound before cramming it back inside me. Of course I'd go see how big of a discount the school had gotten the tickets at, but it was extremely unlikely my tiny check would end up being enough.

It took me a moment to realize Mr. Gossil hadn't ended his announcement. "...those wishing to be entered into the drawing should stop by the office between today and noon tomorrow."

In the face of the near-universal apathy expressed by the rest of the student body, it took my mind several seconds to process exactly what had been said. I grabbed Brandon's arm and shook it to get his attention. "Did he just say they were drawing for free tickets?"

Brandon looked slightly amused. Cassie, who I'd just interrupted, looked very much not amused. "I think so. I wasn't paying very close attention, but I think he did."

The sound that came out of my mouth was disturbingly close to a squeal, but I was too excited to care. I waved goodbye as I stood and headed towards the doors.

Amazingly enough, there was already a line in the office by the time I got there. Either the nerds who liked musicals didn't actually eat in the lunchroom, or some of the people who maintained a cool, disinterested facade actually wanted to see it. My enthusiasm ebbed lower and lower as I waited in line behind a number of people who it turned out didn't even want to see the show, but figured that this would be a great chance to get away from their parents for the better part of twelve hours.

By the time I signed my name to a brightly-colored pink slip of paper, dropped it into the box, and walked out past the ridiculously-long line of people still waiting to enter the drawing, I knew for a certainty that I wasn't going. They'd posted the cost of the tickets, and I'd been right. My paycheck wasn't going to cut it.

I was still trying to decide whether or not to head back into the cafeteria, when the first bell rang, signaling a fitting end to a disappointment-filled lunch.

History wasn't any better, and we had a sub for Physics. Alec actually walked into class, saw Mrs. Alexander wasn't there, and then turned around and left. It was possibly the most brazen act of class cutting I'd ever seen, and somehow it didn't surprise me in the least. Even so, I spent the rest of the hour stewing while working on the pointless, busywork assignment the sub handed out.

Mrs. Tiggs still hadn't finished grading our tests, which meant I still had no idea how I'd done.

By the time I finally half-collapsed at my normal table in the tutor lab, all I could think about was how nice it would be to see Brandon one more time as he drove me home. I looked around to verify that all of the usual suspects were there. Geeks, check. Jocks, check. Rachel and her sinister sidekick James, check.

I smiled at Rachel and then flipped open my math book. Everything went just like normal, and promptly at five I closed my binder and started stuffing books into my backpack. I looked up to find Rachel standing in front of my table.

"Are you ready? James had to leave early, but don't worry, we've still got a ride home."

I think I managed to keep the disappointment off of my face. Rachel at least didn't seem to notice. Somehow I'd lost track of the fact that it was a Wednesday, and Brandon therefore wouldn't be taking me home.

"Great. Britney's been avoiding me like the plague. I didn't even see her leave today."

I'd never noticed that Rachel's laugh was possibly the prettiest I'd ever heard. Tinkling bells and all that aside, it really did sound like the kind of laugh you'd hear described for the princess of a fairy tale. Had I really never heard her laugh before, or was it just that she hadn't ever meant it before?

"She left about five minutes before James did."

"Still chatting up her prime candidate for the big dance?"

Rachel nodded as we skirted the last two tables between us and the one exterior door in the tutor lab.

"Yep, she's definitely settled on Tim Parsons, who's perfect if you like your men fairly handsome, moderately popular, and built like an ox."

I wanted to protest, but if anything Rachel was being too kind. I'd seen Tim trying to sound out the captions underneath the pictures in Sports Illustrated of his favorite pro football players.

I was just about to ask who we were going to ride with, more as a way of changing the subject than anything else, when movement off to my right answered the question.

"Alec!"

The last thing I was expecting out of Rachel was for her to all but run towards Alec with her arms out as if expecting a hug. Even so, that was less surprising than the fact that Alec accepted the hug, turning slightly to the side to receive her, but still reaching out with his left arm to pull her in close, albeit only briefly.

"You didn't think I'd forget, did you?"

"Not forget, no, just maybe be a little late."

As abruptly as that, the interplay between the two siblings ended, leaving an uncomfortable silence as odd as the affection from a moment before.

We walked to Alec's car in silence, the pair of them apparently lost in their own thoughts, and me wondering why Alec had agreed to give me a ride home. I wasn't enough of a car aficionado to recognize the vehicle other than the fact that it was a matte gray and had the kind of smooth, exotic lines all of the high-end vehicles seemed to be striving for right now. Rachel slipped in the backseat while I was still wondering how this seemingly low-profile ride matched up against Brandon's Mustang.

"Did you enter the drawing for Les Misérables tickets?"

I looked over to find Rachel sitting in the middle of the seat, happily leaning forward so she could talk to us. "Yes, but so did everyone else. My chances are so dismal they're not even worth mentioning."

Rachel looked like she was going to argue, or say something cheerful, but the back of my mind had been trying to figure out how she could be even with us, but still sitting in the back seat. I did a quick check to verify my suspicion.

"Rachel, you should be wearing your seatbelt."

"Why? It isn't like anyone is going to pull us over and give us a ticket."

It was more difficult than I expected to formulate a coherent answer while fighting off the first quivering indications of another attack.

"She's right, Rachel. You should be buckled in."

I expected her to argue with him. No girl on the planet liked it when her older brother sided with her friends against her, but Rachel just frowned a little before scooting back so she could do up her seatbelt.

Was she really that scared of him? I stole a glance at him out of the corner of my eye. He didn't look threatening, well, at least no more so than usual. Anyone with that many muscles was at least a little threatening. But he was just sitting there casually, driving along, seemingly without a care in the world. In fact, he wasn't buckled in either.

"Isn't that a bit hypocritical? I mean you tell her to buckle up, but you're not buckled up yourself."

Alec shrugged. "Yes, I suppose it does look hypocritical at that. Let's just say Rachel would be missed if we hit another car, but nobody would need to miss me."

The answer was like something you'd expect from a politician. It conveyed absolutely no information, and his supreme confidence was infuriating.

Luckily, I wouldn't have to hold my tongue for very long. We were already gliding around the last bend in the road before our lane. I expected Alec to slow to a stop and make me walk like James had. He slowed, but just enough to make the turn down the dusty lane.

Rachel jumped out of the car as soon as it slowed down and opened my door for me. "Enjoy the rest of your night, and don't lose hope on Les Misérables. You never know when you're going to beat the odds."

Shaking my head in amazement at Rachel's unfailing optimism, I turned to thank Alec for the ride. He was scowling a little again, which almost made me get out without saying anything. My thanks received only a nod in return, and then Rachel was waving goodbye as they backed down the lane.

The Jeep was gone, of course. I wiped away the beginnings of perspiration as I climbed our steps. It was still hot enough outside that I knew it was going to be miserable inside.

By the time I reached the door I was contemplating just finding a decent tree and spending the afternoon outside. The sight of a white envelope, barely visible against the off-white door, was enough to drive those thoughts out of my head.

It had my name on the side that'd been facing the door. I pulled it down as I walked inside the house. Mom was gone, there wasn't any reason I couldn't read whatever was in the envelope in the living room, but I found myself quickly climbing up our creaky stairs and closing my bedroom door behind me.

I tore the envelope open and pulled out a piece of heavy paper, almost like parchment. The writing was elegant, a kind of flowing script that was different from anything I'd ever seen, but which paled against the sheer artistry of the sigil positioned at the bottom of the note.

Adriana,

Your words of thanks were altogether unexpected, but decidedly appreciated. You're most welcome for whatever small part I might have played in helping events to unfold as they would have in a perfect world.

My actions were not such as to merit any large boon from you, but still I must ask one. Please never show this note to anyone. I ask not for myself, but for the others such knowledge could affect.

BROKEN

I hope your circumstances continue on much as they are now, but on the chance they do not, I can be reached by leaving a note in the hollow of the lightning-struck tree half a mile to the east of your house.

Chapter 15

My alarm pulled me out of the strangest night of sleep I'd ever experienced. Maybe I'd just been overtired, or possibly the strange, symbol on the note, inked into the place where a signature normally would've been, had reminded me of the other truly alien experience so far in my life.

Whatever the reason, it felt like I'd spent all night on the edge of one of the incredible, vivid dreams. I kept catching glimpses of the characteristic soft glow out of the corner of my eye, but hadn't ever actually slipped into a full-blown dream. It'd left me feeling very unsatisfied.

I rolled over and pulled the note out from its hiding place in my dresser. I had the words memorized already; the symbol was what I wanted now. The note was proof of the existence of our benefactor, but the sigil on the bottom of the page was a clue to his identity. It was incredibly intricate and completely different than anything I'd ever seen.

Once again I traced the sharp edges and smooth swirls with my eyes, marveling at the way it hinted at further complexity lurking just out of sight.

With a sigh of resignation I hid the note once again and pulled myself out of bed. Convinced as I was that Brandon was our benefactor, I no longer felt any qualms about trusting him to come pick me up.

I waited in the living room until I saw him pull up, and then skipped out to meet him with a smile. He reached over and opened my door, but some of the usual casualness was missing from his smile.

"Something wrong?"

Brandon spared a momentary glance from the road, just enough to give me a querying look. "What do you mean?"

"I don't know. It isn't anything I can really put a name too, but I'm usually pretty good at reading people, and something seems to be bothering you. Or maybe just distracting you."

The smile was back, and at near normal intensity. "Distracting is as good a description as any. Some things have been a little different than normal. Nothing to worry about, it just got me thinking."

Before my move to Sanctuary I probably would've pried just a little in an attempt to get whatever it was out in the open, but I didn't press him. I had too many secrets of my own now, secrets I didn't want anyone looking at too closely until I'd had a chance to work through them.

Brandon pulled into his normal parking spot, cut the engine and grabbed my hand before I could open the door. "Hey, you'd tell me if you knew about anything I should know, right? Anything odd or out of the ordinary?"

For a second nothing made sense. Brandon was the one who was saving us, and if that wasn't out of the ordinary, I didn't know what would be. Only he'd said in his note not to say anything to anyone. Of course. He was testing me, making sure I was going to keep quiet about what he'd done. Probably because he didn't want any of the praise for such a selfless act.

I was usually a pretty lousy liar, but it isn't really a lie if you both know the truth. "Brandon, you can trust me. There isn't anything odd going on. At least nothing odder than normal for Sanctuary."

Brandon looked at me for several seconds, and then chuckled. "You're right, compared to other places we do tend towards oddness. It's the small town effect, I think."

Something about his voice was a little different than normal. "You've lived somewhere else, somewhere bigger?"

The wistfulness was gone; the smile was back full force. "Not really. I've visited a few larger cities, but never for long enough to get the full feel for what it must be like to live in a Minneapolis or a New York. Someday maybe though."

This time I was going to pry, but he preempted my question. "It looks like we'd better be going or we'll both be late."

Les Misérables. I managed to put the impending drawing more or less out of my mind for the first half of the day, but I actually missed Britney's constant gossip. There was almost no redeeming value to most of what she said, but it did have the benefit of being distracting. By the time lunch finally came around I needed some kind of distraction. This was my only chance to see Les Misérables performed live before I turned forty.

Unfortunately, while the conversation at Brandon's table was plentiful, it wasn't very distracting. I was quickly realizing that Brandon's friends weren't very nice. I'd pretty much known Cassie was a wench, but Vincent seemed even meaner.

While a story about how someone tricked some poor girl into thinking he was going to ask her out was highly illuminating, it wasn't particularly the kind of thing I wanted to dwell on. Especially considering how many parallels there were between her story, and mine.

I kept looking at the clock, and the later it got, the more certain I was that Principal Gossil was just about to get on the loudspeaker and call out the winners of the drawing. The last two minutes of lunch dragged on forever, but then the bell rang and I was left sitting stunned as Brandon and his friends stood to go.

I let Brandon help me to my feet, hardly noticing the way his touch left my hand tingling, and headed off to class. It was stupid, but I couldn't help feeling this was yet another sign I wasn't going to win a ticket.

I tried to shake the feeling during History, but was still fighting it when I walked into Physics. In a departure from his normal routine, Alec was already seated when I arrived. I flipped open my notebook and tried to distract myself with a brief sketch, only to tear the page out and ball it up as the bell rang.

I looked up to see Alec staring at me, which just made me mad. It was completely unfair. I wasn't going to get to go to Les Misérables, but he was rich enough to fly to New York and book the whole theater.

As Mrs. Alexander stood up to take roll, a burst of static silenced us all. "It's my pleasure to read off the names of the five winners in our drawing for tickets to Les Misérables."

"The first winner is Pam White."

Somewhere down the hall I heard someone yell, and then an entire class broke out into cheers. I knew I should be happy for Pam, but I was too busy wishing everyone would quiet down so we could hear the next name.

BROKEN

Mrs. Alexander shut the door, muting the roar as Principal Gossil continued with a slight rustle of papers. "Also winning a ticket to Les Misérables next weekend, Mr. Andrew Webbs."

A couple of half-hearted cheers broke out towards the front of the class, but they were short-lived. Andrew wasn't in the class, and his friends were probably spending almost as much time thinking about their odds of still winning, as I was.

I only had three chances left, three in two hundred assuming that everyone else in the school had entered the drawing, which was virtually guaranteed.

"And the third lucky person is Suzanne Bergerman."

And my chances were down to two, with even worse odds than I'd had a second before. My hands hurt, only when I looked down to see why, it was because my fingernails were digging into my palms. The blood was pounding so furiously in my ears that I couldn't hear the next name read. I could tell it wasn't mine though because nobody turned back to congratulate me.

There was only one name left to be read, and I knew that it wasn't going to be mine. I'd never been that lucky in my entire life. As quickly as that my pulse slowed and my fists relaxed.

I could clearly hear as Principal Gossil cleared his throat and continued. "The fifth winner is Ms. Adriana Paige."

The cheer from my classmates wasn't nearly as loud as the one for Pam, but it didn't matter. I'd won a ticket. Me, the person who never won anything, was going to get to see the greatest musical of all time.

I smiled and thanked everyone who yelled back congratulations, and then turned to find Alec staring at me.

"Congratulations, Adriana. Les Misérables is one of the best. I hope you enjoy it."

I thanked him sweetly, and even managed a smile, but I wanted to tell him he was a jerk. I'd been desperate to win a ticket, and he had to take yet another opportunity to rub in the fact that he'd already seen it. That he was rich enough to see it anywhere in the world as often as he wanted to.

Even my desire to tell Alec off wasn't strong enough to overcome the pure joy at having won. The next two hours floated by, and before I would've believed it possible, I found myself heading towards the tutoring lab. Rachel met me outside the door, her face lit up with a smile even more striking than her usual expression.

"You won. I'm so excited that you won. Guess what. I traded tickets with Suzanne Bergerman, so we get to sit together!"

Life couldn't get any better. I was going to Les Misérables with Rachel, and I only had two more hours before Brandon would be taking me home.

Chapter 16

My time with Brandon blurred by too quickly. It was like the time between when he picked me up and dropped me off didn't even exist. One moment I'd be blah and mundane, then next I'd be with him and the world was perfect. When I was by myself, it was hard to believe it all hadn't been a dream.

Thursday morning flew by, it was like I blinked and it was already time for Mrs. Campbell's class. A number of the other girls, and even a couple of the guys, stopped by my desk before the bell rang to congratulate me on winning the last ticket to Les Misérables. Britney wasn't one of them. I caught her glaring at me a couple of times out of the corner of my eye.

Under normal circumstances I probably would've felt guilty, or at least wished things had worked out differently. Today, I was fully prepared to acknowledge Britney as the spoiled, self-centered brat she was.

The bell rang and then Mrs. Campbell's lecture was over in record time. I even finished my assignment a good ten minutes before class was scheduled to end. I was absently sketching what I expected the inside of the opera house to look like, when a tap on my shoulder pulled me out of my reverie.

"I'm so sorry, Mrs. Campbell. I finished early, but I should have started on one of the catch-up assignments. I just didn't want to get into a whole new subject with only ten minutes left."

Her smile was much more understanding than normal for a classroom situation. It took the sting out of the words that were probably just for the people close enough to overhear.

"Don't you worry, Miss Paige, I'll let you know when I don't think you're keeping up. Seeing as you are done though, would you please run something over to Mrs. North? I'd do it, but I need to go to a special projects meeting today during lunch."

As quickly as that, my books were in my backpack and I was on my way to the second story of the school, which housed music, sketching, and all the other forms of art lesser mortals like me would never master.

The journey would've been completely unremarkable except that I happened to glance into one of the classrooms just before I found

Mrs. North's room. Even a brief glance screamed art students. There were at least twenty people sitting in front of contraptions that looked like a cross between an easel and a desk, and most of them had the look of intense concentration I'd come to associate with Mom attempting to frame a picture.

The notable exception was Alec, who I almost didn't recognize. I hadn't expected to see him in an art class, but more than that was the way his face seemed transformed. He'd always been gorgeous. I could dislike, even hate him, and still acknowledge that he made my heart go pitter-patter, but this was something else. He looked so happy, so at peace with the world, that for the brief moment between when I saw him and when I recognized him, I thought I'd seen an angel.

I'd always thought that intense look of concentration was the sign of a true artist. Maybe it still was. Maybe whatever he was drawing was absolute crap. Maybe the masters like Michelangelo and da Vinci had completed their greatest works with expressions very similar to what everyone else in the class was sporting. Still, I couldn't help envy such contentment.

I dropped off my bundle of papers at Mrs. North's class, and started back towards my locker. I couldn't help trying to catch another glimpse of the art class as I walked past. I'd been hoping to see Alec again, but hadn't expected him to look up as I craned my neck to see inside.

I stumbled a little in surprise. He was still gorgeous, but the simple joy was gone. He no longer looked like something that couldn't exist in this world, but even with anger etched on his features my heart still skipped a beat. I ducked around the corner and started down the stairs, my embarrassment at being caught staring giving way to anger. It didn't make any sense. I'd never done anything to him. Did he really hate me so much just because I'd told him off about not protecting Rachel?

Cassie was waiting for me at my locker when I got there. "Brandon wanted me to stop by and let you know he had a few things to take care of, so he won't see you during lunch. You can still come sit with us if you want."

The words were right. If I'd been reading them off of a page in a book, I probably would've believed them, but the way she delivered them left no doubt in my mind. She didn't want me at their table. The only reason she'd stopped by my locker was because Brandon had told her to.

"Thanks, but I have some studying to do. I'd better just find a quiet corner."

The smile I received was sickly sweet, but left me with the impression I'd just failed a test. "Okay, we'll see you another day then?"

I pulled out my Spanish and Biology books, more because they were the two subjects I was doing the worst in than out of any real desire to study them, and wandered the halls until Mr. Whethers took pity on me and asked if I wanted to study in his classroom.

Sitting there all by myself felt so lonely. When you boiled it all down, I had a grand total of two friends in Sanctuary. Rachel and Brandon, both of who seemed to dislike the other, and neither of whom I was really sure I could count on. It was fine to only have two friends, or even just one friend if you knew they would do everything they possibly could to make sure they wouldn't let you down. It was entirely different when you weren't sure you could trust the people around you.

Brandon was too good to be true. I pretty much expected any day now he'd come to his senses and realize he could do a lot better. Right or not, it's hard to really become emotionally invested when you feel like that.

Rachel on the other hand should have been the perfect friend, but I got the feeling she'd always choose her brother over me. I felt guilty for holding that against her, family *should* be important. Cindi's friends back in Minnesota had probably felt similarly, but I'd always been really careful not to make her choose between me and them. Alec seemed like the type who'd force a decision just because he could.

I felt my heart go crazy at the same time tears started gathering at the corner of my eyes. It was stupid to have risked a panic attack when I was already borderline depressed, but that was what I was looking at now.

I'd picked a seat that wasn't visible from the doorway, so I just put my head down and let the twin traumas run their course. By the time I was feeling steady enough to leave the classroom, I had just enough time to make it to the bathroom and try to clean myself up before lunch ended.

The rest of the day went in starts and stutters. I went from answering a question about the economy of post-Civil War Georgia, to watching Alec start putting together rough plans for our next group project.

I had just enough time to notice he seemed relieved I wasn't trying to get in his way, and then Spanish was finishing up and I was headed to the tutoring lab. Most Friday afternoon sessions were pretty sparsely attended. Today was no different, which was a good thing since I probably wouldn't have done a very good job of explaining anything.

Mrs. Campbell shut everything down before my shift started, and sent me home with a concerned look in her eye. Rachel skipped over to my table while I was still trying to get my books put away.

"Guess what. I'm bringing pizza on the bus so we'll have something to eat on the way to Les Misérables. I can't wait. My first time going to Les Misérables, and my first road trip on a bus."

"You've never actually been on a school bus before, have you?"

Rachel blushed a little bit. "Well, no not really. It should be fun still though, right?"

I found myself returning her smile. You really couldn't spend any time around Rachel and not find yourself smiling. "Well, I've heard about bus trips that were extremely fun, but I've never been on one before. For me it's always been way too much time crammed into a relatively small space with fifty or sixty other people and no bathroom. Still, if any bus trip is going to be fun, it'd be this one."

Rachel handed me my last book, and waved to Isaac, who was just now getting up from his table.

"Hello, Adriana. I assume you'll need a ride home today?"

It was the first time Isaac had actually spoken to me, and I was surprised at how well-spoken he was. His voice sounded like a superbly-tuned cello. I filed the information away as further evidence he wasn't really our age.

"Yes please, Brandon can only take me home on Tuesdays and Thursdays."

It wasn't my imagination; Isaac flinched slightly, and Rachel's smile momentarily turned plastic. I mentally kicked myself for having once again stepped squarely between the Capulets and Montagues.

Isaac recovered with admirable speed, smiling as he gestured us forward. "Well, then, after you."

It wasn't until Rachel and Isaac were driving away that I realized she'd completely pulled me out of my funk. I still didn't know that I could really depend on her, but at least I knew she'd try her hardest.

Chapter 17

I reached out groggily to turn off my alarm, and then wished it was still the weekend so I wouldn't have to get up and go to school.

I finished off my normal morning routine with a pair of aspirin from the bathroom cupboard. I didn't usually like taking drugs of any kind, but I had a sharp headache building already.

I shuffled downstairs, waved a speechless hello to Mom, grabbed my lunch, bag, and books as I absently wondered why there was a cupcake on the counter with a lit candle. Mom has always been paranoid about open flames. She'd nearly burned down the house as a kid.

I was halfway to the front door before Mom grabbed my arm and turned me back towards the kitchen. "I can't believe you. You really would have left without realizing it was your birthday?"

Ugh. No wonder I had a headache. My brain must have been working overtime in an effort to block out the fact I was now another year older. "Thanks, Mom."

I blew out the candle, and turned to leave again, but didn't even get to take a step this time.

"Hold on there. Do you always skip breakfast now?"

Mom had somehow spontaneously developed these weird memories featuring me as a morning person. I personally couldn't remember a time when I'd actually liked getting up. I didn't necessarily hate the mornings, but we weren't really on a first-name basis. More like acquaintances than friends.

"You both used to be down in the kitchen eating breakfast at the crack of dawn almost every morning. Now it's like you don't even want to roll out of bed."

She used to like mornings. I'd tagged along just because it hadn't seemed right to put a damper on such enthusiasm. Trust Mom to bring that up on my birthday. I swayed just a little. Today it didn't seem quite as bad, as long as I didn't think of her actual name.

"Mom, I don't want to be late. Thanks a bunch for the cupcake. Can we wait to celebrate until after school?"

Now it was her turn to look guilty and fidget just a little bit. "Actually, that's why I wanted to talk to you this morning. I've been shooting that new place I left you the note about. The one that bunch of kids your age told me about. Anyways, it's the best place I've found so far. I've been shooting it at pretty much all hours, but I think I need to get higher up for the shot I want."

I knew exactly where this was going. Actually, I was kind of relieved she wasn't going to be around this afternoon. Birthdays are supposed to be special. Dad had always understood that and done an amazing job of surprising us with something new and unusual on our birthdays. Mom had always felt like a round of happy birthdays and a cake more than met the requirements for birthday specialness. It was going to be hard enough missing Dad on the one day guaranteed to make me think of him. It would've been worse if Mom was around constantly making comparisons between what she was doing and what Dad would've done.

"...so this is the only day he can help me, and if I don't get some help climbing, then I'll never make it high enough to get the shot for the tourism booklet. You understand, don't you, sweetie?"

I nodded, and managed a fairly convincing smile.

"Okay, then. Well there's a present for you in the living room, but since you didn't want to celebrate until after school, you'll have to wait to open it."

I could definitely hear the rumble of a high-performance engine. I nodded again, and turned to go, hopeful that I could avoid the inevitable question of why Brandon was coming to pick me up in the mornings as well as dropping me off most afternoons. Unfortunately, Mom's hearing was nearly as good as mine, and she was walking towards the windows before I managed to get the door open.

"Adri, who's that?"

It was obviously one of those leading questions designed to see whether or not I'd try to lie. I shrugged. "His name is Brandon; he picks me up sometimes in the morning."

I was saved from dealing with her response by Brandon's knock.

"Hello, Adriana, Mrs. Paige."

I never thought I'd see the like. Mom's face lost its stern 'I'm doing this for your own good' look, and instead transformed into something not very different from what I saw every time I watched the girls my age look at Brandon.

"Well, hello. You're Brandon?"

Fifteen minutes later, I was still trying to believe things had gone so well. I'd expected Mom to put her foot down and tell Brandon I'd be riding the bus to school every morning, starting today. Instead, she'd shaken Brandon's hand, smiled way more than usual, and hurried us out the door so we wouldn't be late for school.

"I don't know what kind of magic you just used on my mom, but whatever it was, you should do it again. Heck, use your powers on her every time you stop by. That was amazing!"

Brandon chuckled and reached over to run a finger across my palm. "I didn't do anything special. Your mom seems like a very sensible person."

I almost choked. "I love my mom, but she's the least sensible person ever. She spends half of her time in a different universe entirely, and only occasionally worries about the same kinds of things as other parents."

"Ah, a dreamer, but one who still freaks out when it comes to her daughter and boys. Maybe she was just struck by my obvious good nature."

I shook my head as we pulled into the parking lot. "Please. You're just about everything she's worried about in a guy. Rich, handsome, popular. The only thing you could change to scare her worse would be to join the football team and be the star quarterback."

His smile was so beautiful it made my heart ache. "Well, in that case I'm glad I never tried out for the varsity team. I'd hate to make things any more difficult for you."

Brandon gently captured my arm as we slipped inside the school. "Speaking of stars, I happened to read them last night and they told me a secret."

"Oh, really? Do tell, I always love to hear a good secret."

There was a new twinkle in his eye as he shook his head. "Oh, it wasn't a secret from you, just one you hadn't shared with me. Happy birthday. I've got a multi-part present in the works, but it's taking a bit longer to wrap it all up, so you may have to wait a little."

As quickly as that, he winked and turned to catch up with Cassie, leaving me in a state of near shock. He'd been inside the house, but hadn't been able to see the kitchen, so he hadn't seen the cupcake and candle. I'd done web searches on my name and birth date before and never had it return anything legit, so he couldn't have found it out that way. Even that would've been an unheard-of level of effort coming from a guy, but however he really had learned it was my birthday must have been even harder than that.

I felt like I was floating on a cloud as I hurried off to Biology. The feeling lasted exactly as long as it took me to sit down, listen to Mrs. Sorenson tell us all that she'd finished grading our tests, and then see the big, self-satisfied 'D' sitting at the top of my paper.

For a second it felt as though my heart had stopped beating. I'd never done worse than a 'B' on any assignment or test since I'd finished up

Kindergarten. I couldn't take this home and show my mom. Head in the clouds half of the time or not, she'd still freak out. Heck, I was already freaking out enough for the both of us. This was going on my high school transcript. The one colleges would be looking at. The one that might have gotten me a scholarship. Only now I'd be lucky to pull a 'C' out of the class.

I tried to control my breathing. This wasn't the end of the world. I was almost done catching up in Algebra, so I'd have a ton more time. If I really worked hard, maybe I'd be okay. Most teachers would still offer some kind of extra credit if you begged hard enough.

I spent the next hour mapping out exactly how I was going to salvage my college prospects, and had more or less pulled myself together by the time English ended. My newfound dedication to excellence meant I outdid myself in Algebra. I finished up the day's homework, and made it more than halfway through one of my makeup assignments by the time Mrs. Campbell stopped off at my desk.

"Care to run another errand for me, Adriana?"

I didn't really want to. Not when I'd just discovered I had more studying to do than was humanly possible. Still, Mrs. Campbell had always been super nice, if equally stern, and there was only ten more minutes of class left. Besides, I'd been so intrigued by the sight of

Alec drawing that I wanted to see him like that again. If he could take such joy in the creation process, maybe he wasn't as bad as he seemed. The only way to know for sure was to see him with all of the masks off again.

"Sure, I'd love to. Mrs. North again?"

I ignored the spate of nasty looks shot my way, gathered my books, accepted the bundle of papers, and hurried off to the stairs. It was later than last time, so unless I was quick the bell was going to ring before I made it back down the stairs. The congestion was bad in the halls, but for some reason it was twice as bad around stairs.

Apparently I was hurrying just a little too fast. I tripped just before I hit the first step, and almost went crashing down the flight that led to the basement. Luckily I was just quick enough to grab the banister and save myself from a broken neck. I didn't quite manage to avoid twisting my ankle though, so I limped all the way up to the second floor.

Trying to be as casual as possible, I looked into the art room as I hobbled by, but they'd rearranged their stations, and someone's easel was in the way now.

The sprained ankle had slowed me down enough that there was no way I was going to make it back to my locker before the bell rang. Still, I tried to be gracious when it went off just as I handed Mrs. North the papers.

BROKEN

Based on the number of classrooms on the second floor, and the narrowness of the stairs, there was no point in trying to wait the crowd out. I gritted my teeth and limped out into the surge of bodies.

Surprisingly enough, there were more familiar faces than expected. As I grabbed the handrail on the right, I noticed Isaac several feet ahead of me. Of course, it's hard to miss someone nearly six feet tall and almost as well-muscled as Alec. Even if he was partially hidden by Vincent, who was strutting along a little higher up the stairs with all of his usual arrogance.

If Isaac had been the one close enough to reach out and touch, I probably would've tried to get his attention and said hi. With Vincent, I just stayed quiet and hoped he wouldn't notice me.

I didn't want to risk tripping and making my ankle worse, so I was paying especially close attention to where my feet were going. If I hadn't been looking down, I would have completely missed it. I still almost thought I'd imagined it, but there was no denying that Vincent's foot snaked out and nudged the ankle of the kid in front of him just hard enough to trip the smaller guy.

The result was all out of proportion to what I expected. The smaller boy fell forward, careening towards the banister with so much force he knocked people in front of him out of the way.

Just before I left elementary school someone had read us a newspaper article about some poor guy being pushed over a railing and falling to his death. I'd had nightmares for months. Dreams where the stairs had turned slick and I'd slid all the way down them. Dreams where the banister hadn't even been there and the stairs had become impossibly narrow, and nightmares where I'd somehow stumbled and started to fall over the edge of the railing.

This was like all of those dreams put together, only happening to someone else. A couple of kids reached out, but the only people who could've really stopped him had already been bowled over.

Time slowed down for me as he hit the railing and started over it. His feet came up and his torso was hanging in the void when someone reached over and grabbed his arm. I heard a grunt of effort, saw him stop moving, and only then realized it was Ben who'd nearly died.

In the split second between Ben being gently placed back on the stairs, and everyone starting to breathe again, I followed the arm that'd saved him back to see who the hero was. Isaac met my gaze as he let go of Ben and then he looked up at Vincent with a stare that was somehow both calm and challenging at the same time.

"What are you looking at, freak?" It was hard to believe Vincent could be so nonchalant after having almost killed someone. It'd been an accident obviously, but still that wasn't the kind of thing you just shook off.

All of the kids that'd been rushing forward to congratulate Isaac for his heroic save started backing away. Anxious to avoid the fight, I tried to move with the crowd, but felt a flash of pain as my abused ankle protested.

For a second I couldn't think about anything other than the agony. When I managed to get my eyes to focus again, Vincent was only a couple of inches away from Isaac and hissing something too quiet for me to make out.

Whatever it was, Vincent was all but foaming at the mouth while Isaac was so controlled it was hard to believe a fight was about to break out. As admirable as Isaac's calm was, I was actually wishing he was a little more worked up. I'd seen plenty of fights where the guy who got the first hit in won. Vincent was going to throw the first punch, and then Isaac was going to go down like a house of cards.

Something Vincent said must've been particularly vile. Isaac's expression shifted for just a second. They were circling now, both amazingly graceful considering that they were still on the stairs.

Everyone stepped back a little further. I hobbled up a stair or two in an effort to avoid getting in the way.

I'd heard of tension so thick you could cut it with a knife, but this was the first time I'd ever experienced it. It felt like there was electricity surging back and forth between Vincent and Isaac, making my skin feel too small.

The tension suddenly flickered like a dying light bulb. "Vincent!"

I was disoriented for a second. The yell had come from behind me, and had torn the two apart faster than I'd believed possible.

The crowd, packed so tightly that I'd been worried someone was going to get pushed over the railing, separated as Alec flowed down the stairs. I'd only thought Isaac and Vincent were graceful. Alec made them look like drunken frat boys.

Vincent spun around so fast it almost looked like he was going to fall down and then backed away from both of them like a cornered animal. It was hard to decide whether my excitement at seeing the biggest jerk I'd ever met humbled outweighed my dislike for Alec, who'd pretty much locked up the honor of being the second biggest jerk.

A surge of dread washed through me as Vincent backed closer to the wall in an effort to maintain his distance from Alec.

I half expected for the incredible tension I'd been feeling before to disappear, but instead it morphed slightly. If I hadn't known it was absolutely absurd, I would've said it felt like there was a tingly wind blowing down the stairs, pushing Vincent along before it.

Isaac moved slightly. It was a small change of position, but somehow incredibly menacing. It wasn't until Vincent froze in place that I realized Isaac's shift had kept Vincent squarely between him and Alec. It was like watching a pair of wolves bringing down an elk. I'd seen gangs work together like this before, but it seemed strangely out of place in Sanctuary.

I was positive there was going to be a fight after all, but then Vincent grabbed some poor freshman, shoved him into Isaac, and pushed his way downstairs as Isaac caught the human missile.

As soon as Vincent was safely out of sight, everyone surged forward to congratulate Isaac on having saved Ben, and Ben on having not died.

The near fight between Isaac and Vincent and then Alec's intervention seemed to be the buzz for the next two hours. It appeared that a lot of other people felt the same way that I did. Alec was plenty prickly and stuck up, but that was nothing compared to how much the average student hated Vincent, who seemed to delight in making everyone's life miserable.

The teachers seemed curiously ignorant of everything. Nobody else seemed to think that was unusual, which freaked me out almost as much as Ben having nearly gone over the stairs.

At least I didn't have to listen to all of the gossip during lunch. Once I'd been able to hobble down the stairs, I'd made my way to Mr. Whethers' room, and I'd spent the entire lunch break studying.

I hadn't been especially excited at the prospect of spending that long by myself, but the cafeteria was all the way on the other side of the school. Limping over there listening to Vincent run his mouth and then coming all the way back here for History wouldn't be worth it.

History being what it was, I probably heard about as much in that one hour as most everyone else did during the whole rest of the day. Mr. Simms seemed especially dense, and pretty much let everyone do whatever they wanted for the entire class.

In deference to my new dedication to academic excellence, I finished up the reading, and then opened up my Biology book and started trying to get a handle on all of the items I'd thought I understood, but apparently hadn't.

When the bell rang I limped back to my locker before making my painful way to Physics. I almost turned around and left when I saw the substitute again, but almost two decades of ingrained respect for authority figures propelled me into the room and to my seat.

I happened to look up at the exact moment that Alec appeared in the doorway. I expected him to take one look at the sub and turn around like he'd done before, but he registered the presence of a substitute and then came inside regardless.

It didn't make sense until the first girl all but fainted as he walked past her desk. Of course. He didn't like substitutes, and figured he had better places to be, but the draw of hero worship after having almost double-teamed Vincent was just too much to resist.

The sub took a desultory roll, and then waved his hands at us. "Her notes say you're all supposed to be able to work on some kind of group project. Just keep it to a dull roar."

It was like releasing a bunch of kids in a candy store and telling them to sample whatever they wanted. Every single girl in the classroom but me made an instant beeline towards Alec's desk. The guys were a little slower, but not by much. For a while I tried to ignore all of the poorly disguised gushing about how brave Alec was, or attempts by the guys to recreate exactly what Alec would've done if Vincent had gone ahead and thrown a punch.

After fifteen minutes I finally gave up, closed my book and flipped open my notebook. Our physics class was about the most sedate, nerdy group of people I'd yet met. If they were this worked up about the fight, it was a good thing I didn't share any other classes with Alec. The rest of the school must be three or four times as bad.

Sketching helped block out all of the inane conversation that'd taken over the other corner of the room. It was amazing how easily I was able to zone out while drawing. Once again, I didn't try to guide my hand, just let my subconscious create a horizon and start fleshing out a body of water and droopy trees around it.

The sound of a hand coming down hard on a desk pulled me from my refuge. "I told you all to keep it to a dull roar. I want everyone back to your seats."

A couple people looked like they wanted to give the sub a hard time, but these were all the kids who were hoping to make it into the top ten percent of their graduating class. None of them really had a disobedient bone in their body. They grudgingly returned to their seats and left Alec by himself.

I picked my pencil back up and started drawing again, only to be disturbed by someone clearing their throat. Alec was looking down at me with something almost like a smile playing at the corner of his lips. For a second I couldn't blame the other girls for swarming him over. He was so attractive it was hard to remember he was such a jerk.

I forced myself to stop wondering if anyone else in the entire world had such incredibly blue eyes, and tilted my head to the side questioningly.

"Sorry, I can tell you're not really in the mood to work on our project, especially with all of the racket today, but I saw you limping down the stairs just before lunch. Are you okay?"

It was almost convincing. If he hadn't mentioned the stairs, and thereby the fight, I might have fallen for it, but he was just looking for more attention.

"I'll be okay. Just a little sprain."

Alec looked like he wanted to say something else, but finally nodded and sat down in the next chair over. It wasn't as good as if he'd gone all the way back to his seat, and it was extremely out of character, but it was better than nothing. I breathed a sigh of relief that he wasn't going to continue fishing for compliments, and returned to my drawing. I knew I should open my books back up and study, but it was starting to take shape, and I figured it was only a few minutes away from becoming recognizable. Once that happened my meager drawing skills would evaporate and I'd have to stop anyways. For whatever reason every time I tried to work on something after I realized what it was, I completely ruined it. One of many reasons why I'd never really pursued drawing.

A short time later I surfaced again and looked down to find a familiar landscape. The body of water had morphed into an oblong pond with a crescent island positioned almost exactly in the center. I still remembered the first time I'd been told a monster had taken a bite out of the island, and that was the reason it was so oddly shaped.

The trees were all familiar too. I'd climbed each and every one of them at least once. The one on the right had taken the longest to conquer. I'd tried climbing it dozens of times over the years before finally making it to the top when I was thirteen. When I'd finally made it as high as I figured was safe, I'd worked my trembling way back down to the ground, and never felt even the slightest inclination to climb it again.

I felt tears start to gather at the corner of my eyes as I remembered all of the good times our family had spent together there. It was like being immersed in everything I'd loved only to have it evaporate when I went to grab my surroundings.

"Hey, that's really pretty good. Is that a real place?"

I nodded, hoping Alec would take the hint implied in my silence. I should have known better.

"What's it called?"

The name slid out of me almost of its own accord. "Monster Lake."

Every single birthday I could remember had involved some kind of trip out to Monster Lake. Picnics had swapped off with treasure hunts and then been replaced by other activities depending on Dad's mood and my age. My subconscious had keyed in on the one scene guaranteed to make me feel miserable.

"Was that close to your house in Minnesota? I..."

Whatever else Alec was saying was lost to the roar in my ears, caused as always by my racing heart. I didn't even have a chance to try and fight the attack. By the time I realized I was in trouble, papers were flying off my desk and the floor was racing up to meet me.

Rather than swimming around in blackness like I normally did when collapsed, this time there was just nothing. One second I was falling, the next I was opening my eyes and looking up at Alec.

"Stand back, everyone, and let me through!"

It took a few seconds to realize the sub was the one yelling. Nobody seemed very interested in making room for him. The reason it took so long for my brain to start working again was that I couldn't seem to think about anything other than Alec.

He was looking down at me with an expression I'd never seen on his face before. I still couldn't read it, but it was new and somehow seemed like it belonged there more than his normal impenetrable mask.

"What's going on? Is she okay?" The sub had finally pushed his way through the crowd, and looked like he was about two steps away from a total panic.

Alec stood, and it wasn't until I went up at the same time that I realized he was carrying me. "I think she'll be fine, but maybe I should get her to the nurse. Just to be sure." Even as he was talking, Alec was moving towards the door.

"There's really no need. I'm fine. I don't need to see the nurse." It was obvious he was going to ignore me. I tried to thrash around enough for him to put me down, but he restrained my arms with a couple of fingers. The motion was so casual I was pretty sure nobody even realized he'd pinned my arms to my stomach with surprising strength.

I thought about kicking, or even screaming, but that would just leave me feeling like a child and give Alec exactly the kind of attention he was probably hoping for.

"You hit your head pretty hard; I really think we should get you to the office. Sir, with your permission?"

The comment about hitting my head settled me down. It wasn't until we were out in the hall that I realized my head didn't hurt. That was probably a really bad sign.

"Let go of my hands."

Alec unpinned my arms, set me down, and then chuckled as I started gingerly probing my scalp. "What are you doing? You didn't actually hit your head. I caught you before you hit the ground."

I started to shake my head and then thought better of it. "Please, every other time I've dropped that quickly I've totally banged myself up. You were on the other side of my desk, there's no way you got all the way around it and managed to catch me before I hit the ground."

The mild amusement on Alec's face froze into something else. "Believe what you will. There's no reason to worry about a concussion."

"Then why did you tell the sub I'd hit my head?"

He looked away for a moment, almost as though deciding whether or not to tell the truth. "I presumed you wouldn't want to stay and be subject to everyone's questions. You seem not to like people prying about your attacks, and you were less happy than usual today. I thought you could use the break."

Apparently he'd decided against the truth option. It was too much for me.

"*I* looked unhappy today? You, who never crack a smile unless you're going to get something out of it, were concerned about the fact I wasn't all smiles and giggles? Maybe you should flunk a test or two. Only it doesn't really count unless your dad, you know, the one who used to make your birthdays really special, is gone."

Alec's mouth opened, closed, and then assumed its normal place in his unreadable mask. He reached out, almost consolingly, but I stepped away before he could make contact.

I knew I should shut up before I said something really unreasonable, but my anger was in the driver's seat now. "Don't try and pretend you're sorry. You were just looking for an excuse to get out of class once all of the hero worship dried up. Well I got you out and you helped me avoid all of the stupid questions everyone would've asked, so we're even."

There was another flicker of something I couldn't quite read in Alec's eyes, but I was long past caring. I turned and limped off, wishing my ankle was in better shape so I could properly stomp.

Spanish arrived much too soon. Since I hadn't gotten in trouble wandering the halls so far, it was a definite temptation to skip the last hour of school too. Unfortunately my luck was bound to give out sooner or later, and then I'd be in even more trouble. The last thing I needed was a record of delinquency to go along with my failing grade in Biology.

Mrs. Tiggs was positively glowing as we all walked into her classroom. She popped out of her chair as soon as the bell rang, and began handing out graded tests. My world started trembling as I turned my test over and saw an 'F' at the top of the page.

'Come see me after class.'

The note felt like the final nail in the coffin of my academic future. My efforts to focus were entirely wasted. It took everything I had just to hold myself together until class ended.

I'd planned on remaining in my seat until everyone else left, but Mrs. Tiggs motioned me to her desk while half the class was still filing out the door.

"It gives me no pleasure to tell you this, but based on your initial test score I think you should prepare yourself for the fact that you're probably going to fail this class. I worried this would be the result of your starting so late in the semester and not having any prior Spanish experience. Unfortunately, it's now too late for you to switch into another class. I'm afraid you'll just have to take the failing grade."

I stood there woodenly for several seconds, unsure whether or not she was through. She finally made a shooing motion and turned back to grading papers. Predictably, there were still a half-dozen other kids in the classroom. They all turned back to the door and started filing out again, but by tomorrow half the school would know exactly how badly I'd just been humiliated.

I found myself just outside the tutor lab with no recollection of having stumbled to my locker, or going by Physics to grab the stuff I'd left there. Still, somehow my Spanish book had disappeared, replaced by my math book. My knees started shaking as I entered the room, but I made it safely to my normal table before they gave out.

"Adri, Adriana? Excuse me." I didn't recognize the girl standing across from me, but based on her uncomfortable expression and the fact that more than one person had turned for the sole purpose of watching us out of the corner of their eyes, she'd been standing there longer than I'd realized.

Apparently my looking up was enough of a response for her to proceed. "I've got a note from Mrs. Campbell. She asked me to deliver it to you."

I managed something that could just barely be construed as a thank you, took the note, and watched her leave. A note from a teacher, even one I liked, didn't seem very important when weighed against failing two of my six classes.

The reoccurring thought of how horrified my Dad would've been that his daughter, 'the smart one,' was going to flunk out of high school was enough to keep me constantly on the edge of a panic attack. The longer that went on the less ability, and even more dangerous, the less desire I'd have to try and fight it off.

I finally opened up the note more out of a need for a distraction than any real inclination to find out what it contained.

Adriana. I'm afraid I've been called into a surprise meeting with the school administration. Normally I wouldn't cancel the tutoring session, but Albert and Peter are both out, and it wouldn't be fair to leave you all by yourself to try and take care of everyone. Go ahead and tell everyone the tutoring session is canceled, and I'll see you tomorrow.

—Nora Campbell

I sat motionless for several seconds before realizing this was the out I needed. If I could pull myself together enough to cancel the lab, I could go home and self-destruct without ruining the scattered shards left of my life.

"The lab has been canceled for today. I'm sorry, everyone, but most of the tutors are sick and Mrs. Campbell had to go to a meeting after school. Everything should be back to normal tomorrow though."

I expected everyone to jump to their feet and all but run out of the room. I didn't expect what I actually got.

"Who are you and why on earth should we believe you? The last thing I want to do is go home and get in trouble for cutting tutoring again."

I opened my mouth to answer, but words wouldn't make their way past the trembling in my chest. I felt tears start threatening to arrive and further humiliate me, but Rachel came to my rescue.

"She's one of the tutors. Patty Sanders, who I happen to know has Mrs. Campbell's class sixth period, just gave her a note. Stay if you want, but she's done exactly what she was supposed to."

I wanted to give Rachel a big hug, or maybe just break into tears right then and there. I managed to just give her a smile, and hold off on the tears until I'd gathered up my stuff and made it out of the room.

Rachel caught up with me before I made it very far. "Adriana, are you okay? Don't you want a ride home?"

I turned towards her to respond and just broke down. She pulled me into an open classroom and gave me a hug while I tried to explain about the two failed tests, my birthday, and how much I missed my Dad and Cindi.

The last bit was especially garbled. I was pretty sure she wasn't getting any of it, but that didn't matter. All that mattered was I was finally able to tell someone. I never really got myself under control; my sobs just subsided enough for me to tell Rachel I wanted to go home.

Isaac was standing right outside the classroom door, and unobtrusively helped Rachel get me to his car where she jumped into the back with me. Even through the haze of tears I could tell he wasn't happy about the seating arrangement, but once again Rachel showed the kind of iron will she'd demonstrated with James. Almost before I knew it we were rolling to a stop in my driveway. I fumbled, for the latch, but Rachel put a hand on my arm before I could get the door open. She handed me a white-wrapped package with a shy smile.

"Hang in there. Oh, and happy birthday. Don't open it now, but I hope you like it."

I whispered thanks as I hugged her goodbye, and then made my halting, limping way into the house. I was only in the house for fifteen minutes before I realized being all by myself was a terrible idea.

At some point I transitioned from just crying to having a full-blown panic attack. It should've terrified me that something new was bringing on an episode, but it was like there was so much else going wrong I couldn't spare any more emotional energy.

I came out of the attack and remained on the floor thinking about all of the good times I'd had with Dad and Cindi. The memories should have made me feel better, but they had the opposite effect. I felt the tears start again as I realized all that goodness and joy was gone from my life forever. As my immunity started to wear off, I gratefully surrendered to the next attack, and the blissful relief it represented.

I knew I was on track to drop back into the funk that'd robbed me of the weeks immediately after they died, but I was still strangely numb in the parts that should have cared.

It seemed like I was on my third iteration, but it might have been the fourth or fifth. I was too detached to care. The knock on the door at least brought me back to myself enough to wonder how long I'd been on the floor.

My ankle hurt so bad, it was all I could do to get myself standing and then hobble the fifteen feet to the door.

When I finally managed to get the door open and found empty space where there should have been a person, I almost swore. Then I saw the incredibly beautiful rose on our porch.

I picked it up, trimmed the bottom inch or so off with a knife, and got it into some water acting out of nothing more than pure habit. Dad had always kept at least a pair of rose bushes alive. He'd loved nothing more than giving Mom roses.

Once I'd safely done my part to help prolong the future life of the gorgeous specimen, I got down to really examining it. I was far from an expert on roses, but I'd looked through pictures of hundreds of different kinds of tea roses, and never seen anything quite like this one. It was as big as some of the largest specimens I'd seen, and had at least fifty percent more petals than most of the 'very full' varieties I was familiar with.

That in and of itself was pretty amazing, but nothing in comparison to the petals themselves.

They were the purest white edged in a breathtaking purple. Equally amazing was just how velvety they were. They looked like the softest thing in the world, and cried out to be touched.

I expected to be disappointed as I leaned in. Most of the prettiest roses aren't actually very fragrant. This one proved a surprise. The normal scent I'd come to associate with roses was there, with the slightest hint of something new, something better than anything I'd ever been exposed to.

I leaned in even closer in an attempt to drink in the fragrance, and heard the rustle of expensive paper as I brushed the note that had been attached to the rose with a simple green ribbon. My name was elegantly scrawled along the outside face in a script I'd only seen one other place.

BROKEN

After a moment's hesitation, I unfolded the parchment.

Your birthday should be a time of happiness. I've spent months looking for a name for this flower, and at the point of giving up, inspiration struck today. Lagrimas del Angel always come at too high a cost. Nothing so exquisite could be otherwise. Please don't despair.

The hand-drawn symbol on the bottom of the page was so familiar it almost felt like a part of me now. He'd saved our house, got Mom a job, and then given me the best birthday present I could've asked for.

I felt my insides clench and knot, but this time it was happiness that brought tears to my eyes. My wavering vision was just up to making out the outline of Rachel's present where I'd left it on the table.

Feeling incredibly ungrateful and thoughtless, I limped over to the table and tore open the delicate wrapping paper. It was a copy of the latest Les Misérables movie, complete with the score from the most recent Broadway production, and a signed picture of the entire cast.

Mom still wasn't home by the time it got dark, but I went to bed truly happy for the first time in ages. Rachel was the best friend a girl could wish for, and Brandon had come through in spades.

Chapter 18

I felt my stomach do handsprings as I walked inside the opera house. The week had flown by much faster than expected. Especially considering how slowly each individual day had dragged along. Most of my waking hours had been spent wondering if Saturday night was ever going to arrive.

My train of thought shattered as I got my first glimpse of the interior of what'd become my own personal Mecca. The exterior of the building had been impressive, complete with statues and sculptures reminiscent of an eighteenth-century opera house, but I hadn't expected the illusion to hold once I passed through the enormous, gilded doors.

I'd been wrong. The floors were a gorgeous marble which drew the eyes to the nearest golden-white wall, and up the elaborate gilded trim towards vaulted ceilings. It was like walking into a palace, complete with painted, spun-sugar clouds, and burgundy drapes made out of rich velvet.

If it wasn't for the press of people pushing me from behind, I probably would've stayed in the front entryway right up until the sound of the orchestra filtered down to me. As it was, I only got a few hurried looks before being rushed along with the rest of the students.

Seeing all of my classmates looking utterly bored as they allowed themselves to be herded through the most amazing building I'd ever seen brought me back to my original train of thought.

I hadn't actually spent every waking moment thinking about Les Misérables. A fair number of those seconds had been spent with Brandon. He'd already been picking me up from school every morning and dropping me off most days. We now spent every lunch together, and he'd started lingering when he dropped me off. It was still only on the days when Mom wasn't home, and I hadn't quite mustered the guts to invite him in, but it'd still been really nice.

Of course it'd been the logical kind of thing to have start happening after someone asked you to the Ashure Day Dance. It was still so amazing someone like Brandon had asked me to go to a dance that half the time I forgot all about it. The other half of the time I had a hard time believing it'd really happened. But it had, and there were more than four dozen roses scattered around our kitchen to prove it.

Predictably, Brandon didn't do anything halfway. I'd gone to school on Tuesday after receiving his amazing, 'anonymous' gift the day before, only to be ambushed at lunch. I'd been anxiously waiting for him at his normal table when a pair of employees from the local florist had walked in, their arms overflowing with roses. I'd been expecting them to stop in front of Jasmin. Instead they'd passed her up and then declined to make a beeline to Cassie either. When they'd started handing the flowers to me, I'd tried to convince them there'd been some kind of mistake.

The sound of 'One Day More' playing on the cell phone nestled in the closest bouquet had been what finally convinced me it was all meant for me. Brandon's voice had been like silk caressing my face when I'd answered the phone.

One minute I was minding my own business trying to pretend like I didn't notice the nasty looks some of Brandon's friends were shooting my way when they thought I wasn't looking, the next I was going to the biggest dance of the year with the most popular guy in school. I'd half thought Cassie was going to rip out my throat.

I walked past a pair of gorgeous, gold-fringed drapes, handed my ticket to a distinguished-looking man in a uniform, and then smiled as he pointed me towards my door.

It was almost a relief to be around strangers again. He'd been polite, but hadn't tried to fawn over me. My being asked out had changed my treatment from almost every girl at school. Half the student body, the more sensible portion it seemed, had all decided that I was some kind of massively stuck-up slut. The other half had decided they needed to be my new best friend if they wanted to get invited to any of the cool parties ever again.

It might not have bothered me except the girls who now hated me were the ones I generally would've gotten along with, at least as much as I ever got along with anyone.

My leaving Brandon's insane bouquet of flowers at the office instead of lugging it around all day should have helped. Apparently they all either thought it was a ploy, or were just too stupid to get the message that I didn't want to jump on the popularity bandwagon. Whatever the reason, I'd gotten three invitations to assorted parties or other activities before school ended. I even got another two as I hobbled back from the office with my roses, which had decreased during their stay there by exactly the number of office ladies.

I'd politely declined each invitation, citing my need to catch up in Biology and Spanish, and made it to tutoring without further mishap.

Another usher, this one thankfully no more fawning than the first, pointed me towards my seat, and I felt my second surge of disappointment for the night. My seat was on the main level, but it was only three rows from the very top, and all the way off to one side. I guess it really wasn't that surprising. If the school was paying for the tickets I should just be glad I hadn't been stuck with a standing room only spot.

Still, as disappointing as it was that the performers were only barely going to be visible, it wasn't as bad as the nagging worry that Rachel wasn't coming after all.

We'd spent almost every second together talking about how much fun we were going to have seeing Les Misérables together. She'd even still been excited about the bus ride.

Given everything she'd said, I'd anxiously waited for her to show up at the departure point. It'd seemed impossible, but as Mrs. Alexander had gently herded me onto the bus, there'd still been no sign of her.

"Maybe she's driving instead of taking the bus down. I seem to remember someone saying her brother had purchased a ticket. He isn't here, so possibly they're going down together."

It'd been a fairly slender thread upon which to hang my hopes. Somehow my dream of seeing Les Misérables had morphed into a dream of seeing Les Misérables with Rachel. We still didn't get to spend much time together, but she was rapidly becoming the only person I could confide in besides Brandon. A boyfriend, or near-boyfriend, was nice, but some things just needed to be shared with another female.

I couldn't tell my mom about my feelings for Brandon or she'd absolutely freak. After spending so much time lying to her about the origin of the almost four dozen roses, I couldn't afford any kind of slip in that regard. She'd thought the single rose, Lagrimas del Angel, as I was calling it now, had been sweet and thoughtful, especially when I'd told her it was from an anonymous admirer.

The other roses had been an entirely different matter. I'd had to do some pretty quick talking to convince her I didn't know who they were from either. All of which meant I still hadn't told her I'd been asked to the Ashure Day Dance.

Luckily, Rachel was the perfect listener, even if she did cringe a little every time I mentioned Brandon. All the things I would've told my mom had instead been shared with Rachel. Best of all, there'd been absolutely no hint that she'd blabbed to anyone else.

I settled deeper into my seat, opening my program as the orchestra started warming up. It was amazing to think the near-chaos currently drifting up from the pit would transform itself into the glorious strains of the Overture in just a few minutes.

I was so intent on the program it should've taken a small explosion to bring my head around, but something caused me to look up as

Alec walked past the drapes. He looked even more gorgeous than normal.

I'd gone back and forth, both with myself, and with Rachel, on how much to dress up. Going in normal street clothes would've cheapened the experience, but I hadn't wanted to stick out too much from the rest of the kids, all of whom I'd been pretty sure would be in shorts and polos.

I'd been right, which had made me glad I'd compromised and come in my one and only sun dress. Alec apparently hadn't gotten the memo. He was in an honest-to-goodness full tux. I wasn't the only one stunned by how good he looked; there was a ripple of turned heads as people noticed his entrance.

He paced the short distance down to the back row of seats with such incredible grace that I felt my mouth go dry. No one person should be so attractive, not when there wasn't enough of him to go around to every single woman in the world. For a few seconds I forgot all about the reasons I didn't like him, and just wished he was sitting in front of me instead of two rows behind me where I couldn't see him.

Then I realized what his arrival really meant. Rachel had stood me up. She wasn't on the bus, and she apparently hadn't come with her brother, so she wasn't coming. I knew I should reserve judgment until I'd given her a chance to explain what'd happened, but it was hard to remember that when faced with Alec's air of superiority.

Rachel was nicer, but she was still a Graves. Maybe this was just a sign of things to come.

Apparently I wasn't the only one put off by Alec's snobbishness. A couple of guys who looked like they were old enough to be in college were rolling their eyes at him. They were whispering and laughing, but positioned as they were closer to Alec than to me, I couldn't make out any of what they were saying.

While I agreed completely with their sentiment, they were so loud they were disturbing at least twenty or thirty people. Hopefully they'd quiet down once the actual show started up.

Judging by the orchestra, it was almost time. I looked back, intending to shoot the obnoxious pair a nasty glare in the hopes it would shut them up, and instead caught Alec's eye. The house lights were still bright enough for me to make out every detail of his perfect face, and yet I was still baffled by his expression. He'd obviously been staring at me, was still staring at me actually, but it wasn't a leer. It was something else, it made me want to blush, or maybe smile and toss my hair. Whatever it was, it left my skin feeling warmer than usual, and more than a little tight.

Even after I looked away with a flush of embarrassment, I still felt like I could feel his eyes watching me. I could feel his presence behind and to the left of me, like a gentle tingle of electricity I could've pointed to even with my eyes closed.

I resisted the urge to look back again as the lights dimmed and the orchestra began the opening strains of the first number.

The actor playing Jean Valjean strode out onto the stage, and even weighed down by chains, he still commanded everyone's attention as though he was a member of the nobility. Each successive character somehow managed to latch onto my heart as they arrived.

Despite the nagging sensation that I could feel Alec behind me, the first few minutes of the play exceeded all my hopes. That all changed when they started 'Lovely Ladies'.

It was my absolute least favorite song on the whole soundtrack. Frankly the whole play would've been better if they'd just left it off. Still, sitting through a song about 'ladies of the night' as my mom still called them, had seemed like a small price to pay for getting to listen to the rest of the play.

By the middle of the song both of the oversexed boys behind me were whispering catcalls.

I felt my ears going red. I wanted nothing more than to sink down into my seat and try to ignore them, but once guys got started on something like that, they never stopped. Some of the people around me were starting to evidence signs of annoyance, but that just spurred the hecklers on to greater heights.

I was so worried they were going to ruin everyone's experience, that I turned around and shot them a dirty look.

"Oh, sweetie, don't you worry, we've been aching to get our hands on you all night. We're saving plenty of loving for you later. Meet us out back after this crap is over and we'll give you a real show."

My mouth dropped open in shock. Nothing was going to get them to shut up now, not when they had such a perfect target. Sitting there staring at them was about the worst of all the choices open to me, but I was too shocked to pull my eyes away.

I felt a surge of heat rush through me as the room wavered slightly. For a second I worried I was going to pass out, but movement behind the two punks distracted me from my heaving internal landscape.

There was just enough light for me to see Alec lean forward and put a hand on each troublemaker's shoulder. There was an abortive movement by the two loudmouths, as they tried to spin around and confront him. Granted, the lighting was less than ideal, but it didn't look like Alec was holding onto them very hard. Still, neither of them made it more than a quarter of the way around before being slammed back down into their chairs.

The tingly heat that'd convinced me Alec was staring at me earlier was back, and even more intense. I felt the tiny hairs on my neck stand up as the feeling redoubled yet again. The darker, more vocal of the two opened his mouth and got the first part of a swear word out before ending in a hiss of pain that was almost completely drowned out by a crescendo from the orchestra pit.

Alec leaned forward, whispered something in each of their ears, and then finally let both of them go. I expected them to turn around swinging, or at least swear at him. I didn't expect them to remain in their seats stunned and shaking like trauma victims.

An usher finally arrived to see what all of the commotion was about. The older boys shook themselves and then looked for a second like they were going to try and get Alec kicked out of the theater.

The sense of being caught in some kind of electric sandstorm momentarily intensified, and then faded away as they got up and left.

I felt my mouth drop open again as they scurried out of the theater without once looking back. Alec, who I'd always figured had the depth of an old-style Mickey Mouse cartoon, had just faced down two older boys, and singlehandedly saved my Les Misérables experience.

Valjean launched into 'Who am I?', and almost against my will I was pulled back around to where I could see the stage. Even as enthralled as I was by the music, I made a mental note to thank Alec after the performance. For once I wasn't going to try and get the best of him verbally, I was just going to walk up and thank him.

The sense of being able to feel Alec behind me didn't diminish during the course of the play, if anything it gradually increased almost to the levels it'd been during the face-off with the college boys. Now though, it felt more reassuring than threatening.

The rest of Les Misérables was even better than I'd hoped. Minutes and seconds went by faster than at any other time in my life. As the curtain finally came down, I brushed away the traces of tears that'd appeared on my face during the performance, and turned in my seat as the lights came up.

Alec was gone. The drapes were swaying gently as if they'd been brushed by someone moving quickly, but other than that there was no trace of him.

It wasn't until I'd filed out into the grand foyer, eager to spend a few minutes taking in the gorgeous bronze statues liberally scattered throughout the room, that I realized why I felt so odd. Part of the difference was the normal sensation of having vicariously been part of something larger than life. My head knew all I'd done was sit motionless while performers portrayed a fictional story. The rest of me felt as though I had just risked life and limb, seen people I loved killed, and played a small but tangible part in altering the course of history.

Returning to my mundane, ever so boring life was an incredible letdown, but that didn't explain the hollow sensation that'd lodged itself somewhere between my heart and stomach. Illogical as it sounded, the only explanation for feeling as though a part of me had been ripped out and lost was Alec's having disappeared sometime between the last note and the final bow.

It was unsettling. Even my growing feelings for Brandon didn't hint at that kind of need. It was a pale shadow of what it felt like to lose a family member, but it was made up of too many of the same elements.

One of the chaperons, an over-bleached woman who looked like she was struggling to deny her last eight or nine birthdays, had to call my name at least twice to shake me out of my funk.

I followed everyone else out to the bus, but there wasn't any refuge there. I was just too different from everyone else.

Hour after hour passed in silent misery, until finally the rest of the kids wore themselves out and it quieted down enough for me to lapse into a fitful sleep. I was smack-dab in the middle of a dream about Rachel and Britney when everything changed.

BROKEN

Ever so slowly, the normal dreamscape took on a sharp-edged glow, and then morphed into the breathtaking colors that'd wormed their way even deeper into my heart than I'd realized. I didn't recognize my surroundings, but they were different than any of the places I'd been before. The new scents whipping past me on the breeze were sign enough even if I hadn't been able to detect the subtle differences in the light emanating off of the foliage paving the trail I was walking along.

For the length of the dream I lost myself in the wonder of experiencing the world in all of its amazing depth. Still, even the pure delight in my surroundings wasn't enough to mute the feeling something was missing.

Chapter 19

It seemed like the old karmic scale was still going strong and trying very hard to make up for how great Les Misérables had been. We finally arrived in town after way too many hours of driving and then I had to wait for Mom to come pick me up.

The last chaperon had been about five minutes from throwing in the towel and just taking me home herself by the time Mom finally pulled into the school parking lot. Mom hadn't even apologized. She'd mumbled something about needing to hit one of her 'close' sites while the moon was still high in the sky as she dropped me off at home and then drove off without looking back.

I'd just managed to drop off into a fitful sleep when she came back home and ruined any chance of me catching up on the sleep I'd missed because of the trip. I'd never been able to go back to sleep after being woken up in the morning, but I tried anyways. By the time I finally gave up and got out of bed I was not a happy camper.

I was even less so by the time Mom finally woke up. Rachel not having been at Les Misérables had been preying on my mind the whole time I'd been studying, and since Brandon wouldn't work for girl talk, I needed to hash it all out with my mom.

Only she was so far gone, getting anything out of her was all but impossible. She interrupted partway through my description of what'd happened to ask if I'd noticed when the light outside my bedroom had stopped working. As if I cared when some stupid bulb burned out.

I tried for another fifteen minutes, but once her mind started focusing on a new project, anything less than the domestic version of a tactical nuke had effectively zero chance of catching her attention.

Apparently someone decided that having my mom completely ignore me in my moment of need was going a little too far on the divine retribution. In an effort to try and balance things out the dream angels granted me another vivid dream on Sunday night. It was wonderful. I got to swim around in the most glorious pond known to man. I was somehow faster than normal, and spent what seemed like hours chasing around slivers of light that turned out to be some kind of long, thin fish.

For perhaps the first time in my entire life I didn't mind at all that I'd ended up in a swimsuit so small I might as well have been wearing nothing at all. In fact, the feel of the warm water sliding past my skin was so incredible I almost considered skinny dipping. Of course that'd only lasted for about a nanosecond. Even in a dream, there were things that were just too scary to really entertain.

The dream lasted longer than any of the others before it, but even so it eventually lapsed into a normal, boring dream. Still, I woke up feeling more refreshed and rested than any other time I could remember.

Even more amazing, the feeling was strong enough to carry me through Biology and Mrs. Sorenson's relentless grilling. I did better than expected, but still not as well as I'd hoped. Not considering how much time I'd spent studying. It was like she knew exactly which parts I didn't understand completely, and after letting me start to get a little bit of false confidence, she'd hammer me down again.

Talk about depressing. Still, I was feeling well-prepared for my English test tomorrow and Algebra flew by. By my latest calculations I was only about two weeks from being all caught up.

Lunch was interesting. I was still the odd man out, but it was amusing watching Vincent preen. I never did figure out what it was he'd done, but apparently it had him thinking he was even more of a stud than normal. Whatever it was, it had Brandon pissed, which was a refreshing change. If he had to be friends with some of these people out of responsibility, that was one thing, but letting them continue to be jerks was taking it too far.

Nobody was more surprised than me when Brandon pushed back from the table, scanned the room, and then pulled me to my feet. We spent the rest of lunch pacing around the outside of the school while he worked through whatever was bothering him. When the warning bell finally rang, he turned and looked at me with a considering smile. We stood like that for a good thirty seconds before he reached a single finger up and traced the left side of my face as he leaned in slightly.

It was simultaneously the scariest and most exciting thing I'd ever experienced. Even as I leaned in a little bit myself, my thundering heart seemed to be trying to leap out of my throat solely for the purpose of disrupting what looked very much like it was going to be my first kiss.

Every tiny hair on my body stood up in a shiver of nervousness as he tilted his head to the side, and then he broke off, shaking himself slightly as he gave me a smile.

For a second I thought he was rejecting me, that he'd decided not to kiss me because he wasn't interested. Only the way he reached out for my hand indicated that he really wasn't repulsed by me. It bothered me the entire time I was in History, and then just before I got to Physics it hit me.

He hadn't stopped because he didn't want to kiss me. He stopped because with all of my blushing and near-terror it'd been obvious I wasn't ready to be kissed. It was the ultimate act of chivalry. I more or less floated through my last two classes.

It wasn't until I finally got to tutoring that I started to put more stock in the idea that Rachel had simply chosen not to go to Les Misérables. She looked up, and then away guiltily as I walked in. There wasn't a trace of smile or greeting on her face, an abnormality that hit me hard somewhere in the region of my stomach.

Albert stopped by to say hi, and I used his presence as a distraction.

"It sounds like you're almost caught up."

"Yeah, finally. I've got another two weeks or so, but then I'll be all done with this whole triple math homework garbage."

Albert smiled, and for the first time I noticed how genuine his expressions were. It was almost like he was a different person when he wasn't concentrating on explaining some particularly stubborn math problem to one of the slower students. You know, the ones who still didn't understand why anyone needed to know their multiplication tables.

"And here I had such high hopes for you becoming a true math geek. Granted, you've shown pretty mediocre progress so far. I don't think I've once seen you skip a meal just so you could graph out some new function. Also you've evidenced no inclination to check out old textbooks from the library in an effort to edge out your competition at the next math bowl. Still, I had hoped. I mean being a tutor and all, it seemed like a given."

I stuck out my tongue. "Please, like you really do any of those things. I in fact happen to know that you're in a band that performs occasionally down in Vegas, so don't go trying to pull a fast one on me."

Albert looked genuinely startled, but recovered quickly.

"Hey there, idle, profoundly-untrue comments dropped by Mrs. Campbell in passing conversation don't count. I'm absolutely not a member of Fatal Angst."

"Yes, you are, at least you are until I either decide to dispose of your body, or let your little secret out of the bag because you're not doing your job."

I hadn't heard Mrs. Campbell approach from behind me, and for a second worried she was really angry, but the way Albert chuckled as he cringed in mock fear alleviated my concerns.

Albert pushed his glasses a little ways back up his nose, and then wandered off to help the next person with a red card face up on their desk.

The number of people who proceeded to come into the tutoring lab was nothing less than amazing. Based on overheard conversations, it sounded like there was a perfect storm of tests. Both of the other math teachers were apparently having tests in every single one of their classes, and Mrs. Campbell was having tests in a couple of hers as well.

The resulting number of questions kept us all jumping. I started work half an hour early, and Albert, Peter and Mrs. Campbell all stayed an extra forty-five minutes.

I was helping out an undersized freshman who was having a really hard time understanding the fundamental concepts of the unit she was going to be tested over tomorrow when Mrs. Campbell stopped by. "We're all done. Wait until the end of your normal shift, and then go home. If anyone complains feel free to suggest that they don't leave it until the last minute next time."

There was plenty of grumbling when I announced that the lab was over, but nobody actually said anything. Rachel was waiting for me at the door as everyone else filed out. She looked up guiltily as I made my way over to her.

"Did you have a good day? I haven't seen that many people here ever."

If there was one thing that'd always pissed me off, it was people who refused to own up to their mistakes. In my mind not being where you said you were going to be, especially after being so jazzed about it previously, fit into that category. Rachel wasn't making a good start.

"Why don't we cut to the chase, Rachel? You didn't go to Les Misérables. We spent more than a week planning what we were going to do on the way up and the way back, and you didn't bother to show up."

Rachel's mouth opened and closed a few times. She looked around, but we weren't the only two people in the room. James was barely visible pacing up and down the far end of the hall, so there wasn't any help there either.

"I'm sorry, I really wanted to go. More than anything, but I couldn't."

"That's it? You aren't going to give any kind of real reason? I guess I should at least be glad you aren't going to lie to me. Unless you really didn't ever want to go, and were lying to me all along."

Rachel shrank in on herself a little. It almost looked like she was going to cry, which should have made me feel bad, but I was too mad to care. I'd been miserable the whole way there, and especially the whole way back, and then she wanted to just pretend like none of it had happened.

Rachel's lip trembled slightly as she finally managed to get a response out. "This isn't like you. Why are you doing this?"

Cindi used to do the exact same thing. Her 'woe is me, I don't understand what is happening act' had usually worked with Dad, and it'd always infuriated me. It had much the same effect now.

"This isn't like me? To stand up for myself when I find out who my real friends are? Please, you don't even know me, and apparently I don't know you."

Rachel shook her head in denial. "No, this isn't you. Is Brandon putting you up to this? He isn't what you think, you really shouldn't trust him."

Now she'd gone too far.

"Brandon didn't put me up to anything. Unlike you, I can actually think for myself. I don't know what kind of sick hold Alec has over you, but until you do something about it, you'll never have any real friends. He won't ever let you have one."

She wiped away a pair of tears before they could escape from the corner of her eyes. "You don't know what you're talking about, Adri. You really can't trust Brandon. He's not safe."

"Whatever. Like your brother is any better."

I turned and went out through the exterior door. I was all the way out to the parking lot before I realized that I didn't have a way home. I was still trying to figure out what to do, when I heard the deep roar of a high-performance engine.

Brandon was clear over at the other end of the parking lot, but somehow he saw me and flipped his car around.

"You're looking just a little stranded."

"That obvious?"

His smile was just as radiant and reassuring as always. "Only to someone who happens to know your entire schedule, and who just saw what looked like Rachel and James leave without you."

It was my turn to try and hide a trembling lip as I responded. "Rachel and I had a fight."

Brandon turned his stereo down and motioned me around to the passenger seat. "You okay?"

I managed a smile. "Yeah, I'll be okay. It was just a really bad fight. I've never said those kinds of things to anyone. I don't think there's any going back. She has to hate me."

Brandon shook his head and flashed another of his winning smiles, albeit one with an overtone of sympathy. "I'm sure it isn't as bad as that."

I wanted to disagree, to go into detail about why my life had just taken a turn for the worse, but something about his manner was suddenly distant. I thought about calling him out on it, but with my life suddenly looking like I was all but friendless, that didn't seem like such a good idea. Without really meaning to I'd managed to alienate just about everyone at school.

Brandon already had plenty of reasons not to be with me, it was the height of stupidity to give him any more. I could probably deal with not having a boyfriend, even assuming that was what we were right now. Going half a year without anyone to talk to because my mom was wrapped up with her art and everyone else in the town thought I was stuck-up would be more than I could take.

The thought was enough to leave me speechless for the entire drive home. Brandon seemed content to leave me alone with my thoughts as he sped around the various turns at speeds that normally would've made me protest.

As I went to leave the car, he grabbed me by my back pocket, which nearly made me shriek in surprise. "Hey, you know what you need to put all this in perspective?"

"No, but then I think it's more than just a matter of my perspective being off." My fear of alienating him had almost vanished in the rush of indignation over how he'd grabbed me. I wanted to say something even more snarky, but there was just enough worry left to curb my tongue. Mostly.

"You need to come to the party Friday night."

"You mean the monthly kegger?"

Brandon shook his head, still flashing the grin that made it almost impossible to remain mad at him. "No, the monthly full moon 'kegger' happened last weekend. This is just a party to blow off some steam. We have them sometimes to celebrate things."

"Like what?"

Brandon shook his head as he pulled me back down into my seat. "Nope, if you want to find out, you'll have to come to it with me."

"You know, I don't usually leave conversations midway through. You really can let go of me."

"Maybe, but I'm enjoying holding onto you."

I forcefully removed his hand as I shook my head. "Boys. You're all the same. Okay. Assuming my mom takes off for the night, I'll go, but only on the condition that you behave."

I managed to make it to the door without my knees knocking together, but it was a close thing. I'd been scared sick when he'd been about to kiss me, but it had at least been something I'd been dreaming about off and on for years. I wasn't sure I was ready for the other things he was starting to imply.

Chapter 20

There were a couple of times between Monday and the end of the week where I didn't think I was going to survive having to worry about whether or not I'd be able to sneak out to Brandon's party. My dreams had taken a decidedly odd turn. I'd had the lucid, vivid dreams every single night, but my guilty conscience seemed to be working overtime. At least that was all I could assume. I woke up flustered, with vague memories of Alec. My best guess was that I was trying to defend myself after having argued with his little sister. If I was going to waste my time in the vivid dreams, it would've made more sense to spend them trying to explain my side of what'd happened to Rachel, but apparently I wasn't normal enough for that.

I'd been all set to swallow my pride and thank Alec for shutting up the two kids sitting behind me. Only that'd been before the ride home all by myself on the bus while he sped home in his little luxury car. Maybe I'd still have apologized to him if he'd been in school on Monday. Instead, he'd skipped the entire first half of the week, and by the time I did finally see him, I'd backed myself so far into a corner, I couldn't even meet his eyes during class.

Somehow I'd managed to make it through day after day of isolation. Brandon's friends continued to more or less ignore me, the boys without the trace of spite that I picked up from most of the girls. Britney started another rumor sometime about the middle of the week. Apparently I was now some kind of closet drug addict who was hoping to get Brandon to fund my habit.

Rachel hadn't been back to tutoring since we'd argued, and I was picking up an increasing number of hostile looks from people I didn't even know. Some of them were recognizable as Alec's friends, but most of them were just nameless nerds who apparently had a soft spot for Rachel, or a towering hatred for Brandon's friends.

"Adriana Paige. Have you heard a word I was saying?"

I looked up and blinked a couple of times. "Sorry Mom, I was thinking about school."

"I swear, you've become more absentminded lately than ever before. As much time as you spend studying and thinking about your classes,

I'm surprised they haven't decided to graduate you a year early."

I shrugged uncomfortably. Since Mom hadn't been interested in the things I could safely tell her without getting grounded, school had become a standard excuse for why I was so distracted.

"Speaking of which, when do they send out mid-term reports?"

"I think they do them twice here. We missed the first batch, and the second isn't until later." I still didn't particularly like lying, but seemed to be doing it more and more often.

"Anyways, I was just apologizing for leaving you home alone on a weekend again. I ran into another trio of hikers, and they told me about a new vantage point for that crooked-looking mountain I keep telling you about. It's on the far side, so I'm going to hike as far in as I can while it's still light today so I can make it there tomorrow with plenty of time before sunset. I don't want to make the hike again, so I'll probably spend all of Sunday shooting, and then hike back on Monday."

Mom paused in her preparations to put her hand on my forehead. "You're not coming down with anything, are you? You've been so listless lately. Do you need me to stay home with you?"

There it was, the perfect opportunity to get her to stay home with me. It would get me out of having to spend time with Brandon's increasingly annoying friends, which was what I currently wanted more than almost anything else in the world.

Unfortunately I wanted to spend time with Brandon even more than I wanted to avoid his friends, so there wasn't really a choice.

"I'm fine, Mom. Just feeling a little run down. I'll spend the whole weekend lying around reading and studying. That should fix me right up."

I gave Mom a wan smile, exactly the kind I used when I was really sick, and helped her finish packing. I wasn't sure whether I helped because I was feeling guilty, or because I was worried Brandon would show up before she'd left. Maybe I was just hoping to kill two birds with one stone.

It wasn't until she was finally in the Jeep and backing down our lane that I finally stopped worrying that Brandon was going to pop around the corner. He'd been smugly confident he wouldn't show up before she was gone, but had refused to tell me how he planned on pulling up at my house five minutes after the coast was clear.

Half of me was strongly tempted to dawdle for fifteen or twenty minutes, but with my luck he'd really manage to show up within the next few minutes, and I'd have to scramble to get ready while he waited for me.

With a sigh I ran up to the bathroom, brushed my teeth, gave my hair the once-over, and grabbed a light jacket as I left my room. It wasn't even remotely as cold here as I would be at home by this late in the year, but the oppressive heat had finally started to wane a little. Knowing my luck, if I left it home tonight would be the first time it snowed in Sanctuary in the last two centuries.

More and more excited about the prospect of going to my first real party, I bounced down the stairs and into the kitchen for a drink. I happened to look out the window as I pulled a glass out of the cupboard, and nearly dropped it when I saw Brandon leaning against his car, patiently waiting for me. Before I could move out of sight, he looked up at me with a self-satisfied smile. I nearly dropped the glass again.

Twenty seconds later I was headed out the door. "How did you do that? There was no way you could possibly have timed things that close."

Another smirk as he held my door open for me. "I told you. Great instincts resulting from superior breeding."

"Fine, don't tell me. I didn't really want to know anyway."

Brandon chuckled as he threw the Mustang into reverse and sped out of the lane faster than normal. The stereo clicked over to another song as we flipped around and headed back into town. It was more of the thrumming beats I'd come to associate with Brandon.

"I thought this place was in one of the parks or something. Why are we headed back to town?"

"Wow, you really are a city girl. In order to get far enough not to be busted by the cops we have to go really remote. There isn't any way my car would make it where we need to go. We're headed to Vincent's to hitch a ride in his truck."

'Truck' turned out to be an understatement. I'd marveled more than once since getting to Utah, at just how big some of the pickup trucks I saw driving around were. It seemed like nobody was willing to drive anything around the way it came off of the showroom floor. Everything had bigger wheels, and suspension that lifted it up several inches.

Vincent's truck had more in common with the beasts in monster truck rallies than it did with the souped-up vehicles I'd seen driving around town. The tires were the biggest I'd seen on anything outside of a tractor, and the lift kit on it was so outrageously tall that I was pretty sure someone was going to have to lift me into the cab. By myself it was going to take a rope and climbing shoes. Of course it was black. I couldn't imagine Vincent in anything other than a black vehicle.

Predictably, Vincent was rubbing down his vehicle, but the exercise seemed more targeted to giving him a chance to walk around with his shirt off than it did with cleaning up the already immaculate truck. Based on the way the cheerleader types by the garage were watching him, it was working.

I much preferred Brandon's jeans and tee shirt, tight as it was, over the shorts and shirtless look, but apparently I was in the minority.

I almost hyperventilated when Vincent casually walked out of the house with a pair of beer kegs and tied them down in the bed of his pickup. His house was more on the fringes of town, but it was still in town. What if his parents came home and saw them? For that matter, where had he been hiding them? It wasn't even remotely possible that all of the people who were going to be at the party were old enough to drink without getting arrested.

Brandon looked at my white knuckles and laughed. "Don't worry, nobody's going to make you drink, and we've never been busted by the cops. We'll have you safely back home sometime early tomorrow morning, and your mom will never have the slightest idea you went to such a wild gathering."

As far as reassurance went, it was a pretty lame attempt, but somehow it didn't sound so feeble when it was Brandon saying it. I calmed down enough to marvel at the amount of other baggage Vincent dragged out of the house, and then any chance I might have had to back out vanished as Brandon picked me up and deposited me on the tailgate of Vincent's truck.

"Riding in the back, isn't that illegal?"

The high-maintenance blonde Vincent was helping up next to me rolled her eyes. "Please."

Brandon helped a couple of late arrivals into the pickup, and then closed the tailgate. I half thought he was going to ride up front in the crowded cab, but he instead cleared the sides of the truck in a jump that was almost inhumanly graceful. He crowded in, close enough I could feel my skin start to tingle with anticipation, and then Vincent started the engine and we were off.

In what was probably the only display of maturity and common sense I'd ever seen out of Vincent, he didn't tear off down the freeway at eighty miles per hour. He was still going plenty fast, but at least the wind wasn't deafening. After a few minutes of white-knuckled fear, I was finally able to relax a little, and enjoy the feeling of having Brandon so close while the wind tossed my hair back and forth.

The other girls were studiously ignoring me while they gossiped back and forth about everyone from underclassmen to teachers and other adults in the town. I didn't want to join in the gossip, and Brandon was sprawled out on the pickup bed with his eyes closed. I settled for contemplating the glorious sunset's myriad colors.

We passed some kind of border into one of the parks. Vincent slowed down a little more as I was busy taking in the incredible pinks and purples that were dominating the western sky. It was like someone had splashed glowing paint across a window and then gone back and painted in picture-perfect clouds to complete the scene.

I'd seen plenty of amazing sunsets back home, but there was something about the rugged, almost hostile, skyline here that gave this one a spectacular level of depth. Maybe Mom was right about the west after all. Sure, it was hotter than Satan's kitchen, and a dermatologist's worst nightmare, but the skylines were amazing.

Brandon opened his eyes as I let out a sigh of contentment. "Bored already? We're only halfway there."

As I opened my mouth to respond, Vincent turned off the road onto a trail that hardly looked wide enough for a Geo Metro let alone his monster truck.

I let out a yelp as we dropped down a small hill and then started climbing up the other side of the gully with a small bounce. Brandon chuckled at me, but shifted position enough to brace himself against the two beer kegs, and then reached out and wrapped an arm around me. A couple of the girls who'd been looking especially condescending over my surprise as we'd gone off-road were now obviously disappointed. They were probably wishing it was them instead of me cradled against Brandon's yummy chest. I tried not to radiate too much contentment, but rather suspected I failed.

Vincent wasn't really driving any faster than before, but the fact that we were going up and down slopes I wouldn't have thought could be driven made his current speed reckless. Even with Brandon's arm stopping me from flying out of the pickup, I still had a couple of moments where my heart shot up to the top of my throat. He of course remained frustratingly calm, even when we hit a bump with enough force to nearly send everyone flying out of the bed. The other girls were trying hard to appear nonplussed. They were probably even fooling the boys, but they weren't enjoying themselves.

I was nearly sick by the time the track we were following leveled out, but there was just enough light left for me to enjoy the last of the sunset as we finished up the last ten minutes of the drive. As the final glimmers of color faded away into twilight, Vincent pulled his truck over in a spray of dust, and we were there.

I'd been expecting a lot of people. Even I knew you couldn't finish off two kegs of beer with eight or nine people, but this was crazy. There were already at least thirty people here, and based on the clouds of dust I could now see coming from where we'd just been, there were more people still on their way.

Brandon nimbly jumped out of the truck bed, and then helped me down to the ground as

Vincent came back and manhandled one of the kegs to the edge of the tailgate and tapped it. My first kegger had just officially started.

Cassie showed up in a white pickup a few minutes after the beer started flowing, and popped the panel covering the bed, revealing an astounding row of speakers that promptly started spewing an aggressive mix of drums, guitars and synthesized notes that made Brandon's usual mixes sound like Christmas carols.

In short order there was a roaring fire going, despite the fact it wasn't really cold yet, and people started congregating in groups to talk or dance depending on their preference. Brandon seemed to be one of the former. Dragging along behind him as he slowly worked his way through a third of the school was extremely boring. I honestly couldn't think of a less entertaining way to spend an evening, but I wasn't ready to join the dancers. Most of them seemed to be rapidly losing key items of clothing, and all of them were dancing so close it was hard to tell where one person ended and the other began.

As Brandon handed me another cup of beer, which I started slowly pouring out on the ground as soon as his back was turned, the loneliness really started to hit me.

It would be bearable if I had a friend other than Brandon. It might even be fun to sit back and laugh at some of the antics making an appearance as people got more and more wasted. Instead I was stone cold sober, and the next best thing to completely friendless.

About the time Vincent tapped the second keg, Brandon looked over at me and flashed a thoughtful smile. I would've said nothing could've made up for the last two hours, but it came remarkably close.

"I'm sorry, this isn't any fun for you, is it?"

My listless shrug earned me a chuckle. "Well then, let's change stuff up a little. Care to dance?"

I almost said no, but as he pulled me in towards him, I suddenly realized just how badly I wanted to touch his incredibly hard chest and shoulders. Being wrapped in his arms was so pleasant that I didn't even protest when he pulled me in closer.

My whole body tingled where it touched him, and his cologne, so faint as to be almost imperceptible, was like nothing I'd ever smelled. Almost against my will I found myself pressing up against him so I could drink in the scent.

The music was still way too loud, everyone around us was still ridiculously drunk, but suddenly I couldn't care less.

Someone tried to come up and talk to Brandon as the next song started, but he waved them off, not even pulling his eyes away from mine. I'd thought my heart couldn't race any faster than it already was, but when he started moving his face down closer to mine, it felt like it was going to tear itself free from my chest.

It was happening. I'd fantasized about kissing even back when I thought boys had cooties. I wasn't sure I was any more ready than I'd been out in the parking lot, but I could tell by the way he was moving that he wasn't going to abort this time.

The tingling was even more intense now as I brought my hand up and cupped the side of his face, and then our lips met. It wasn't like I'd imagined. His lips were warm, and they had the slightest hint of softness, but there was more urgency and fierceness to the kiss than expected.

It wasn't as amazing as I'd fantasized, but I was still having a hard time thinking. I tried to pull back and catch my breath, but his arms had become steel cables that pulled me in tighter.

Fear finally overcoming my desire not to look stupid. I started to push away from Brandon. My efforts seemed futile for several seconds, and then his right arm released me. He wasn't letting me go though, his right hand had just repositioned to my stomach while his left arm kept me pinned against him almost as tightly as both hands had just a second before.

It should have been obvious what he had in mind, but it wasn't until his hand was under my shirt and moving upwards that my overloaded mind caught up with events. I tried to protest, tried harder to push myself away from him, but he just held onto me tighter than even before.

His hand was just millimeters away from its target, and I was starting to see stars from lack of air, before I finally remembered some of the tricks my dad had shown me.

I slammed my heel down on his left foot, and then brought my knee upwards towards his crotch, only to hit nothing but air as he spun me around.

"What the crap are you doing?" He wasn't even limping. He seemed more surprised than angry.

"What was I doing? Maybe trying to convince you to keep your hands to yourself, you think?"

As soon as the words came out I started wishing I hadn't said them. This was *Brandon.* Guys like him didn't just drop out of the sky and decide they were interested in chubby little nerds like me.

Brandon's expression hardened, and I suddenly knew there was no going back. Maybe it would've been worth it to let him grope me a little, but done was done.

People were starting to gather around us, Brandon's closest friends, the ones he ate lunch with every day, were all standing behind him, while everyone else filled out the circle.

I looked around for some kind of support from the other girls present, but couldn't find even one sympathetic face. The next thing I knew I was on the ground with my ears ringing and Cassie standing over me.

"...your stupid lies. If you repeat them you'll be sorry. Every single person here will vouch for Brandon."

A couple of people flinched a little at that, like they weren't completely comfortable lying, but Cassie stared them down. Nobody would meet my gaze.

I opened my mouth to protest, and Cassie grabbed me by the front of my jacket and dragged me the better part of twenty feet. My head was still spinning as she leaned down and hissed into my ear.

"Get out of here. Don't wait around, don't ask anyone for a ride. You had your chance and you blew it. He's mine again, and if you're not out of sight in the next five minutes I'll kill you myself and end this stupid experiment once and for all."

I'd only heard that kind of blatant willingness to kill once before, and just like with Jasmin, I was absolutely convinced Cassie was serious. I wanted to get up, to do something other than just lie shaking on the rocks, but my mind was like an appliance with stripped gears. It was spinning but not grabbing onto anything, so nothing was happening.

Cassie picked me up with one hand and gave me a hard shove back towards the road. I almost fell. Considering just how rugged the terrain was, it was a good thing I didn't, because I probably would've broken my neck. It was still a near thing, but once I was moving reflex kept me headed in the right direction.

Tears were flowing freely down my cheeks, and my heart seemed to be missing every second beat, almost like a hole had been torn in it and now it was a battle to continue beating, when it just wanted to quit.

I did fall down when I hit the first slope. There was just enough moonlight to confirm that the pain in my hands and elbow was the result of having all of the skin abraded away. I thought I was going to pass out, or maybe throw up, but I couldn't cry any harder than I already was.

Part of me kept expecting Brandon to come running towards me from the direction of the party. He'd apologize, and explain how he'd wanted to stop Cassie, but he'd been too stunned by what she was doing.

Even the delusional part of my brain that was trying to come up with a way to be rescued couldn't create a plausible scenario from there on. The look he'd given me at the end hadn't been that kind of shocked gaze.

Cassie's threat was too vivid. Instead of curling up on the ground where I'd fallen, I pulled myself back up and continued to stumble along in the direction I thought would eventually get me back to the road.

The washed-out landscape mocked me as I realized just how alone I was. Rachel didn't like me anymore, she'd never forgive me. I'd managed to alienate everyone from Alec's group, and now Brandon had tossed me aside like so much trash.

It was too much. I collapsed onto all fours, hardly noticing the burning pain from my damaged palms, and let the racking sobs take over.

I probably would've stayed there all night if not for the howling. It'd been going for several seconds before it pulled me back from the mental abyss I'd been so eagerly approaching.

I looked around blankly for several more heartbeats before I finally managed to place the noise. Wolves. There weren't supposed to be any wolves in the area, but there wasn't any ignoring my ears.

I numbly pulled myself back up, and began stumbling back towards the party, only to stop as another howl echoed down through the canyon.

It was between me and everyone else. I turned and started into a shuffling run. Maybe the wolf would be attracted to the noise and light. Maybe I'd be able to get far enough away it wouldn't smell me.

I'd only been moving for about a minute before another howl sent chills running down my spine. It sounded like a different wolf, and it was closer than the first one. I tried to run faster, but all that time studiously avoiding exercise was working against me. I topped a slight rise and then tripped as the ground wasn't where I expected it to be.

BROKEN

My jacket saved me from picking up any really serious scrapes this time, but just before I finished tumbling to a stop I slammed my head into a crescent-shaped rock. My vision swam in and out of focus, but I struggled to my feet, only to nearly fall again as my right ankle all but collapsed under me.

They were definitely closer now. They'd stopped howling, but I could still hear them.

I somehow found myself on my back again, looking up at the biggest wolf I'd ever seen. TV had given me the impression that a wolf shouldn't be much bigger than a German Shepherd. These guys were roughly the size of a small pony, one nearly black, the other more of a gray color, both with yellowish eyes, and lips pulled back to show teeth the size of my fingers.

Most of my jeans had been torn away from my right calf, which was bleeding fairly profusely, but I didn't feel any pain. It was like my mind had finally torn loose from the moorings that usually held it in contact with reality. I was going to die, ripped to shreds by the same impossible animals that had killed the hikers a few months ago, but I just couldn't bring myself to care.

Nobody would even miss me.

The black wolf was inching towards me now, growling low in its throat. I could see its haunches tense up, and then it was airborne, hurtling towards me almost faster than I could follow.

Only it didn't hit me. A patch of night had interposed itself between me and the wolf. My vision still wasn't up to making out fine details, and everything was moving too quickly to follow. The growling seemed to be in three parts now, which didn't make any sense because the patch of night was vaguely man-shaped, if impossibly big.

There was a yelp as one of the wolves was tossed into the side of the canyon with enough force that I could feel it from where I was lying. A shower of sparks lit up the night as the second wolf dodged away from my defender, and then impossibly the first wolf was back and darting in as I heard jaws snap shut on something.

The black shadow staggered back, nearly falling under the combined weight of its two opponents. A second later another yelp was cut short as one of the wolves fell away to lie motionless on the ground.

My head was throbbing so bad I blacked out for a moment, and missed the end of the fight. When I opened my eyes back up, the indistinct shadow was moving smoothly towards me. I opened my mouth to thank him, and then felt as though my world had been pulled out from underneath me.

The shadow went from my savior to a nightmarish being. It was easily eight feet tall, covered in thick fur, and had bloody claws as long as my hands tipping the ends of its fingers.

BROKEN

My vision was still swimming enough that I almost couldn't believe what I was seeing. Even so, there was no way to ignore the bloodstained mouth as it got closer. I had a moment to realize I was still going to die all alone, and then the blackness came for me.

Chapter 21

I woke up expecting to see pale blue eyes burning a hole through me. Haunting eyes set above terrible fangs. Instead I found myself lying atop a gigantic bed in a room I didn't recognize.

The sheer shock at still being alive prevented my mind from working very well. It took several minutes before all of the other relatively inconsequential details started filtering in. My hands were bandaged, as was my elbow and right calf. My dirty, ripped jeans and shirt had been replaced with clean clothes that were only a little too small.

That last fact should have alarmed me more than it did. Somehow being stripped down by a stranger paled in comparison to a near-death hallucination involving wolves and a monster straight out of a science fiction movie.

The bedroom was possibly the nicest room I'd ever been in. A movie star or millionaire would have had a hard time topping this place for sheer decadence. The walls were paneled in some kind of rare, doubtless expensive imported hardwood.

The bookcases that covered the majority of the wall space seemed to be made out of the same kind of wood, and were filled with more books than I'd seen in the local bookstore the one time I'd convinced Britney to stop by on our way home after school. They were all hardbound, with leather bindings and engraved covers.

There was a stereo system off in one corner, hooked up to a laptop and some kind of portable music player. I had to look around the room twice before I finally spotted the speakers to the system. They were built into the walls and ceiling, and based on their number and varying sizes I had a sneaking suspicion they'd produce nearly as much volume as the monsters professional DJs brought to dances. Based on the amount of money involved in setting up such a system in the first place, they probably cranked all that out without even the slightest hint of distortion.

As impressive as the stereo no doubt was, it was all of those shelves filled with books that finally pulled me off of the bed and onto the incredibly lush, maroon carpet. Emerson, Ayn Rand, Shakespeare, and Tolstoy were all present. Whoever lived here was either incredibly well read, or a complete poser who bought books just for show.

Almost scared to find out which it was, I reached over and pulled out the copy of Mary Shelley's Frankenstein, and opened it up to find a well-cared-for book that'd still obviously been read several times.

I carefully slid the book back into its spot and then noticed the faintest glimmer of light coming from an open doorway off to my right. It was an art gallery. One covered in pictures that were eerily familiar, all with a circular signature at the bottom right hand corner. They were mostly of mundane kinds of things, landscapes, or people, but there were overtones that caressed a hidden chord inside my soul. Everything was done in drab, painfully boring colors, overlaid with incredibly vibrant, hues that were almost unreal in their perfection.

It wasn't until I'd moved around a corner and entered what looked like a new phase for the painter that I figured out why the paintings looked so familiar despite the fact that I'd never seen any of the places or people depicted. The realization hit with such force that it distracted me from the familiarity of the signature.

The new pieces were all breathtaking. The drab colors were gone, leaving scenes made up of multi-hued strands of light. It was like waking up and having someone tell you they'd been reading your mind. The pieces weren't of specific places or events from my dreams, but they were an exact match for how they'd looked and felt.

BROKEN

I felt my hands start to shake. It was like I'd had too much forced on me too quickly. I wanted to just collapse and let unconsciousness overcome me, but something pulled me onward towards the next series of pictures, and then the next after that. I wanted to stop. Each piece opened up another fragment of my soul, revealing a new pain that I'd kept hidden for the last few months.

The last picture was next to a door, which I opened almost without realizing I was doing so. The organized confusion of a true artist met my gaze. I'd seen it with my mom, when she was so driven to complete a shot that she couldn't be bothered to clean up after herself. She left just enough structure to the mess to find needed tools, but didn't waste any effort on anything that wouldn't help her with her great aim.

Brushes were scattered everywhere, old and new canvases stacked in the corners of the studio, and flecks of paint had found their way onto almost every visible surface. The rich smell of paint was nearly overpowering, but I noticed it only in passing as I made a beeline towards the easel that dominated the center of the space.

The painting was still wet, right down to the signature which had been done in the palest green. The scene was from the point of view of someone looking into a bedroom window, darker than most of the later stuff I'd just looked at. The centerpiece, done in a dimmer light than what I remembered from my dreams, was the sleeping figure. She was delicate-looking. A tiny figure, a being of light temporarily clothed in flesh, one who seemed almost at the point of breaking out of her mortal husk.

She was so breathtakingly beautiful it was several seconds before I noticed the other, nearly unformed details of the room. They were so indistinct it took me a full minute to place them. Once I did, my eyes darted back to the sleeping figure, the gorgeous one whose features I now recognized as Cindi's. Only it couldn't be Cindi because the room was mine, the one here in Sanctuary.

My pulse racing, I refused to look at the signature again. I now knew what it was, but if I ignored it maybe I could ignore the ramifications of everything I'd just learned. The room was swimming as my battered psyche finally took one blow too many, but I fought the attack with everything I had left. I couldn't afford to be found here collapsed on the floor. I had to get away before he realized I was awake.

My shoes were at the foot of the bed; I grabbed them, but didn't put them on. I needed to be quiet, more now than ever. I crept to the other end of the suite, passing a curious collection of items ranging from a mundane, if expensive-looking, desk, to an intricately tooled broadsword, black with age, and sized as though made for a giant.

BROKEN

I finally found the exit and was halfway down the hall when I heard voices for the first time. While it didn't sound like anyone was out-and-out yelling, they weren't the calm voices of friendly conversation. I quickly reversed direction, and found an external door less than a minute later. The voices had faded away to nearly nothing as I'd gotten further away from them, but all of a sudden they peaked into a full-blown yelling match, punctuated with an incredible crash that sent a tremor through the entire house.

Any thoughts I'd had about trying to find a phone and calling 911 vanished as full flight instinct took a hold. A few seconds later I was outside and running. The moon was so obscured by clouds it provided only minimal light, but even the poor visibility couldn't convince me to slow my flight through the near jungle waiting outside the house.

I could barely make out the stone path that led through the garden, but I stumbled along it as quickly as I could with my sprained ankle, deciding between branches in the path completely at random.

I'd only been running for a few seconds when lightning tore its first gash in the night sky and opened up the way for a monsoon-like rainstorm. Within a few seconds the cold rain was falling so hard that I couldn't see even a few feet ahead of me. I started shivering instantly. As much as my body had been through in the last few hours, I needed to find shelter before I got chilled.

The next lightning strike was so close it lit the entire sky up. The telltale flash of glass up ahead was just enough to guide me to a door that was nearly hidden by the rampant foliage.

I pulled the door open with less effort than expected, and slipped inside. The heady fragrance of flowers told me immediately what I'd stumbled across. "As if there wasn't enough greenery outside, he's got to have an entire greenhouse too."

The abrupt lessening of the rain assaulting the glass roof brought back my sense of urgency. Nobody could possibly find me while the most intense rainstorm since Noah had sealed up the ark was going on, but I couldn't stay here once it stopped. I slipped my battered shoes onto my abused feet, and turned to leave just as the door opened of its own accord.

I fell back in amazement as he stepped into the pool of light that'd materialized as the clouds parted. The jeans were mundane, perfect, but completely normal for all that they were snug in all the right places and loose everywhere else. The shirt, unbuttoned in his haste to follow me, was also perfectly normal, entirely believable. Everything else, however, was too surreal to really grasp. The sculpted stomach and chest were exactly like I'd secretly imagined they would be, but my gaze was pulled instead up to the massive bandage covering most of Alec's shoulder. The bandage alone should have told me I hadn't been hallucinating, but the fragments of memory didn't coalesce until I saw his eyes. The amazing, pale blue eyes were the final, poetic piece of evidence threatening to shred my sanity.

I'd never really liked Alec, but I never suspected he was an actual monster.

It was too much to process so quickly. When Alec took a careful step towards me, all I could think of was that I'd just seen those same eyes hovering above bloodstained fangs. I shrank back away from him, and saw his face go from calm to expressionless in a barely detectable flicker.

I'd opened my mouth, maybe to apologize, or possibly to scream for help, but it snapped shut at Alec's response. Moving faster than I would have believed possible, he spun around and fled through the door. Between one heartbeat and the next he disappeared into the darkness, letting the door slam shut with enough force that the glass in the ceiling should have come down in a rain of razor-edged shards.

The flowers closest to me swayed slightly from the force of the vibrations, pulling my gaze towards them. I felt my heart skip a couple of times and tears start to flood my eyes as I took in beautiful white petals edged in an amazing shade of purple.

Lagrimas del Angel. The whole greenhouse was filled with them, and suddenly I couldn't ignore the significance of the circular signature on the paintings anymore. I hurried outside, looked desperately from side to side for some hint of which way he'd gone, and then headed off to the right towards the sound of shattering pottery.

Just before I was about to give up hope of finding him, I heard another crash and turned into a small grotto. The sight of rock walls nearly covered by a swath of greenery caused me to pull up with a suddenness that only barely saved me from tumbling into the small reflecting pool off to one side. Alec froze at my appearance, a large planter that easily weighed as much as I did dangling from one hand. The shards of pottery strewn about the grotto answered any questions I might have had regarding its imminent fate.

Neither of us moved for several seconds, and then he turned towards me with a glare.

"Go away!"

The command was so forceful it was almost more than I could do to stop myself from turning and running away in terror, but I held my ground.

"Leave. Leave now and I won't follow you."

The anger was still there, but now there were other emotions, one of which I could identify, one of which I knew how to handle.

"It was you the whole time, wasn't it? The bank. The mayor. Were you responsible for the Les Misérables tickets too?"

"Why? What possible difference does it make one way or the other?"

The words had lost most of their force, but none of the feeling behind them. "Because I want to understand. Why me? Why would you do all of that for me?"

"You really don't understand? You saved Rachel from a beating. If for no other reason, then for that."

I took a careful step forward and placed a hand on his arm. He absently let the huge flower pot drop, but didn't step away from me.

"That isn't why you did it though. Is it?"

Alec finally shook his head. "No, I just did it for you. Maybe not so much at first, but I couldn't get you out of my mind. You were everywhere I looked. In my class, at lunch, even in my dreams. I couldn't get away from you."

I felt my heart skip another beat. Everything good that I'd attributed to Brandon had been Alec all along. I didn't understand what I'd seen a few hours ago, but he wasn't a monster. The amount of hurt in his voice took him out of the category of frightening. I moved a little closer. "Do you still want me to leave?"

"Do you want to leave? I won't stop you if you do. If you can convince your mom to leave town there's even a chance you'll be safe from Brandon."

Shivers worked their way down my spine as some of the pieces clicked into place. "He's like you, isn't he?"

Alec's laugh was a bitter, humorless thing. "You mean a monster? Yes, we both feel the call of the moon. Does that scare you?"

I shook my head. "No. I guess a little, but not like it should. You wouldn't hurt me after everything you've done for us."

"I could kill you without even meaning to. You're so fragile. All it would take is an accident, a momentary loss of control. I really am a monster."

"No, you're not. I don't understand what you are, but you aren't a monster. Brandon is. Vincent, Cassie. They're all monsters, but you aren't."

Alec finally let his eyes fully meet mine. "How can you know that when sometimes I'm not sure myself?"

Almost without realizing it, I moved my hand from his arm to his stomach, and then wrapped both arms around him and pressed my face into his rock-hard chest.

"Thank you for saving my life. Were those wolves some of Brandon's friends?"

I felt him nod. "Simon and Nathanial."

"I didn't know them that well, they mostly ignored me, but I didn't think they'd kill me."

Alec finally put his arms around me. He hugged me like I was made out of fine china, but it was a start. The tingling sensation I'd always felt around Brandon was back, stronger than ever. Despite the incredibly grave nature of everything that'd happened in the last few hours, I felt mildly euphoric. Maybe this was what people were talking about when they said they were buzzed.

"Maybe they weren't going to kill you. I can't say for sure, but they've both killed people before. I couldn't take the chance that they weren't just playing around. I had to stop them."

I thought for a moment that my knees were going to collapse on me. I carefully reached up and brushed the bandage on his shoulder. "They could've killed you?"

Alec shrugged. "I came out okay all things considered."

He was going to have to rethink this deflection thing, but now didn't seem like the time to get pushy. I forced a measure of gaiety into my voice and smiled up at him. "Well, I'm glad things turned out the way they did. Otherwise we'd both be dead."

Alec flinched slightly, and then looked at the grotto. "I suppose I'd better clean this up or Donovan is going to be very unhappy with me."

"Who's Don...." I felt my mouth drop as I finally recognized my surroundings. "I've been here before. In my dream. Then I drew it, which I didn't understand because I only ever draw real places, and this was imaginary. Only it wasn't, but there wasn't any way for me to know..."

I turned around, expecting to have to field a barrage of questions, but Alec was calmly watching me. "Isn't that odd? Doesn't that make you want to know what's going on?"

He was debating whether or not to lie to me. I could see it in his eyes. Funny how I'd never realized how expressive they were.

"Don't lie to me."

Alec sighed, and then shrugged. "I'm not sure what to tell you. There's so much you don't know, and most of it I can't tell you. More importantly, you're better off not knowing."

I waited for several seconds, expecting him to go on, and then finally realized the matter was closed as far as he was concerned. "Hold on there. You can't just leave me in the dark about all of this. I'm in up to my neck; you have to at least let me know what I've fallen into."

He was shaking his head again. "I'm sorry, I know this has to be hard, but you don't belong in this world. You admitted yourself that you don't know anything about us. It was a mistake for me to let you get involved. I'm going to remedy that right now. We'll get you home, and then your mom is going to get an offer that's too good to pass up. With any luck you'll both be out of town within a couple days. I think I can arrange it so neither of you will be back for a year or two. That should be more than enough time for this all to resolve itself one way or another."

I felt my eyes go wide with panic as I realized what he was proposing. "Wait. No. You can't do that." I tried to grab a hold of his arm, but he'd already taken several steps away. The pleasant tingly feeling was gone, but that loss was nothing against the sense of cold abandonment rushing through me.

I tried to step forward, tried to follow him, but my vision was dimming and my heart felt like it was about to explode. I managed a single step before my knees collapsed and the ground jumped up to meet me.

Consciousness was slow returning. When my eyes finally fluttered open, I was surprised to find myself in Alec's arms once again.

"Are you okay?"

He tried to set me down, to stand me up on my feet, but I grabbed onto him as tightly as my shaking arms were able. "Don't leave me. Please don't make me go."

I didn't realize I was crying until I tried to talk. It was embarrassing, but was I too worried about being sent away to care. Any amount of ridicule would be worthwhile if it meant being able to stay with Alec. He obviously still wasn't convinced though.

"Adri, you don't understand. This is the only way to keep you safe. I can't protect you here. I can't even protect my own family."

He was still trying to disengage my arms from around his neck, but it was obvious he didn't want to hurt me, and I was holding on with everything I had.

"No, *you* don't understand. This whole time I thought I was in love with Brandon, I didn't even know him. You did so much for us and didn't even hate me when I was so rude. I've been so stupid, please don't send me away."

I was halfway to another attack before Alec finally put a finger to my lips and nodded. "Very well. I should send you away for your own protection, but I'm too selfish to do what's best for you. Maybe later I'll be able to do what's right, but not right now, not so soon."

Chapter 22

Rachel met us at the door with a shy smile that let me know any hard feelings would evaporate instantly if I wanted to be friends again.

Alec put me down with a slight start as soon as he saw his sister. I reluctantly let go of him, and covered the last few feet under my own power. I gave Rachel a hug as soon as she was within arm's reach.

"I'm so sorry. I've been incredibly dumb."

She waved the explanation away. "Brandon's fooled people smarter than both of us put together. The hardest part was not being able to tell you anything."

Alec started to open the door, but Rachel put a hand on his arm. "The rest of the pack is back. Jasmin already told them what happened. It doesn't look good."

I had my mouth open and was halfway to asking what was going on when I saw Alec's expression, and swallowed my words. He didn't look any different than normal, in fact if I'd been standing forty or fifty feet away from him I'd probably have still thought he was just as calm and in control as always. This close, I could feel the anger radiating off of him.

I almost took a step back when he turned towards me. "I realize it's unreasonable to ask you to trust me right now, but I'm going to need you to do so. Can you remain quiet for the next few minutes?"

I wanted to ask why, but it was obvious we didn't have the time for a lengthy explanation. I nodded. "I trust you. After everything you've done, I know you wouldn't hurt me."

Alec turned towards Rachel, but she shook her head before he could even open his mouth. "You don't even need to ask. I'll follow your lead, and try to look brave."

He threw the door open and stalked into the house. Rachel grabbed my hand and pulled me along behind her.

A group of familiar faces was waiting for us in the largest living room I'd ever seen. It took me several seconds to match identities to the rain-soaked group staring at me with such hostility.

Jasmin was standing in the center, and didn't even wait for me to get fully in the room before she started talking.

"She goes back to Brandon tonight. It's a long shot, but it's better than nothing. She brought it on herself so there isn't any reason to cry over what might happen."

Alec shook his head. "Unacceptable. She wasn't properly his. There was no bond of Ja'tell, and consequently we have no obligation to return her to him."

Jasmin opened her mouth to say something else, but a tiny brunette, probably Jessica, interrupted her. "Alec, we have to do this. None of us are stupid; we know what's going to happen. You killed two members of his pack."

There was steel in Alec's voice that I'd never heard before. "Still unacceptable. You've all aired your opinions; you can retire to your beds now."

James looked up from where he'd been slouching against the wall, and I suddenly realized that he wasn't shaking from cold. He was so furious it looked like he was only seconds away from exploding.

A very pretty Hispanic girl placed a gentle hand on his arm, but he shook her hand off and let out a sound that was uncomfortably close to a growl. "You selfish jerk. You've been mooning over her for weeks. You've got her now, but at what cost? This isn't open to discussion. We're taking her back to Brandon and asking for leniency."

In an effort to see better, Rachel and I had moved slightly to the side. Alec reached back without looking and moved us directly behind him. It wasn't until his arm brushed me that I realized he was shaking ever so slightly himself.

"There's only one way you're going to touch her, James. Are you really ready to take that step?"

I felt shivers run down me as I realized just how easily everything could boil over into deadly violence. The tension in the room pulsed out in waves, skittering many-legged across my skin like something that belonged under a rock somewhere.

The feeling intensified even more as first Jessica and then Jasmin picked up the same strange, near epileptic quiver. James let out a low, grating growl, and my stomach dropped as he looked up with eyes that weren't the unremarkable brown they'd been just a second before. The hot yellow eyes of a predator were looking out of James' familiar face, changing it into something threatening and inhuman.

Answering growls from Jasmin and Jessica seemed to snap something inside of Alec. His tremble became more pronounced. There was a ripping sound, and when I looked down at his hands, they'd been replaced by the same wickedly-sharp claws I remembered from the night before.

I must have let out a gasp, because Rachel tightened her grasp on me and moved closer. She might have whispered something comforting, but I couldn't hear it past the thunder of my own heartbeat.

All three of them were moving towards us now. It was so inhumanly smooth and slow the motion was almost imperceptible, but I was certain they were stalking us. Stalking me. As soon as they got close enough to cover the remaining distance in a single bound, they'd attack, and if Alec had been sorely pressed fighting two of his kind last night, three were almost certain to kill him.

Rachel pulled me around behind her and spoke with a calm that seemed too concrete to be real. "Jasmin, please don't do this. I'm not going to move. She doesn't mean anything to you. What about me?"

Jasmin stopped moving. She was still shaking, and when she looked up at me, her eyes still bubbled with hate, but they were human again instead of the pale, ice blue from a moment before.

With a visible effort of will, Jasmin closed her eyes, calmed her shaking body, and then turned and quickly walked out of the room.

I was just tall enough to see over Rachel and take in what was going on in the rest of the room. James' eyes were still yellow, and he was still inching his way towards me, obviously undeterred by Jasmin's defection.

The Hispanic girl carefully closed the distance between them, and then placed her slender, perfect dark hand on James' arm once again as she leaned in and whispered something in his ear. For a moment it seemed he was going to shake her off again but then he shuddered, shot Alec another dirty look, and stormed out of the room. The tiny form following after him looked like a fragile schooner trailing along the edge of a hurricane.

The room seemed so calm after James disappeared that for a second I forgot Jessica was still half-crouched in the center of the room. Alec hadn't forgotten, and if the waves of tension and energy rolling off of him weren't as strong as the combined effects coming from all four of them, it still felt like the walls should explode outwards.

Jessica seemed to shrink in on herself, and then she turned and ran away with a final hiss of defiance. Isaac looked up at Alec from the corner where he'd been quietly standing. Alec's almost imperceptible nod sent him in the same direction as Jessica.

Whatever meager survival instincts I had left chose that moment to finally kick in, and I felt my knees begin to give way. Rachel let out a high-pitched sound that had all of the surprise of a squeal, but none of the excitement. Apparently Alec knew how to interpret it. He turned back and caught me again before I could hit the ground.

"There isn't anything to worry about now. Go ahead and catch your breath."

As pleasant as it was to be in his arms again, I was starting to worry he'd get tired of it. I pushed him away as soon as I was reasonably confident my knees would support me. "What's going on? Why are they so scared of Brandon?"

Alec shook his head. "This isn't the time; we need to get you back home to your mom. It would be most unfortunate if she were to arrive and find you gone."

My mind was still a little fuzzy, but it was working well enough for me to know he was wrong. "No. She's not going to be home until Sunday. There isn't any reason to go back there yet."

I looked around for Rachel, but she'd disappeared sometime between when I'd started falling, and when I'd thought to thank her.

"You mean she wasn't planning on coming back until Sunday. Once Brandon gets involved in things, they tend not to go as expected."

I wanted to ask questions, but Rachel appeared from a hallway. "He's right, Adriana. You need to be home in case your mom returns sooner than expected. Things are going to get plenty weird enough over the next couple of weeks. You don't want to start out with your mom already mad at you."

Feeling very small inside at the thought of going back by myself, I nodded. Alec apparently read the meaning of my sudden change in expression. "Don't worry; I'm not going to send you back alone. We'll make sure nothing happens to you."

Too scared to even muster a "yeah right, they all hate me," I simply waited while Alec flipped open an ultra-slender cellphone, and made two calls. He spoke too quietly for me to make out exactly what was being said. It seemed like he was giving orders though, and that they weren't being received very well.

A few minutes later Alec bundled me into the back seat of an unfamiliar car, which rapidly filled up as first Jasmin, Isaac and the tiny Hispanic girl arrived. Jasmin completely ignored me as she climbed into the car; Isaac gave me a polite, if somewhat cool nod. The Hispanic girl gave me an honest-to-goodness smile as she slipped behind the steering wheel and started the engine. In what was one of the most thoughtful things that'd happened all night, she turned the heater on full as she pulled out of the driveway.

The drive into town, and then back out to my house was quiet, but luckily didn't take as long as normal. Apparently her timidness stopped well short of observing the speed limit. Alec, Isaac, and Jasmin all jumped out of the car as soon as my house was in sight. The car was still doing at least twenty miles per hour when they bailed. They faded into the darkened landscape about the time we rolled to a stop.

I went to open the door, but a delicate brown hand stopped me. "I'm sorry you've had such a rough night. James and the others will come around eventually. Till then just continue being brave and trust Alec. He really will move the *cielos* to protect you."

She had a thick, beautiful Spanish accent. For a second I was torn between complimenting her on it and asking her what *cielos* meant. I finally just settled on faking a smile and thanking her. She smiled at me. "No need to thank me. My name is Dominic by the way."

A few seconds later I was standing alone, nervously facing my house. Alec suddenly appeared at my side. I jumped a little at the surprise.

"I'm sorry, I didn't mean to scare you."

I shrugged as my breathing started to slow down again. "It's okay. Where were you?"

"Scouting. We had to make sure Brandon's pack wasn't waiting for us."

"How can you be sure? They could be hidden anywhere."

Alec shook his head, his eyes strangely gentle. "No, if they were hanging around outside we'd be able to smell them."

"So not only are you faster and stronger than normal people, you've also got noses like real wolves?"

"Of a sort. That's not really important though. Let's get you inside."

I nodded and started towards the door, only to blink as Alec stepped in front of me. "May I have permission to enter and make sure it's safe inside?"

I slowed down, suddenly terrified at the thought of Brandon and his friends waiting inside for me. "I thought you said you'd be able to smell them if they were here."

"If they were outside, yes. Under normal circumstances we'd be able to determine whether or not they'd been here in the last few days, but the rainstorm last night was strong enough to wash away all of that."

Alec waited patiently as I tried to get a grip on myself. As soon as I nodded he disappeared through the door. A few seconds later he was back. "It's safe; there's no trace of them."

He held the door open for me, and then slipped outside. "You need to erase any evidence that you weren't here all night. Take a shower, change into some of your own clothes, and then go to sleep. We'll keep watch outside until your mom gets back."

I opened my mouth to ask what would happen after that, but he was already gone, moving so quickly through the darkness that I wasn't even sure which direction he'd headed.

I locked the door for the first time since we'd arrived in Sanctuary, turned on all the downstairs lights, and then slowly walked upstairs. It was crazy to be scared that Alec had somehow missed someone, but I couldn't shake the feeling I was being watched. Once I finally made it upstairs, I checked both rooms, and the bathroom, before finally relaxing a little.

I showered quickly, carefully making sure the smell of alcohol and cigarette smoke was out of my hair, and then changed into clean clothes and collapsed onto my bed. I was exhausted, but I couldn't fall asleep. Every time I closed my eyes, I saw dark shapes hurtling towards me.

After looking at the clock for the thousandth time, I finally got up and went downstairs. The lights were still blazing, just as I'd left them. I debated for several seconds before opening the door and stepping out into the darkness. Somehow the porch light didn't reach out as far into the yard as I'd remembered.

Alec appeared on the edge of the light with such suddenness that a startled yelp escaped me despite my best efforts.

"I'm sorry, I didn't mean to frighten you."

Strangely enough, I believed him. He was moving with the same, over-controlled care I'd seen him use around Rachel. "It's okay, it must be really limiting to always have to pretend you're slow and normal."

His expression took on an alien cast, as he shrugged.

"Actually I've spent so much of my life trying to hide the unusual aspects of my nature, it's usually effortless. For some reason, I forget myself around you."

There was something to his voice, but even after he'd hinted at having strong feelings for me, it was hard to really believe it all. At least not without an outright admission on his part.

Seeking to distract myself from a thoroughly useless train of thought, I looked around, trying vainly to pierce the curtain of black hanging around the feeble circle of light. "Are they out there waiting now?"

Alec shook his head. "No, I'd already have come and carried you away if any of Brandon's people were around. Barring that, you'd hear us fighting. Mere doors and windows wouldn't do much to muffle the sound."

"You'd be fighting, because of me."

Alec slowly crossed the distance between us, and took my shoulders in his hands. "Please don't try and take the blame for this. We've been on a collision course with Brandon's pack for years."

His touch was intoxicating. I could feel warm tingles start from my shoulders and work their way down my arms. A full two seconds of silence passed before I realized he'd asked me why I'd come downstairs. "I can't sleep. I've been trying, but I'm too wound up to do anything but just lie there. I thought I'd come downstairs and talk to you instead. I mean, unless it's bothering you. You know, keeping you from patrolling or something."

That last bit hadn't really been planned. I'd wanted to come downstairs and talk to him, but wouldn't have dreamt of just saying it outright. Maybe it was the natural high I got simply from being around him.

Alec's smile was brief, but it felt like the first one I'd seen since he'd been forced to save me. I couldn't blame him for being worried about how this was going to further strain already tense relations with Brandon's pack. Still, the transforming expression made me realize just how badly I'd missed his other face, the one that wasn't stern and serious all of the time.

"No, you're not bothering me in the slightest. Jasmin or Isaac either one could easily keep watch. Our sense of smell and hearing are good enough that it's all but impossible for even other wolves to catch us unawares. They're here more in the role of bodyguards. If Brandon's people do show up, it'll likely take all three of us to get you away safely."

"So you don't mind? You'll stay here and talk to me?"

Alec paused for several seconds, which wasn't promising. Then again, he hadn't released my shoulders yet, so maybe there was still some hope. "I'm not sure that's the best idea. You really need your sleep. The whole purpose of this little exercise is to convince your mom you've been safely home this entire time. If you crash later in the day, she's going to know you didn't sleep tonight."

"Maybe if you stayed with me it would help me sleep." I almost couldn't believe those words were really coming out of my mouth. I wanted to blame it on how close he was standing, or how tired I was, or anything else that might be remotely believable, but based on how serious his face had just become, it was too late to take it all back.

"That doesn't strike me as being a much better solution."

I felt my neck and face begin to burn from embarrassment. I took a step back, and reached for the door, hoping to beat a quick retreat before I could humiliate myself further, but he stopped me with a surprisingly gentle hand. "I'm sorry; that didn't come out as intended. If it would help you sleep, of course I'll come upstairs and sit with you. It's the least I can do after allowing you to be dragged into this mess."

Alec followed me upstairs, and then slid down the wall to sit on the floor as I sat down on my bed. As soon as I was comfortable he reached up and flipped off the light.

"Hey, I can't see you now."

His laugh was like silk. It reached out, and smoothed away the last of the embarrassment. "The deal was I would come up here so you could sleep. You aren't going to fall asleep if the light is on and you're staring at me."

"Fine, the light can be off, but I get to ask you questions still, and you need to start giving me real answers."

The chuckle was a little more resigned, but he didn't argue, so I launched into my first question before I'd really thought it through. "What...I mean, you're all so different..." I trailed off into silence worried he was going to be mad.

"I think you meant to ask what I am." Alec sighed, but it wasn't an angry sigh, so I nodded, forgetting for a moment that he couldn't see me in the darkness.

"We share a little in common with a bunch of different legends, but none get it quite right. In short, we're shape shifters, people who can take the form of animals."

I'd already seen that for myself, but it was strangely exhilarating to hear him admit it. "You mean like werewolves?"

There was a hiss of sound, as if I'd just hit him. For a second I worried I'd made him angry. "No, not like werewolves."

I waited for him to elaborate. When the silence grew too uncomfortable I was the first to crack, just like always. "Did I say something wrong?"

Alec's voice was surprisingly gentle. "No, you've nothing to feel sorry about. I should tell you though that calling a shape shifter a werewolf is the kind of insult that nearly always results in a fight, and often even a death."

I felt momentarily like I'd been hit. Alec was waiting for me to respond, but I couldn't bring myself to say anything.

"I'm sorry; I didn't mean to scare you. I forget sometimes how much more violent my world is."

I wasn't any less shocked, but his tone was so apologetic I couldn't help but smile.

"That's better; I much prefer the happy Adri face to the scared Adri."

"Wait, you could see me smile? I guess that all follows, better hearing, better sense of smell. Of course you'd have better vision too."

It wasn't until I heard the note of longing in my voice that I realized what I was missing. Alec didn't have that same advantage, and I could feel him waiting expectantly.

"Sorry, it's just that this all makes me think of these amazing dreams I've been having since I arrived. I'm transported to various places, but in every case I can hear and smell better than I can in real life. Not only that, everything is glowing. Only that isn't the right word for it. Mostly there's just light coming out of the people and the plants and animals. It's so beautiful. Funny your having more acute senses would make me think of that."

Alec sighed. "It's bordering on stuff I shouldn't tell you, but you deserve to know. You've just described exactly how we perceive the world. The colors are all more vibrant, the breeze is more alive with scents than anyone could ever know."

I felt my heart speed up a little as things started falling into place. "Your paintings. That explains them. You were superimposing what you see over top of what someone like me would see. Only how would you know what things look like to us?"

Alec's chuckle held more than a little resignation in its timbre. "You are amazing. Anyone else waking up in a strange place would've run away as soon as they regained consciousness. At the very least, you should have started screaming. Instead you wander around, take in some rather feeble attempts at art, and then sneak out without saying a word."

Secure in the knowledge he could see me, I stuck my tongue out at him. "Hey, my survival instincts, or lack thereof aren't the point. Stop trying to distract me."

"I suppose I deserved that. It's just more than a little unsettling how quickly you're putting pieces together. There really are things that aren't safe for you to know. Among them, the reason why it isn't safe for you to know them."

I waited expectantly, and he finally resumed. "To answer your question, I wasn't always like this. When I was younger I saw exactly the way that you do. Even now, my vision is more like yours when I'm in this form. I still see incredibly well, and there's just the slightest hint of light from living things, but nothing like what you saw in the dreams."

"So you work from memory mostly then? That and trying to make what you see when you're in human form even more drab than what you really see?"

"That about sums it up, although I didn't really expect you to pick up on that last part so quickly. You're remarkably perceptive."

I felt my face heat at the compliment. I quickly looked for something worthy of a chuckle to change the subject. "So what does a seventeen-year-old shape shifter spend his time doing?"

I succeeded with my goal of making him laugh. "Well, I spend a ridiculous amount of time trying to keep my friends away from each other's throats. We've got some pretty strong personalities, and it's nearly a full-time job stopping minor disagreements from boiling over into something bigger. Apart from that, I spend an hour or two every day vetting Donovan's management of the family assets. He does an incredible job with everything, but even so, there are certain things I have to approve myself."

"Who's Donovan?"

Another chuckle. "That's one of the most difficult questions you've asked so far. He likes to call himself our butler, but that doesn't even begin to describe him. He does take care of most of the duties a typical butler would assume, but he's also our financial manager and long-time family friend. I'm excited for you to meet him tomorrow. I think you'll like him."

"Yeah, but will he like me?" I sat up in bed, excited to finally be getting real details about Alec's life.

"Please lie back down. You have to at least be trying to sleep. Otherwise I'm heading back downstairs. And don't pout. It won't influence me in the slightest."

"It's just *sooo* hard for my merely human ears to hear you from so far away. Maybe if you were to move over here I wouldn't have to strain to catch every word."

It was so blatantly coy, I almost couldn't believe I was saying it. It *had* been said though. All there was left to do was hope he didn't decide I was the biggest loser to ever walk the earth. The extended silence was almost enough to make me decide he was going to get up and leave.

"All right, I'll come over and lean against your bed, but you really need to try and sleep. You've got to be nearly exhausted."

"What about you, mister superhero shape shifter? You've been up longer than I have. I'm not the only one who needs to sleep." I tried not to let my voice get too sing-song, but I felt a completely irrational thrill as he quietly crossed over to my side of the room.

"That's actually one of the benefits of my condition. I don't actually need normal amounts of sleep. An hour or two per night is usually more than enough."

Having him so close to me was somehow both exhilarating and soothing at the same time. I could feel the tense, knotty parts of me start to relax for the first time since Simon and Nathanial tried to kill me. As exhaustion started to finally eat through all of the nervous energy that'd been fueling me, it was all I could do to follow what Alec was saying. Still, I wasn't ready to go to sleep. It felt like he'd disappear if I closed my eyes.

"So you don't need to sleep. What do you do with all the rest of your time?"

Alec was close enough now that I could see his smile. It reached out and wrapped itself around me like a warm blanket. "Well, I do spend a fairly significant amount of time each day sitting in class. Kind of like someone else I know."

"Unacceptable. I've added that up in my head, and you've still got several hours each day that you haven't accounted for." Despite my best efforts, I was mumbling so badly I wasn't sure anything I'd said was comprehensible.

Somewhere in there I'd closed my eyes, so I felt a sluggish, tired kind of surprise when he gently brushed his fingers across the side of my face. The sensation was so feathery I almost opened my eyes to verify that he'd really touched me. It was too much effort. Besides, I didn't really want to know if he hadn't touched me, it was better to just go on pretending he had.

"I'm afraid that really is the balance of my time. I spend time with Rachel of course. Then there are a few odd minutes where I squeeze in some reading, or a bit of painting."

"They're beautiful. Best I've seen. Ever."

I imagined I could hear him smile. "Thank you. I'm afraid mostly all I see is the flaws. Even with the most perfect subjects, I still generally fail to capture their true essence."

"But not all?"

"No, not all of them."

It was getting harder and harder to string thoughts together in a comprehensible manner. "Sounds fulfilling. Busy, but fulfilling."

Alec waited so long to respond that I nearly drifted off. "It's always seemed fulfilling. At least until recently."

I wanted to know what he meant, but couldn't muster the willpower. I already felt myself starting to drift away. Even the feeling of him caressing my check again wasn't enough to bring me all the way back to full alertness.

"Somehow that all changed after you arrived. Little by little I started to realize just how empty my life really was. I wish I could come right out and say it while you're awake. I don't want that life anymore. I don't really want any life that doesn't involve you."

Part of me wanted to scream for joy, to jump up out of my bed and wrap myself around Alec as tightly as I could, but I was just too far gone. I half thought I was dreaming it all. As I finally let sleep pull me down into darkness, I almost thought I heard Alec say one last thing. The tone was so vulnerable and hesitant he almost sounded like another person.

"The truth is, I've fallen well and truly in love with you."

Chapter 23

Someone was calling my name, but I really didn't want to wake up. I was still so tired, and I'd had the most wonderful dreams. They were a little foggy now, but they seemed to have involved Alec coming to my rescue, and then holding my hand as I went to sleep.

It wasn't until I finally placed the familiar voice that everything started coming back to me. I sat up with an abruptness that nearly knocked Alec off of his perch on the edge of my bed. Him still being there, looking at me with a barely restrained amusement glimmering in his eyes, calmed my racing pulse.

"You're still here."

"You sound disappointed. Do you want me to leave?" His expression had taken on the guarded blankness I still hadn't learned how to read, so I wasn't sure whether he was joking or not.

"No, not disappointed, just surprised. I figured I'd wake up and find everything had just been one amazing, crazy dream."

I'd hoped that my reassurance would make the mask drop, but if anything Alec was looking at me even more seriously.

"Would you prefer things to take that course?"

It took me several heartbeats to understand what he was getting at, long seconds in which his face grew increasingly remote. "No, how could you think that? Why would I possibly want to have you vanish when I've just now finally found out it's you who's been watching over my mom and me since we got here?"

Alec looked away for a moment, and then stood up and walked over to the window. "It would be for the best, you know. I could arrange for you both to leave the state, and never have to come back to Sanctuary again. You'd be safer."

I felt my mouth drop open as his words hit me with almost physical force. I wanted to turn and run away, but the quasi-dream from the night before was just barely vivid enough to keep me in the room.

"Is that what you want? Not what's best for me, or what you think is best for me, but what you really want?"

The silence seemed to stretch into hours before Alec finally shook his head.

"Good, because I don't want to leave. You said last night that your life felt meaningless before I came here, well, mine was even worse. The only thing that's kept me sane has been your behind-the-scenes help. I want to stay with you. I want to be with you."

Alec studied me for a moment longer, and then nodded, a short, choppy motion with little if any of his usual grace. "Very well then. It's just after ten o'clock. Your mom is about to pull into the driveway. Do your best to convince her you spent the night safely at home. We'll stay here and watch over the two of you. Also, if you can convince her it's safe to leave on an extended trip, that would be very helpful. Once she's gone, I'll come back for you."

I opened my mouth to ask him what he meant, only to be distracted by the sound of the Jeep's engine as it rolled to a stop on the cement pad.

As I looked back, Alec's eyes captured me. "You're sure this is what you want?"

I managed a nod, and then the downstairs door crashed open. "Adri, honey. Where are you?"

Alec was gone when I looked back. Only the slight sway of my curtains gave evidence he'd just casually jumped out of my second-story window.

I heard Mom's equipment bags hit the floor one after another. The sound of her tromping up the stairs finally roused me from my state of shock.

"I'm in my room, Mom."

Apparently the sound of my voice was at least slightly reassuring, she was only a little wild-eyed by the time she opened the door and stuck her head in my room.

"Oh, there you are, dear. I was worried you were gone."

I forced a chuckle. "Please, Mom. Where else would I be? Saturdays are one of my only two chances all week to actually sleep in. It isn't like I'm going to climb out of bed at the crack of dawn and go hiking or something."

Mom's chuckle was almost genuine. If Alec hadn't implied she was going to suspect I'd been up to no good, I probably wouldn't have even noticed how off she sounded.

"You're right, dear. I shouldn't have doubted you. I just had a few kids come hiking past this morning talking about this massive party the entire school was at last night. I know it's completely irrational, but I kept thinking about you there with all that alcohol."

I was so nervous about answering her question that I didn't realize she was headed over to shut my window until she was already so close that there was no hope of intercepting her. Hopefully Alec had kept moving after he'd jumped. Otherwise Mom's questions were about to get a bit more pointed.

"Mom, how could you think that? I've never even had the slightest desire to do something like that." The lies were starting to add up, but Alec had acted like it was important not to be grounded right now. That and I really didn't want to get into the kind of trouble the truth would bring.

"That's a good point, but you can't blame me for being worried, sweetie. I mean with this new boyfriend of yours. You know I don't trust boys who drive sports cars. Especially not the really cute ones who have a way of making every female in sight go all gooey on the inside."

She slid the window shut with a sigh, rather than screaming in shock, so Alec wasn't lying on the ground with a pair of broken legs.

Apparently Brandon's charms were enough to make Mom forget herself while he was around, but not so great as to keep her from worrying when he wasn't. I shrugged uncomfortably. "He's not my boyfriend, Mom. I mean he wasn't really ever my boyfriend, but even less so now."

Mom looked away from the skyline, a new batch of concern painted across her features. "I'm so sorry, dear. I didn't particularly approve of him, but I wasn't going to get really vocal about it. Not when he was your first boyfriend. What happened?"

I didn't have to pretend to be hurt and disappointed. Even knowing that Alec was everything I'd thought Brandon was, I still felt used and disappointed. "I just wasn't what he was looking for. He made it very clear the last time I saw him."

Mom crossed the distance from the window and wrapped her arms around me. "Teenage boys are so cruel. I'm sorry. Do you want to go out for ice cream this afternoon?"

My smile came much easier than it would have if Alec hadn't magically come into my life. "That is the time-honored method for dealing with breakups."

Whatever Mom had been planning on saying was interrupted by the perky jingle of her cell phone. She shot me an apologetic look as she answered it, but I already knew Mr. Peters had taken to calling her at unusual times to get updates on where she was at with her shots for the tourism brochure.

"This is she. Yes, I'm doing well, thanks, may I ask who's calling? Yes, I am a photographer. Why yes, I did have a couple of pieces that I submitted last year, but they never got printed. No, I've never heard of...yes, of course. Well, that's really not my area of expertise. I might know of a person or two who might be interested in helping you out..."

Mom's face was nearly as surprised as the time Dad had come home from work and announced he'd just taken the next two days off and we were going up to St. Cloud for a vacation starting in twenty minutes. I wasn't sure who'd called, or what exactly they were after, but it was looking like she was going to have a really good story to tell when she managed to get off of the phone.

"I appreciate your interest, but as I said, that really isn't the kind of thing I do. Oh. Well, I have commitments here, projects I'm working on. For three weeks?" She looked at me with wide eyes. "I'd have to confirm that. Can I call you back in half an hour?"

Mom stood there with the phone up against her ear for several seconds before shaking herself and looking at me. "That was some kind of promoter. She wants me to go out and shoot a fashion show in Paris. For a week and a half, and then another one in Italy. I've never heard of either of the shows, but she's offering me twenty thousand dollars for just three weeks."

I felt my eyes go wide at the idea of something so unbelievable happening to us, and then even wider as I realized this must be what Alec had been referring to. 'Convince her it's fine for her to leave' indeed. He hadn't been kidding about getting us out of the country.

"Mom, you have to go! This is the biggest opportunity ever!"

She looked doubtful. "Sweetie, I know it seems exciting, and heaven knows we could use the money, but that just isn't my kind of thing."

I shrugged. "Yeah, but once you've had some paying photography jobs it's sure to help land others. It isn't your ideal kind of work, but it's still a good start, and you never know where it might lead."

"I can't leave you here alone. Not only that, I've still got the brochure to do."

Obviously I was going to have to work harder. "Mom, I'll be fine. Just think of it as an extended hike. You'll even have cell phone coverage, so you can check in with me as often as you want." At least I hoped we'd be able to arrange that somehow. "As for the brochure, you've got scads of great shots already. Maybe if you call up Mr. Peters you'll be able to work something out."

Actually I was positive Mr. Peters would be amiable to the idea. At least he would be if Alec had remembered to work whatever magic he'd used on the Mayor the first time. Of course it was possible he'd forgotten to make the arrangements, but somehow I doubted it.

Mom looked like she was starting to waver. "It does seem like a great opportunity, but there just isn't any good way to know for sure it's legitimate."

That didn't sound like Alec at all. "Are you sure, Mom? They didn't arrange anything you could use to verify they're for real?"

I suddenly realized why parents got such a big kick out of catching their kids doing something wrong. Mom looked so sheepish I almost laughed.

"Well, he did say he'd arrange for an immediate advance to be wired over to our bank, but it's closed on Saturdays, and it isn't like I can go calling up the bank president for something trivial like that."

I opened my mouth, still unsure what to say in response to her latest excuse, only to be interrupted by her cell phone again.

"Yes, this is she. Mr. Kard? Oh, hello. A wire? Really? I didn't realize you even had anyone working today."

Mom listened for several more seconds and then hung up. "They just sent the money. Apparently it's for real. The bank president was just calling to tell me the money has been confirmed, subject to my accepting the job."

Now was the time to strike. "Mom, go call Mr. Peters, and I'll start pulling your stuff together."

It's amazing how quickly you can pack when it's for someone else, and they aren't around to tell you what you can or can't throw into their suitcase. Even with my lack of sleep starting to catch up with me, I was still essentially done by the time Mom wandered into her room, staring at her phone like she wasn't sure it was really possible for it to have just told her what she'd just heard.

"He says it's fine. He'll swing by next week to pick up the shots I think are the most promising, and then he'll see if he can't put the brochure together from that."

She noticed the suitcases and the empty hangers for the first time. "Honey, there isn't any reason to be in such a hurry. We haven't really decided to take the job yet, and even if we do,

I'm sure we won't be able to arrange a flight for another day or two."

Right. If Alec really had arranged this incredible trip, literally overnight, he'd have her on a plane much faster than anyone else would've believed possible.

"Mom, we've already gone through every single one of your objections, and they've all been taken care of. I'll be fine, the brochure will still be completed on schedule, and the job is as real as it gets. The only thing left to do is call them back and accept before they decide to offer it to someone else."

It obviously hadn't crossed Mom's mind that they might decide to go with someone else. Waffling over whether or not to take the job was one thing when she was sure she'd have it in the end. It was entirely different when it might cost her the biggest break she'd ever had. She nodded jerkily as she stepped out of the room, already dialing.

I felt my eyelids drooping by the time she came back. "They want me to leave right now. She said she's already arranged for a charter plane out of St. George. If I leave in the next ten minutes, we can make the flight out of Salt Lake International with something like half an hour to spare."

We both sat there in silence for a few seconds as everything sank in, and then Mom exploded into motion. She ran downstairs to repack her photography equipment, all the while yelling upstairs to verify that I'd packed all of the other essentials she was going to need.

Almost before I'd even finished assimilating how quickly Alec had pulled everything together, Mom was backing down the lane as I waved goodbye.

Alec appeared within thirty seconds of Mom's departure, Isaac close behind him. "We need to go. One of Brandon's people just got close enough to smell us. They left before we could tell for sure who it was, but the odds of them coming back with lots of help just went through the roof. If we're still around when they do, things will get ugly."

Part of me wanted to break down into a gibbering wreck. The rest of me just nodded calmly, and turned to head upstairs as Isaac politely passed me, apparently on his way to the kitchen. Alec gently grasped my shoulder before I'd even managed to take a step.

"There isn't time. We have to go now."

As soon as we were out the front door, Alec motioned for me to jump on his back, and then we were off with a speed I suspected an Olympic athlete couldn't have matched. The lane between our house and the road flew by faster than I'd ever driven it in a car.

The wind created by our passage was strong enough to make my eyes tear up, but I resisted the urge to close them. I occasionally saw shadowy shapes darting through the trees ahead or to either side of us, but there wasn't any way to be sure it was Isaac and Jasmin instead of Brandon and his entire pack.

A faint howl from behind us caused Alec to put on another terrifying burst of speed as we left the lane and turned to parallel the road. The sight of branches clawing at us as we slipped by them with little more than inches to spare was too much. I finally closed my eyes and ducked down as close to Alec's neck as I could get.

With one less sense distracting me, the rest of them kicked into high gear. I could feel every step, including the occasional slide as the rough gravel we were running on wasn't up to bearing our combined weight without slipping. The bitter taste of fear along the back of my tongue was surprisingly strong, but even so I found my thoughts dwelling on the sheer pleasure of having my arms wrapped around Alec's rock-hard upper body.

The high-pitched scream of a performance engine pulled me away from my absurd musings. James' blue and white Accord passed us doing the better part of twice the legal speed limit, and then flipped around with the distinctive squeal of overworked tires.

Alec veered up onto the road as I looked back to find that even as fast as he was running, the Accord was still gaining on us at a prodigious rate.

As the car pulled even with us, Alec smoothly reached over, pulled the passenger door open, pried me off of his back, and slid me into the front seat without losing even a single step.

If everything had happened at something approaching normal speed, I probably would've started hyperventilating, but it was all so quick my mind didn't have a chance to fully register what was going on before I was safely ensconced next to James.

Jasmin and Isaac appeared alongside the road, materializing where there'd only been trees a half-second before. Faster than I would have believed possible, all three of the shape shifters piled into the moving car, and then James stomped on the gas hard enough to break triple digits before slowing slightly for the first turn.

The mirror on my side of the car was perfectly positioned for me to be able to see three or four flashes of tawny brown sliding through the trees before the winding road carried us out of sight.

Alec nodded as I looked back and met his eyes. "They were pretty close. There weren't that many of them, but they could've decided to push the issue regardless."

I spent the rest of the trip, expecting someone to jump out of the trees, but faster than I'd have believed possible, the wrought iron gates I'd noticed on our trip out last night were swinging open, and we were turning off onto Alec's asphalt lane.

A distinguished-looking gentleman in his fifties was waiting for us as we screeched to a stop. His slightly disapproving frown hinted at decades of practice letting his 'bosses' know when they'd just crossed some kind of line, all the while never crossing any himself.

The shape shifters all exited the car, most before it had even stopped moving, and then Jessica and Dominic both appeared as I made my comparatively slow way out of the vehicle.

"...everyone's okay. I was somewhat worried about taking so much of our strength away. I'm glad it worked out."

Alec turned towards the older man as I made my hesitant way over to the group. "Donovan, this is the young lady we hosted last night. Adri, this is Donovan."

Feeling even more awkward than normal, I stuck out my hand, only to feel my eyes widen as he gracefully took my hand in his own, and bent down to brush his lips across it.

"My sincere apologies that we weren't better hosts. Please let me know if there is anything you need to make your stay here more comfortable."

I stammered out a thanks as Donovan released my hand. The rest of Alec's friends were already disappearing, Isaac and Jessica around back towards the garden, while James and

Dominic were already inside his car, and backing down the lane.

Alec took my hand as Donovan opened the front door for us. He walked with a definite limp, one that was all the more painful when contrasted against his otherwise graceful movements. I looked questioningly at Alec, but he shook his head, so I stayed quiet as he led me into the house.

Rachel was waiting for us in a luxuriously-furnished sitting room. "Mother's been asking for you, Alec. I told her you'd be back soon, but she's worried."

"I suppose this is a good opportunity to introduce Adriana."

For the first time since I'd found out about Alec's secret, Rachel was looking uncertain. She was suddenly the old Rachel I knew from school instead of the confident young woman who'd helped face down three terrifying shape shifters intent on sending me back to Brandon.

"Are you sure, Alec? I could go help her get settled into the Lilac Room."

Alec's smile was gentle. It reminded me of how Mom looked when I offered to take care of some especially undesirable duty she'd been procrastinating.

"No, Mother's still the mistress of this house. We've waited too long as it is. If we don't take care of it now it may be another week or two before we have a chance, and

Donovan will be severely disappointed in both of us."

They were both smiling now, as if at some shared joke, but that didn't help defuse the sudden feeling of nervousness sweeping through me. Rachel followed us down a series of corridors, and then waited as Alec knocked on a plain, oak door.

A half-second passed, and then responding to something too faint for me to hear, Alec gently opened the door. A slightly tilted eyebrow seemed to ask Rachel if she wanted to come inside, but she shook her head, now with the slightest of quivers to her chin.

Whatever I was expecting from Alec and Rachel's reactions, I didn't get it. The airy, sunlit room we walked into was almost like being outside. There were a number of plants scattered about the space, some resting on the floor, others on a variety of slender stands. The effect was ethereal. It was hard to imagine that any of the spun-metal stands could support anything more substantial than a box of Kleenex.

It wasn't until we were further inside that I realized there was an entire alcove off to one side, almost completely dominated by a black grand piano. The piano was so breathtaking it was several seconds before I realized there was someone sitting at it.

"Alec. I'm so glad you're safe. Rachel was going on and on about some kind of problem with the pack. She's so excitable. I told her everything would be fine, but she worries so. Your dad was the same way. Always going on and on about some crisis or another, but nothing ever really materialized."

Alec's mom was tiny. It was easy to see where Rachel got her slight frame from, but there was more than just genetics at work. I'd never seen someone with so little extra flesh on their bones, at least not outside a hospital. It seemed she should be wearing a hospital gown instead of the white, flower-print summer dress I was almost sure cost more than my whole wardrobe.

"We're experiencing a time of more than usual difficulty, Mother, but that isn't why I've come by. I wanted to present my friend Adriana to you. She'll be staying with us for the next few weeks."

I got a distracted smile. "That's nice, dear. You remind me so much of your father. So serious and worried all the time. Oh, how I miss him."

Alec let his mother take both of his hands in hers. "I know you do, Mother. Rachel and I miss him too."

Alec's mom tossed her head. "You barely remember him. Rachel's a good girl, but she was so young when he died. She can't really miss him. Not like I miss him."

For a second I thought he was going to argue with her. His tired smile had the feel of resignation, of something that'd been well argued over the years.

"Will you play something for us, Mother? Adriana hasn't had the pleasure of listening to your songs."

I'd rarely seen anyone change moods so quickly. "No. You know it isn't ready. I'll tell you when I've perfected it. Yes, you can bring Rachel, but I can't let anyone listen to it before it's ready."

Alec bowed his head in acquiescence, grasping my hand as he turned to leave. His mother grabbed his arm before he could complete the motion. He halted instantly, despite there being no way she was strong enough to stop him. I doubted she had enough grip strength to slow even me down.

"Don't be angry with me, Alec. You're all I have left."

"I'm not angry, Mother, but you're wrong. You have much more left than just me."

She shook her head with a youthful smile. "Such a good boy."

Rachel, tears coursing down her face, stormed off as Alec pulled his mother's door shut behind us.

I started to follow her, but Alec recaptured my hand in his. "She just needs a little time. Donovan will alert Jasmin."

My surprise must have bled through to my face. Alec's smile had a tinge of sadness to it as he led me away. "There's still a lot you don't know about all of the others. There's much I could tell you about Jasmin, but it isn't my story to share. Suffice it to say only Dominic has a greater capacity for empathy."

I wanted to ask what Alec meant, but it was more and more obvious he wasn't going to answer anything he didn't want to. We walked in comfortable silence for several minutes before turning off into what I could only assume was the Lilac Room.

Donovan looked up as we entered the suite. "I trust your mother was well, sir?"

Alec nodded, a short choppy motion that eloquently conveyed his desire not to discuss the matter. He turned towards me, only to break off as a cell phone rang.

"It's for you, probably your mom. Pretend you're home, I'll explain once you're finished."

I almost dropped the phone, and probably wouldn't have managed to figure out how to answer the call in time if he hadn't reached over and pushed the green button for me.

"Hello?"

"Adri, honey, are you sure this is a good idea? I haven't gotten on the charter plane yet, there's still time to call this off if you're uneasy about being alone for so long."

The last place I wanted her right now was home though, so it was easier than normal to lie.

"Mom, this is the chance of a lifetime. Don't worry about me, I'll be fine."

There was a long pause as her dreams warred with normal maternal instincts. I could hear a plane start up in the background by the time she finally responded.

"Okay, honey. If you're sure, then we'll do it, but if anything comes up just call me. I'll keep my cell phone with me all the time, and I made them promise to fly me back no questions asked if it became necessary."

I stifled a laugh at the idea of Mom making a twelve-hour flight back to the US because I stubbed my toe, and instead tried to interject even more sincerity into my voice.

"I'll be fine, Mom. I even promise to stay out of trouble. Have a safe flight."

I stared at the cell phone for several seconds before looking up at Alec, who was just putting a cell phone that could have been the twin to the one I was holding away.

"You redirected our calls?"

"Correct. That's what Isaac was doing in the kitchen after your mom left. I thought it might come to this, so I had him bring along some of his toys. You'll want to change the message sometime tonight, so you can let it roll to the voice mail if she calls while you're at school."

"You really do think of everything, don't you?"

His smile was surprisingly bashful. "I don't think you can go that far, but I try to anticipate most eventualities." The smile disappeared, and his face seemed to put on additional years. "For most of my life, there's been quite a bit riding on my ability to do so."

Seeking to break the tension, I pointed to his phone. "You got a call too?"

"Yes. I'm afraid something has come up. Will you be okay here for a few hours?"

Normal human response was to make a little white lie, but I got the feeling I wouldn't be able to get away with lying to Alec.

"I rather suspect whatever 'came up' is important enough I'll just have to be okay."

He flinched a little, like maybe my aim had been a little too true. He looked for a moment like he was going to say something, but then his phone started vibrating again, and he simply nodded as he turned and walked away, moving much faster by himself than he did when I was with him.

As I stared at the empty space where he'd been standing just a second before, I felt my chest start to constrict, and my breathing speed up. The sense of terror racing along my synapses was completely irrational, and extraordinarily powerful. Just as the room began to spin crazily around me, I felt a gentle touch on my shoulder.

"Mistress Paige, is there anything I can get you? Something to eat perhaps? Or if you'd rather, I can show you to the theater."

I chopped off a hysterical burst of laughter just before it managed to emerge full force and totally embarrass me. Of course Alec had a theater in his house. Probably a pool and a gym too. Along with a half-dozen other amenities I'd never think of, but that the ultra-rich simply couldn't do without.

I pulled my erratic, pointless thoughts back into a compact, nearly sensible ball, and shook my head as I did my best to give him a genuine smile. "No thanks. I probably won't be hungry for several hours still. Is there a library in the house perhaps?"

Donovan's smile had a surprising touch of mischief to it. "Actually, you could say that we have two. In a manner of speaking."

I felt a more genuine smile working its way across my face. "Could we go to one of them? I really should be doing my homework, but I'd much rather just curl up with a good book."

Donovan picked up the cell phone that I, unsure whether or not it was really mine, had left on the bed, and handed it to me. "I believe you'll want to keep this with you at all times. Otherwise it won't be able to fulfill its assigned purpose. And yes, we can most definitely go to one of the libraries. In fact, I believe you'll find the smaller one quite satisfactory. It has a copy of every textbook currently in use at your high school, in case you reconsider."

There were more turns than I had any hope of ever remembering, but eventually we made it to a familiar-looking door. At a nod from Donovan I pushed it open, and then as the furnishings registered, I turned back around. "This is Alec's room. I couldn't possibly..."

Donovan shook his head. "Young Mr. Graves instructed that you were to have every convenience. I'm sure that included access to what we all jokingly call the second library. Besides, this is where you'll find the copies of all your textbooks."

It must have been obvious I wasn't convinced, but Donovan wasn't dissuaded. He pointed to the cell phone, still grasped uncomfortably in my hand. "In the event that you need something, it is likely you can just say my name and I'll hear you. If not, that wonderfully infernal device is, I believe, programmed to call me if you hold down the number nine. I am of course completely at your service."

I opened my mouth to protest, but moving much too quickly, even with his painful-looking limp, to be a normal human, he'd already vanished around the corner.

I stood awkwardly in the doorway for several minutes, but I couldn't resist the draw of all those books forever. I finally broke down and started tracing various spines as I decided which one I'd start with. Unfortunately I found the textbooks before I made a final decision, and then guilt over how poorly I was doing in Biology and Spanish won out.

I was halfway through my second re-read of my Biology chapter when I heard a quiet knock at the door. Rachel giggled a little at my guilty start. "Don't worry; it's just fine that you're here. I ran into Donovan and he told me where to find you. I just wanted to apologize for earlier."

I shook my head violently. "No, you don't have anything to be sorry about. It...well, it was all so horrid. I can't imagine how hard it must be for you."

Rachel stopped me before I could say anything else. "It's pretty rough, but not for the reasons you think. Mom isn't entirely healthy. Hasn't been since our father was killed. It isn't really her fault she behaves the way she does. When we humans get involved with shape shifters sometimes we pay a pretty serious price."

It took me several seconds to understand why Rachel's words seemed so odd. Ever since learning Alec's secret I'd assumed everyone here was a shape shifter. Only I hadn't ever felt the underlying hint of power and energy from her that I'd come to associate with Alec and the others.

"Wait, you're not a shape shifter? How is that possible?"

Rachel's expression as she tried to understand my question was so surprised it actually managed to lighten the mood.

"Oh, I forget sometimes how much you don't know. I'm normal, and Mom's normal, but everyone else is a shape shifter. Human-shape shifter marriages almost never happen, but when they do the kids can go either way. Alec became a shape shifter, and I'm just a run-of-the-mill girl without even a single superpower."

We sat in silence for several seconds as I tried to process how that new piece of information fit in with everything else I already knew. The obvious, if somewhat selfish, implication was that maybe it really was possible for someone like Alec to want to be with someone like me. There were plenty of other things to think about though.

"Wow, is that hard? I mean living with people who can do all those things?"

Rachel's shrug was surprisingly sincere. "It was a bit at first, especially right after Alec first started manifesting. Okay, maybe I was crazy jealous then, and again a couple of years later when it became apparent I wasn't going to manifest anything, but I got over it."

My raised eyebrow was completely involuntary, and apparently more eloquent than I'd realized. At least it earned me another laugh. "It wasn't like it was easy or anything, but Donovan gave me some good advice when things were the worst. I don't remember his exact words, but essentially it came down to the fact that there'll always be people who're better than me at something. Even gaining super powers wouldn't change that. What's important is that I do the best I can with what I've been given. As crazy as it sounds, Alec's pack needs me."

I mentally reached around for something similar and then finally nodded. "I guess I can understand that. My mom would have a hard time functioning without me, so I try to do the best I can at taking care of her."

Rachel's smile lit the room up. "That's it exactly. Anyways, I mostly just wanted to stop by and see if us girls can take you shopping tomorrow."

The non sequitur really threw me for a loop. "I left my money at home. I'm not much of a shopper anyways."

That last part sounded pretty weak even to me.

"Don't be silly. Alec hustled you out of your house so quickly you didn't get to bring anything but the clothes on your back. Jasmin's clothes will fit you pretty well, but that's only a short-term solution. We need to get you stuff to wear, and since it was Alec who created this mess, it's only fair he be the one to pay."

I was absolutely sure there was no way I was ever going to fit into anything Jasmin owned, but girls being girls, there was no point in protesting. Regardless of the truth, Rachel would be obliged to say I was just as skinny as Jasmin.

"I don't think Alec exactly got me into all of this. It was more like my own stupidity that landed me in this particular batch of trouble."

"Please, as if any girl who didn't know what a jerk Brandon was would've done anything different. He's gorgeous. It isn't until you realize just how hollow he is that anyone has a chance of resisting him."

There wasn't really any response to that. "So, what's going to happen now? I mean with Brandon's pack? Everyone seemed really worried last night."

"I'm not sure. Not really. It won't be straightforward; nothing involving Brandon ever is. His pack is bigger, but we've always had the laws on our side before this..." Rachel broke off as my eyes got bigger. "Sorry, that's touching on some of the things I'm not supposed to tell you."

I shrugged, pretending indifference. "How soon will we know if it's really bad or just a little bad?"

"I don't know. Things were already pretty tense. That's probably where Alec is right now actually. Brandon's people are always skirting around the edge of our territory, but tonight they'll be out in greater numbers than normal. If things don't boil over now, it's pretty much guaranteed that there will be some kind of confrontation Monday at school."

The word *confrontation* reached out and grabbed me. It took a second before I realized it was dragging up memories of the near-fight between Alec and half his pack. "What happened last night...it was for real, wasn't it?"

Rachel didn't ask what I meant; she didn't even bat an eye. "I'm afraid so. Don't hate the others too much. Sometimes when you're that scared it's hard to keep things in perspective. Now that they've calmed down a little nobody would really trade you to Brandon on the tiny chance it might smooth things over. Not when we'll eventually end up in exactly the same spot."

"It felt kind of like a game of capture the flag, with me as the flag." It wasn't the most flattering comparison ever invented, but at least it allowed me to try and convince myself I'd imagined the near-violence.

Rachel's laugh was short and bitter. "That would be quite the understatement. I've known all five of them for quite a while. Most of them my whole life. Even so, I don't really know what it's like to be a shape shifter. Most of the time it just means they're faster and stronger than me. That they can heal from things that would kill me almost instantly. Sometimes though, the other side of their nature shows through."

I felt my heart speed up as Rachel met my eyes with more gravity even than normal. "They aren't always completely in control, Adri. They try, and some of them are really good. Alec is probably the most controlled person I've ever met, and Isaac is so disciplined he's almost immune to the power plays. Even so, sometimes it's like they operate on a shorter fuse than the rest of us."

My throat was so dry it took me two attempts to clear it. "Could Alec have won?" The question stuck in my throat, reluctant to come out. It felt disloyal to Alec but I had to know.

"I don't know. Individually Alec could take any of them. There's a reason he's dominant to all of the rest of them. James is a hybrid too. He isn't even second in the pack because Isaac is a better fighter than him, but he makes for a strong third. Jasmin is essentially fourth, although sometimes she gets away with bossing James and even Isaac around. Apparently she's a lot tougher than a normal wolf should be, and she's just crazy enough to fight to the death over something that the other two don't think is really all that important. Jessica is pretty much the most submissive, not by temperament, but because she's the weakest fighter we've got."

I felt my eyes go wide at all the new terms, but kept my mouth shut because I was worried Rachel would clam up if I started asking questions.

"I'm pretty sure Alec could take two of them, but not all three. They knew that, which was part of the reason they were pushing so hard."

I felt shivers crawl up my spine, but what could someone say after something like that? Rachel reached over and gave me a hug. "Try not to think about it too much. Just remember that Alec's dominant to everyone here, and he'd die for either of us without even a heartbeat's worth of hesitation."

After Rachel left I spent the next hour trying to get comfortable in Alec's desk chair. It was likely the discomfort was more due to the subject matter than the chair, but I just couldn't get comfortable. I finally moved my books over to the bed and sprawled out on it. Spanish, Math, History, Biology, English. The subjects all blurred together as the hours passed by in a blur of academic exhaustion.

I wanted to go to sleep long before dark, but couldn't justify it, so I just kept grinding along. I'd long ago learned that changing subjects and studying something new was almost as good as a break, so I swapped out books on a regular basis, and persevered despite increasingly-frequent head bobs.

The attack came as a complete surprise. One moment I was quietly studying, an instant later hordes of shape shifters were pouring into the mansion. Most of them looked just like Simon and Nathanial, pony-sized wolves moving with blinding speed as they tore through doors and raced down halls.

Brandon came in immediately behind the first batch of wolves. There was no way I could've known that the gray monster who casually sliced through walls and two-by-fours with his wickedly curved claws was Brandon, but I was somehow certain. He was built just like Alec had been Friday night, only so much bigger that he had to crouch forward to avoid hitting his head on the unusually high ceilings.

Donovan faced off against one of the first wolves, but it was obvious he was no match for the grace and power of his opponent. The gentle, aging butler was knocked to the ground between one heartbeat and the next. I was mercifully spared from seeing the wreckage left when Brandon's wolves moved on, but there was no doubt in my mind that Donovan was dead.

Screams, distant enough that they had to be coming from the other wing of the house, reached out and pierced my heart. There wasn't any way to be sure whether or not it was Rachel or her mother, but ultimately it didn't really matter. Brandon was going to kill all of us.

Another door caved in under a blow from Brandon's fist, and I suddenly realized that he was now standing in the Lilac Room. "Spread out and find her."

The words were nearly unintelligible, coming as they did from a throat that shared little in common with Homo sapiens, but the venom behind them was unmistakable.

I fled the bed where I'd been studying, and hid in Alec's studio, but I could hear them getting closer, the dissident melody of growls, howls, and destruction growing stronger as they rampaged through the house.

Terror stretched time out, but even so it felt as though only seconds had passed before I felt Brandon enter Alec's suite. I crouched frozen on the floor as my death crept ever closer. As Brandon crashed through the studio's far wall in an explosion of plaster and lumber, I tried to shield my eyes, only to find that I couldn't move.

The incongruity of being restrained when I couldn't see anything constraining my movements was enough to finally snap me back to wakefulness, but it was still several seconds before I stopped thrashing and realized it'd just been an extraordinarily terrifying nightmare.

As soon as I stopped moving, the iron band around my arms relaxed and slipped away. "Are you okay? I'm sorry about that, I was afraid you were going to hurt yourself."

Alec's even tones caressed me like a calming breeze. I finally oriented myself enough to realize that the warm, solid surface my back was resting against wasn't a wall.

"I'm sorry. It was a nightmare." My voice came out raw and scratchy, like I'd been talking for hours, or possibly just screaming for the last minute or so. I wanted to tell him about what had happened, but now that I was awake my fears felt foolish. I tried to distract myself by looking around, and then felt my face heat up as I realized I'd fallen asleep in Alec's room.

"I'm so sorry, Alec. Donovan and Rachel told me you had copies of our textbooks in here. I was studying and must have fallen asleep. Please don't think..." I felt tears start to gather at the corner of my eyes, but there wasn't any way to tell whether they were attributable to simple terror, acute embarrassment, or a combination of the two.

Alec's arm was back, and he gently hugged me against his chest. "It was all just a dream, and you don't have anything to be sorry about. I don't mind you being here. I'm sorry I had to leave you alone for so long, it was inexcusable."

I wanted to say something, wanted to tell Alec he didn't need to worry about me, that I'd spent enough time by myself lately to be happy with my own company, but the words wouldn't come out. The sheer pleasure at having him hold me so close was like a drug. I could feel the pleasant, tingly sensation I'd started associating with his touch, and it was like the best full-body massage, tied up with chocolate and reading a classic.

Unaware of my mild state of euphoria, Alec continued on. "Actually, I owe you another apology. When I returned and found you here I meant to carry you to your room. I was only going to sit down for a second, but apparently I was more exhausted than I realized. I hope you don't think my actions are inappropriate."

I managed to slowly shake my head no, despite my lassitude. Alec waited several seconds, and then sighed. "Well, I suppose I'd better get you off to bed."

The words initially didn't mean anything to me. I heard them, but my mind refused to assign meanings to the sounds. It wasn't until he'd moved his arm and rolled out of bed with his characteristic speed and grace that I finally realized he meant to take me to the Lilac Room and then return here to sleep.

I suddenly had a hard time breathing. The idea of lying alone in the dark, in the very room I'd just seen Brandon demolish, sent my heart into an erratic rhythm. If there'd been an EMT present they'd have already been charging up the defibrillator.

Alec turned around while I was still trying to get my throat to work again. "You stopped breathing. What's wrong?"

The tears his touch had dried up a few seconds before were back, and just seconds away from escaping the corners of my eyes by the time I finally pulled myself up onto my knees and managed to speak.

"Please don't send me there. Not after my dream."

There was just enough moonlight trickling into the room for me to see his expression change. My stomach seemed to reach up and wrap itself around my heart as I realized it was the expression he used when it was important to him that people not know what he was thinking.

"I'm not sure that's the best idea."

The tears finally made their escape as I crumpled back onto the bed. "You're right. I'm so sorry to be such a bother." The words were broken by gasping sobs, but they were understandable, if only just barely.

Alec's hand on my shoulder just made me try to roll away. I didn't want his pity. Not after everything else he'd already done for me. Guilting him into helping me more just felt wrong.

He captured me in his iron grip, stopping me from getting up and running away. "Adriana Paige, it isn't that I don't want to be with you. I want it more than anything else right now. *That's* why I'm not sure it's such a good idea."

His face had somehow gotten so close to mine that I could see his eyes, and they were dead serious. I'd never noticed how clear his eyes were. They were the purest blue I'd ever seen, and looking into them was like trying to plumb the depths of a bottomless spring. I could see further into him than I ever could with Brandon, and there wasn't any deception there.

I nodded, and then buried my face against his chest as I cried myself out. It was several minutes before I was able to speak again.

"You're so ready to send me away it's hard to believe sometimes that you really want me here."

Alec stroked the side of my face, ending by tucking a strand of hair back in place behind my ear. "I really want nothing as badly as I want you here. If I were to be completely selfish I'd never have even made the offer, but that wouldn't have been fair to you."

I snuggled closer to him. "Well, I just want to log my vote for you to be more selfish."

Alec's dry chuckle hinted at old hurts. "According to my father, we shape shifters were created specifically for the purpose of not being selfish, of watching out for the dayborn even at the expense of our own desires."

"You miss your dad. I can tell it in your voice."

His shrug would've been imperceptible except for the fact his arms were still wrapped around me. "I do. I don't really remember him, but I've read through his journals dozens of times. It seems crazy to miss what you never knew, but there are days when I really wish he were still around to give me advice. I think that's what I missed the most. That and his stories."

I smiled. "That sounds nice. We never got stories at my house. Dad played with us plenty, but bedtime was bedtime."

"Donovan said Dad used to tell me stories every night. After Dad died Donovan took over telling them to both Rachel and me. It wasn't until after I grew up that I found out they were legends about where we came from. That we weren't normal like everyone else."

"Like the...dayborn? What did you mean earlier?"

Alec was quiet for so long that I thought maybe he wasn't going to answer. "That touches on the things you shouldn't know."

"Please. It will help me go to sleep. I need something else to think about." It was a bit of a white lie. As soon as he'd touched me everything else ceased to matter.

"Once upon a time the Sun and the Earth loved each other. So much so that the Sun sent her children down to live upon the Earth's face."

I was relaxing so quickly that I wasn't sure how much longer I would be able to stay awake, but his story was already different than any other I'd heard, and I resolved I wasn't going to miss any of it. As long as he was willing to talk I was going to fight off sleep.

"Something happened though to break the bonds between the Sun and the Earth. Some say the Earth insulted the Sun, who is incredibly vain. Others believe the Sun's children marred the face of the Earth, and that when she refused to discipline her wayward family, the Earth swore in his wrath to destroy them."

Alec adjusted his pillow and continued. "Whatever the cause, it's commonly held that this was the point at which the Earth ceased to be a paradise. Bountiful gardens were replaced by weeds and thorns. Hurt and betrayed, the Sun distanced herself from the Earth, lessening the number of life-giving rays warming his surface. Possibly that was his plan. If she'd totally abandoned him then her children would've all died."

I felt my eyelids begin to flutter, as my breathing slowed to match Alec's.

"Whether that was his intent or not, the Sun didn't completely abandon him, either out of respect for what they'd shared, or possibly out of concern for her children. Once it became apparent that the Earth and Sun were through with each other, the Moon began to court her. Doomed to touch only briefly during the rare solar eclipses, they nevertheless became beloved, one to the other. The greatest sign of the Moon's devotion to the Sun came about when he sent his children down to the Earth to watch over and protect the sunborn, or dayborn as they are most often called."

Alec's pause was long enough that I think I nodded off, but the sound of his voice once he resumed talking pulled me back awake.

"Originally there were just two of the moonborn, a pair of brothers called Adjam and Inock. Unbeknown to the Moon, the Earth had anticipated his great gesture of love, and sent forth a plague upon the land. As Adjam, the elder of the brothers, descended from the heavens and touched down upon the Earth, he collapsed to the ground in pain. Despite his agony as the very bones of his body rearranged themselves, he managed to call out a warning to Inock, to flee back to the Moon. The love of

Inock for Adjam was so great that he rushed to his brother's side, where he too fell victim to the Earth's plague."

I wanted so very badly to remain awake, but wrapped comfortably in the warmth of Alec's arms, I couldn't fight off exhaustion any longer, and I felt myself drift off into dreams of two brothers who survived the plague, rising from the ground after seven days, one a wolf, the other a jaguar.

Chapter 24

I'd been awake for several minutes before I finally remembered where I was. I rolled over, opened my eyes, groaning when I saw that the other side of the bed was empty.

Who knew what Alec thought. He'd obviously fled his own room to avoid talking to me when I finally woke up.

Donovan's gentle knock and appearance at the door pulled me up short before I could really get going on the self-loathing. "Good morning Mistress Paige, I hope you slept well."

He limped into the room with his odd, somehow graceful lurch, and then set down a tray filled with eggs, French toast, orange juice and everything else you'd expect if you were to go to IHOP and order their 'everything but the kitchen sink' special.

While I was still trying to catalog everything on the tray, Donovan laid out a full set of clothes, everything either in unopened manufacturer's plastic bags, or with price tags still attached.

"Mistress Rachel thought you might desire a change of clothes seeing as how Master Alec carried you off without providing proper time for you to pack your things. I pray though that you not think too harshly of him. It was he who prepared your breakfast. A small act of atonement, but still a start nonetheless."

It was all so surprising that it took me a moment to find my voice. "Thank you, Donovan. Have I slept in too long?"

A gentle smile met my inquiry. "Those of us who don't require normal amounts of sleep have all been up for quite some time, with the exception of Master Alec, who remained abed for an uncharacteristic length of time, but the rest of the house is just now waking. In fact I rather suspect you have just enough time to shower and eat before Mistress Rachel will be pounding on the door, as it were, in excitement for your upcoming trip into town."

A groan escaped me despite my best efforts. Donovan was too polite to ask outright, but I had to respond to his raised eyebrow or he might think I didn't want to talk to Rachel. "I'm sorry, Donovan, it's just that I *really* hate shopping."

"Ah, yes. Might I suggest that possibly is due to the fact you've never pursued the activity in the right company?"

Right company indeed. I'd expected it would just be Rachel and I, and that we'd make a quick run in to Sanctuary, which seemed silly seeing as how my house was just as close as town was. I was wrong on both accounts.

The *company*, as Donovan had dubbed it, also included Dominic and Jasmin. Dominic had smiled shyly in my direction as we'd climbed into an ostentatious black Mercedes. Jasmin just looked like she'd rather be anywhere than on babysitting duty.

Rachel had explained that Alec didn't want us delicate, fragile girls traveling alone, so he'd assigned us bodyguards, who happened to also be female and delicate-looking, but who weren't nearly as fragile.

Also, it turned out we weren't going to Sanctuary, or St. George, or even anywhere in Utah, a fact I didn't realize until we'd been on the road for twenty minutes.

"Oh, Adri, don't be silly. You can't do real shopping in Sanctuary. Besides, Alec wouldn't have let the four of us go alone if we'd been planning on staying so close to Brandon's territory. Vegas was definitely the best option given the time restrictions we're under."

I'd settled in for a long trip, only to realize as we crossed the state line that Jasmin was positively shattering the speed limit. I managed to limit myself to a single gulp, when I saw just how fast she was going, but everyone else was so relaxed that I finally managed to unclench my fists and join back in the conversation. It helped that the Mercedes was so smooth, and that I knew Jasmin had reflexes and reaction time that would've made any Indy racer insanely jealous.

Apparently there wasn't a single cop on duty, because we made it into downtown Vegas in what I was sure was record time. It had to be. Jasmin hadn't dropped below triple digits until we were less then fifteen minutes from exiting the interstate.

It wasn't until we hit the first store that I started to get an idea of what Donovan had been hinting at. The shyness Rachel normally exhibited at school was replaced by supreme confidence the moment we crossed the threshold of the first store. Armani, Versace, Prada, we conducted a tour de force of them all along with others whose names I didn't even recognize.

The shopping trip was ostensibly for me, but Rachel cajoled both Jasmin and Dominic into dressing rooms on more than one occasion. Amazingly enough, everything she picked out for them fit so perfectly that I began to agree with them that there wasn't much point in even trying anything on.

The first store we stopped at didn't take us seriously until Rachel pulled out a black

American Express, after which every sales person in the entire place lined up to assist us.

Once we each sported a bag or two from some ridiculously over-priced store, things went much more smoothly. I tried on a variety of jeans, blouses, shirts, skirts, dresses, and just about every other article of clothing imaginable. I drew the line at a swimsuit, since there was no way on earth I'd ever wear one, and then felt so bad at how crushed Rachel was that I let her drag me into a store full of formals. It was a mistake because I soon found myself being zipped into a delicate, green dress that I was absolutely positive wasn't going to survive the experience of trying to wrap itself around me.

"Oh, it's perfect, Adri. We have to get it."

I avoided looking at the mirror. It seemed like a crime to defile such a pretty dress, and I wanted to remember it like it had looked on the hanger, all shimmery and wispy. I did risk a look down at the price tag. My heart actually skipped a beat. That was more than some people spent on their first car.

"Rachel, you've already bought me way too much. I can't let you get this. Not only will I never wear it, you could practically feed small countries with what you'd have to pay for all this."

She started to pout, but I'd already been taken by that tactic once today, and caving in had just landed me in deeper trouble. "I'm serious, Rachel; we are not walking out of the store with this dress. You can throw a temper tantrum if you want, but I'm not giving in."

Rachel glared at me for several seconds, and then suddenly smiled. "Okay, Adri. I mean I was just trying to do something nice for you, but if you're going to be like that, we'll leave it here."

Her grin didn't engender trust, but when I opened my mouth to call her on it, she forestalled me with an upraised hand. "I swear. We'll go home and leave the dress here."

The pout came back out for a moment. "But, if you're not going to let me buy this for you, I'm going to need to compensate by buying something for Jasmin."

Rachel flounced off, followed by a frowning Jasmin, leaving Dominic to help me out of the straitjacket I was currently using as a dress.

Chapter 25

I slowly stretched, and then turned over and smiled when I found Alec lying on top of the covers.

"Good morning, beautiful." As always, his voice sent shivers down my spine.

By the time we'd arrived home, it was ridiculously late, and I'd barely managed to stay awake long enough to bolt down a little dinner after Donovan had helped us unload our haul. I'd then done the single most gutsy thing of my entire existence. I'd quietly followed Alec back to his room and then asked if I could sleep there again.

He'd given me another of those long looks that seemed to say he thought it was a bad idea, but that he couldn't bring himself to deny my request. Not with everything else he couldn't do for me.

"Please, I must look horrid. If you'd known I could look this bad, you'd never have bothered saving me from Simon and Nathanial."

Alec cocked his head to the side, as if trying to decide how to respond to my half-serious jest.

"Actually I was completely serious. You are beautiful."

I waited for the inevitable joke, or backhanded compliment to follow, but he seemed happy to just stop there. For once in my life I managed to be smart and do the same.

"So what's the agenda for today?"

Alec stretched and then shrugged. "School, just like every Monday."

My groan brought a smile to his face. "I can ship pesky parents out of the country, but if you start a wholesale program of cutting class your mom will find out when she gets back."

"So I just go about my day like normal, pretending like I don't know Brandon's a psychopath who just happens to be able to change shapes at will and rip big holes in brick walls?"

I finally rolled out of bed, and started picking through the pile of bags from our shopping trip, hoping to find something that wouldn't make it look like I'd just won the lottery or robbed a bank.

"Now you know how Rachel feels. I'm afraid that with only a couple of differences, it'll be business as usual."

I finally settled on a white button-up, and headed to the bathroom so I could change.

"So are you going to tell me what the differences are, or is that part of the stuff I'm not allowed to know?"

Alec's chuckle was muffled by the closed door, but still brought a smile to my face. "The biggest difference will be that we're going to have to shuffle some class schedules to make sure Brandon and his pack don't have access to you or Rachel. Everything else is just kind of a corollary to that. At least one pack member will need to be with you whenever you leave the house."

I spit out the toothpaste currently prohibiting me from being able to respond, and swung the door open. "Alec, it's the middle of the semester. We can't just walk into the office and tell them we want to change our schedules. It doesn't work that way."

After seeing Vincent's 'accident', and knowing he'd probably been trying to kill or at least seriously injure Ben just for the fun of it, I couldn't really argue with Alec. Rachel seemed relatively unfazed by the idea of bodyguards, but I wasn't especially excited about yet another point of difference between me and everyone else. Still, school was both better and worse than expected.

As Alec had intimated, the day started out with a trip to the office. Not just me, not even just me and Alec. The entire pack trooped into the room, filling it with impeccably dressed, mostly gorgeous, shape shifters, who gave off a perceptible tingle of energy if you knew what to look for.

I'd really thought Alec was tilting at windmills right up until he politely, but firmly asked for a brief meeting with the principal and was ushered into the other man's office five seconds later. Alec drew the blinds, which didn't do anything to muffle the principal's raised voice. Fifteen minutes later, after the unmistakable feeling of Alec's power had crested to the point where it almost felt like there was a breeze blowing from the office, we were all sitting down with the bewildered school counselor and playing musical classes. Only it turned out Rachel and I were the only ones not changing our schedules. I started to protest being treated differently than everyone else, only to feel my mouth click shut as Rachel shook her head at me.

It wasn't until Alec was walking me to Biology that I finally got an explanation. "You and Rachel are the ones who need the most sleep, ergo you don't change classes."

"That's crazy." I would've stopped. You can't really have a good disagreement while you're walking down the hall, but we happened to be holding hands, which he used to keep me moving along. And here I'd been so excited back in the councilor's office when he'd taken my hand.

"It's not crazy. Everyone who swaps classes is going to be doing double homework for the duration. Assignments for their old class, which they presumably still want to get credit for, and assignments for the new class so as not to make any more waves than necessary with their temporary teacher. It only makes sense to place that burden on the ones who can most easily deal with it."

That last part had been said in a near whisper, due to the fact that we were right outside Mrs. Sorenson's class. Everything he was saying made sense, but didn't resolve the real reason I was so worried.

"I can help. I could switch at least one class and still keep up."

Alec shook his head. "Adriana, you're struggling in two classes already. How do you propose to handle yet another set of homework?"

I felt my mouth slam shut. He knew everything about everyone, but it still somehow caught me by surprise that he knew so much about me.

"But they'll hate me even more." I already wished I could take it back, but it was too late.

It took less than half a second for him to figure out who I was talking about.

"They don't hate you. A few of them are scared almost senseless, but nobody hates you."

"They were willing to kill me. They wanted to trade me back to Brandon." It came out as something less than a whisper, but apparently Alec's hearing was acute enough to catch that too.

Alec drew me close, heedless of the open door and the twenty staring kids. He placed the side of his face against mine and whispered into my ear. "I'm not going to let anything happen to you. If there's a way to keep you safe I'll find it."

The feel of his breath caressing my cheek sent tingles racing through my entire body, but even that couldn't completely reassure me. Still, I gave it my best effort, and if my smile wasn't entirely convincing, it was at least good enough to temporarily reassure Alec.

I followed him into class, pausing while he handed his note to Mrs. Sorenson. It was almost worth all of the craziness and exhaustion of the last seventy-two hours to see her eyebrows rise in astonishment as she read the innocuous piece of paper essentially giving Alec carte blanche in her classroom.

"This is highly irregular, Mr. Graves. In fact I don't believe the administration can legitimately expect me to comply."

Alec's smile could have been used to sweeten pretty much any beverage you could imagine. "I promise not to get in the way. In fact if you could just find us a couple of desks in the back corner you'll hardly know we're here."

The look she shot me was so venomous for a second I thought my heart was going to stop.

"Ms. Paige has an assigned seat towards the front of the class. Based on her scholastic performance to date it would be highly irresponsible of me as an educator to allow her to change seats."

I was just far enough off to the side to watch as Alec's eyes very slowly and pointedly drifted down to stare at the note in her hands. For a second I wasn't sure she'd gotten the hint, but then those same hands clenched reflexively, nearly tearing the note before she caught herself and smoothed it back out.

"Ms. Bellarose, please move up to Ms. Paige's old seat."

Alec politely collected his note and led me to our seats.

Any enjoyment I'd just experienced as a result of seeing one of my least-favorite teachers put in her place quickly soured as she started the class and launched into her usual barrage of questions designed to demonstrate my stupidity.

Alec had apparently gotten under her skin even more than I'd realized. She abandoned her usual practice of stopping once I missed my first question, and instead continued to grill me, her smile growing each time I failed to answer something correctly.

My earlier commitment to rededicate myself to school notwithstanding, the weekend hadn't exactly been conducive to mastering the intricacies of our latest subject. Her smile was wide indeed by the time the bell finally released me to flee in defeat and embarrassment.

Alec paced me all the way back to my locker. "Is that normal for her?"

I started to laugh, only to cut the motion short as I realized there was a better than even chance I'd end up crying instead. I settled for just nodding as I swapped books and slammed my locker shut.

Alec pursed his lips for a second and then nodded, not at me, but at whatever decision he'd just made. "We'd better get you to your next class. Dealing with that will have to wait until later."

I wanted to ask what he meant, but the halls were already full of other students, and I was pretty sure he'd tell me when he was ready and not a moment sooner anyways.

With a sigh, I followed him into the crowd. A few minutes later I'd been handed off to my next babysitter, James this time, and was safely ensconced in Mr. Whethers' class.

Mr. Whethers looked more than a little confused after reading James' note, but he simply added James' name to his roll, and then absently waved the two of us towards seats. I would've enjoyed English if not for the wildfire buzz created by my little scene with Alec outside of Biology. Mr. Whethers repeatedly asked various clumps of giggling and or staring girls to be quiet, but his efforts were largely wasted.

BROKEN

As time went on the speculation grew both wilder and louder rather than petering out as any normal person would've expected. The former was probably due to an almost complete lack of anything resembling actual fact. The volume was no doubt designed to see if they could draw a reaction out of me and thereby figure out how I'd gone from dating one of the two most popular boys in school to dating the other one in the space of just one weekend.

The prevailing opinion among the popular girls off to the left was that I was the biggest slut ever. The equally vindictive but more scholastically minded group in front of us was convinced I was just playing with Alec in an attempt to make Brandon jealous.

It was all so far off that part of me wanted to laugh. I couldn't care less if Brandon was jealous, and Alec hadn't even kissed me yet. Even so, hearing my name said with such disdain by so many different people took its toll over the course of the class, and before long I was once again fighting the urge to break down and cry.

Luckily by the end of the class, Mr. Whethers had become so frustrated with the complete lack of attention being paid him by the gossipers, he'd actually started writing them up for detention.

As class finally ended, James cracked one of the first smiles I'd ever seen grace his face. "Wow. I never would've thought anyone could push old Whethers so far. He just set a school record for the most detentions assigned in a single class."

With James' considerable frame opening a route through the crowded hallway, it took almost no time to make it to my locker.

Jasmin was waiting for me, and if she didn't exactly look overwhelmed with joy, she at least wasn't scowling.

We were just outside Mrs. Campbell's class when a muted hiss from Jasmin alerted me to impending danger. I didn't realize what was happening until I felt the rising tingle of energy wash over me. It was both warmer and weaker than normal, and for the first time I realized that Jasmin's power was different than what I'd felt from Alec. It arced back and forth between us with a fury that jolted me all the way down to the soles of my feet as Vincent and Cassie came into sight.

The answering surges of power from the two rival shape shifters made my hair stand on end as Jasmin shoved me into the classroom, moving with only slightly more than human speed. I probably should have cleared out of the way, but despite there being nothing I could do to help Jasmin if it came to an open fight, I wasn't going to abandon her.

As Vincent and Cassie got closer, something about them seemed off. It is amazing how the mind focuses in on minutia when things get really scary, but I couldn't think of anything else until I realized it was their eyes. Cassie's had gone a pale, unearthly green, while Vincent's had deepened into a near black. If eyes really were the windows to the soul, he'd become so twisted and warped there wasn't much left that could truly be considered human.

The halls had emptied remarkably fast, especially considering how much gossip there was for the rumor mill. It was almost like some primitive survival instinct had kicked in and steered everyone away from ground zero.

With the two of them so much closer, I could feel their energy beating at Jasmin and me. It was all I could do now to remain motionless as they entered what even I knew was striking range of Jasmin.

"Awfully exposed out here, aren't you, precious?"

Vincent's voice was a low, unnatural thing, pitched so it was just barely audible for humans.

Cassie's expression made my stomach tighten up and my gorge rise. It wasn't right for a girl to look at another girl like that. Like she couldn't wait to watch Vincent do all kinds of terrible things.

"Payback sucks, doesn't it?"

Jasmin's complete stillness was an eerie counterpoint to the waves of power still beating at me. I somehow knew she was just seconds away from springing when the sound of running footsteps caused all three to turn.

Alec appeared around the corner, followed by Isaac, just a split second before Brandon sauntered into view from the opposite direction.

The tingly feeling grew exponentially more powerful with so many more shape shifters present. Rubbing my arms did nothing to ward off the feeling that entire colonies of insects were skittering across my skin.

Mr. Rindell's appearance forestalled what I'd been sure would turn into a full-blown fight. He sized up the situation with the canny eye of an educator who'd seen more fights over his career than most gang leaders. "Class is about to start, and if every one of you isn't where you're supposed to be before the bell rings, you'll have detention for the next month."

Vincent's hiss was still almost inaudible. "This isn't over."

I felt my knees almost collapse as the two packs slowly backed away from each other, and Jasmin joined me inside the classroom.

Mrs. Campbell gave the two of us a considering look after reading Jasmin's note, but sent us off to a pair of empty seats at the back of the classroom without comment. We were starting a new unit, but I couldn't concentrate on the lecture.

Alec's unshakable calm over the last few days had mostly convinced me the other members of his pack had been overreacting. Somehow I'd ~~me~~ to believe the coming dispute with

Brandon's pack would be resolved as easily as a normal teenage dispute.

After experiencing such intense, barely restrained violence, I was starting to see just how ludicrous that'd been. People had already died over what was going on here. It hadn't been real, either because I hadn't examined Simon and Nathanial's lifeless bodies, or maybe because I was repressing the experience like I'd done with so many other parts of my life lately.

I could feel my mind trying to shut down, hoping to cushion me from the worst implications of what was coming. I knew it was going to be bad, could feel it in a sickening, only-seconds-away-from-vomiting kind of way, but couldn't follow the chain of logic through to the very end.

I let Jasmin help me pull my books together, and then numbly followed her out to the hallway. Alec and the rest of the pack were waiting for us at my locker. Jasmin calmly opened my locker and put my things away while I was still trying to come to terms with everything.

Alec took my hand. "Are you okay?"

I shook my head. "This is going to be really bad, isn't it?"

His silence validated my belief, probably even more than he realized. "I'd...we'd...spare you it if we could."

It was my turn to shake my head. "No, this is my fault. I belong here, not cowering in a corner somewhere."

Rachel hugged me from one side while Dominic placed a gentle, dark hand on my other shoulder, and then we were off.

Brandon, and what must have amounted to his entire pack, were waiting for us just off school property. The two leaders faced off as everyone else fanned out around them. Jasmin, Isaac, and the others all maintained calm exteriors that were markedly different than the eager, often sadistic expressions of Brandon's people.

"I demand satisfaction on behalf of my pack for the two of our number that you brutally murdered. This is within my rights under the laws that bind us. I demand two lives for the two lives robbed me."

Brandon's expression was confident and a little smug, and I somehow didn't doubt in the slightest that he'd expected Alec to calmly hand over two people to be executed.

Alec hadn't even flinched at the demand. "Your wolves were lawbreakers who were executed before they could break further laws. The protection of the people, of the secrets that guard our nature from the dayborn, represents a law that supersedes any question of territory or dominance."

The energy suddenly rolling off of the gathered shape shifters nearly drove me to my knees as Alec continued.

"By their actions Adriana Paige learned of our nature, and it was only by the grace of the

Maker that I was able to stop them from killing her. Their deaths were an unavoidable price to save an innocent."

Some of the faces across the circle from me flinched a little, and I had a moment to wonder if Brandon hadn't told them the truth about what'd happened.

"Her life belonged to me, it was mine to dispose of as I saw fit."

I opened my mouth to protest, but closed it at a sharp jab in the ribs from Rachel.

"The ancient laws don't support her life being a disposable commodity, extinguished at your whim. Not even the bond of Ja'tell provides you with that right."

Brandon's grin was wider even than before. "Ah, but those aren't the laws under which we labor now, are they? She's mine, and I have every right to do whatever I wish to her. Her presence among your pack is a direct affront to my rights and honor. I could demand your life, be glad I'm only requiring two of your pack."

Alec shook his head, face more emotionless than even a second before. "By the same laws set down by Adjam and Inock when they first took mates from among the dayborn, I challenge your bond of Ja'tell. I challenge your standing among the people, and your personal honor. The dispute between us is such as can only be settled by blood."

For a brief second it seemed Brandon had been taken by surprise, but he regained his equilibrium while I was still trying to understand what was being said. He closed the distance between himself and Alec with such quickness that for a second I thought they were going to fight then and there.

For the first time I realized just how much bigger Brandon was than Alec. I'd never seen them so close together. They were so careful not to cross paths, it was possible this was a true first, but seeing them now there was no way to get around the fact that Brandon was at least two inches taller, as well as being broader and more muscular. I'd seen Alec shirtless, and he had the incredible physique of a swimsuit model, but Brandon's was that of a professional body builder. Either of them dwarfed me, but Brandon gave off an air of menace that even Alec's controlled power couldn't offset.

Brandon's next few words came out in a low growl that I couldn't make out, and then he slowly backed away from Alec before he and the rest of his pack disappeared from sight.

I finished processing everything about the time Alec turned and walked back. I opened my mouth to protest, but he shook his head at me as we all fell into formation around him.

From what little I knew about Alec's pack, it wasn't uncommon for them to spend time together without the kind of chest-beating byplay that was so much a part of Brandon's group, but our lunch table was even more subdued than I'd expected.

Faced with an almost complete lack of conversation, I didn't have the courage to ask some of the questions on my mind. It wasn't until I'd followed Isaac to my history class that I finally worked up the nerve to find out more of what was going on.

Once the substitute had called roll, and then more or less turned the class loose for a 'group study session', I turned to Isaac and whispered my first question.

"This fight between Alec and Brandon, it's for real? I mean they aren't just going to fight until first blood, are they?"

Isaac's nod was hesitant, like he knew I was headed towards things he wasn't supposed to tell me. "I'm afraid the contest is quite serious, but still nothing for you to worry about."

That didn't add up in the slightest. "I don't believe you. At least not the part about it not being anything to worry about. You all wouldn't have been so worried about Alec bringing me home Friday night if this was all no big deal. None of you have argued with Alec about anything since then, but Friday night James, Jasmin and Jessica were all ready to rip my head off over his express orders."

The nod I received this time was even slower than the first. I waited for Isaac to say something, but he seemed unwilling to give away anything I hadn't already figured out for myself.

"Can he win? Alec, I mean. Can he ki...beat Brandon?"

Isaac's sigh was eloquent. "I'm forbidden to speak on these things. To do so risks no small amount of Alec's displeasure."

"But you're going to anyways, aren't you?"

"It is right that you know the sacrifice undertaken on your behalf, both by Alec, and by the rest of our family. The one because of his feelings for you, the other because of our respect and love for Alec."

"It's true then; he can't win."

"While it isn't impossible, it's unlikely. Alec is a remarkable fighter, to hear Donovan speak of it, he's possibly even almost the equal of his father, but Brandon's strength and speed have not seen a match in centuries. It's likely Brandon will emerge the victor."

Even though, or possibly exactly because it was what I'd suspected, the words sent slivers of ice through me. My heart seemed to be having a hard time maintaining a steady rhythm, but I forced myself not to give into the panic attack that was promising temporary relief from the horror of my life.

With what I'd just been told, I should be able to put some of the pieces together. "Once Alec is dead, there'll be repercussions for everyone else?"

Again the short, reluctant nod. I had so many questions I still wanted answered, but it didn't seem fair to get Isaac in any more trouble than he was already in.

"Will you be okay? I mean with Alec. He's not going to torture you or anything for telling me, is he?"

Isaac's smile somehow completed his face. Funny how I'd never thought there was anything wrong with it before, but after finally being rewarded with something more than his normal, serious countenance, I had the first hint why he was one of Rachel's favorites among the pack.

"It's likely I'll be exceedingly sore for the next few days, and my ego, such as it is, will likely take quite the beating, but our Kir'shan, our Alpha as you would say, isn't a bad sort."

That was a relief. It also meant I knew exactly what I was going to do when I saw Alec next.

Half an hour later, I was following him down the hall towards Physics and wishing I'd had more time to prepare. Alec slowed as we finally arrived outside the door to Mrs. Alexander's classroom. I carefully craned my head around him, half expecting to see Brandon's entire pack waiting to ambush us. Instead the pause seemed to have been caused by the fact Mrs. Alexander had been replaced by a sub.

"Do you mind if we don't go to Physics today?" Alec's question should have been lost in the clamor of all of the kids walking by us, but I picked his voice out as easily as if we'd been alone together in the forest. Was that another mystical power granted to alpha shape shifters, or just because I was so hyper-aware of him?

"I thought you said we'd get in trouble if we started cutting school."

His easy, graceful shrug pulled his black polo shirt tight across his shoulders. It seemed impossible that anyone could be so well built and tightly ripped that you'd be able to see every muscle through his clothing, but there he was.

"I may have exaggerated slightly. Odds are that I can convince the secretaries to make your absence here disappear, and mine hardly matters."

I throttled down my first impulse, the almost overwhelming desire to say yes, to do anything required to spend more time with him, and instead focused on the opportunity to get inside his head, to learn some of the things moving him.

"But that isn't why you want to skip."

"No, I find that I'm strangely unconcerned right now with what the future may bring, and this seems entirely too good an opportunity to waste on a substitute that knows even less about physics than we do."

I returned his smile, and grabbed his hand, tugging him in the direction of the outside door. We didn't go far, stopping in a little cluster of trees no more than fifty feet from the school.

"So is this nearly complete disregard for consequences typical?"

Alec gazed at me with one of his indecipherable looks for several seconds. Feeling more than a little self-conscious, I tried to let go of his hand and scoot a little further away, but he maintained his grasp. "Please don't. I didn't mean to make you nervous. It's just that you continue to surprise me."

"It's more than a little creepy how you all can do that. Are all shape shifters born with the ability to read people's minds?"

The smile was back, gentle and teasing. "Minds no, scents yes. The human body is quite marvelous in how many different systems it recruits to match its mood."

The way Brandon had always known exactly the right thing to say at any given time suddenly made sense. Alec let me process his latest little tidbit of information, and then continued.

"Actually, none of us are born with any unusual abilities. All of the changes tend to show up more or less around puberty. And no, disregard for the consequences of my actions isn't typical. In fact I've spent nearly a decade weighing almost every word."

"So dashing off to rescue an admittedly stupid teenage girl and landing yourself in a fight to the death that you probably can't win isn't how you normally run your life. Why did you do it then?"

Again the silence, but this time, more completely enveloped as I was by the tingly warmth that seemed synonymous with being in his presence, I was content to wait.

"Apparently Isaac's decided there are a few things you should know. Don't try and tell me it wasn't him, you didn't know that particular piece of information an hour ago, and nobody else has had the opportunity to tell secrets."

I felt myself tense up in worry, but he waved my worries away. "In answer to the core of your question, Jasmin thinks it's because I've finally gone over the edge, that in essence I've snapped due to the stress, and this, 'obsession,' as she terms it, is merely a novel way of committing suicide."

My heart started racing again, but he wasn't done. "The other school of thought is that I'm more of a healer than anyone realized, and that I couldn't resist your obvious need."

He'd lost me there. "Wait, what do you mean?"

Alec paused for several seconds before answering. "You glow. All of the time. Until now we always thought someone had to be a shape shifter to do that."

"But I'm just a normal person. Why would I appear different than anyone else?"

Alec's shrug was enough to send my heart racing again, but not enough to distract me from his words. "With shape shifters, we believe it's because the animating energy, the soul if you will, burns more brightly than normal. I think it's tied in with what allows us to shift forms. With you, there isn't any obvious reason, but I think that Dominic has probably hit upon the root of the matter."

His pause this time wasn't just to collect his thoughts; I could tell he was tempted not to tell me whatever he was thinking.

"You know that our legends indicate a belief we were created in order to watch over and protect humans? Well, Dominic believes that your light represents a defense mechanism. We don't know of any accounts where humans have burned so brightly, but it's possible the primitive parts of you, the ones that remember what it was like to be watched over by our kind, hit upon a way to call for help from us, while not admitting a problem to your own kind."

He was being so vague that it took me several seconds to follow the explanation to its logical conclusion. "So you're saying that I was, am, so broken I glow so your people would be able to pull me aside and fix me."

His nod was hesitant, but my wan smile seemed to reassure him somewhat.

"I guess that makes sense. Nobody likes to be told there's something wrong with them, but I can't exactly say everything is just Jim Dandy. Not when I still collapse at the mere mention of what I've lost."

The silence wasn't as comfortable now. I had to break it, even if it meant further examining all of the holes inside me that I'd spent so many months struggling to ignore.

"So you're just one of those guys that can't resist trying to help the broken girls, huh?"

"No. That's Dominic's theory, I didn't say it was mine. I did what I did because when I close my eyes I still see you there."

My heart jumped up to my throat, but in a good way.

"I don't know why, not really. Your incredible, unearthly beauty helps, as does your stubborn determination to continue soldiering on, despite how badly you've been hurt. That doesn't explain it all though. Neither does the fact that you stepped in and saved Rachel from a beating I couldn't stop."

He reached up and tucked a stray hair behind my left ear. "Whatever the reason, since your arrival here, I just feel like parts of me that were missing have come back home. Even when I thought you were some kind of...rogue...shape shifter come to destroy my pack, I was still drawn to you."

My stupid eyes were tearing up again. Sometimes being a girl really sucked. Boys never seemed to have their bodies betray them in front of other people like we did. The most gorgeous, kind boy I'd ever met had just professed his love to me, and strangely enough it made what I had to do next both harder and easier.

"Alec, what if I were to go back to Brandon? Would that stop everything from going wrong? I mean, then you wouldn't have been poaching his property or whatever you call it."

It was bad enough that my heart was shattering as I said it, the look in Alec's face made everything a hundred times worse. For a second I thought the earth was shaking, but it was Alec, trembling much like he'd done Friday night.

A loud crack from beside us made me jump. Alec looked at the branch, easily as thick as my arm, which he'd just torn from the tree we were leaning against. He stopped shaking as he considered what he'd done to the poor tree.

"You're saying that because you're worried for me? Not because you really want to go back to him?"

I shook my head, as confused by his reaction, by how close he'd come to losing control, as I was by my not having felt threatened. "No, I want to stay, but how can I knowing it will mean you're going to be fighting to the death?"

Alec tossed the branch away with a sigh. "I've spent years learning control, but sometimes I still forget just how breakable everything around me is. If you go back to Brandon, you support his claim that you belong to him, and I'd still be forced to challenge him. If I didn't, he would be justified in killing whichever two of my friends he wants."

"So there's no way you can avoid fighting him?"

Alec's smile was more bittersweet than normal. "No, but it's not too late to save you. I can have you on a flight to Paris tonight. It's the only way to guarantee your safety."

I shook my head. "I'm not leaving. I believe you when you say my going back to Brandon won't solve anything, but I'm not going to run away and leave you all to deal with the mess I created. I wish you'd stop asking me to."

His gaze was long and steady, but finally he nodded. "You have as much right to see this through as anyone else does, but it's almost certainly going to get a lot uglier before it's over. Your freedom is going to be incredibly restricted, at least as bad as it was today. We'll escort you to school, stay just long enough to ensure we don't get in trouble, and then hurry back to our territory. At least if Brandon's pack does come after us there, we're within our rights to do something about it."

I opened my mouth to comment on the fact that Brandon's pack was roughly twice the size of ours, only to realize that scurrying back home kind of precluded continuing to help out at the tutor lab.

"What about helping Mrs. Campbell?"

It shouldn't have surprised me that Alec thought it over for several seconds before shaking his head. Whatever else he was, he wasn't the thoughtless jerk Brandon had proven himself to be.

"I'm sorry, Adriana. I wish we could, for Rachel's sake as well as yours, but it's just too risky. Fewer witnesses means more chance Brandon's people will try to arrange for something to happen. There are just too many of them for us to meet them in a stand-up fight and come out unscathed."

I didn't like it. Mrs. Campbell was the only teacher who'd taken an active interest in my wellbeing, but I could see his point. I managed to do at least a passable job hiding my near frown as I nodded in acceptance.

"Can I have just a few minutes today after school to tell her?"

Alec's hand was warm on my face as he nodded. "You're amazing. All the things being taken away from you just because you got involved with the wrong crowd, and you just do what has to be done. Of course you can have a few minutes. I'm sorry to make you do this."

I wanted to tell him it was less than he was doing. To say it was the least I could do considering this was all my fault, but the unabashed bliss of having him touch me was overwhelming. It took surprising effort to string coherent thoughts together. Before I managed to do so successfully, he sighed and helped me to my feet.

"We'd better get back or you'll miss Spanish."

Based on how badly Biology had gone, I was dreading Spanish with even more fervor than normal. I felt incredibly better when it was Dominic who was waiting with a smile for us at my locker. Alec let go of my hand with an actual look of regret.

Mrs. Tiggs seemed to have read whatever memo Mrs. Sorenson had been working off of earlier. She started out the hour by asking me a question I was positive wasn't in any of the chapters I'd ever read.

The class' collective mouth dropped in astonishment as Dominic called her on it. "But Mrs. Tiggs, isn't that covered in Chapter 18? I mean, I just started the class obviously, but it just seems confusing. Your syllabus says we're talking about the preterit today."

The only other person I'd ever met who could've even come close to pulling off such an innocent expression was Rachel, and I wasn't sure even she could compete with Dominic today. If I'd found her standing in front of a broken window with a rock in her hand, and she'd told me she had no idea why the window had shattered, all the while flashing me that look, I would've believed her.

Mrs. Tiggs apparently wasn't quite so gullible. "It's a reasonable question, as the two subjects are highly related. One could almost say they're so close to the same thing that any distinction is purely arbitrary."

Now Dominic looked both innocent and confused. "But why are they so far apart in the book then? I mean my Spanish book in the school before I came here had them pretty widely spaced too."

It was masterful. I'm not even sure the rest of the class realized the pattern, but Mrs. Tiggs caught on about halfway through the hour. Every time she was snippy with me, Dominic made her look like the idiot we all suspected she was.

As the bell rang, and we exited the first truly instructive Spanish class all semester, I pulled Dominic off to the side. "That was amazing. Thank you, but you can't keep doing that or she's going to fail you."

Dominic sagged a little against me. "I don't think she will. Not after the rest of the class realizes she has a hard time reading the book herself. Even if she does, it doesn't really matter. I never expected to finish junior high, let alone graduate from high school. Besides, James is always talking about dropping out and just getting his GED. Maybe I'll follow suit."

She stiffened slightly as I hugged her, but then smiled and returned the gesture with an earnestness that made me think she hadn't had much in the way of hugs in her life.

"Well, I hope it doesn't come to that, but thanks again. I may still flunk out, but seeing the expression on her face makes it worthwhile."

Was it possible to be both shy and confident at the same time? If it was, Dominic's fluid, expressive face pulled it off.

"Nonsense. Once we undo all of the damage from her teaching you, you'll do so well even she won't flunk you."

It went against everything past experience with Mrs. Tiggs had taught me, but I almost believed her.

Chapter 26

It was amazing how quickly my classes flew by when I had a friend, or at least a protector, with me at all times. Then again all of Monday had flown by, not just the school portion of the day, so it really shouldn't have been a surprise today was doing likewise.

After Spanish, Jasmin had escorted me to Mrs. Campbell's class. Telling her I wasn't going to be able to help out at the lab anymore had been one of the harder things I'd ever done, but she'd been surprisingly understanding. We'd scheduled my makeup test for the next day and I'd left with the sneaking suspicion she'd guessed more about what was really going on in Sanctuary than either pack would've liked. I'd been busy contemplating what Mrs. Campbell might have really figured out as we left the building, only to have Jasmin interrupt my musings with an apology of all things.

She didn't get into specifics, and it was obvious she was still worried about the coming showdown with Brandon, but I was pretty sure she really was sorry. It didn't make us best friends and she was still an enigma, but it was a start. It even gave me hope maybe Jessica and James might eventually come around.

I was still reeling in surprise as we walked out to the parking lot and met up with the rest of the pack, or rather the rest of the pack minus Alec. He'd shown up several minutes later, looking very satisfied with himself, but obviously unwilling to answer any questions. As we caravanned home, I realized the collection of vehicles carrying us back to Alec's estate probably cost more than my house.

Donovan had met us at the door and conducted us to the dining room, where Alec and his friends devoured a sizable meal. Even back when I'd had a more substantial appetite, I still couldn't have kept up with the wolves. Even the girls packed away more food than I would've believed possible for such slender frames. I mentally shrugged and added it to the list of shape shifter benefits. Able to eat like a complete pig and still slip into size zero jeans.

Dominic spent a couple hours after dinner helping me with Spanish. She probably would've spent even longer with me, but Mom called, so Dominic slipped out to give me some privacy. I fielded something like a hundred questions about school, reassured her two or three times that she wasn't a terrible mother, and promised yet again to stay one hundred percent out of trouble while she was gone. I was beginning to wonder if I was ever going to get off the phone when she finally decided, ultra-late shoot tomorrow or not, she'd better go to bed.

By the time I finally finished up the rest of my studying, decided I was ready for my catch-up test in Mrs. Campbell's class tomorrow, and spent a few minutes with Rachel, I was well and truly exhausted.

I thought about going back to the Lilac Room, but it would've just been because I was worried about what everyone else was thinking. I'd been raised to believe good little girls didn't spend the night with boys. Not even boys who were so gentlemanly it was sometimes painful.

I still believed that, but my desire to be with Alec had devoured the parts of my brain that used logic and reason to decide things. I wanted to be with him while he slept, even if it was only for a couple of hours. Everyone in the pack already knew I'd spent the night. In the end, the reasonable part of me never had a chance.

Waking up next to Alec fully vindicated my decision. He'd greeted me with his typical, heart-stopping smile and I'd leaned in to kiss him before I'd even realized I was in motion. He'd pulled back, but his expression at least wasn't reproachful.

I wanted to force the issue, wanted it so badly I could feel the desire bubbling inside me, but even more than my natural shyness, the thought of him pulling away again, this time in disgust, was too much to contemplate.

Once we got to school, I'd found the rampant gossip had subsided to a dull rumble, but the few undecided votes had come down solidly on the side of everyone else. Some people hated me for using Brandon, others hated me for playing Alec, while a small, but decidedly upwardly-mobile group disliked me for achieving not just one, but both of the conquests they'd been dreaming of since grade school. In the end, it didn't really matter why everyone disliked me. Still, only the fact that Alec's pack closed ranks around me kept the situation from becoming unbearable.

Biology went better than it had since my first day in Sanctuary, largely because Alec seemed to have developed a postdoctorate knowledge of Biology. Also he didn't have a single qualm when it came to using that knowledge to deflect questions aimed at me. Mrs. Sorenson tried three different times to make me look stupid before finally giving up and getting down to the business of teaching.

She continued to shoot us nasty looks throughout the class, but I hardly noticed. Alec spent the rest of the class time writing questions for me in the margins of my notebook. By the time I'd described my grandparents, kindergarten teacher, and top three most embarrassing moments, I wanted to get a chance to ask some questions of my own, but he just shook his head and passed me my notebook back with a new set of quickly-jotted queries. The sentences should have been a careless mess based on the speed with which he was writing. Instead they turned out more even and carefully constructed than anything I'd ever been able to accomplish.

I'm the Alpha here; you can ask your questions when I finish with mine.

The flippant, humorous nature of his response was so atypical, and yet still quintessentially Alec. I nearly broke into a fit of laughter that would've gotten us both in even more trouble with Mrs. Sorenson.

I roll my eyes at you...a lot. So once you're done, I get to ask you any question? No restrictions?

That was nearly a deal breaker, I could see it by the way his initial smile at my 'rolled eyes' faded away into his more characteristic seriousness. He contemplated his response for a good fifteen seconds, which was probably something like two hours in shape shifter time, before finally touching his pen to the paper again and then passing my notebook back.

It's a deal. When I finish up with my questions, you can ask whatever you want. Of course if your question is something that's going to get you into trouble, I reserve the right to pack you onto a plane and send you off to safety once I'm done answering.

I stuck my tongue out at him, for real this time, as I wrote down my response. *Bully*. Still, all in all it was a win for me. Once he'd dug up every painful moment from my childhood, I was going to get to finally start learning about him. His pack too of course, but most importantly, I'd finally know more of what made Alec Graves tick.

A couple of hours later at lunch, Mrs. Campbell had met the appearance of Rachel, Alec, and the rest of the pack with a raised eyebrow and a disbelieving headshake, but simply motioned them all over to the other side of the room, and handed me my test.

Despite having spent weeks preparing for my makeup exam, I was still a little nervous until I started working the first problem. Forty minutes later I handed Mrs. Campbell a completed test, and got the extreme pleasure of watching her grade it and write a large, crimson 'A' on the front page.

I was so excited I nearly squealed in delight. I managed to restrain myself, just barely, only to giggle as Rachel dropped her lunch and squealed for me. Dominic's gentle smile wasn't quite as enthusiastic, but I already knew her subdued reaction wasn't any less heartfelt. Throw in Jasmin's congratulations, which seemed to indicate the passing grade had been nothing less than inevitable, with Alec taking my hand as soon as I sat down, and Jessica and James' lack of response didn't matter at all.

With Isaac's reassuring presence at my side in History, I weathered the renewed gossip, apparently occasioned by the entire pack's absence during lunch for the second day in a row, and soon found myself reunited with Alec in Physics.

As luck would have it, Mrs. Alexander was gone again, and the substitute was typically clueless about what we were supposed to be doing. Alec of course spent the whole class unearthing other little bits of embarrassing information. I'd never experienced anything like it, every question I answered spawned two more, and he invariably seemed to figure out the underlying reasons I'd done a given thing, or reacted a certain way.

I'd just finished describing my failed tryout for the school's production of To Kill a Mockingbird, when he hit me with a completely unexpected question.

"So tell me about both your best date and your worst date before you came here."

I felt my skin instantly heat up, and looked down, unable to meet his gaze. He let me sit there for a couple of seconds, and then reached out and used one gentle finger to nudge my chin up.

"What's the matter, afraid I'll be jealous?"

I shook my head, fighting the urge to look back down. "No, there isn't anything to be jealous of. I'd never been on a single date before

Sanctuary, and you know all about what's happened since I arrived."

His smile was surprisingly reassuring. "That sounds like the easiest one I've asked you yet. Why the sudden bashfulness?"

My throat seemed to be spending an awful lot of the time lately constricted down to the point where speech was all but impossible. It was even worse than usual now. I thought maybe he'd have moved on to something else by the time I was able to talk again, but he was still patiently waiting when I managed to make myself look up again.

It was tempting to lie and tell him I was just thinking about Cindi, the only one in the family who'd ever really had any luck in the dating department, but that wasn't fair. Besides, it would only put off the dreaded day. Eventually he'd find out what I was really like.

When the words finally made it out, they seemed to fight me the whole way, clawing at my throat with such force that by the time they finally exited my mouth, they were the barest hint of a whisper. "Because I'm worried once you realize just how much of a loser I was back home, how much of a loser I still am, you'll decide you don't belong with me."

"Why would you not dating very much have any impact on how I feel about you?"

"Because in addition to being the most thoughtful boy I've ever met, you also happen to be rich enough to buy a small country. You're so incredibly gorgeous girls swoon when you walk into a room. How can I possibly compete against the kinds of girls who'll continue throwing themselves at you for as long as you're breathing?"

Anger managed to accomplish what all of the swallowing hadn't. The diatribe that'd started out nearly inaudible had grown in volume until by the end I was hissing loud enough the people closest to us turned around in curiosity.

Alec calmly captured my wildly gesturing hands, immobilizing them with a casual strength that made me feel like a child.

"Please don't do that."

He continued on before I could open my mouth. "The fact you didn't date until recently doesn't mean you're some kind of nerd. Even if it did, that wouldn't matter to me. Also, other girls who may or may not find me attractive are irrelevant. I don't want them, I want you."

Even I could tell that I wasn't doing a very good job pretending I believed him.

Alec recaptured one of my hands in his, and then leaned back, lazily exuding confidence. "It's okay that you don't believe me yet, I'm equal to the challenge of convincing you."

He smiled at my shrug, but now that we weren't arguing about the inevitable fact he was eventually going to leave me, my mind was free to start working again.

"Don't do what?"

For the first time ever, I'd managed to catch him by surprise. It took him several seconds to figure out what I was talking about.

"Your hands, you tend to talk with them when you're excited or angry, and it's very distracting. I mean for us. All of the motion results in a hundred tiny signals flooding my brain as my instincts try to decide whether you're prey to be chased, or a bigger predator that I need to flee from."

I felt my eyes go wide as I realized what he was saying. It made me think of the stray kitten we'd taken in for a few months when I was five. Cindi and I had spent hours teasing it with pieces of string, watching its tiny head dart back and forth from one to the other as it tried to decide whether to pounce on them, or dart away and hide under the bed.

It'd been really amusing when it had been a half-pound kitten, but the thought of having a two-hundred-plus pound wolf attacking me because I'd triggered some kind of fight or flight instinct wasn't so funny.

"Oh, I didn't realize it was a problem. I'll stop."

Alec laughed. "It isn't actually that bad. More like an itch you can't quite reach. Although, if you ever want to drive Jessica absolutely crazy, spend a few minutes around her fidgeting. She's the most naturally high-strung out of anyone besides Jasmin. The fact she's also a submissive only makes things worse."

It was terribly vindictive, and wonderfully appealing. I felt a smile tugging at the ends of my mouth. "She won't eat me if I do that?"

His chuckle pulled my smile wider. "No. If you're really worried about it just make sure that one of the others are in the room at the same time with you."

"Now that has some real possibilities."

I was still rolling the thought around in my mind when the bell rang and Alec pulled me to my feet.

We swapped out our books and were halfway to Spanish when Vincent and Brandon strode into view. Moving so smoothly I was positive that nobody else even realized anything was wrong, Alec swung me around so he was between them and me.

The tension ratcheted up in step with the rolling waves of energy, as Brandon and Vincent drew nearer. They split up when they saw us, casually positioning themselves so Alec couldn't protect me from both of them.

I felt my knees stop working as I took in Brandon's lazy, confident smile, and Vincent's sick, eager expression, but the gentle pressure of Alec's grasp on my hand kept me from falling down. I looked up at Alec, hoping for a reassuring smile, but his face had taken on the expressionless mask he used to guard his thoughts.

I tried to slow down, but Alec kept moving forward, never altering his speed in the slightest as he pulled me directly towards Vincent.

It seemed incredible that the few other people still in the hall couldn't feel the surge of energy as Vincent stepped directly in front of us and placed his hand on Alec's chest. The sudden spike was enough to make my hair stand on end, but Jim Hansen hurried by without any indication there was something out of the ordinary.

"You're in our way, half-breed."

I felt Alec's grasp tighten slightly, but considering the crushing strength he was capable of, it was the closest thing imaginable to a non-response.

Brandon was coming up behind Vincent, as Alec reached up and placed his own hand on Vincent's chest, with another, stronger flash of power. The ripple of skin and bone was so quick for a second I couldn't believe what I was seeing, but there it was. Alec's hand and fingers had elongated, turning into a hairless replica of the deadly claw that'd terrified me just a few days before.

Vincent's bulk was such that it screened Alec's movements from passersby, as those razor-sharp claws sank just the barest distance into his chest. Alec spoke for the first time, and the even tone of his words was a stark contrast to the winds of power that seemed almost ready to throw me across the hall.

"You forget yourself, mutt. As the leader of another pack, I'm due more respect than that. Should you or your dominant wish to push things further, I guarantee that your heart will decorate the floor before he can come to your aid."

Brandon stopped moving as Alec's words carried to him. He was probably weighing odds and tabulating the probable cost of the various courses of action available to him. Vincent's life was likely a relatively small component in the grand equation.

Dominic's presence as she stepped around the corner seemed to be the deciding factor. Brandon gave us another lazy smile as he stepped slowly backwards to give us more room.

Alec's tone was still conversational as he shoved Vincent backwards and allowed his hand to return to normal. "The harassment of my people stops now."

"Now why would we do a thing like that when we all know you're a dead man?"

Dominic stopped just outside of what I was starting to understand was pouncing range for people who happened to have supernatural strength, as Alec gave Brandon a cold smile.

"If I ever really decide the outcome is a foregone conclusion, you'd better start watching out for your people. You'd be surprised just how many of them could disappear if I no longer worried about the consequences of my actions."

The tingle of Alec's power lessened slightly once we were out of sight, but it still hadn't dropped off completely by the time we were standing in front of Mrs. Tiggs' classroom.

I could still feel the faintest traces of his power long after he'd finally let my hand go with obvious reluctance and strode off, leaving Dominic and I to find our seats.

The pack was more subdued than normal on the way home. Everyone splintered off into smaller component parts as soon as we passed the wrought-iron gate signaling the entrance to the Graves estate.

Donovan was waiting patiently inside the door, but he took one look at the bristling bundle of energy that was Alec, and obviously revised his plans on the spot. "Shall I have dinner delayed, Master Alec, Mistress Rachel?"

"I'll take mine later, Donovan, but please don't let that inconvenience the rest of the household. I'll be out in the garden if anyone needs me."

Alec took a pair of quick steps down the hall, and then turned back and looked at me. "Would you care to join me, Adriana?"

It wasn't until we'd been sitting in a secluded corner of the sprawling, green sanctuary for nearly half an hour that Alec finally relaxed.

There wasn't any visible change to his demeanor, but one second tingles of lightning were dancing along my skin, and in the next heartbeat the unseen world settled into a sleepy calm.

"Will you do me the honor of allowing me to escort you to the Ashure Day festivities?"

The question caught me so much by surprise that the tiny ant I'd been watching managed to drag his heavy burden of leaves halfway across the nearest flagstone before I managed a response.

"Is this because of earlier? Because I told you I don't expect you to stay with me?"

Apparently it was his turn to spend some time pondering his reply. My six-legged friend was joined by another of his kind, and they were manfully working their way up the hill towards a tree.

"I've actually wanted to ask you for quite a while. Hearing that Brandon was taking you was harder for me to accept than you might imagine. My asking you now has nothing to do with our conversation from earlier today."

"Why are you doing it now then? I half expected you to try and send me out of the country again. An invitation to the local equivalent to Prom was the last thing on my mind."

The pair of ants disappeared, hidden among the lush grass that somehow managed not to look out of place here on the edges of the desert.

I was starting to realize that the best way to get information out of a guy was to wait him out. Sometimes applying a little judicious pressure here or there helped, but it was largely just a matter of letting them work through whatever internal barriers stopped them from sharing their feelings.

"My taking you to the dance is one of the more selfish things I could be doing. It represents so much of what I want, but is wrong for you on almost every level. I guess I've just decided I'm tired of trying to be good when I have so little time left."

"Why is that selfish? Most people would think you were being quite charitable taking the new girl to the big dance when you could have your pick of anyone in the school and half the females in the state."

Alec slowly reached over and took my hand for the first time since we'd sat down. The sudden surge of tingly, pleasant energy nearly distracted me from the fact he was very carefully not meeting my eyes.

"Can you feel that? I mean, it feels good, doesn't it?"

I felt smiles tug at the corner of my lips as a giggle bubbled in my chest. "I think it's supposed to feel good, silly."

My laughter died at his lack of matching mirth. "Have you ever wondered about my mom? I mean, why she's the way she is?"

Definitely not a time for funniness apparently. "What do you mean? I've only met her the one time. She seemed normal enough. I guess a little distracted..."

The chuckle I'd been waiting for surfaced, but it wasn't at all like his normal laugh. It was as if someone had sucked all of the joy and goodness out of the sound I'd grown to crave on a nearly subconscious level, and left a twisted shell.

"She's definitely distracted. You could even say utterly disconnected from the world. Completely free from the present, always living in the past."

"I don't understand how any of this ties together."

He looked up at me for the first time, and the tortured look in his eyes made me hold onto his hand as tightly as I was able.

"It's all the same thing. Our touch, my touch, it's like a drug. It's addictive, subtly, so subtly most humans never even realize what is happening to them. I've seen what it's done to my mother. How can I say I love you if I turn around and do the same thing to you?"

For a second I couldn't even think. He'd just used the 'L-word', and my heart felt like it was tearing itself apart inside my chest. In the subtle shadings we girls used to measure commitment, it wasn't as good as if he'd come right out and said, 'I love you Adriana Paige', but it was still pretty good, and it was a complete first for me.

Once I made it past the second part of his statement, I was able to start considering the first part of what he'd said. It was horrifying and amazing all at once, and it made complete sense. His mom was living in memories because the real world was just a pale shadow of her life with his father.

Alec seemed to take my silence as condemnation, or possibly just agreement with his self-condemnation. "We're where the legends of succubi originated. Irresistible demons who drain their victims dry, who leave their lovers a hollow shell of what they were before."

I'd finally worked through things enough inside my mind, to respond, but he bulldozed right over me. "Do you understand now? My getting closer to you is the ultimate form of self-gratification. It's the worst possible thing I could do to you. If you somehow survive everything that's about to happen, it would leave you forever hungering for another touch, but never able to fulfill that desire."

I placed a hand on his lips before he could ramp back up to another diatribe. "None of that matters. All I want is to be with you, and if we're as likely to all die as you seem to think we are, then the state of my mind after you're gone is hardly something worth wasting worry on. I accept your invitation. As much as I hate the very thought of going to any formal dance, I can think of nothing better than going with you."

"That's the addiction, the Ja'tell bond talking."

Now that I knew his concerns, it was hard not to notice just how distracting the feel of his lips under my fingers was. Just how pleasant it was to have his hand cupped over mine. It was with an incredible amount of regret that I let go of him, and put several inches of empty air between us. It didn't help much; I could still feel his energy caressing the exposed pieces of my skin.

"There, I'm not touching you, and I still want to go to the dance with you. Want it more than anything else."

That wasn't completely true. I wanted him to kiss me even more than I wanted to go to the Ashure Day Dance. Having him touch me in other ways was pretty high on the list too, but maybe that was just psychosomatic. He didn't need to know that. I really did want to spend time with him. Even if he wasn't going to touch me, being with him was better than being anywhere else.

"This is a mistake. The worst kind of mistake because we both know it's wrong and we don't care."

"I don't think it's a mistake. I don't even think it is wrong."

"But if you did, would you care?"

"Probably not, but that doesn't change the fact that this is what I want to do."

His sigh was ample evidence he didn't believe me. It probably didn't help that I'd moved in closer as I finished speaking, but I was already worrying about something else he'd said.

"Alec, everyone keeps talking as though this fight is soon, but I've never heard an actual date."

He finally wrapped his arms back around me, but it was a subconscious move, as if he was trying to protect me from what he was going to have to say next.

"It's after the dance. The night of the new moon, an hour or two after the Ashure Day celebration ends."

I was suddenly even more grateful we were going to the dance together. If I only had a couple of weeks to live, then I wanted to spend every possible second with him.

Chapter 27

I groaned as Alec circled two of my biology essays and handed them back to me. "You're doing much better, but you're missing a couple of key components here and here."

"Has anyone ever told you you're a brutal taskmaster?"

His smile took away some of the sting over just how careful he was being not to touch me lately. It was like he had a split personality. When he was thinking about it, he was ultra-careful not to do anything to deepen the Ja'tell bond. Other times, usually when he was thinking about something else, he'd unconsciously reach out to me.

I still wasn't sure which option I preferred. Every moment we spent together made me want to touch him that much more, but the idea of being addicted to anyone, even him, was more than a little unsettling.

"Sure, Rachel tells me I'm entirely unreasonable on at least a daily basis."

I stuck my tongue out at him, and started back through the book in search of the missing information. There were so many other ways I'd rather be spending our time together, but he was adamant I not fall further behind in my classes.

I looked up to ask for a hint, and found him staring off into space. "Penny for your thoughts?"

His smile was a half-hearted thing. "Mother is playing again. She just finished up with 'Courtship', so the next one will be 'Welcoming'."

It was amazing how quickly I could forget his supernatural abilities. Most of the time he seemed so normal. If you could consider any gorgeous, well-built boy who happened to be interested in me normal. Every so often though he'd do something that should be impossible.

Alec's smile was slightly apologetic. "Sorry about that. Would you like to listen as well?"

My confusion earned me a chuckle. Alec reached over to the bedside table and picked up a remote that had more buttons on it than most laptops. A split second later piano music flooded the room through the myriad of speakers mounted on the ceiling.

The piece Alec's mother was playing was incredibly beautiful, full of lilting chords of joy that seemed to stumble over each other in a cheerful effort to outdo their predecessors in greeting the audience.

Five minutes later, she started the number over again, playing with variations on the minor notes, and Alec silenced the speakers with another click of his remote.

"It's beautiful. I never realized she was so good, Alec. I mean, it's the most incredible thing I've ever heard."

His smile was a combination of pride and regret. "Mother says it represents my birth. She was always an excellent performer. Donovan says she would've been nationally acclaimed if she'd chosen to pursue a career instead of marrying my father. She didn't begin composing until after he was gone."

In what was for me a rare display of common sense over curiosity, I shelved the rest of my questions and looked for something I could use to help him sidestep the memories.

"Growing up surrounded by this, and neither you or Rachel play an instrument?"

Alec shook his head. "I've never had the finesse to play anything. Rachel took violin lessons for more than a year. I think she wanted to be able to play with mother. That was when she begged me to wire the house for sound. Donovan and I spent two weeks setting up mics in Mom's studio, and then another couple of weeks running sound into every other room of the house. She kept insisting it was so she could monitor Mother on the rare occasions when nobody else was home, but I used to hear her trying to play along to 'Courtship'."

The trace of a smile on Alec's face lulled me into a false sense of security. "She doesn't play now though. I've been into her room, and there's no violin there."

"No, she doesn't play anymore. She stopped playing shortly after Mom finished up the piece you just heard."

His expression was so serious now that I almost stopped him before he could continue. "She stopped when she realized that 'Welcoming' was the only celebration of childbirth mother was going to write."

I felt my smile sour, and tried to turn away, but Alec caught my chin and gently pulled my face up, forcing me to meet his gaze.

"You don't need to feel embarrassed. It's not something that's easy to talk about. It's even harder for Rachel to discuss, but sometimes those things still need to be examined. It's actually a relief to tell you. There are so many open secrets around here. It comes from living in such close quarters, from everyone being able to hear what's said anywhere in the house. It feels good to be able to share them with you."

I returned his smile and tried not to focus on questions of just how much of the fluttering in my stomach was due to natural attraction for him, and how much was due to mystical heebie-jeebies.

"For my part, I'm just glad you're telling me something for once instead of continuing to keep me in the dark."

He released my chin and ran a finger down the side of my face. "Well, then I'm afraid I'll have to trade upon your current satisfaction to beg your leave. As much as I'd rather stay here and bask in your beauty, it's time for more training."

I tried to keep the disappointment from my face, but his expression fell a little despite my best efforts.

"You're unhappy with me?"

"No. I mean not really unhappy, at least not with you. Maybe with the situation. I just feel left out of everything that's going on. I know you don't want to get me any more deeply involved with 'dangerous information', but it really sucks sometimes."

Alec gazed at me for several seconds, and then sighed. "If you would like to come watch, you may. Give us half an hour, and then ask Donovan to show you the way."

I felt my face break into a huge smile, but he held a hand up to forestall my thanks.

"This is all still very much against my better judgment, but I'm finding it increasingly hard to refuse you the things you want the most."

"Somehow I find that hard to believe. Even if it were true, you're hardly the type to give away the upper hand by coming out and telling me so."

Alec's eyes had taken on the serious, resigned expression that'd become disturbingly commonplace lately.

"I know. I think that last part bothers me the most, but I find myself doing so nevertheless. Make sure you wait at least half an hour. There's a definite element of danger to all of this."

I must have checked the clock sixteen times during the last five minutes of the obligatory half-hour. The sensible, grownup part of me was arguing for another five minutes just to make sure, but I told that part to take a flying leap and all but ran through the house looking for Donovan.

"Yes, mistress? Do you need something?"

"Donovan, Alec said I could go watch them work out. Will you take me to wherever they are?"

He dried his hands on a blisteringly white towel, and nodded. "Of course. I believe they are in the north end of the valley. Right this way."

We made good time, even with Donovan's jerky, oftentimes painful gait, but the estate was even bigger than I'd realized. We walked for several minutes before rounding a corner and finding the entrance to a hedge maze.

"We're very nearly there. The maze serves as a final barrier against unwelcome eyes."

I was lost within seconds, before we'd made more than four or five turns. "No wonder Alec laughed when I threatened to try and follow him. I'd starve to death before anyone found me."

Donovan's laugh was surprisingly relaxed. I'd only ever seen him with a serious, if respectful expression. Even Rachel's frequent teasing hadn't ever managed to crack his 'working face'.

"I hardly think that would be the case. While you may very well have lost your way, it would have been a small matter for one of the others to track you down. You have, if I may say so, a very distinctive smell. It reminds me of a type of sage brush that hasn't grown here in quite some time."

His sigh was more felt than heard, and it put me in mind of mountains, redwoods, and other ancient things.

"Donovan, can I ask you a question?"

"Of course, mistress. I'm afraid there are many which I won't be able to answer, but it would be a delight to share those things which haven't been forbidden me."

"You're really old, aren't you?"

His hesitation was brief, so much so I almost thought I'd imagined it. "Yes, Mistress Paige, I'm quite old."

"Older than Sanctuary?"

This time there wasn't any doubt. He'd definitely hesitated. It stretched out long enough that for a moment I didn't think he was going to answer, but then he nodded, a long deliberate motion that left no question but that it was a confirmation.

I wanted to ask more, but didn't want to venture into the kinds of things that would get him in trouble with Alec. We walked for another minute or so before I was struck with the silliness of someone who was old enough to be my great grandfather calling me 'Mistress Paige.'

"Donovan, you could just call me Adri if you want."

"That would hardly be appropriate, mistress."

"It just seems silly. I mean, I'm not really part of the family or anything, so there isn't really a need, is there?"

Donovan's smile was incredibly gentle as he shook his head in disagreement. "You're very much a part of the family, and if I may be so bold, I'm quite delighted by your inclusion. I've not seen Mistress Rachel or Master Alec this content in more years than I like to think about. For my part, I hope to have the continued pleasure of your company for a very long time."

I felt myself blushing. I hated how easily my face heated up, but a little thing like my imminent death was hardly going to change that.

"Thanks, Donovan. Not just for that either. I haven't properly thanked you for how nice you've been to me."

Donovan waved away my thanks. "That is no more or less than my duty to a member of the family, and with that, we've arrived."

BROKEN

The Graves estate was cradled between two spurs, and we'd finally traversed the length of the estate to arrive where the spurs joined the mountain. The north end of the valley was a terraced masterpiece that was remarkably green despite the complete lack of visible water. Large trees of a type I didn't recognize towered on each side, shooting up dozens of feet before branching out into an interlocking canopy that cut the harsh sunlight down to a greenish haze that swayed with the gentle motion of a breeze too slight for me to feel.

A gravel pathway cut its winding way between real, live grass before terminating in a sandy courtyard that my eyes had been avoiding, almost as though my mind wasn't ready to deal with what it knew it would see there.

The pack had turned at our appearance and six sets of unblinking, inhuman eyes stared up at me.

A low growl sounded from one of the throats, and Donovan edged in front of me as the largest of the figures turned and struck out at another of the shape shifters with blurring speed.

A startled yelp bounced off of the valley walls, and then Donovan relaxed slightly and started forward. "We should be safe now. Master Alec seems to have things well in hand."

His word choice didn't inspire an overabundance of confidence, but I could hardly turn and run away after begging to be allowed to come watch.

The path seemed to shrink as we were walking, and almost too quickly sand replaced the crunch of gravel under our feet.

I recognized Alec's humanoid form from before, a massive, black, heavily furred tower of muscle, claws and fangs. I might have pulled back at his approach, but the eyes, even with their vertical pupils were still undeniably his. A paler, more icy blue than I was used to, but it was still him looking out at me from the other side.

Everyone else was harder to pick out, but I gave it my best shot. Isaac was probably the bluish-black hybrid who was nearly as big as Alec. His utter stillness in comparison to the constant motion of the rest of the pack was too much like his normal self-mastery for it to be anyone else.

The other hybrid, the gray one with his teeth showing and just the barest hint of a growl had to be James. Jessica was obviously the smallest of the wolves. She paced back and forth, her eyes never leaving me as she made it entirely evident she'd like nothing more than to give into countless millennia of instincts, and just rip my throat out in a single lightning-fast bound.

It wasn't until I tried to decide which of the two remaining wolves was Dominic, that I realized the next smallest figure wasn't a wolf at all. The pitch-black shadow that padded towards me was some kind of cross between a leopard and a jaguar.

A low growl rippled up out of Alec's throat as the large cat got closer, but she dropped to the ground and rolled onto her back. I started forward, but Donovan's hand closed around my arm, pulling me up short.

Alec's gaze never left the prostrate shape shifter. He let her remain on the ground for several seconds, and then his chin dropped in an unmistakable nod.

Moving with what had to be exaggerated care for someone capable of such speed, she rolled back onto her paws and crossed the remaining distance between us. Donovan released my arm as she reared up and placed her front paws on my shoulders. The colorless eyes didn't match any of the pack's human form, but they had Dominic's gentleness.

She dropped back down and butted her head against my hand. I started petting her out of reflex, but when I slowed down out of embarrassment, she butted my hand again. After a few seconds she turned and slipped away, disappearing into the trees in a matter of seconds.

The rest of the pack waited expectantly, milling about partially hidden by Alec's towering figure. I turned to ask Donovan what to do next, only to have the words torn away from me as a surge of power washed over me from where Dominic had disappeared. A momentary ripple of stillness swept through the pack, and then Dominic reappeared, this time walking on two legs.

I'd been too overwhelmed by everything else to really register the fact that everyone was wearing some form of stretchy clothing. I'd never thought about how changing shapes must make for difficulty when it came to clothing choices, but it appeared someone had solved the problem.

Dom's black outfit had perfectly matched her fur, and whatever it was, it had shrunk down to fit her four-legged form, while still having enough elasticity to expand out to cover her person shape. The girl's clothes had an elastic band of some kind at their necks, legs and arms, while the boys were wearing a pants-like number which cinched down over their waist, as well as just above the knees.

My preoccupation over what everyone was wearing gave Dom a chance to cover the distance between us. Donovan smiled as Dom reached us. "I'll leave her in your care then, Mistress Sanchez?"

Alec watched Donovan leave, and then turned back to the pack and chivvied them back into motion. I grabbed onto Dom's hand with enough force to bruise a normal person as Isaac and James turned on each other with a sudden ferocity that left me breathless.

"It's okay. They're training, sparring if you will."

It was hard to believe what I was watching was anything less than an all-out bid to kill each other. Isaac ducked a vicious swipe from James, and then knocked the smaller hybrid over with a backhand blow I was pretty sure would've crushed rock.

Dominic winced a little as the blow landed and her boyfriend hit with earth-shattering force.

"Are you sure? I mean, it looks pretty real to me."

"They're definitely being careful not to kill each other. Isaac could've connected with his claws instead of his fist."

Jasmin and Jessica were circling each other now. It reminded me of a fight I'd seen between two feral dogs while I was still in grade school. The dogs had circled for five or ten seconds, and then one had thrown himself at the other. A neighbor had broken the fight up with a few thrown stones before it'd come to a grisly end, but it'd been obvious once the first dog had latched onto his opponent's throat that it was only a matter of time before the smaller dog would've died.

This was exactly the same, only it happened faster as Jasmin blurred into motion. One moment she was growling at Jess from a distance of more than five feet, the next instant she was on top of Jess, and her teeth were latched around the smaller wolf's throat.

Dominic's hand tightened on mine as Jess began to whine, but Alec took a menacing step forward and Jasmin released Jessica with another growl.

"She didn't want to let go, did she?"

Dom looked for a second like she wasn't going to answer, but she finally shook her head. "It's harder to control the instincts, the beast inside us, if you will, while we're in an alternate form. Hybrid, wolf, cat, to one extent or another, we become the beast, and if there's one thing animals have figured out, it's that you don't survive by letting a beaten opponent live to learn from their mistakes."

I felt a shudder go through me at what she was saying. "So Alec wasn't kidding when he said it wasn't safe for me to be here?"

"You're probably not in any more danger today than you were that first night. Jessica isn't any fonder of you now than she was then. I've been working with James every day since then, but he hasn't really come around yet, so he is still a bit of a problem. Luckily, with Alec and Isaac both firmly on your side, and Jasmin starting to develop a liking for you, there isn't a thing those two can really do about it. As long as Alec is very careful to stay between the two of them and you, you really don't have a reason to worry."

"He let you get close to me."

Dom's smile was incredibly winning. "Ah, but Donovan was still with you, and not only do I like you more than any of the others, I'm also a cat, so in this case my instincts aren't quite as worrisome."

"You're different from the others then? I mean, they can't change into cats, can they?"

She shook her head, attention still mostly on the fighting taking place on the far end of the sand court.

"We're from different bloodlines. If you believe the legends, Adjam became the first wolf, and Inock the first of the big cats. Alec and the others descended from Adjam, and I'm a descendant of Inock."

It all seemed so impossible, legends brought to life and paraded before my incredulous eyes, and yet there was no arguing with the truth. It was starting to sink in that I needed to come to terms with all of the natural implications. Things like the fact that some or all of my attraction to Alec was based on his ability to addict humans to him, intentionally or not.

James and Jessica were squared off against Alec now while Isaac and Jasmin watched. I'd thought everyone else moved fast, but Alec was even faster. He actually dodged Jess' jump, causing her to latch onto nothing more than thin air, while he spun around and hit James with a blow to the chest that had to have broken ribs.

"Alec's a good leader. Maybe the best. This kind of exercise would be impossible in nearly any other pack, but it's the only thing that's kept us alive in the face of Brandon's larger pack."

I didn't want her to say anything she wasn't supposed to, especially not if Alec was having as hard of a time controlling the anger that seemed to be part and parcel of the new shapes everyone was wearing, but I was desperate to start understanding some of what was going on.

Dominic must've looked away from the fight long enough to see the questions on my face. "It's hard to understand just how important the pack structure is. The question of who is dominant and who is subordinate drives so much of what we do. Even so, it's not nearly as bad as other packs, other places. Alec's established clear dominance to everyone else here, but he still probably couldn't make his gentler rules stick if it weren't for the fact that Isaac backs him almost without question."

The object of our discussion was currently backing away from James while trying to keep Jessica from circling around behind him. I finally realized what I'd always thought of as grace was really an economy of motion. It was like he was saving every possible bit of energy because he never knew when he'd find it necessary to burn up his reserves in a blaze of violence.

Even as I watched, he spun around, plucking Jessica out of the air, grabbing her by the head mid-leap as she sought to find purchase on this throat. He tried to spin back around to meet James' rush, but the smaller hybrid knocked him down with a crash. Isaac and Jasmin were there in a blink, tearing the other two wolves off of Alec before the conflict could turn deadly.

I couldn't breathe until the dust settled, and Alec rolled back up to his feet, dripping blood from a large gash in his side. Dominic heard my sudden gasp and reached over to reassure me.

"He's okay. We heal fast, and he heals faster than most."

"So this isn't normal?"

Dom shook her head again. "No, in most packs, any confrontation ends in violence. Generally there are a whole host of dominants who want to become the alpha. This would usually turn into a real dominance fight, with the other two doing their very best to kill him before turning on each other to fight over the spoils."

"That's terrible."

Her nod was sad. "I told you he was special. All of that hard-won civilization tends to flake and chip away when we're that close to our beast. Alec always does what's right though. No matter what it costs him personally."

Dom's words were timely. Before hearing them I would've watched Alec's near-stillness with unconcern, but now, seeing the way Jasmin and Isaac split their attention between Alec and the wolves they'd just pulled off of him, I could nearly see the effort he was exerting to shove aside the instincts demanding the death of the wolves who'd marked him, who'd questioned his supremacy.

With a shudder, he relaxed again, and Jessica approached, dropping to her stomach to crawl the last little ways, and then rolling onto her back. James dropped down on all fours, grounding the wicked-looking claws tipping his hands, and then it seemed all was forgiven.

My suspicions were confirmed when Dom sighed with relief. It hadn't just been my imagination. Alec's will had been sufficient to the task, but its victory hadn't been assured. It was a terrible risk to run, one that apparently put a big fat target on his chest for anyone in the pack who wasn't happy with how things were currently running, but Alec ran it regardless. He ran it again and again because doing so gave his pack a slight chance of survival, and he couldn't deny them that chance, not when there was something he could do to put it within their reach.

That wasn't the kind of person who'd take advantage of my human weakness to seduce me. In fact, it was all too likely he was going to fight my every effort to bring us closer together precisely because he didn't want to take advantage of me. I was suddenly very certain though that I was going to wage that war. I couldn't not want him, not love him, any more than he could do less than his best to keep his family from harm.

Chapter 28

Alec was completely drenched in sweat, and I still wanted to throw myself at him so badly my teeth hurt. It shouldn't be possible for someone to look so good dressed in what amounted to little more than loose, extra-stretchy sweatpants.

"How was training?" It was hard to sound casual. The urge to kiss him had become almost overpowering in the last few days. He knew me better on every level imaginable than anyone outside my immediate family ever had, and all I could think about right now was how much I wanted to touch him.

"Fairly well, all things considered. We took it easy though..." I'd gotten used to the idea that he left a substantial number of thoughts unsaid out of a desire to protect me from knowing too much. I didn't like it, but I'd learned to accept it. He didn't need to finish that particular sentence though. They'd gone easy because today was

Ashure Day, and once the dance finished up, he'd be facing off against Brandon, and it would be stupid to tire himself out when he was going to be fighting for his life.

It was a thought pretty much guaranteed to stifle a conversation, but I managed a smile. "Only you would come back dripping in sweat and say you took it easy."

Alec's smile was a bit strained at the edges, but the tenderness on his face was genuine. "I don't know what I'd have done without you these last few weeks."

My heart went pitter-patter, but still mindful of the fact that throwing myself at him would just result in him freaking out and keeping me at arm's length, I managed not to go all gooey on the outside too. Unfortunately the effort meant I was slow responding. He moved on before I got anything out.

"How's your homework coming?"

Now I did frown at him. "I think my mind's going to explode if I look at my Biology book even just one more time this weekend. Other than that things are great."

Alec's chuckle seemed to reach out and caress me. "I take it you'd be up for a brief field trip then?"

My ears must have perked up. For all that we'd spent an incredible amount of time together over the last little bit, he hadn't *taken* me anywhere.

"A field trip sounds great. Except I have to be back at least three hours before the dance, or Rachel and Jasmin will eat me. At least that's what they said, and I tend to believe them."

Alec crossed over to me and ran a finger down the side of my face. "Only you could manage to make a joke out of having fallen in with monsters."

I shrugged. "What else is a girl to do?"

Alec's reply shrug mirrored mine exactly and yet still turned the movement into something far more graceful and eloquent than what I'd managed.

"Be that as it may, I think you don't give yourself enough credit for just how amazing you are."

I felt myself start to blush as Alec disappeared into the bathroom.

Monsters I could handle, motorcycles were something else entirely. I'd almost backed out when Alec told me we'd be taking his bullet bike, but I didn't want him to know I really was a complete wuss.

All of which explained how I'd ended up on Alec's shiny, blue Yamaha R1 with my arms locked around him in a death grip. Apparently I'd given away at least some of my fear though, because Alec took the first half of our forty-minute drive at a positively sedate pace, or at least what qualified as a sedate pace on a machine that could go from zero to sixty much faster than any of the exotic sports cars Alec and his friends usually drove.

Just as I finally started to enjoy leaning with Alec while zipping around turns at what I was starting to suspect were triple digit speeds, he pulled off behind a ramshackle, old building and held a finger to his lips. I held my breath and tried my best to try and figure out what he was listening for, but encased as I was by the blue helmet he'd insisted on, I would've been lucky to notice if a herd of elephants had been hot on our trail.

Several seconds passed, and then Alec smiled at me again and backed the bike into the building, which was every bit as decrepit-looking on the inside as it'd been on the outside.

"Are we here?"

"Disappointed?"

I felt my skin heat up again, but managed to stick my tongue out.

"No, we're not quite there yet, but before we continue on, I need your promise not to discuss this with anyone. Not even the rest of the pack."

I was taken aback with his sudden intensity, and part of me wanted to bristle at the implication I couldn't be trusted with a secret. His expression softened a little as he reached into the small bag mounted on the fuel tank, and handed me a bottle of water. I hadn't even realized I was thirsty until that second.

"I'm sorry, Adriana. I know I can depend on you, this is just important enough that I needed to make sure you understood what's riding on your discretion."

I finished with the first third of the bottle, and then nodded. "I won't say anything. What exactly are we going to see?"

"Not a what, but a who."

Much like he'd done when we'd been fleeing from my house, Alec picked me up and then slung me around so I could wrap my legs around his waist, and my arms around his neck and chest. This time Alec wasn't sprinting, but he still set out at a pace that made conversation impossible, so I just relaxed into him and enjoyed being so close for a second time today.

Once we stopped, I slid down Alec's back and looked around. The tiny cabin set back into the rocks before us blended into the hillside so well, I probably wouldn't have noticed it if Alec hadn't stopped so close.

As soon as he was confident I could stand unaided, Alec gave me a reassuring smile, and then knocked gently on the door.

The woman who appeared a few seconds later seemed frail in a way that somehow wasn't attributable to her graying hair, or slender frame. It wasn't until she released Alec from a hug, and slowly moved back into the cabin, that

I realized it was how she moved that made her seem so old. Her motions reminded me of how my grandfather had moved the last few years before he'd died. Slowly, and with extra care, as if a careless action would leave him crumpled on the floor, racked with pain.

"Mallory, I'd like to introduce you to Adriana Paige. Adriana, Mallory."

I smiled, and gingerly offered my hand to her, which she clasped in both of hers. "I'm very happy to finally get to meet you, young lady. Alec is better company than most, but it's nice to have a new face around here."

I felt myself warming to her immediately, even more so as she ushered us into her small sitting room and clucked over me, all the while proclaiming that I was far too skinny. It was exactly the kind of thing you'd expect your grandma to say, but I almost believed her.

Alec helped both of us down into our chairs, and then smiled as Mallory waved him off. "You go ahead and do your chores. We girls will just get to know each other, and then once you're done, you can bring me up to speed on the latest developments."

We passed several seconds in silence after Alec disappeared, and then Mallory turned back towards me with a twinkle in her eyes. "So it finally happened?"

"I'm sorry; I don't understand what you mean."

"Alec's finally fallen in love, and with such a lovely girl. I was half worried he was going to spend the rest of his life so mired in responsibility, he'd never let himself notice anyone."

I was flabbergasted, but my lack of response didn't faze her in the slightest.

"I take it he finally realized you aren't a shape shifter then?"

Apparently my astonishment leaked through to my expression, that or maybe she could just smell the shock on me. Whatever the reason, her smile took on new intensity, and she slowly reached out and clasped my hand again.

"I'm sorry; I spend so much of my time alone with my thoughts that they develop well-worn grooves. I forget sometimes that other people haven't been privy to the endless hours of speculation that got me from one point to another."

There was something about her touch that distracted me. Not in a bad way, almost like the tickle you get in the back of your mind when you know you're missing out on some key point of plot in a suspense novel.

"You glow much more brightly than any human I've ever met, but you don't feel like a shape shifter, so you're either a very powerful Fir'shan, one strong enough to mask your nature from Alec, as well as me, or you're a very extraordinary human. Alec wouldn't have brought you here until he was sure it was the latter."

I closed my mouth in astonishment. "I didn't realize Alec had talked to anyone about me. Actually I think you just let more drop in a few sentences than he's told me all week. Alec claims it's because I could be put in danger just by knowing certain things, but I think he's still just not quite sure he can trust me."

Mallory slowly leaned back in her chair, and then shook her head. "No, it isn't because he doesn't trust you. If he didn't trust you, he wouldn't have brought you here. He'd trust Isaac or Jasmin with his or even Rachel's life, but neither of them know about me. In fact, bringing you here expands the circle of people who know about me to a grand total of three. He trusts you, more than just trusts you, but he's right. There are a number of things you shouldn't know just yet."

Mallory smiled again in response to my heavy sigh. "I know that must be hard to swallow. I'll tell you what. Go ahead and ask away, and if I think you should know the answer to any of your questions, I'll just tell you and devil take the consequences."

It seemed too good to be true. "Aren't you scared of what will happen when Alec finds out that I know more than I'm supposed to?"

"And how's he going to find out, youngster? From how long it took them to unload my most recent food shipment, he won't be back anytime soon, and I'm certainly not planning on telling him. Are you going to let our little cat out of the bag?"

I started to shake my head, but honesty prevailed before I could finish the motion. "I mean I'm not planning on it, but I'm not very good at lying or keeping secrets. Especially not from Alec."

Mallory's chuckle was that of a much younger woman. "That bothers you a little, doesn't it?"

"Sometimes. A little. I just hate being such an open book to everyone."

"Try not to let it get to you too much. As hard as it may be for you to believe, Alec's even better at reading people than most of us. There are several of the pack there at the house who are nearly as bothered by that as you are."

The familiar feel to her touch suddenly fell into place. It was hard to believe that I'd spent so long with her and not realized that she was a shape shifter until she'd said as much.

"Ah, and the first question you want to know is how come you didn't realize I was a shape shifter, isn't it?"

I nodded, surprised at her insight, but more or less resigned to the fact that I was never going to have any kind of secret ever again.

"Partly it's because I'm so old, but it also has a little bit to do with the fact that I've spent the last couple of decades concealing my presence from others. I suppose it has become a habit to hide the more unusual aspects of my nature. I guess all that practice has made me better at it than most of the shape shifters you've run into so far."

It made sense, but didn't really help me fill in any of the broad holes that had been bothering me for so long. Mallory gave me several seconds to ponder her answer before continuing.

"How is the rest of the pack? Alec will tell me, but he'll filter his answer through what he thinks I'm able to hear, not necessarily what I need to hear."

"They're worried. Jessica and James seem to be the most unsettled by everything that's happened, but I think everyone is more or less concerned. Is there someone in particular that you were curious about?"

Mallory hesitated for a moment, and then nodded. "How does Donovan seem to be doing?"

The question took me completely by surprise. There was no reason it should have, but it was the last thing I expected her to ask me.

"He's good, I think. I mean I haven't been there very long, and I don't know him or anyone else very well, so it's hard to tell. As long as there isn't any kind of public fight with massive amounts of bloodshed, I probably wouldn't know that everyone is at each other's throats, but Donovan seems happy. He's always pleasant."

The expression on Mallory's face tugged on my heartstrings. The open vulnerability there made me cast about for additional tidbits to tell her.

"He's one of my favorites. Rachel and I were already friends, so it made sense that she'd be nice to me, and Dominic at least knew who I was, but Donovan was nice to me right from the start. It's almost like he approves of me where some of the others aren't so sure Alec's dating me is a very good idea."

Mallory's expression was far away as she spoke. "Yes, he would approve of the two of you. He's the consummate man servant, so very professional that you probably wouldn't ever know it if he didn't like you, but I'm sure he does. He approved of Alec's father's choice even back when most of the pack was still energetically opposed to the idea. He's always been one to see truly."

"You are, I mean, you were close?"

Her smile turned sad. "Actually, neither. We weren't close when there was an opportunity for closeness, and now that I'd like very few things more than to be close to him, there's no real opportunity for us to become so."

She patted my hand as she shrugged. "It's rather ironic how things work out sometimes, but that's not fair on my part. I'm sure there are things you would much rather learn of than how I came to be in my present circumstances."

"Actually, that's part of what I want to understand. I mean I didn't come here wanting to learn your story specifically, but there's so much history I don't know. There's this shared past that I'm not a part of. It's like, oh, I don't know, I think maybe learning about the past will help me understand what's going on right now."

Mallory's sigh seemed to allude to every one of her presumably substantial years. "How very perceptive. The past is very much driving what's happening right now, but so much of the past is tied up with the very things from which Alec's trying to protect you."

I was bubbling with questions, but sensing that now wasn't the time to push, I sat back and waited in silence while she decided exactly how much to tell me.

"Alec's father was killed nearly two decades ago. I don't remember everything about that night, I wasn't even conscious for a large part of the happenings, but the pieces I do remember are sharper than they should be. Sharper in my mind now maybe than even when they happened."

Her hand gripped mine with a fragile strength that hinted at the vibrant, powerful woman she'd been back then. Back before the years had worn at her.

"The pack was huge back then. Much larger even than Brandon's is today, but all of that might didn't save Alec's father that night. There was a nightmare of blood and death, and when the sun finally touched the earth again the next morning, a full third of our number were dead, and most of those who remained were crippled. I would've been one of the former, except for Donovan."

The questions continued to bubble up inside me, but I throttled them down, suppressing them rather than risking an interruption which might cause her to not finish.

"At great risk to himself he carried me away from the site of the battle, running and swimming more miles than I care to think about. Eventually his strength finally gave way, and when he couldn't even crawl anymore, he found a cave and did his best to ensure I wouldn't die from exposure. As soon as he was able to move again, he went back and I haven't seen him since."

"But how?" The question just kind of popped out before I could think. It could've been taken as the worst kind of insensitivity; Mallory just gave my hand another squeeze.

"He hasn't always been crippled. In fact he used to be a delightful dancer. His injuries were sustained at the hands of the individuals who killed Alec's father, the same ones who wanted to kill me, and who tortured Donovan for days before finally accepting that I'd died from the wounds that left me like this."

Mallory shrugged, slowly and painfully in response to my questioning look. "My scars aren't readily visible, but they're there. That's why Alec is forced to come move the food he has sent to me. The scar tissue built up around my heart tends to pull in painful ways when my pulse starts racing. I tend not to worry about it all that much, but Alec fears it's a sign of deeper problems. I generally humor him and leave the heavy lifting for his visits, and we both pretend he doesn't know about the small garden I keep in a nearby cave."

I opened my mouth, but just simply didn't know what to say. The horror of being trapped in a body that was riddled with old injuries was something thousands of people faced every day, but it seemed even more of a shame for someone who'd once been so vital and strong.

Mallory's smile held only the faintest hint of regret. "No need to feel sorry for me. I've had a good run. A much better one than most of my friends did. If I haven't managed to accomplish what I was sent down to do in the course of almost a hundred and fifty years, then I've nobody to blame but myself."

"Still, I'm sorry. You seem much too nice of a person to have had all of that happen to you."

"Nonsense. If I am kind, it's no doubt because of those very experiences that I would've been the most desperate to avoid. I think most of the best people are that way exactly because of the things they've endured. Individuals like Dominic, Rachel, and Jasmin don't just happen. They're the result of a native goodness being tempered and refined by terrible experiences."

Mallory suddenly doubled over in a fit of coughing that left her white and shaking. I jumped to my feet and almost ran for Alec, but she grabbed my hand with more of that fragile strength, and pulled me back down.

"There isn't anything he can do for me, child, and unless I'm very much mistaken he's more than normally worried right now. He's in no kind of way needing yet more to fret about. Just let me catch my breath and I'll be as right as ever."

Several minutes later, once the renewed bout of coughing had subsided, Mallory looked back up at me with wan features.

"How did it happen? What brought things between Brandon and our Alec to a head?"

"It was my fault. I'd been dating Brandon, and we went to a party. Only while we were there he tried to do things I wasn't comfortable with. When I told him no, he—they—threw me out and told me to find my own way home."

It was harder to relate the story than I'd expected, but Mallory's cluck of disapproval over Brandon's actions helped a little. It made me hope that maybe she wasn't going to hate me for bringing ruin to Alec and the others.

"I was stumbling in the dark when Simon and Nathanial came for me, only I didn't know it was them, I just saw two enormous wolves running me down. If Alec hadn't stopped them I think they probably would've killed me."

"Undoubtedly, but don't let it bother you, sweetie. This has been all but inevitable since Alec's father died. From the moment they were born, I could tell that both Alec and Brandon had been gifted with uncommon potential for power."

My blank look apparently made her take pity on me. "I'm sorry. I forget you're not aware of my special gift. I see inside people. Shape shifters really, but every once in a while normal humans as well. I can see their potential, and when they develop gifts, I can see the shape those gifts have taken."

"Gifts?"

"The most powerful of the Fir'shan, the hybrids as the younger generation calls them, occasionally develop unusual abilities. Alec's father's was that of being able to heal himself more rapidly than normal, even for our kind. Thanatas, the legendary king who defeated the southerners, was said to be able to mold his own body, making powerful changes that made him unbeatable in combat."

Mallory's explanation was tickling the back of my mind. "Is that why Brandon's unbeatable?"

"Nobody is unbeatable, but yes, that's why Brandon is such a formidable adversary. His gift is more prosaic than most, it's just increased strength and speed, but that makes him more than a match for most normal hybrids."

"That's why Alec had more food than normal dropped off here then? Because he really doesn't think he can win?"

Mallory pondered for several seconds, before finally shrugging. "That may be unduly pessimistic. He's detail-oriented enough that part of it's probably just an insurance policy for me in case he doesn't prevail, but there is a kernel of truth to your concern. Alec is an incredible fighter, but Brandon's like hasn't been seen in centuries."

"Why are you telling me all this? I've been with the others for almost two whole weeks, and nobody's hinted that there were hybrids with special powers."

Mallory patted my hand again. "I probably wouldn't have complicated things this way save for the fact that for only the third time in my long life, I've looked inside a human, and seen something outside of the ordinary there."

"Wait, you mean me? I've got a power? I'm about as ordinary as you can get."

"Hardly ordinary. Have you had more of the dreams since Alec rescued you?"

"How can they be a power? They're gorgeous, but nothing cool like what you described."

Mallory started to answer, only to break off as she was overcome with another coughing fit. Thankfully this one was less intense.

"Many of the gifts aren't flashy like Brandon's strength. In fact, I suspect that many of the Fir'shan actually develop gifts but never realize it because they're of a less powerful nature, and are mistaken for luck, or uncommonly sharp instincts. Your gift seems to be that of sharing dreams."

I gasped as I realized what Alec must have suspected for quite some time. "You mean that was really him in my dreams?"

"Indeed. That's part of why he was so concerned you might be a powerful Fir'shan posing as a normal human."

A tiny sound just outside the door preempted my next question. Alec carefully maneuvered a pair of huge metal baskets in through the door. I felt my eyes go wide as I realized that they were full of hundreds of cans of food. I didn't even want to guess at how much weight was in each basket, but as Alec cleared the door it was obvious that the slow speed that he'd been moving at had only been due to him not wanting to hit anything. He moved like they weighed no more than a couple of pillows as he crossed the cabin and set them down in front of what must be the food pantry.

"That was almost as quick as normal."

Alec nodded in response to Mallory's observation. "I've been lifting weights for a while, but present circumstances dictated a more aggressive program."

He opened the door to the pantry, and started putting cans away, but Mallory waved him off. "You'll put them in the wrong spots. Just leave that, and I'll put it away later. Don't go all mulish on me, I may be old and feeble, but I'm still able to move a can of food. Come over here and let me look at you."

Alec came back towards us with an air of resignation. Mallory tenderly accepted the letter he produced from a pocket somewhere, and then waited while Alec knelt in front of her.

I felt a tingle of power as Mallory reached out and placed her hands on either side of his face. The power surged, and Alec's heavy, cool power was joined by something light and laughing.

Several seconds later, Mallory released Alec with a sigh and fell back in obvious exhaustion. Alec watched intently until she shook her head, and then the mask fell for just a second before he locked it back in place, hiding the disappointment that for the slimmest of moments had been plainly written on his expression.

Mallory reached out, as if to take Alec's hand, but he gently set her hands back on her lap. "Nothing's changed. We'll just proceed as before. Rest now, and should the worst come to pass I'll send Donovan to you."

A few seconds later Alec and I were outside the cabin, walking back in the direction of the waiting motorcycle. I reached out to take his hand, and felt a glimmer of relief when he didn't reject the gesture as he had with Mallory.

"Alec, was the letter from Donovan?"

I had to repeat the question again before he shook himself and nodded. "I've been running letters back and forth between the two of them since I was ten. I don't come out here very much, but I make the trip as often as it's safe to do so. They both live for those letters."

We walked in silence for several more seconds before I got the nerve up to verify my interpretation of what I'd just seen.

"She was just looking inside you to see if you've developed a power yet, wasn't she?"

Alec helped me over an especially daunting rock and then nodded. "And nothing has changed. She's been telling me for years now that I have the potential to develop a fairly spectacular gift, one that should it choose to manifest in a useful form, could be more than a match for Brandon's strength. Apparently I'm still right on the point of developing said gift, only our time has run out. I fight Brandon tonight. Besides, even if I were to develop a gift this instant, most of them require practice to master, and I'm not going to have a chance to do any of that."

"I'm sorry. It's my fault that this all happened."

Alec stopped and tugged me around to face him. "Don't be sorry. I wish this had happened a long time ago. We kept stalling, kept waiting for me to develop the ability to stand Brandon off, and it was the wrong thing to do. I should have challenged him when Simon and Nathanial killed the tourists, should have slapped Vincent down the day he almost killed Ben, should have done something a thousand times over, but I just kept waiting. Well, I'm finally done waiting, and it's a relief. I'll fight Brandon tonight, and one way or another things will finally be resolved."

I shook my head in denial, unable to contemplate the horror of what he was discussing, but he gently stopped me before I could complete the motion.

"This isn't your fault. Even if it was, it wouldn't matter because spending the last two weeks with you would've been more than worth the price."

Chapter 29

The dress hadn't entirely been real inside my mind. Even after Rachel finally admitted she'd purchased the dress from our Vegas trip, and had it sent here, it'd been hard to believe I was really going to be wearing it at the dance. It was hard to still be disbelieving when it was hanging from the door just a few feet from me, but I was giving the effort my best shot. Its green, silky beauty seemed to be mocking me. There was no way I was going to be able to pull off a dress like that. Even assuming it didn't fall off of me, I was still going to look like a walrus.

"Stop fidgeting, Adri. It's just a dance, not a funeral, and if you don't hold still your makeup isn't going to turn out right."

Rachel poked me in the ribs, and then went back to work on the last few details of my 'new and improved' look. I'd actually been trying to sneak a look in the mirror to find out how everything was shaping up, but it wasn't worth trying to explain. With the pall that'd descended over the pack once we'd made it back, it was almost certain she wouldn't believe me. Nobody even knew where we'd gone, but they'd keyed off of our mood faster than I would've believed possible. The results hadn't been good.

Jasmin stepped back around behind Dominic as I was watching, and for the first time I got a good idea of how the massively piled style Jasmin had been working on for the last half hour was going to turn out.

Dominic frowned at my gasp. "Oh no, I really look that horrid?"

"No, you're gorgeous. All of you are amazingly gorgeous. I suddenly feel uglier than normal."

I wasn't sure my reassurance had been prompt enough, but Jasmin jumped in with a self-satisfied smile. "She's right, about how beautiful you look, Dom, if not about how pretty she is. James is going to pant when he sees you."

Rachel had started prepping for the dance early, doing first her own makeup, and then Jasmin's while I was still gone with Alec. By the time I'd returned, Rachel's youthful features had taken on a mature cast that'd make all kinds of boys wish they'd taken a risk and asked Alec's little sister out.

Jasmin had about the least reason out of any girl alive to be an expert hair dresser since her naturally wavy hair could just air dry and still look like she'd spent hours working on it, but an expert she was. The results of her efforts on Rachel's behalf were nothing less than spectacular, and the casual-looking knot of curls and twists was wispy in all the right places.

Even with Rachel currently an order of magnitude hotter than normal, Jasmin still captured the prize. Rachel's work on her behalf had resulted in a makeup job that was so incredibly understated, even us girls had a hard time detecting it. Her wavy brunette hair had been straightened and pulled back in what looked like an attempt to let some other girls shine for a change, but it just made her look like a goddess who'd decided to spend the night slumming.

Given who she'd spent the last hour being surrounded by, it was no wonder Dominic was worried she was the ugly step sister. She needn't have worried. Her features were even more exotic than Jasmin's, and Rachel had chosen bright colors that made her stand out much more than usual. James' macho cool really was going to finally crack tonight.

Maybe I could pull the dress off after all. Everyone would be so busy looking at the other three girls that they wouldn't even notice me. It wasn't ideal, but it was better than nothing.

A quiet knock brought us all around to find Jessica waiting at the door, her makeup and hair partway done, a dress bag slung over her arm.

"Can I join you guys?"

Her voice was scratchy, and her eyes were red from crying, but she was putting on a brave face, and Rachel didn't even hesitate.

"Of course, Jess. We figured you wanted some privacy with Isaac, or we would've dragged you over here hours ago."

The rest of us were quick to pipe in, but at least on my side, the sentiment was a little half-hearted. Unlike Jasmin, Jessica never had come around, never made her peace with the fact that because of me things were going to go downhill in a hurry after tonight. I'd tried to get both Rachel and Dominic to explain why she hated me so much, but neither would give me a real explanation. Rachel would always just get mad and say there was no excuse for how Jess was acting. Dominic always refused to say anything other than that Jessica had been through her own set of struggles, and had her reasons for her behavior.

"I'll be done with Dom in just a moment, Jess, then I'll fix your hair while Rachel finishes up with Adri."

The nickname should have hurt, but somehow it wasn't as bad when the pack used it. It was almost like having a new family, one without all of the grief-poisoned memories that popped up every time I really thought about Dad or Cindi.

Faster than I would've believed possible, we were all in our dresses, and waiting in the living room for the boys to make their appearance. Jasmin and Rachel had worked what I was pretty sure was actual magic. Even Jessica was nothing less than stunning, and I didn't look as bad as normal.

Jasmin's backless black dress and shoulder-length gloves had streaks of blue that brought out her eyes, while Dominic's tight, red gown seemed to give her the confidence and poise you'd expect from someone so gorgeous and utterly exotic.

Jess had opted for a sleeveless silver number that flared out at the bottom so much I wasn't sure how Isaac would be able to walk next to her without stepping on the shimmery material. Rachel's mauve dress was probably the most conservative of all, neither over-snug, nor especially low-cut. It had seemed entirely out of character considering what she'd purchased for the rest of us, but when I'd asked, she'd just grimaced and said Alec would've made her stay home if she'd chosen anything more daring.

None of which helped me feel any more comfortable in the tight, strapless wonder Rachel had been so excited to give me. Even with all of the weight I'd lost since the accident, it still felt like the material was fighting a losing battle to stretch itself over my frame.

I'd been hoping to be able to put off actually putting the dress on for at least another half hour, but when my makeup had finally been pronounced satisfactory, Jasmin had studied me for a few minutes, pulled my hair back, secured it with a pair of silver combs I was worried might actually contain genuine diamonds, and then helped Rachel cram me into the dress.

If Jessica hadn't grudgingly complimented me on just how good my hair looked, I might have suspected Jasmin was trying to purposefully make me look worse than the other girls. Dominic and Rachel had to tell me I looked good, that was an unwritten girl-rule regardless of what species you were. Jessica had no such imperative, so I was forced to conclude Jasmin had done the best she could considering what she had to work with, and resigned myself to being the homely one in the group.

Still, seeing all of the other girls in one place, fully decked out in the kind of shoes I'd always wanted to wear, but never been able to pull off, was even more intimidating. I was once again psyching myself up to be seen in public, when Donovan limped into the room and cleared his throat.

"The gentlemen have at long last arrived."

Isaac was the first one through the door, looking particularly 007 in a tux that amazingly enough had the occasional silver thread that matched perfectly with Jessica's dress. I looked up from his outfit just in time to see a flash of concern melt away into relief.

I had just a moment to wonder at the novelty of Isaac showing that much emotion all at one time, and then James stalked through the door in a tux that was so cutting edge, that I wasn't sure if there was anything else like it anywhere in the States. The shimmery nature of the fabric combined with an unusually angular, sharp cut to make it different than anything else I'd ever seen. I worked my way up from the blindingly-polished black shoes, to the splash of deep red peeking out of his chest pocket, and somewhere along the way decided I loved the tux.

As amazing as James' and Isaac's tuxes were, I was already looking past them, craning my neck to see down the hall in a vain effort to catch a glimpse of Alec. There was no reason for my heart to be pounding away so furiously in my chest, but unlikely or not, my body at least seemed convinced he was going to change his mind and leave me standing here by myself.

Rachel looked up from her conversation with Jasmin just long enough to give me a reassuring smile, and then I heard the barest whisper of sound. I spun around with a speed that gave lie to all of my pathetic attempts to pretend like I hadn't been worried.

Alec was standing in the doorway, having crossed the distance down the hall faster than I would've believed possible, appearing almost as if by sorcery.

His shoes were every bit as shiny as James', leading up to slacks that could've been mistaken for shiny, but were actually something else, something with more depth than anything I'd seen before. The coat was made out of the same material, tailored tightly enough it managed to emphasize rather than conceal his massive shoulders and chest.

His pocket square matched his bow-tie, both of which were the exact shade of green used on my dress. It wasn't a masculine color by almost any standard, but he made it his, and there wasn't anything about him that could be described as anything other than manly.

Having stalled as long as I could, I finally looked up past his perfect lips and met his twinkling eyes. A smile tugged at the corner of his mouth as he walked towards me, and it wasn't until he stopped and held out his hand that I realized it hadn't been empty this whole time.

"Rachel said you needed some shoes."

While I was still struggling to get thoughts to coalesce into words, Alec smoothly went down onto one knee, and picked up my left foot. The work of art he slipped onto my foot was so beautiful I felt bad letting it touch the ground. I held it up for a second, admiring the way the lights played off its gentle curves while I convinced myself nobody was going to throw me into jail for defiling it by using it for its intended function.

Glass, or possibly something else perfectly transparent. It was hard to tell for sure what it was from so far away, but it wasn't plastic. The cool ovals where the sole had been cut away to reveal the material underneath told me that much. Whatever it was, it'd been created in layers. The outermost material was achingly clear, while the inner layers seemed increasingly less so.

Alec waited, another smile playing about his lips, while I came to terms with the shoes. He then deftly slipped the other shoe onto my right foot, and steadied me as I tried to adjust to suddenly being almost six inches taller.

"They're perfect. Thank you."

Rachel ducked around her brother so she could see the shoes and then smiled before leaning in to whisper.

"Mom wore those to the Ashure Day Dance, the one where she fell in love with Dad."

I pulled back in protest, but Alec's grasp on my hand tightened just enough to stop me.

"She wanted you to wear them. They were meant to be worn again tonight."

My head was still spinning as Alec offered me his arm and led me out of the room. There was a limo, easily the largest vehicle I'd ever seen, waiting for us outside. We piled into it with plenty of room to spare. The bar was fully stocked, but Alec shook his head at Rachel when she made as if to reach for a drink. Nobody else seemed even the slightest bit interested in the prospect of alcohol.

Rachel sat back with a pout and then turned and whispered in my ear. "Stupid shape shifters. None of them can get drunk, so they deprive the rest of us of the best parts of being young and stupid."

Once we arrived at the park, I did my best to pretend obliviousness to all of the gasps and stares as we trickled out of the limo. It was a good thing Alec had such a steady arm, it was all I could do not to stumble as I took in the transformation that'd taken place. Our group glided up to the covered pavilion, surrounded in a pocket of silence as the rest of the crowd turned to see who'd just arrived. Alec produced tickets for all of us from a pocket somewhere while I was still taking in the sheer number of lights that'd been assembled for the occasion.

The decorations inside the pavilion were amazing. Swathes of silk gave the open-air building an ethereal feel, while candles and other light sources created a soft illumination. I didn't have to possess preternatural hearing to catch whispers about the city having received a very large, very anonymous donation just a few days before. The committee had obviously chosen to spend it on decorations.

My newfound height put me closer to Alec's ear. I only had to tug on his arm a little bit to get him down to where I could whisper to him.

"That was you, wasn't it?"

"What if it was?"

"It's too much. I mean it's really nice, incredibly gorgeous in fact, but it must have cost you a fortune."

Alec shrugged. "A paltry sum if it helps ensure a perfect night for you."

"You've done so much. I mean the dress, the shoes, and now this. Thank you, but you really shouldn't have."

His smile was back, and for some reason it nearly pulled tears out of me. "I'm glad you like it. The fact that everyone else gets to participate is nice, but really it's all for you. Of course I did make a couple of stipulations."

The music started up before I could ask what he meant. Almost before I realized what was going on, I found myself twirling through some kind of modified waltz. For the first time in my life, I was glad Dad had drilled me for all of those weeks when I'd turned twelve. My first dance had still been complete and utter misery, but at least I managed not to trip over my own feet as Alec led me around the room in time to archaic music.

The rest of the pack fell into formation around us, all dancing much more proficiently than me. James and Dominic led the way, with Jasmin and Rachel dancing off to our left. Amazingly enough, Isaac and Jessica were far and away the best; he was leading her through steps that were at least twice as hard as anything we were trying.

For maybe the first time I'd ever seen, Jessica was happy. She seemed completely in her element, utterly oblivious to the number of people watching her every move, and I felt just a little of my resentment dissolve.

"You're all such good dancers. How did that happen?"

Alec released my waist and spun me out and back in without missing a single step. I wished I could be so lucky, only the fact that his arm was like an iron bar allowed me to keep my misstep from resulting in a fall, or possibly a sprained ankle. "Donovan has very inflexible standards when it comes to some things. Dancing happens to be one of them. In fact, I don't think I'll ever forget the expression on Jasmin's face when he told her she could go clubbing all she wanted *after* he judged her suitably proficient in real dancing. He said he wouldn't have her 'seduced by throbbing beats and soulless contact' before he'd at least exposed her to proper dance steps."

I felt a giggle surge past my lips, and pressed them tight before I could completely embarrass myself. "That's amazing. My dad thought knowing how to dance would make my first dance easier. It turned out to be a complete waste of time. Nobody asked me to dance and his lessons wouldn't have helped even if they had.

Still, now I wish I'd done a better job of learning."

Alec nodded, but there was a distracted air to the gesture. I waited while we made another quarter of a journey, him gracefully, me not quite so much, around the floor, before opening my mouth to speak, but he beat me to it.

"I don't suppose either of us talk about our dads much. I'm not pushing, but if you ever need to talk about him, about what happened, I'll listen. I'll even try to suppress the natural male instinct to present advice or solutions."

I missed another step, but I wasn't fighting off a panic attack, I was just shocked that his words hadn't triggered one. Maybe it was just a function of the simple passage of time, but that didn't feel like the right answer. Wrapped inside his right arm as I was, the pleasant tingle surging through me wherever our skin touched, it seemed utterly impossible anything could ever have that kind of power to hurt me again.

I regained my footing, and it wasn't until Alec ceased moving that I realized the music had stopped. "Sorry, the stipulation was two decent songs, and then the DJ could play three of whatever he was in the mood for."

"It's okay, I actually need to sit down for a minute." The words came out as a reflex, designed to let boys gracefully bow out of having to keep dancing with me, but a slight tremor in my legs put some truth to the polite lie. I really was tired.

Even more surprising was the way that Alec held onto my hand as he led me over to a line of chairs. He was normally so careful not to prolong physical contact.

Rachel and Jasmin were waiting for us as we reached the chairs.

"Big brother, will you please take Jasmin out on the dance floor so she can get some practice following? I tried to lead last time and she kept tripping me."

Alec gave me a considering look, and then nodded as I faked a smile at him and gestured my assent. Rachel turned to me as I suppressed a stab of jealousy.

"I swear she's going to explode if Ben doesn't show up. Considering that dances are about the last place he'd ever go of his own free will, I think the odds are better than even that she'll leave little pieces of herself all over the park before the night is over."

The revelation was like being hit by a Volvo. Somehow I'd assumed that all of the things Brandon had told me were lies.

"Wait, she really does like Ben? I mean Brandon said she did, but I just assumed it was a lie like everything else he told me."

Rachel patted my hand. "Brandon's lies are so convincing precisely because he's so careful to mix a healthy serving of truth in there to go along with the false. She's liked Ben for almost as long as I can remember. I think it all started when they both ended up at the school nurse together with broken bones due to 'falling down the stairs.'"

I felt a shiver course through me at the thought of what Rachel was implying. Watching Jasmin twirl through moves that seemed to be a modification of East Coast Swing, it was hard to believe anyone so self-possessed could've had that kind of childhood.

I thought about asking for more details, but it felt wrong, like reading someone else's e-mail. Besides, I was pretty sure Rachel would tell me it was Jasmin's story, and I'd just have to go to her with my questions.

The music picked up slightly, and Jasmin and Alec sped up with it. They were moving so quickly now it almost seemed they were better than Isaac and Jessica. A quick visual search laid that question to rest though. I could just make out Isaac's towering form across the pavilion in the corner where they'd apparently gone to find room for some of their more impressive moves.

It seemed amazing to me that they were willing to move so quickly around normal, uninformed humans, but apparently they figured professional dancers were at least as quick. I shook my head and turned back to Rachel, only to feel my throat constrict as I saw Britney.

Not only was she wearing a tight, black dress that made her look at least twice as hot as me, she also happened to be draped across Brandon's arm. I was so caught up watching Britney that it took me several seconds to notice the differences in her date. Brandon had always exuded a sense of confidence, but sometime since I'd last seen him, it had morphed into something even more aggressive. He still cut through crowds, but people weren't moving out of his way out of deference anymore. Instead they were dodging away to avoid being run over.

I felt the fine hair on the back of my neck stand on end, but was distracted by Alec's return before I could figure out what else had changed about Brandon. Jasmin pulled Rachel to her feet, and gently pushed her towards Alec before casually taking a seat next to me.

It was a careful act. I'd spent way too much time with the pack to believe any of them had failed to notice Brandon's entrance. My gaze wandered back to where Vincent and Cassie were arrogantly walking through the door. Where Brandon had chosen a fairly traditional black tux, Vincent had selected a silvery masterpiece that probably cost only half as much as the former's outfit, but which practically screamed for attention.

Cassie trailed along half a step behind Vincent, in a gray evening gown that was equal parts material and skin. Backless and strapless, combined with some fairly daring cutouts. She could probably have made a run for royalty if she hadn't topped the dress off with a scowl. She didn't look happy to be on Vincent's arm instead of pressed up against Brandon.

Jasmin elbowed me in the ribs, distracting me before I could start in on whomever it was that happened to be following along behind Cassie.

"Just ignore them. Even Brandon won't try anything with this many witnesses around. It's just more dominance games."

I nodded. It made sense, but it was all I could do to keep my eyes grounded despite the cold prickles running up and down my spine. Actual conversation was just too much, so I sat quietly with my head slightly bowed while the song ran its course.

Alec's fingers gently pulled my chin up as the music ended.

"Dance with me?"

I mustered a brave smile as I nodded and let him lead me out onto the dance floor. It was a slow song this time, and Alec didn't protest when I abandoned all pretense of actual dancing, and just leaned into him hungrily. The reassurance I was seeking was weaker than normal. The solid feel of his body was just as permanent as always, but there was no tingle where our skin touched.

Almost as though sensing my thoughts, Alec hugged me tightly and buried his chin in my hair. "I know you don't want to hear this, but it isn't too late for you to change your mind. Even now, it'd be a relatively simple thing to have you halfway across the country by the time the challenge actually occurs."

The thought of what was coming filled me with dread, but I shook my head. As scary as all of this was, I knew flying away and never knowing what'd happened would be worse. Alec was probably going to die, and all of the rest of us with him, but if he didn't, if the pack somehow managed to survive the coming crisis, I wanted to be there.

Alec was more than capable of sending me away and then never letting me know he'd survived. There was a constant war inside him over what to do with me and I couldn't afford to give up my one advantage. He seemed less able to contemplate cutting me out of his life when I was around. I planned on playing that card for all it was worth. I was staying and that was it.

Alec sighed, presumably in resignation, and then suddenly my legs were thrown up in front of me as he picked me up with inhuman speed. Only the steady pressure of Alec's arm around my waist kept me from screaming, and then I was back on my feet, and being carefully, but firmly shoved through a tangled knot of bodies.

My shoes had never been intended to allow ankles to withstand that kind of punishment. Even just walking had been risky, so it wasn't a surprise when my right foot slipped, and a sharp knife of pain shot through that ankle as it collapsed under me.

Dealing with blinding agony hadn't ever been my strong point. I opened my mouth to scream, only to find that no sound would come out. The world was still spinning, but I was oriented just enough to realize that Dominic had her hand over my mouth and nose.

I pulled at her arm, but the effort was completely futile. Rising panic over not being able to breathe made me hammer at the iron bar pressing me against her, but she never looked away from whatever had captured her concentration.

Rachel suddenly appeared off to my right, and she put her finger to her lips, and then sank all ten fingernails into Dominic's arm. The sudden absence of the support I'd been unconsciously using to keep weight off of my right foot resulted in tear-jerking pain as the damaged appendage touched down, but I gritted my teeth and managed to keep it down to a hiss.

Rachel draped my arm over her shoulders, and then dragged me forward a couple of awkward, hopping steps. A couple of heartbeats passed before I realized the pool of shadow before us was Jessica. She had her eyes closed and was rocking back and forth as Rachel carefully pulled her to us.

I mirrored Rachel's actions, wrapping my free arm around Jess as I whipped my head back and forth in an effort to figure out what was going on. We were pressed up against one corner of the pavilion, with what I assumed was the rest of the pack between us and everyone else.

For a moment the wall of bodies precluded figuring out what was going on, but then Isaac shifted slightly to the left, and I saw Brandon and Vincent through the gap. The pools of black where Vincent's eyes should have been finally made me aware of the prickle of energy arcing back and forth between the two rival groups.

I couldn't imagine what it must feel like where Alec or Brandon were standing. Even just the fringe of power dancing over my arms and shoulders was enough to make me profoundly grateful I wasn't any closer to the epicenter.

Vincent's sadistic smile sent shivers down my spine, but it was nothing compared to Brandon's expression. I'd known for a couple of weeks now that what the outside world saw was nothing more than a mask, but I hadn't realized just what was under the facade.

Now I knew. It was like he'd spent the last few days peeling back some of the layers that'd hidden him, and the sheer inhumanity waiting underneath completely distracted me from the throbbing in my ankle.

He held Britney before him, ostensibly caressing her, but in reality using her as a shield, his dark eyes daring Alec to attack.

Britney was apparently unable to sense the crackling power surrounding her. She looked completely unconcerned, ecstatic even to be where she was, clasped in Brandon's left arm.

Brandon's lips drew back, but it wasn't in a smile, it was the human equivalent to showing his hackles.

"Break it up! You kids back off!"

The words seemed to float in from far away. They certainly didn't have an effect on any of the shape shifters. Vincent was moving too slowly for my human eyes to detect any change, but I was sure he was closer now than the last time I'd looked.

The feeling of insects marching across my skin intensified as James started shaking. Jasmin and Dominic both followed suit within seconds, and the feeling doubled as several of Brandon's wolves went into near convulsions.

"I said break it up!"

Mr. Paterson shoved his way past a pair of Brandon's wolves, and for a split second I thought they were going to turn and kill him. A heartbeat before they moved a low, barely perceptible growl washed over the entire scene.

I realized that the sound was coming from Alec, spreading out from him in ripples of calm. As the noise touched the shaking wolves in either pack, they calmed down, saving Mr. Paterson from injury he'd never even seen coming.

"This ends now. I don't care who started what, you guys are done dancing. Alec, you and your friends leave now. Brandon, you guys are out of here in the exact opposite direction and I mean now."

For several seconds nobody moved.

"I'm not talking because I like the sound of my own voice, people. If you leave now, I'll forget this ever happened. If someone doesn't start moving in the next three seconds, I'll see the whole lot of you expelled and brought up on charges."

Mr. Paterson was still too new to know what he was dealing with. For a moment it looked like Brandon was going to let Vincent knock the teacher into a wall, but then he gestured Vincent back. Brandon's pack relaxed slightly, and then, presumably acting on a signal from Alec that I couldn't see, Dominic and Jasmin fell back to help Jess and I.

Even with Dominic under my right arm, I couldn't hop along without jostling my ankle, and I felt tears gathering in the corners of my eyes again. Alec carefully lifted me into his arms before I took more than two or three hops.

Jasmin had her cell phone out before she'd even made it to the stairs, and the sound of a massive engine under hard acceleration heralded the arrival of our limo.

I leaned back in my seat as everyone else settled into their spots. Alec pulled out his pocket square and used it to dab away my tears. "I'm sorry. I didn't mean to set you down so hard."

Jasmin interrupted before I could say anything. "Any slower and you'd have been cut off from the rest of us by those mutts."

My confusion must have been obvious. Dominic looked up from Jess. "Vincent and Cassie cut Jess and Isaac off from the rest of us."

Rachel leaned in so she could whisper. "Jess is terrified of what Vincent and Brandon will do to her if they get a chance. She collapsed, and then everyone stormed the area."

The limo hit a particularly nasty bump, and a wave of pain drove questions about what exactly Brandon had threatened out of my mind. I'd never noticed how bad the roads between school and Alec's house were. Each jostle sent waves of agony up my leg, and Jess's quiet sobs kept time to my suppressed gasps.

It was one of the worst half hours of my life, and by the time we made it to Alec's house, I felt like I'd been wrung out. Alec yelled for Donovan and the first-aid kit as he carried me inside, and set me down in the living room.

Donovan appeared a few seconds later, and edged Alec out of the way. He stripped off my shoe and then his prodding fingers brought another couple hisses out of me as he checked for a break. Apparently satisfied with whatever he'd found, he pulled out a syringe and filled it from a little vial while Alec gently scrubbed my ankle down with an alcohol pad.

"Fortuitously, it's not broken, but I'm afraid it's one of the uglier sprains I've seen. I can take care of the pain though."

There was a reason I'd never had the slightest inclination to give blood, but fear of needles or not, I couldn't bring myself to protest, so I just shut my eyes and gripped Alec's hand as Donovan stuck the needle in several different locations.

The blessed numbness quickly spread out to encompass my entire foot. Working with a sure quickness any surgeon would have envied, Donovan wrapped my ankle and then examined his handiwork with a nod of approval.

"That should take care of the pain and immobilize it so it can begin healing, but it is vitally important that you don't put any weight on it, Mistress Paige."

Alec gripped Donovan's shoulder in thanks, and then nodded as Donovan excused himself to go see to Jess.

"We should go too. Poor Jess."

Alec shook his head. "They've already got her mostly settled down. James and Dom have already split off, and Jasmin and Rachel will leave next. She just needs some time. Time and Isaac."

Once again it boggled my mind that they could all live with so little privacy. Alec interrupted my thoughts.

"I'm sorry to have ruined your night. I wanted it to be perfect. I should have known that wasn't possible. Not with everything hanging over our heads."

It felt funny to smile. The gesture belonged with perfect times, not ones in which people other than me were having nervous breakdowns. Then again, a bad night with Alec still somehow managed to beat most other good nights.

"Everything was almost perfect. If there was anything less than ideal, it wasn't your fault."

"Still, I'd like to make it up to you."

He looked down at my ankle and then smiled with a hint of mischievousness. "I suppose dancing is out, but I think I've got something that'll do just about as well."

Alec carefully picked me up before I could respond. A few seconds later we were outside, traveling through the darkness with a breakneck speed that would've been suicidal with merely human vision.

I was completely lost by the time we came around a corner and my inferior eyes were finally able to see the first hints of light up ahead.

Alec slowed, to prolong the suspense as we got closer. Even so, it was only a few more steps before the grotto materialized out of the darkness before us.

I'd thought it'd been breathtaking two weeks ago bathed in the light of the full moon. I'd been amazed at its lush beauty the couple of times I'd snuck back during the daylight. Neither of those compared to what greeted me now.

Soft light came from dozens of floating lamps that'd been placed in the pool, all of which gave off an aching, white luminescence that seemed perfectly matched to the brilliant white of the rose petals scattered over the surface of the water.

It wasn't until we got closer that I could make out the purple edging to the petals.

"Lagrimas."

Alec's voice was husky. "Nothing else would be appropriate. Not for you, not tonight."

As we continued forward I was able to make out the other additions to the grotto. The hundreds of petals had been joined by a dozen of their potted sisters. Their rich, heavenly scent filled the air from scores of perfect, tall buds, and I found myself leaning forward slightly in Alec's arms in an effort to capture more of its essence.

Alec circled the pool and then stopped before a wooden easel that'd escaped my notice. The subtle tinkling of the tiny waterfall behind us was suddenly joined by a slight, but definitely cooling breeze that dove down into the grotto before making its way back out using the path we'd just followed in.

It didn't seem fair for things to cool off now when it was so inconvenient after so many weeks of oppressive heat. I was still musing over the injustice of it all when Alec shifted me around so I was held in just one arm.

"There's something I'd like you to have. Something I hope will help you remember what you mean to me..."

He trailed off, and then seemingly at a loss for words, reached out and lifted the black velvet that'd been covering the painting. Another graceful gesture flipped on the set of soft lights surrounding its border.

As always with Alec's paintings, it took me a second before I could shift my perspective enough to translate the beautiful formations of light into something I could tie to the drab, dreary world I inhabited.

It was the same grotto where we now stood. The warm glow from the climbing ivory and roses formed a backdrop awash in the silvery light of a full moon. Just visible off to one side was the pool, alive with enough microscopic life to give it a pale glow of its own to compliment the off-center reflection of a hundred tiny lights.

A few seconds later I finally recognized that the subject of the piece was a female, reaching out towards the point of view with glowing hands.

"She's beautiful. It's how I always imagined an angel would appear."

Alec was silent for so long I finally tore my gaze from his masterpiece long enough to find that he was staring at me with surprise.

"It's you, Adri. Of course it's beautiful."

For a second I couldn't breathe. It seemed so utterly impossible. Maybe it could've been a painting of Cindi, but not one of me. I couldn't possibly be the gorgeous figure he'd brought to life on his canvas.

I opened my mouth to protest, and then the expression on her face finally registered for me. Compassion. Acceptance of the viewer, combined with an obvious desire to mend grievous hurts. It was exactly how I remembered feeling. My questing eyes finally found the last, missing piece. There was the gratitude. Misplaced on her perfect face. Wrong on the features of someone who couldn't possibly need help from a mere mortal, but still there.

"It's so beautiful. I don't know what to say. Are you sure you want to give it up?"

Alec looked back up at me, and his eyes were filled with incredible need. I was suddenly struck by the similarities to the me he'd painted, and what I saw written on his face.

It seemed impossible he would be unsure, that a glorious being like him could ever need anything I could provide, but I couldn't deny it was there.

There was no way of knowing what it was, but I didn't care. Whatever it was he needed I wanted to give him. I opened my mouth to say as much, but my vocal chords wouldn't cooperate.

I was still trying to verbalize my feelings, when his free hand came down to my chin and gently pulled it up. My heart stuttered and threatened to quit as his lips slowly came down to meet mine.

My only other experience had been so terrible that I nearly panicked, but before I could formulate a protest, or even decide if a protest was what I wanted, our flesh touched. The contact immediately drove every other thought from my mind.

His lips were the perfect combination of firm and soft, and the heart that'd been all but stopped a second before sped up to heart attack rates, slamming itself against my chest in an effort to get closer to him.

All of my senses were blending together. I couldn't tell if he smelled incredible, tasted like heaven, or if it was all just a side effect of the energy which had gone from tingling to crackling as soon as our faces touched.

My inhibitions, the ones that'd always kept me from acting on the occasional amorous impulse, evaporated sometime in the first half second, and I found myself with both arms wrapped around his neck, clinging to him with all my strength.

Later I'd probably claim it was to steady myself against the wave of dizziness, but right now I knew it was because I wanted him more than anything I'd ever experienced.

Alec pulled me away, held me at arm's length while I gasped for air, and then once I calmed down a little, he smiled and pulled me in close again, just for a hug this time.

I tried to turn it into a kiss, but he deftly avoided my attempt, burying his face in my hair. "I'd like to, I truly would, but I don't think that would be fair to you. Even letting that happen was a mistake. I've never come so close to losing control."

He wasn't breathing hard, and normally a comment like that would've made me doubt his feelings for me, but what I'd just felt was too powerful to deny. I could still see traces of desire in his eyes; and for the first time since I'd met him, I was absolutely positive he wasn't ever going to leave me.

"I don't think it was a mistake. I want to kiss you again, but I'll behave."

"You like the painting then?"

I nodded, and then shivered. It's amazing how a near complete loss of physical control can burn through your energy reserves.

Alec frowned. "I'm sorry. I forget sometimes how much easier it is for you and Rachel to catch a chill. Let's get you inside where it's a bit more temperate."

It seemed like such a waste, leaving the grotto after all the work that'd been put into transforming it, but Alec waved away my protests. He easily cradled me in one arm, while carefully picking up my painting with his free hand.

A short time later, we were back inside the house and headed towards his room. Cuddled up against his chest with the familiar, warm tingle caressing my skin, my system apparently decided I was completely safe, and started shutting down. I was doing a fairly respectable job of hiding my drooping eyelids, but all my efforts were undone by the prodigious yawn that ambushed me as he set me down on the bed.

"I'm not tired, I promise."

His eyebrow arched in disbelief as I pulled him down onto the bed, and I found myself admitting the truth.

"Okay, I might be a little tired, but it isn't a big deal. I want to spend as much time with you as possible. After all, it isn't like I'm going to be able to really get much rest between now and whenever we need to leave for the challenge."

His wonderfully expressive face froze into the stony mask he wore so often with the rest of the world.

"You weren't planning on bringing me, were you?"

"It's not safe, Adri. I don't want to leave you anymore than you want to be left, but it's the only option."

"No, it isn't, just bring me along."

His fist clenched, knotting up the covers next to my head, but I was long past worrying he'd lose control of his beast and hurt me by accident.

"You heard Mallory. The odds are very good that I'm not coming back. If the worst happens, the rest of the pack may very well have to try and fight their way out of there. They won't be able to get you out, they'll be lucky to survive even fleeing unencumbered. I can't ask them to run that gauntlet carrying you the whole way."

I ran my finger along his cheek, mirroring the motion he'd done to me so many times. "Then don't ask them. You'll either win, in which case it doesn't matter whether I'm there or not, or else I don't care what happens."

Both fists were knotted now, and unless I was very much mistaken, there was just the barest hint of a shake there as well.

"Don't be ridiculous, Adri. You should know at least a little by now what they're capable of. I can't let you expose yourself to the kinds of things Vincent or Brandon would...it's out of the question."

Mom had always gone on and on about how nurturing I was. When she was less happy with me, she tended to focus more on just how stubborn I could be. It wasn't always obvious what would set off a bout of 'stiff neck' as she referred to it, but the only people who'd ever successfully talked me into a 'reasonable, rational' response had been Dad and Cindi.

I could feel that same core of iron making its presence known right now. I wasn't going to be deprived of however much time I had left with him. I wasn't going to be losing this argument.

"Alec, I need to be there with you tonight. If you leave me here, I'll head out on my own and look for you."

The shake was definitely there, and getting more pronounced.

"I'll order Donovan to keep you here."

"You can try. He may even do it, but I don't think so. He's far too much the gentleman to keep a lady captive against her will. Even if he does, do you really think he can watch over me every second?"

With a sharp tearing sound, Alec's right hand elongated into the viciously clawed weapon of his hybrid form. It shredded the comforter and mattress just a few inches from my head. I gave him my best lop-sided smile and kissed his arm.

"You're not going to scare me off with cheap tricks. This is important."

His eyes were an intense blue, paler than normal. They were Alec's eyes, but they were also the eyes of his beast, and I suddenly realized the dominance stuff wasn't just a game. There was a feral part of Alec that didn't play well with others, that would kill or be killed in turn rather than have his will thwarted.

A complex collage of emotions flooded through my system as I tried to process what that meant, and whether or not I needed to be scared. As suddenly as it'd changed before,

Alec's fist relaxed, shrinking back into its normal size and shape like melting snow.

"All right. You can come. I don't like it. Don't like knowing you're guaranteed not to survive my passing, but it's your choice."

I was too busy being amazed by how quickly he'd stopped shaking, how rapidly his eyes had gone back to normal to really wonder whether or not it was all just an elaborate ruse designed to lull me into a false sense of security so he could trap me here.

"Not that I'm complaining, mind you, but why the sudden change?"

Alec gave me a lopsided smile of his own. "My death is nearly certain, but there's always a chance I'll somehow survive. As unlikely as that is, I don't want to survive and then find I've poisoned you against me. I won't stop you."

I felt things I hadn't realized were knotted up relax inside me. When my voice finally came out it was smaller than normal.

"Thank you."

Alec shrugged and gave me another smile. "You must have driven your parents crazy with that refusal to back down."

"I suppose I might have frustrated them a time or two."

"And to think Rachel says *I'm* stubborn."

I started to smile, but stopped as he cocked his head to the side in what was unmistakably a listening posture.

"What's the matter? What do you hear?"

"Jasmin just left."

"What's wrong with that?"

"It's not safe for her to leave the estate. Brandon's pack could be waiting for her."

He started to move, but I held onto him.

"Alec, she'll probably be okay. I know it isn't the best idea but please don't stop her. Not tonight."

It was like I could see the thoughts dart around as he put pieces together, and I was suddenly torn between telling him in the hopes it would buy Jasmin her last night with Ben, and trying to keep her secret.

My heart raced until he finally relaxed and sank back down with me.

"Please don't let on that you know. I wasn't supposed to say anything. I just couldn't let you go after her."

The immediate crisis past, I could have lost myself looking at his features, but a slow smile suddenly reminded me of the only other person I knew that could pack so much pain in such a simple gesture.

"What about Rachel, Alec? Where is she?"

I hadn't thought his expression could become anymore bittersweet. I was wrong. "Rachel doesn't have anyone either, but she's still suffering from a deeper hurt. She's with my mother."

My confusion must have been more than usually self-evident as I sat up. "No, Mother isn't going through a good episode. She's asleep. Rachel crept into her room and crawled into bed with her. It's a poor substitute for what she aches for, but it's all Mother can offer right now."

"Alec, there must be something we can do."

He gently captured my hands, stilling their frantic motion and shook his head. "Not right now. Rachel cherishes her few remaining illusions. One of the most important is the pretense that nobody knows just how hard it is sometimes for her to be the only human in a house full of shape shifters."

I felt my lips trembling, and he freed one of his hands to brush it lightly across my mouth. "You've been a godsend for her, Adri. As badly as it hurts each time she sneaks away, it hasn't happened nearly as often since you got here. She's been improving ever since you moved into town, and the rate of change has increased over the last two weeks."

"I suppose we make quite the pair, her and I. Two shattered little dolls trying our best to make sure the pieces don't blow away and leave us with nothing. An imposition to everyone around us."

He hugged me to him as he shook his head. "Not an imposition. Never that."

It felt wrong to try and kiss Alec right now. I didn't want to make light of Rachel's hurt, or Jasmin's loneliness, but his presence was too great a temptation to pass up. My face started out in the hollow of his neck, drinking in the ambrosia of his scent, and then moved up towards his lips without conscious decision on my part.

Our lips met, and it felt like a warm, pleasant surge of electricity washed from my head down to the tips of my toes. My head started spinning almost instantly, only my hand on his chest, and his arms around my waist kept me from losing my balance completely. As it was, I still fell into him, overcome by weakness as my heart stopped beating altogether.

No more than a second or two of breathlessness could have possibly passed, but Alec pulled away, firmly holding me at arm's length.

"You need to get some sleep. Regardless of how the fight turns out, you'll need to be well-rested."

My best longing look didn't seem to be having any effect on him, so I finally nodded and relaxed back onto the bed.

"I guess I did promise to behave myself. I don't think I'll be able to sleep, but if you'll tell me another story I'll at least try..."

Apparently satisfied by my promise, Alec joined me on the bed and pulled me close. I was still chilled enough from being outside for the warmth of his arms to feel good.

"Adjam and Inock found that the dayborn had lost all knowledge of their loving mother, and that they reacted poorly to Inock's plague form. Neither brother was able to maintain their original forms for more than a few hours at a time, and although Adjam was able to blend in with the animals found in the area, there was nothing like Inock's feline body nearby, and he was chased and hunted by many of the dayborn, for they thought him a demon."

Alec's breath caressed the back of my neck even as his quiet, velvety baritone reached inside my head and smoothed away the tensions that'd been keeping me from seeking sleep. I knew there'd been a reason for being so scared, but I just couldn't bring myself to care about it now.

"The brothers watched the dayborn for many turnings, but although they learned many things, they found themselves unable to learn the dayborns' language. Even worse, the dayborn hunters were becoming ever more skilled at tracking Inock, and they began to press him sorely."

I felt as though I was drifting. The bed no longer mattered, or even seemed to exist. All that mattered was the story and the warm drowsiness that increased with each breath.

"Adjam saw his brother's frustration grow, but he never suspected just how strong it'd become until two hunters brought Inock to bay, and he turned on them. Inock killed the first hunter and would have done likewise to the second, but Adjam sprang upon his brother, knocking him away before the second man could be harmed."

Alec's fingers slowly caressed my stomach as he spoke. It should have tickled, but instead it lulled me even further towards oblivion.

"And thereby the full effect of the Earth's curse was felt. Trapped as they were in their beast forms, neither brother could talk to the other, and the resulting confrontation quickly spun out of control. Hours later Adjam was left bleeding and broken as his brother disappeared into the night."

Alec's soothing voice continued on, but I'd lost the ability to listen. My mind floated off into visions of a battered wolf who dragged himself over to a brook before collapsing on the bank, streaked with mud. Just before the blackness carried me completely away, a willowy girl appeared from behind a thicket of trees and timidly approached the bleeding figure.

Chapter 30

The cool night air dimpled my skin despite the warmth of Alec's chest. We'd been walking for quite a while before I came fully awake.

Dominic and Jasmin had shaken me awake, and then helped me out of my dress and into jeans and a white shirt.

Donovan had been waiting in the hall just outside Alec's room. He'd pressed objects into Dom and Jasmin's hands, and then brushed his lips across the back of my hand. He slipped away, and then we'd entered a brightly-lit room filled with the rest of the pack.

Alec had picked me up and carried me out to a massive SUV that I'd never seen before. Everyone piled in, and despite the seriousness of rapidly approaching events, I fell back asleep somewhere en route to our destination.

Apparently you couldn't drive all the way though, because we were walking again, or at least some of us were. I could just make out Isaac off a little ways into the darkness. He was in hybrid form and moving with a ground-devouring gait that was deceptively smooth. Flashes of movement off to either side of us, lower to the ground, made me sure the girls were all following along on four legs.

Alec shifted me around as he realized I was awake. "We've still got nearly half an hour, you should get some more sleep if you can."

I tried to argue but couldn't find the strength. A while later the flash of light as James and Isaac lit flares pulled me back awake.

It took several seconds for my eyes to adjust, and then I started being able to pick out individual shapes in the darkness. Alec set me down as Vincent appeared, a towering, furred figure illuminated by the light of the flares that'd been planted on either side of the cleared space. His dark eyes drank in the light as he surveyed us with his typical boundless arrogance.

A horde of shifting figures milled about just outside of the twin circles of light. The rest of Brandon's pack and they seemed to have grown in number since the dance.

Jasmin and Dominic crowded up against me, one on either side, and I let my hands brush against their heads. The feel of their fur, one short and soft, the other long and coarse, anchored me before the surreal strangeness of the scene could carry me away.

The tingle of shape shifter power was as strong as I'd ever felt it, jumping from multiple sources, arcing around me as it unsuccessfully looked for a place to ground out. For the first time, I was able to accurately pick out the individual signatures that made it up.

Jess was off to the left, white hot with mixed anger and fear, stabilized only by the cool, controlled pillar of power that was Isaac. Jasmin almost hummed under my fingertips like barely-leashed violence, while my other hand drank from the still pond that was Dominic, her mere presence feeding me comfort.

I'd just finished identifying the raging beast to the right as James, when Brandon stepped into the light.

He looked like some kind of pagan god, smeared all over with blood, an uneven circle drawn on his chest, filled with sharp, angry lines that didn't mean anything to me, but which made the wolves around me tense and growl.

"While I appreciate the sentiment, it really is far too late to secure absolution by bringing me the girl."

His voice had changed, becoming deeper and harsher, with elements that didn't sound like they could come from any human throat. He stepped forward, and I felt my chest seize up. The transformation I'd sensed the beginnings of at the dance had run its course now and any question as to why someone as cultured as

Brandon would associate with a near-psychopath like Vincent was put to rest.

He was shaking now, quivering with the need to kill, and I realized that it didn't matter whether the darkness inside Brandon had created Vincent or just attracted him to orbit in his sphere like a small moon. It was enough to know that Vincent's was the lesser evil.

"Adri is here solely as a witness."

Alec's voice was huskier than normal, but still carried most of its velvety perfection. As I looked at him, I realized I wasn't feeling any power arcing from him. Everything centered on him now, but he wasn't adding to the storm. The wolves behind Brandon growled as Alec stepped forward.

"Ah, and here I'd thought you'd once again settled on a course of appeasement." Brandon's features were hollow, almost skeletal in the harsh chemical light.

"No. We've come for one purpose and one only. No more murdered hikers, no more convenient accidents. This ends tonight."

Brandon worked more mockery into a simple clap than most of us could carry off with a full cast of supporting actors.

"Always observing the old forms, aren't you, Alec. Well now it's time for a whole new batch."

One second Brandon was a human, the next he was a huge monstrosity, a thing that normally dwelt in the bottom, most primitive parts of the mind, venturing out only to star prominently in nightmares.

The rush of power beat back at our entire pack. If it'd been a physical wind it would've knocked me over. Intangible or not, it still staggered me and only my grip on Jasmin and Dom kept me from dropping to my knees.

Alec stood motionless for a pair of seconds, and then seemed to explode and melt back into himself. I blinked, and his human body had been replaced with the hybrid form that'd saved my life once before.

Only this time he wasn't fighting wolves, he was fighting another hybrid, and Brandon towered over him.

There was another ripple of movement on the other side of the light. Jasmin and Dom both pulled away from me, joining the other three, facing outward in preparation for the inevitable attack.

Vincent's dark form inched slightly closer, but Brandon's growl froze his henchman in place. The complete stillness that resulted was suddenly shattered by a flash of heat lightning off to the east, and when the spots cleared from my vision, the two hybrids were a blur of motion.

Merely human eyes never could've hoped to follow all of the action. I got the feeling Alec's technique was superior. He moved from spot to spot, motion to motion with the smooth economy of a tree bending before the wind, but if he was a tree, Brandon was the hurricane.

Flare-light reflected off of deadly claws, and blood splattered the earth as Brandon drove Alec before him. Gashes appeared on both leaders, wetly glistening in the green light, but they were more numerous on Alec than on Brandon.

I expected the unseen plane to mirror the fight I was so desperately trying to track with my inferior vision. There should have been titanic clashes of power, ants marching up and down my skin from being far too close to ground zero, but there weren't.

Brandon's energy beat down on Alec, beat down on all of us, but although I could feel the answering flare of power from the rest of the pack, Alec remained silent, dancing away from the worst bursts of metaphorical death at the same time he dodged Brandon's fangs.

The flares were almost dead, but there was just enough light for me to see the smaller figure reel away from the larger as a vicious slash sank home in Alec's chest. Time stretched and pulled like taffy, and I had plenty of time to watch Alec fall, to feel splatters of hot liquid even standing so far away.

A scream ripped itself free from my throat, and it suddenly seemed we really were caught up in a hurricane. As the flares finally died, the pulsing pressure, the pins and needles disappeared as well. Only that wasn't quite the term for it. The power, the energy that'd become more than oppressive, was sucked towards Alec and Brandon, dragging with it my strength, and the unnatural vitality of the rest of the pack.

I felt a lance of pain sink into my back, mirroring the jolt in my ankle, as all five shape shifters collapsed around me. I knew with a certainty I was going to die, that we were all going to die, but that didn't matter. It was only right that my existence cease within heartbeats of Alec's.

Chapter 31

As the normal grogginess of sleep wore off, I realized just how thirsty I was. I reached for a drink, hissing a little as my stitches pulled against the still-healing skin, but the glass of orange juice remained steadfastly just beyond my fingertips.

Alec appeared immediately, paint-speckled and undeniably alive, from where he'd been working in his studio. "I really wish you'd just call for me when you need something. All of this moving around isn't going to help your back heal any more quickly."

"You're not letting your injuries slow *you* down."

It was a losing argument, but I hated being cooped up in bed all the time, and it was the only argument I had. Alec paused for a second to look down at the long, thick bandage wrapped around his middle. The gash of white cutting across his darkly tanned skin was uncomfortably similar to what I imagined his wound must have looked like just after Brandon had inflicted it.

He sighed, but there wasn't any real frustration to the sound. "Our cases are hardly comparable. You know I heal more quickly than you do."

An upraised finger cut me off before I could latch onto my last remaining point. "The fact that your injury was less severe is really quite immaterial. Even the fact that shape shifter-inflicted wounds don't heal as quickly as normal for me is really a small matter when compared to just how much blood you lost before we got the bleeding staunched."

And there was the real rub. Alec was well on his way to being fully healed, while I still had fits of dizziness every time I tried to stand. I even had to have Jasmin or Dom help me to the bathroom.

There was no good way to know how long I'd lain there with a branch stuck through my back, but it'd been long enough for even a relatively small wound to result in near fatal blood loss. I'd been nearly unconscious from the pain, so I didn't remember any of what had happened next, but Alec had reluctantly filled in most of the details.

Apparently the stress of the fight had finally awakened his potential, and his power was a real humdinger. The metaphysical hurricane that'd knocked me to the ground had actually been Alec pulling power from all of the shape shifters and humans in the area.

The experience had been nearly as overwhelming for Alec as it had been for the rest of us. He'd recovered just in time to find Brandon grimly pulling himself along on all fours. Luckily Alec had recovered more quickly, and once Brandon was deprived of the strength and speed *his* power had bestowed upon him, Alec had been more than a match for him, even wounded and exhausted.

Brandon's end had been quick, and if Alec hadn't realized my blood was slowly leaking out onto the ground, the rest of Brandon's pack would've likewise been quickly sorted out. Instead, Alec had stumbled over, shifted back to human form, and got the bleeding slowed to a point where I wasn't in imminent danger of death.

Unfortunately that'd been all the delay Brandon's pack had needed to make a run for it. Isaac, James and Jasmin were trying to track down the worst of the lot, the ones who'd taken an active part in Brandon's atrocities, but it was slow going.

Part of the job had been resolved when Cassie and two other wolves had tried to circle around and attack the estate. Luckily Isaac and the others had stumbled onto them. The fight had been brief and bloody. None of our guys had escaped unharmed, but they were all going to make a full recovery, and the same couldn't be said for Cassie or the others.

I shivered a little at the thought, and Alec looked up with concern on his face. "Do you need another blanket?"

"No, I'm fine, just a little worried about Jasmin and the boys."

Now he did frown. He wasn't excited that he had to stay here instead of leading the tracking group. I personally was glad he couldn't go along, and not just because it was dangerous work. I wasn't positive he'd really come to terms with having killed Brandon.

"They'll be fine. You need to worry about getting better, and nothing else."

My pout met with just as much success as it usually did. After a second or two I gave up and nodded.

"Okay, I promise to be good and concentrate on getting better, if you'll come keep me company."

The flash of emotion, barely visible in Alec's eyes, was a source of hope and despair all at once. Eagerness, desire. Both curbed by the same iron will that'd continued fighting long past where most people would've given up and died.

I patted the bed next to me, wincing slightly as even that simple motion pulled on things that weren't meant to be pulled on. He stared at me for several seconds, and then sat down on the bed. I waited, and then when I was sure that was as close as he planned on getting, I slid closer, resting my head on his arm. As long as I was careful not to go too far, not to touch too much of him, I could get away with that much.

His half-imagined sigh sent little trills of satisfaction through me. He wasn't going to initiate contact. If I didn't know with an absolute certainty that he wanted to be with me, I would've despaired already. Still, Dominic had been right so many days ago. Alec was worth it, and as long as he still loved me, I was going to do my best to help him see that we belonged together.

Human or shape shifter, homely or gorgeous, none of that mattered. All that mattered was he made my heart beat faster, and I could no longer imagine my life without him. I guess you call that love.